MISFIT ALPHA

CURSED WORLD BOOK 5

STEPHANIE FOXE

STEEL FOX MEDIA LLC

The Foxey Betas

A big thank you to my ART (Advanced Reader Team). Their advice cleaned up the book and helped me to be more confident launching a new series.

Terri Adkisson, Samantha Rooney, Larry Diaz Tushman, Karen Hollyhead, Jen Plumstead, David Ravita, Stephanie Johnson, Tami Cowles, Morgan Davis

To Jessica, thank you so much for your kind words when you sent back the edited manuscript. After a year of doubt and discouragement, it was a much needed boost.

CONTENTS

CHAPTER 1

AMBER

Amber woke with a gasp, her fingers tightening around the Seed of Life. She still had it. The journey back had been rougher than the trip into the fae realm, and for a time, she hadn't been sure if she'd lost it.

Ceri hovered over her, frowning with concern. "You okay?"

"Yeah. That just took more out of me than I expected." She sat upright and lifted the Seed of Life with trembling hands. Its light and warmth filled the room.

Ceri knelt in front of her, eyes locked on the seed. "That thing has an insane amount of magic in it."

"Understatement of the century," Tessa said in awe. "Are you absolutely sure we should destroy it and not...use it?"

"Don't even start," Ceri warned with a frown.

"It has the power to restore the fae realm to its former glory," Amber whispered, sorrow for what Kadrithan and all the fae had to give up forming a lump in her throat. She'd do almost anything to save him from this. "They wouldn't ask us to destroy it if there was another way."

The door opened. "She back yet--" Derek froze, his jaw dropping open. "Is that it?"

"Yep." Amber tried to stand but found her legs still too wobbly for the task. "I don't know how Kadrithan makes that trip so often."

Ceri pulled her up to her feet. "I could feel the strain through the pack bond the longer you were there. It was odd, almost as if…" She waved her hand as if brushing aside the thought. "The important thing is that we have it. Evangeline is still feeding, but she'll be ready in time."

Amber nodded. "We finally have a chance to get ahead of them. They don't know we have this. They don't know we can break the curse."

"They have to suspect it," Tessa objected, raising a brow. "These guys have been in power for ages. You really think they won't attack again?"

"All our allies are still here, and now the MIA has joined us. If they attack, we'll just defend ourselves. We'll be ready." Amber sounded surer than she felt, but now was not the time to show doubt. They couldn't turn back now after coming so far and fighting so hard.

"Are Kadrithan and Zerestria going to be rejoining us soon?" Ceri asked.

"I don't know. He didn't sound very confident. He said he had to get somewhere safe but wasn't sure he could. The fae are under attack."

"We need to wait until twilight. So…" Ceri glanced at the clock. "Four more hours. If Kadrithan was fleeing somewhere, there's a chance he could get to safety and still have time to be here for the curse-breaking. It just feels…wrong to do it without him."

"Tell me about it." Amber pressed her lips together, the memory of his kiss and the desperate way he held onto her filling her with fear. It had felt like a goodbye.

The door opened again, and Genevieve hurried inside, firmly shutting the door behind her. "Ito is being a pain, and everyone wants an update."

Amber sighed and handed the seed to Ceri, strangely reluctant to part with it. She shook off the impulse. "I'll talk to them. They deserve to be filled in after everything they've risked helping us. Especially since this isn't over."

Derek patted her shoulder. "I'll go with you and help answer any questions I can."

"Ditto," Genevieve said with a firm nod. "They just need to see you're still here and still working on things. Also, you're the only one that can muzzle Ito."

Amber frowned. "Is he really that bad?"

"He's..." Genevieve pursed her lips as she hesitated over what to say. "Grumpy as hell and entirely too pessimistic."

"Great." Amber dragged a hand down her face. "That's the last thing we need right now."

"We've got this." Ceri gave her elbow a quick squeeze. "Go do your leadership thing, and me and Tessa can go talk to Evangeline to make sure we're ready to go on time."

Amber straightened her shoulders and led Genevieve and Derek back out into the hall. A wise friend had once told her that, as alpha, she didn't get to hide in her room like a pouty teenager when bad things started happening. She had to be out there with her pack and all the other people depending on her. She would be strong for them.

CHAPTER 2

KADRITHAN

Kadrithan walked down the narrow hallway. It had taken him a few hours to get there, and every muscle in his body ached. There was no time to rest, though. The walls shook under the endless assault. *Death trap,* he thought. The last city of the fae would be their grave. Even if the curse was broken in time…He shook his head and forced his attention back to the present.

Zerestria stepped out of the shadows just ahead of him. "Were you able to retrieve it?" she asked, her shoulders stiff with anticipation.

"Yes." He nodded once. "The pack has it, and they will be breaking the curse at twilight, as the prophecy instructed."

She closed her eyes and let out a breath of relief. "Then it is out of our hands."

"Are the elders here?"

"Yes." She straightened her shoulders and nodded her head toward the throne room. "They're waiting."

He followed her into the heart of the fortress, where the same men and women that had advised his parents now sat debating the future of a dying people.

Zerestria opened the door, and the conversation ahead of them fell silent for a moment.

"Were you successful?" one of the elders asked.

"Yes," Kadrithan replied as he and Zerestria took their seats in the circle in the center of the room. The throne sat empty, looming over them like a gravestone.

"The curse will be broken at twilight, or it will not." Zerestria's serene appearance was belied by the white-knuckled grip of her hands on the arms of her chair. "We must remain calm so that our people can retain hope." Her gaze moved to him. "Perhaps it is time we give them a king once again."

Kadrithan stiffened but kept his face blank. "The elders have served the people since the fall of the fae. I see no reason to upend that in the midst of this chaos."

Murmurs of agreement and disagreement flowed through the gathered elders. He could not blame the doubters for their lack of support. After so many years hiding away and working behind the scenes, they had every reason to consider him unfit to take the crown. The fae did not know him, and the memories of their previous king had faded over the centuries.

A brief rap on the door silenced the conversations. Zerestria waved toward one of the two guards, and she opened the door, admitting one of the remaining captains.

He bowed then stood stiffly before them, his face pale and dripping with sweat. "They have broken the outer gate."

Kadrithan let his eyes slip shut for one moment as the gravity of the situation hit him. It was no longer a matter of *if* their enemies stormed the keep. It was a matter of *when*. When he opened his eyes, Zerestria's gaze was heavy on him. The last of his resistance dissolved. Whether he wanted it or not, the burden of leadership fell to him. He stood. "We will not die huddled in a hole in the ground. I will lead whatever remains of the army through the inner gate."

Zerestria stood as well. "Then go as their *king,* Kadrithan. Do not leave the throne empty in the final hour."

The elders that had objected only minutes earlier now remained silent.

"Are there any objections? I will not hold it against you now, or for whatever future remains to us," Kadrithan asked, his voice even though he felt anything but.

"No," one of the dissenters spoke up. "Any concern for how this may play out in the future is pointless now. We have let fear rule us long enough."

Zerestria waited, her gaze touching each of them. "Then it is decided." She walked to the throne and lifted the crown from its seat. It had not been touched since it was placed there after his parents' deaths.

He approached the throne, dread settling in his gut like a stone. The other elders trailed behind him. A memory of approaching the throne as a child flashed through his mind. This place had been wondrous back then. Now the shadows were filled with ghosts.

"Kneel," Zerestria commanded.

He complied, bowing his head and willing his hands not to shake.

"Who does the king serve?" she asked.

"The fae." His hand curled into a fist.

"Do you swear to rule with honor and mercy and strive to always provide for the fae?"

"I do."

"So it is witnessed." The crown's heavy weight pressed against his skull uncomfortably, much like the idea of being king. He'd never felt worthy. Never had time to be properly prepared for the position. It had seemed right to let the elders rule. Even now, this was the last thing he wanted, but like many things, his wants were superseded by the needs of the fae. He rose and turned to face the elders.

"Long live the King!" Zerestria's voice echoed through the near-empty hall.

The elders echoed her words, but they all knew that was not to be. He was the last king of a doomed race.

CHAPTER 3

AMBER

Amber stared at the horizon. The sun crept lower every minute like the sand in an hourglass. They didn't have long before they would attempt to break the curse. Anticipation and a deep sense of foreboding made it hard to stand still. Her fingers tapped against her crossed arms. It was almost peaceful though, this moment alone. So, of course, Ito had to come ruin it.

Ito's hands were clasped behind his back in a white-knuckled grip. He stood near her shoulder for a moment before speaking. "What do you intend to do with my pack once you have broken this curse?"

"Do with your pack?" She frowned and shook her head. "Nothing."

His eyes darted to her face. "You're lying. You'll want us to keep fighting for you in this war you're starting."

She turned to face him. "Anyone *willing* to join us and fight back is welcome to, but if you think for a moment I intend to draft unwilling people into this, then you don't know me at all. Bram is arranging a safe place that anyone in your pack, including yourself, will be free to go to. With your home destroyed, I think you can agree it's not really safe to stay."

"I've informed the pack they may leave if they wish. Another alpha from the council has offered to take them in. If I get my way, I'll be the only one left trapped with you." He held her gaze in an unspoken challenge. Based on the hate simmering behind his eyes, she thought he really expected her to get angry, as if he'd thwarted her master plan.

"Good. I wouldn't want anyone to feel like they had no choice. I hope they're happy whatever they end up deciding." A sharp tug on the pack bond made her look over her shoulder. Ceri held up both hands––ten minutes left. She nodded and turned back to Ito. "Anything else on your mind?"

"No." He spun on his heel and walked away.

Amber moved to follow but stopped in her tracks as her demon mark warmed. She caught Ceri's attention and motioned at her demon mark.

Ceri hesitated then nodded, mouthing, "Hurry."

"Glad I caught you alone."

She turned to face Kadrithan. He looked different, somehow. His features weren't quite in focus, and his clothes were drab. He had always taken the time to make the details interesting when he appeared for her. "We're ready. We'll be breaking the curse in about ten minutes. Are you staying to watch?"

The corners of his mouth lifted as he shook his head, but she couldn't call it a smile. "That's good. I can't stay, but there are a few things I need to tell you, just in case."

"What do you mean, just––"

He pressed a cold finger to her lips. "There is money in these accounts." He lifted her other hand and pressed a piece of paper into it. "For your pack and for Evangeline, if you need it."

She accepted it reluctantly and nodded. Something was very, very wrong. "Why are you giving me this?"

"In The Market, there is a vendor named Rhiannon. She keeps the history of the fae. Whenever it is safe, it would be good for people to know the truth about who we were. I don't want it forgotten."

She waited to be sure he was done. "Why are you talking like you're about to die?"

"I'm not going to die. The fae are perfectly safe where we are as long as it takes you to break the curse. It's just a precaution in case it takes me longer than expected to find you after the curse is broken."

"You promise?"

"I swore I'd never lie to you again." He pressed his hand to her mark with a sad smile. "I have to go now."

We need you over here. Genevieve's urgency and excitement zinged through her mind.

"Me too," she said with a sigh.

Kadrithan opened his mouth to say something else but closed it quickly and stepped away. He held her gaze as he vanished into a puff of smoke.

Pain shot through her chest. Her skin turned to ice and her heart raced as she struggled to take a breath. Gravity seemed to double as her knees hit the ground. Amber yanked the neck of her shirt down. The demon mark twisted, then faded completely. Her awareness of Kadrithan vanished.

Panic bubbled up in her. *No, no, no.*

Genevieve's voice sounded distant, even though her beta's hands were on her shoulders. She had no idea when Genevieve got to her. Hadn't she been alone?

"Amber!" Genevieve shook her again. "What the hell is happening?"

Her words caught in her throat. She hadn't fulfilled her demon mark. He hadn't asked her to do anything. And the curse hadn't been broken yet. That left only one option. She met Genevieve's worried gaze. "He lied to me."

"What?"

"Kadrithan swore on his mark that he'd never lie to me again after he finally told us about the fae." Her hand went to the now empty spot on her chest. "But he lied to me when he said they were safe and that he'd find me after we broke the curse. He *lied*." A helpless rage drove away the shock. "That *son of a bitch*."

Genevieve shook her again. "Look at me." Amber forced her eyes back to Genevieve. "We are going to break this curse, then you can find him and give him a good slap."

She ground her teeth together. "Okay."

"But you have to reign these emotions in, alright? You're projecting really hard right now."

Amber leaned into the pack bond and found her pain and anger reflected back at her, but beneath that her pack's strength. Their steady love and concern. Bit by bit, she shielded them from the overwhelming emotions churning within her. They had to get through this. If he––no. She couldn't even let herself think it. They would get through this, and she would find Kadrithan. "Let's get this over with."

Amber walked side by side with Genevieve toward the gathering. Ceri and her coven stood with Evangeline, preparing to break the curse as the sun sank in the sky behind them.

It was nearly twilight.

CHAPTER 4

CERI

Ceri kept a calm demeanor, but inside she was a bundle of nerves and frustration. Amber's panic was filtering through the pack bond. The last thing they needed was more complications. This was already going to be difficult.

She knelt and pressed her hands to the ground. Her magic sank into the dirt and formed two circles. The largest would be for the coven, while the inner circle would be for her, Evangeline, and Deward.

The ritual she intended to perform was straightforward, as it often was for spells of this magnitude. However, that did not mean it would be easy. Her eyes flicked to Evangeline, who stood apart from the rest of the group.

Evangeline had insisted Saraqael couldn't touch her within the Crux of Realms, and perhaps she was right. After all, he would have snatched her rather than sending his incubi to grab her in person if it had been possible. The only thing that didn't make sense to Ceri, and never had, was that Evangeline had been persuaded to trust him at all. The girl was hard-headed, unreasonable, and sometimes downright belligerent. There was a chance that Saraqael had entranced her. If not fully, then just enough to push her into something she never would have otherwise agreed to.

Tessa stood from where she was laying out the sage and candles. "What are you brooding over?"

"Evangeline was stupid."

Tessa snorted. "Harsh, but probably true. Weren't you a little stupid at that age?"

"Yeah, but..." Ceri shook her head. "The first time Evangeline ran away, it was to protect her mother and the rest of us. She ran away thinking she'd be caught and killed, but hey, at least it would all be over. But this time she left *with* the people that had been hunting her. And took her mother to them."

"So, you think Saraqael used a little mind voodoo on her?" Tessa wiggled her fingers.

"Yeah, I kinda do think that." She sighed. With twilight quickly approaching, there was no time to alter their plan. Since Deward had been able to follow Evangeline last time, she knew they could use that connection to do it again. But this time they'd be able to communicate with her. In a place like that, out of the physical realm, magic was harder to control. They had planned for everything they could. Still... "I'll be right back."

"All right, boss lady."

They hadn't let Evangeline out of their sight since recovering her. It hadn't improved her mood one bit, but the girl also hadn't tried to force the issue. Behind the rage-filled front, Ceri knew she just felt guilty about everything.

Evangeline looked up as she approached. "It's not quite twilight."

"I know." Ceri pulled the bracelet out of her pocket and handed it to her.

Evangeline's face hardened as she inspected the protective rune hanging from it. "You think he screwed with my brain?"

"Maybe. It would have been subtle."

Evangeline ground her teeth together and shoved the bracelet at Ceri. "I'm not interested in your trying to make me feel better--"

"This is not about your feelings." Ceri pushed her hand away. "Take it. Wear it. Don't jeopardize our chances because of your pride."

Evangeline yanked the bracelet on. "Fine."

A gentle nudge from Genevieve drew Ceri's attention. She was approaching with Amber, whose face was flushed with anger. Leaving Evangeline to stew in whatever guilt trip she was determined to cling to, Ceri walked over to meet them. The sun was barely visible over the horizon. They had only minutes left.

"What's up?" she asked, eyes flicking back and forth from Gen to Amber.

"Kadrithan isn't coming."

Ceri frowned. "Seriously? Is he hurt?" This was everything he had worked for years. It made no sense.

"I think the incubi are trying to kill the last of the fae." Amber's hand rubbed at her chest. "That's why we aren't under attack right now. It doesn't matter if we break the curse if every single fae is dead."

"We'll work as fast as we can. It shouldn't take long once Evangeline is pulled into the Crux of Realms."

A muscle in Amber's jaw twitched as she ground her teeth together. "This has to work."

"It *will* work." Ceri pulled her into a tight hug, not caring who was watching. "Have a little faith."

"Not to bust up this moment, but twilight isn't going to wait." Genevieve tapped the time on her phone pointedly. "Is everything good to go?"

Ceri stepped back and nodded. "Yes. Defenses set up?"

"As well as they can be," Amber said as she visibly pulled herself together. The flickering emotions that had been leaking through the pack bond ceased abruptly.

Derek jogged over and held her gaze for a moment. "Be safe."

"You too." Ceri took a step back then turned and hurried away before her emotions overwhelmed her. Derek would be fine. She would be fine. They were at the end of all this chaos. Now was not the time to falter.

Deward and Tommy were waiting for her near the coven. Deward's cloudy eyes were wide and flicked from side to side as if he was watching something. "So many things are converging here. It's like a storm."

Tommy's mouth was set in a grim line. "You sure you don't want the rest of the pack to go with you?"

"Yeah, I'm sure. We could be attacked. We need you to have our back." Ceri gave his arm a quick squeeze.

"All right." He clapped a hand on Deward's shoulder and gave her a nod. "I'll stop pulling an Amber and worrying over you guys."

"*I heard that!*" Amber complained, flipping them off and waving the finger.

Tommy jogged away, leaving Deward with her. The troll still seemed distracted and uncharacteristically edgy.

"I'll do my best to keep you safe," Ceri said, laying a hand on his arm as they stepped into the circle.

"I'm not concerned for myself."

"Then what is it?"

His brows drew together. "I can't see the light in Evangeline anymore."

"Do you think she'll betray us again?"

"No. She wants this curse broken and the incubi crippled as much as we do. Maybe more. This is a different problem entirely." He shook his head. "No purpose in worrying over it now. There's no going back."

Ceri pushed her shoulders back and nodded. "You can sit right here." Deward moved to the designated spot as she searched for Evangeline near the edge of the coven and nodded.

Evangeline walked over and sat down across from him. Her face was flushed, having recently fed, but the dark rings around her eyes showed how exhausted she still was. "Really cutting it close, aren't we?"

Ceri ignored the comment and inspected everything that had been laid out. Nothing was missing, despite the anxious worry that had settled in the pit of her stomach.

Still driven by the prophecy, Deward was their best link to Evangeline. The last time he'd tried to follow her to the Crux of Realms, he'd gotten stuck in the spirit realm. They couldn't risk being separated from Evangeline again. The coven had to be there with her, if at all possible. The only way to ensure that was to temporarily bind the three of them together, and the pack bond she shared with Deward was a strong connection. Deward's connection to Evangeline through the prophecy was weaker, but it would be enough if they amplified it.

"You both ready?" Ceri asked quietly.

They nodded. Deward seemed perfectly calm, but Evangeline was practically vibrating with anticipation.

Ceri took her place within the circle. Deward and Evangeline sat on the other two points of the triangle within the inner circle. In a silver container between them were dried rowan berries. The rowan tree, which was the unifying symbol of their pack tattoo, would increase their connection to the spirits as well as help protect them.

Though she tried to keep her hands steady, her fingers trembled as she lifted the pouch that held the Seed of Life from her bag. She loosened the drawstring and dropped it out onto her palm. Its light filled the inner circle but stopped at the boundary. Grass rose up from the dirt and wound around their legs.

"Bound to the Seed of Life; hope of the Givers." Ceri set it in front of Evangeline then lifted the Angellical stone from her purse. It was ice cold against her skin. "Bound to the Angellical Stone; sin of the Curse Makers."

She set it next to the first item and lit the sage. The sweet smoke swirled around them, providing her a measure of calm. She had to focus on what she knew: magic. It was all she could control. The last of the golden rays faded into soft blues as darkness crept in around them. "Magic's price satisfied through sacrifice."

With the still-smoldering sage, she lit the ground rowan berries. The flame sputtered over the red powder before fully igniting. "As long as both persist, so shall the curse endure. Only the eternal flame can purge that which it has made within the Crux of Realms."

She breathed in the mingled scents and sank into her magic. "As long as we remain in this circle, we are connected and protected." She rested her hands on her knees. The fire glowed between them, pulsing as their hearts began to beat in sync. She blinked, and their vision merged, showing her what each of them saw at the same time. Through Deward, the magic building around Evangeline glowed like white fire. But within her, there was only darkness.

"That is disorienting as hell," Evangeline muttered as she picked up both objects, holding them tight in her fists.

"Just breathe. You'll adjust."

Before Evangeline could voice any further complaints, the magic that tied her to the Crux of Realms swelled abruptly within Ceri. It filled the circle, wrapping around all three of them, and yanked them into darkness.

CHAPTER 5

EVANGELINE

Twilight had muted the harsh colors of the desert to her left. It looked beautiful for once. The dunes were draped in shadows that pooled in the valleys like lakes of indigo. Evangeline pulled her eyes away from it reluctantly. She didn't want to look to her right. She knew who awaited her there.

Saraqael met her gaze, and the bracelet warmed against her wrist. His expression was warm, as if he expected to fall back into the same role he'd filled before his betrayal. As if she'd trust him all over again. Ceri had been right. That bastard had entranced her, and he was trying again. "Hello, daughter."

"That won't work anymore."

He pursed his lips and let out a sigh. "What a pity. It would have saved me so much trouble."

"I'm going to kill you." She didn't shout at him, though she wanted to. She didn't lunge at him, either. It would have been pointless.

He tilted his head to the side, a bemused smile tugging at the corners of his mouth. "You will try."

She turned away from him and looked down at the items still clutched in her hands. "I think it's kind of poetic that you've given me the power to do this." Magic pulsed within her, eager to be unleashed. "Or maybe it's just karma."

"This won't save anyone. The fae will be dead soon, if they aren't already. You will die as well."

She snorted and shook her head. He was desperate. Panicking. The arrogant bastard was practically begging her not to do this. "Guess we all have to die eventually. At least I'll die having served the purpose I was born for."

Evangeline lifted the Seed of Life. It pulsed with so much magic and potential, warming her all the way through. It really was a shame she had to destroy it. The Angellical stone, however, she couldn't wait to burn. The thing felt like death in her hand.

Part of her wanted to savor this moment, but the rational part of her brain was screaming that they were running out of time. It was now or never. Evangeline lifted both items overhead and unleashed her birthright. Pure white fire erupted from her palms.

There was no ritual. No magic words that could end this. Only brute force and the same sacrifice that cursed the fae in the first place. The hope of the Givers and the sin of the Curse Makers had to be destroyed.

The Seed of Life sparked and shuddered as the fire ate away at its protective shell. The Angellical stone cracked in half. Blood oozed out like molten lava and dripped from her closed fist as she heard the distant screams of the souls that had been sacrificed to create it.

Her hands shook as she struggled to maintain the flow of magic. Even freshly fed, this strained the limits of her control. Tremors ran up her legs, and her entire body began to tremble...except... She tore her gaze away from the burning items. It wasn't her body that was shaking. It was everything.

A snowflake landed on her cheek, melting instantly into a rivulet of water that trailed down her face. Another joined it, then another and another, until a swirling blizzard surrounded her. This shouldn't be possible. Nothing could touch her here.

Her feet slipped, almost causing her to lose her balance completely. She looked down and found sand beneath her feet. A cool breeze blew the snow away, and the scent of grass and fresh water filled her nose instead. Her eyes went wide as she swung her gaze around to Saraqael. A smile spread across his face. He lunged for her.

CHAPTER 6

CERI

Ceri had no time to think or plan. Only react. She thrust out a hand as she cast a panicked spell. A shield flared into place as Saraqael's attack struck near Evangeline. Light blinded her, but she didn't stop moving. She had no idea how long the realms would be merged like this or how far-reaching the effect was. She had to reach Evangeline before Saraqael did.

The coven's distant chants filled the air, and a larger shield sprung up around her, Evangeline, and Deward. Ceri's feet slipped as she moved from snow to sand. Sudden heat washed over her, a stark contrast to the chill of the spirit realm.

She whirled around, and Deward was gone. She couldn't see Evangeline, either. There was only empty desert. Panic threatened to overwhelm her for a moment, but she pushed it aside and sat down, pressing her palms to the ground. No matter where she was, she was connected to the pack and Evangeline.

Ceri focused on her heartbeat. It raced alongside Evangeline's. The girl was in danger. *"Visus!"* Evangeline's vision overlaid her own, but it wasn't clear. Flashes of light blinded her, and Ceri was forced to end the connection.

Think, Ceri commanded herself. There was a way out of this. A way to protect Evangeline from Saraqael.

The surrounding air began to shake. Sand lifted from the ground, vibrating together until a roar filled her ears. Snow blew in from behind her, but ahead of her, the fabric of the realm split open, revealing a green field. Ceri lunged for it.

As her feet hit grass, she glanced over her shoulder. Deward was tumbling into the fae realm behind her. Before she had a chance to get his attention, Saraqael turned to her. He was stunningly beautiful. His face seemed carved from marble, and his eyes were bluer than the clear skies overhead. But his mouth was twisted into a snarl as he swung his hand toward her.

White flames swept toward her in a wave that seared the grass. She lifted her palms and pulled on the pack's strength to protect herself. A great gust of wind blew in from behind her and drove a wedge through the fire. Heat blasted over her, drying the sweat from her face, but it didn't burn her. She couldn't hope to overpower Saraqael, but she could divert his attacks.

But if they switched realms again…Deward would not be able to. She ground her teeth together. There had to be a way to protect both him and Evangeline.

The answer came to her in a flash as the air began to shake again. Without hesitation, Ceri flung herself at Saraqael. She collided with him, catching the incubus completely off-guard. Her momentum forced them backward as the realms shifted once again. His foot caught on a rock buried in the snow, and they tumbled down the icy slope. He grabbed her arm, and the tattoo on her thigh burned with searing pain as he poured considerable power into his efforts to entrance her.

Ceri drove her knee straight up and connected with the vulnerable place between his legs. His grip loosened just enough for her to wrench her arm free. The quick motion sent her sliding through the snow.

She flung a handful of snow into the air as she cast a spell. The ice crystals hardened and shot toward Saraqael, obscuring his vision briefly as she darted to the side. She had to stay close enough to drag him with her again, if at all possible. It wouldn't be so easy to take him by surprise this time, though.

Darkness erupted from the ground and wrapped around her legs. She sank into it like quicksand.

Saraqael prowled toward her. "You cannot stop me from reaching my daughter."

A loud keening split the air, and thunder cracked overhead. The familiar bobbing light of the owl spirit rushed toward her. But it was not alone. Hundreds of them were tumbling down the hill toward her and Saraqael in a glowing tidal wave.

The incubus glanced back with a frown. He lifted his hands, and a wall of white fire rolled up the slope toward them, but the spirits burst through as if it didn't exist. Saraqael was forced to turn and face them.

Ceri used the distraction to struggle against the darkness wrapped around her legs. She'd fought against this before, and so had Amber. Sinking into the pack bond, she reached for her alpha's strength and knowledge. Amber's power burned through her, along with her fear and rage. The pack was fighting. The incubus had attacked after all, and Ceri hadn't noticed it until now because of her own desperate situation. She nearly lost her hold on the pack bond as worry for them threatened to overwhelm her. Derek needed her. They all did.

With a shake of her head, Ceri refocused, grabbed the darkness with clawed fingers, and ripped through it as the spirits rolled over both Saraqael and her. She had to finish *this* fight before she could help the others.

Ceri Ceri Ceri. The spirits' frenzied whispers made her head ache. They were trying to help, but it was too much all at once. She pushed forward, the darkness still grasping at her as she moved.

Summoned wind blew her hair into her face, but the spirits parted before her, clearing a path to Saraqael. He wielded a sword made of the same white fire that Evangeline was using to break the curse. With every swing of his blade, he cut through several spirits. Their cries rippled through the air in a palpable wave.

She lunged for him but moved backward instead of forward. The realms were shifting again. She'd been too slow. As she fell backward toward the fae realm, Deward stumbled into view about a dozen yards away. There was no way to reach him or protect him. He'd have to face Saraqael alone.

CHAPTER 7

EVANGELINE

Evangeline stayed on her knees as sand shifted to grass beneath her. Sweat dripped down her brow, and her arms shook with exhaustion. The Seed's ashes smoldered in her left hand, still pulsing with magic, which she greedily absorbed. Without its help, she would have already collapsed.

The Angellical Stone had cracked, but she saw now that its black center remained intact. There was something inside it... something bad. And it wanted out. Gritting her teeth together, she tightened her grip on it and forced the eternal flame to burn even hotter in her hand. Almost instantly, the realms shifted again. They were moving faster now.

Snow blurred her vision as she looked up, but Deward's silhouette was clear. As was Saraqael's. The troll and incubus moved back and forth in a violent dance as Deward narrowly avoided the attacks volleyed at him.

"Shit." The stupid troll shouldn't even be here. But he was. And he was going to die if she didn't protect him. She had no idea how he was dodging anything considering he was blind.

Struggling to her feet, Evangeline took a step toward them, but her legs gave out beneath her. She couldn't continue channeling this much magic *and* help Deward. It just wasn't possible. She'd have to choose between helping him or breaking the curse.

A blow connected with Deward's arm, knocking him flat on his back. Evangeline watched in horror, frozen in indecision. This was their only chance to break the curse, but she couldn't just watch as someone else was killed right in front of her. Her fingers tightened around the Angellical Stone. There had to be a way to do both. There had to be--

The air shuddered around her, but instead of pulling her to a different realm like she expected, Ceri was spit out practically on top of her. The witch's full focus was on Deward. Ceri sprinted past her and flung out a spell just in time to thwart Saraqael's final blow.

Evangeline let out a harsh sigh of relief and shut her eyes, blocking out the fight in front of her. No matter what happened next, she had to finish breaking the damn curse. Then she'd kill Saraqael.

A high-pitched wailing startled her back into awareness. Spirits swarmed Saraqael and her two friends. Ceri cast a bright spell as she scrambled away from Saraqael with Deward leaning heavily against her shoulder.

"You have to finish this!" Ceri shouted, her blue eyes wide with fear.

"I'm trying, but I'm not strong enough!" Evangeline shouted back.

Ceri slid to a stop in front of her and wrapped a hand around her arm. Evangeline felt *power* flow into her. The depth of the shaman's and the pack's magic was awe-inspiring. This was more than anything she'd ever imagined. It was enough to end this.

Her body and mind strained against the agony of channeling so much magic, but she did not relent. This had to end. It had to. A blood vessel in her eye popped as she screamed. The edges of her vision grew dark. She wouldn't make it.

Another hand wrapped around her wrist--Deward's--and the strain lessened as if he'd taken a weight off her shoulders. The magic flared within all three of them and burst free through her palms. Her eyes fluttered open. Saraqael had broken free of the spirits. His brilliantly white wings spread wide as he leaped into the air and dove straight toward them. She grinned. He was too late.

The Angellical Stone shattered. A piercing shriek rent the air as the pain of thousands of souls was released. The sacrifice that had powered the centuries old curse was undone. Snow, grass, desert, and the vampire's backyard all swirled together, connected only by the moon overhead. Twilight had ended. Her eyes focused on the stars overhead.

On blood and flame that fell from the sky.

On light and darkness.

On death.

She was falling, too.

CHAPTER 8

AMBER

Amber's teeth snapped together with a jarring crack. The incubus's throat had been right there. She had no idea how she'd missed. Her muscles tensed as she instinctively prepared for their counterattack, but nothing happened. The incubus that had been right in front of her was...gone.

The fur on her spine stood on end as she took a hesitant step back and looked around. A cold wind washed over the now-quiet battlefield. She and her allies all stood frozen in shock. Every single incubus had vanished. Without a trace.

Is this some kind of illusion? Genevieve asked through the bond. *They can't really be gone.*

I don't— Amber's reply was cut off as an explosion knocked them all off their feet. Scalding heat washed over her body, leaving her cold as it vanished. She forced herself upright. The coven had been knocked out of the circle. None of them were moving.

Fire streaked across the night sky. Someone screamed, though Amber wasn't sure if she'd heard it or simply felt it through the pack bond. Her legs shook as she sprinted toward the coven. The fight had taken all their strength--even drawing on the power of the packs as Alpha Dominus.

"Ceri!" Derek shouted, the panic clear in his voice. She was hurt, and they could all sense it. Her brother searched through the coven with increasing fear then spun in a circle. "Where is she?"

Amber slid to a stop behind him and stared in horror at the blank space where Ceri, Deward, and Evangeline all should have been. "Did you see where any of them went?"

Derek shook his head, staring blankly at the inner circle. The sage still smoldered there, its smoke curling up in a strange, jagged spiral. "No."

Tommy and Genevieve slid to a stop next to her and shook Deward. "What happened to them?"

"I don't know. Are any of the witches awake?" Amber glanced back as she asked. A few were twitching, but they all appeared to be unconscious.

"We have to find her," Derek demanded.

"I know." Amber took a deep breath and sank into the pack bond. Ceri and Deward's connection was clear, but nothing else was. There were flashes of pain and confusion, a vague sense of them being far, but nothing concrete. The bond must be exhausted, just like it had been after that fight in Vegas.

"I can't sense where she is." Derek bit out each word in frustration.

"I can't, either. But the pack bond is exhausted. This has happened before. We just need a chance to rest. And we have to figure out what happened. Where is Tessa? She was the one helping Ceri plan."

"I'll find her," Genevieve volunteered, turning away immediately to search through the witches.

Derek's frustration and fear threatened to overwhelm her. She grabbed his arm and yanked him into a tight hug. "We will find her. She will be okay."

"You can't know that."

"I trust her and Deward to protect themselves. That's all we can do in this moment, okay? Have a little faith."

He nodded awkwardly but pulled away.

"Let's get them all into the house," Amber said, seeing the need to give them all something to do before the panic set in. "We may need to leave quickly, and we shouldn't just leave them laying on the grass, regardless."

"Are we sure the curse is even broken?" Tommy asked.

Amber hesitated then nodded. "I think it is." She rubbed a hand over the place her demon mark had been. "I hope it is." A snowflake hit Amber's cheek. She looked up in confusion, but the sky was clear.

"Did you feel that?" Tommy rubbed his hands briskly up and down his arms. "It got super cold for a moment."

"No, but a snowflake--" A gust of wind cut her off, and for a moment, she was alone, surrounded by snow. As quickly as it had occurred, she was back with everyone else.

Derek's eyes grew wide. "You vanished."

Amber patted herself down, just to make sure she was awake. "I think...I was in the spirit realm for a second."

"How could you have--" Tommy froze as a shouting began near the house.

A wave of fear rolled through the other packs. The hair on the back of her neck stood on end. "Something is wrong." She met Genevieve's eyes and nodded. It was time to activate the emergency plan. "Derek, go help Genevieve. Tommy, come back and help me with the rest of the coven."

He sprinted away as Amber hurried over to the nearest witch, who lay prone on the ground, her eyes twitching behind the lids. A sound too sharp to be thunder cracked overhead. Amber jerked her head up and saw more fire streaking across the sky like meteors. Even though the sun had set, the whole field was lit up bright as day.

Her hair fluttered as the air was displaced beside her. Bram squinted up at the sky, one long finger tapping against his chin. "What an interesting turn of events."

"Did we accidentally cause the apocalypse?" Amber whispered. She'd expected something dramatic, but not *this*.

"Hopefully not. That would be rather…awkward."

"Awkward? Seriously?" She put her face in her hands and took a deep breath. Now was not the time to get hung up on Bram's weird word choices. She needed to do something. To fix the maybe-apocalypse she'd started. Step one: get the witches to safety. Step two: wake up Tessa and figure out what the hell had happened. Step three: find Ceri and Deward.

Genevieve jogged over, followed closely by Jameson and Greer. Amber yelled out instructions, and the witches were whisked inside in seconds. Jameson's pack spread out toward the perimeter, ready to move into the woods if needed. Greer's pack stayed in place on the other side of the property as their first line of defense in case of attack. Ito's pack and the vampires were stationed around the interior of the property.

They were as ready as they could be for whatever came next.

CHAPTER 9

AMBER

Amber scrubbed blood out from under her fingernails. She wasn't sure who it belonged to anymore. It was likely a mix of enemy and ally. The injured had all been carried inside, and the remaining dead were being identified. They'd only lost a few, but after the battle yesterday, the pain of those deaths was almost unbearable. The mood was subdued. Quiet. Angry.

She met her own gaze in the bathroom mirror. Dark rings highlighted how bloodshot her eyes were. The scars on her cheek stood out, stark against her pale skin. It wasn't dramatic to say she looked awful. But no matter how bad she looked, she felt worse.

The emotional feedback from being connected to so many packs was overwhelming. Grief that wasn't her own tightened her chest, making it hard to breathe. Constant anger echoed through the bond from Ito––something she suspected was intentional. He wanted nothing more than to see her break. To prove he was right and she wasn't strong enough to be Alpha Dominus.

He was right that she hadn't been prepared for the long-lasting consequences of her choice, but she'd be damned if she was going to give up now. What was done was done. She'd find a way to survive it, like she always had. She'd find Ceri, Deward, Evangeline, and Kadrithan. And she'd cut down anyone that tried to stand in her way.

Tommy knocked once then poked his head into the bathroom. "Tessa is starting to twitch and is mumbling. We still can't wake her up, but the twitching is sort of a good sign?"

"It's something." She grabbed a towel off the rack and dried her hands then gestured for Tommy to lead the way. They desperately needed the witches to wake up. The pack bond was still not working quite right. What bothered Amber was that it didn't feel exactly as it had last time it had been exhausted. Something was just...wonky.

Tessa and the other witches were arranged on the left side of the living room floor, while the injured were at the other end. The vampires had helped stem the bleeding from any serious wounds so the werewolves could heal more quickly. The trolls were mostly tending to their own.

Bram rose to his feet as they approached. "Their heartbeats are elevated."

"So they definitely aren't just sleeping." Amber sighed and shoved her hands in her pockets.

"No, this is a magical issue. They must be struggling to re-awaken."

Amber pursed her lips as she thought the problem through. "They were in the spirit realm, I think. Have you ever seen anyone get stuck there?"

"Never simply stuck." Bram tapped a long finger against his chin. "I have seen them trapped there before."

"Deward was trapped once. I got him out, but we had the pack connection, and Ceri helped me get to the spirit realm in the first place." She sighed as Tessa's hand twitched once again. "I have no idea how to get there on my own."

"Perhaps the other shaman we found could help you."

Amber jerked her head up. "What?"

"She said her name was Jean. One of mine found her tied up in a closet. She claimed a sorcerer had tied her up and cut off her finger to use in a spell so that she could take her place."

"Where is she now?"

"We handed her over to the MIB. I believe Agent Icewind took custody of her personally."

"I need to find Gen. We should get her back. She might be able to help with this." Amber automatically reached for the pack bond, only to find it still in a tangle of confusion. Even knowing Genevieve was nearby, it was impossible to sense exactly where she was.

"It's coming right for us!" The frantic shout echoed through the house.

Amber's heart jumped into overdrive as she sprinted toward the source of the warning. They'd barely had a moment to rest. They couldn't survive another attack so soon after the last.

Genevieve burst through the front door. "This way! It's landing in the front yard!"

"What is?" she demanded as she slid to a stop in front of Genevieve.

"One of the fireballs. There were two, but the second veered off at a weird angle."

Amber followed her outside. Sure enough, a single fiery comet was plummeting straight toward them. It was close enough to illuminate the entire area. There was no time to react or prepare. Luckily, everyone had had enough common sense to get out of the way and the front yard was empty.

She had a moment to remember that even when small comets hit, they left a huge crater and sent out a devastating shock wave. Her heart clenched as it plunged to the earth barely a dozen yards away. Amber turned away and shielded Genevieve as she braced herself for a fiery impact, but the comet hit the ground with a dull thunk, and the light blinked out.

"Well, that was anticlimactic." Genevieve peeked over her shoulder. The heady scent of magic filled the air as mist rose up from the strange object.

"About time something was." With adrenaline still pumping wildly through her system, Amber couldn't stop the slight trembling in her limbs. "Now we just need to find out what it was and hope it doesn't explode when we get close."

"I'm feeling optimistic."

"Good, you can go check on it, then."

Genevieve scowled at her. "Not that optimistic."

"I'll check it out," Derek said as he stepped out of the front door behind them. He looked as tired as she felt. "Maybe it'll help us figure out where Ceri is. Somehow."

Amber took a deep breath. "Maybe so. Come on."

Genevieve sighed then jogged to catch up. The scent of magic grew stronger as they approached the unidentified-falling-object. She knew it had to be something unnatural since it had slowed down before hitting the ground. The only thing they didn't know was if it was dangerous.

"Spread out." Amber approached it head-on while Genevieve and Derek circled around. There was no crater, just a mist that obscured whatever had fallen there.

Ito broke away from the gathered crowd and strode after them as if he couldn't let Amber and her pack show him up. The mist drifted slowly away as they crept closer. A shape became visible on the ground, but it wasn't anything like she had expected.

Tommy froze. "That's a person."

Pale wings were crumpled around the woman's frail body. She looked...malnourished. And breakable. Not at all close to how the "angels" had always presented themselves.

"It's a succubus," Amber whispered.

Her foot twitched, and they all jerked away in alarm. "Help... me..." The succubus's eyes opened. She reached a shaking hand toward Genevieve but didn't have the strength to move her arm far.

"I'll kill it." Ito drew a blade from his waistband and took a step toward the creature.

"No!" Genevieve flung herself between the werewolf and the trembling succubus. "We need to talk to her. We have no clue what's going on."

"They are masters of illusions and lies, able to control us with a simple touch. There is nothing to learn from any of them," Ito spat out.

"She can't hurt us. We're protected against their influence. And look at her! She can barely move." Genevieve threw her arms in the air in frustration.

"Her appearance could be false!" Ito retorted. "There is no point in taking the risk."

"We can't just execute every incubus and succubus we come across."

"We can and we should." Ito took another step forward, fingers tightening around his knife.

"Kill it!" someone from the crowd jeered behind them. Support echoed up around him, mingled with very few objections. Anger and fear welled up from the gathered packs like a tidal wave. It would only take a single spark, and they'd be lost to the violence brewing in their hearts.

"*Enough!*" Amber's voice boomed over the chaos. Everyone grew silent. "We have no idea what the ramifications of breaking this curse are right now. To find out, we may have to talk to the incubi. We are not going to kill them on sight. Just as before, we'll defend ourselves if necessary, but that's it."

Amber gave Tommy and Derek each a short nod. She needed them to watch their backs. They were in a bad spot and surrounded by Ito's pack. She couldn't afford to split her attention.

Ito grew still for a moment, but a ripple went through the bond between them. Something in his intentions shifted, and she *felt* him make the decision. "I never should have trusted you."

"Don't do this. Not now," she whispered.

"I have to. Before you can lead us further on this path of destruction." Clutching the knife tightly in his fist, he leaped at her. Amber threw herself back and narrowly dodged the first jab of his blade. She hadn't expected him to attack in human form. As wolves, they were narrowly matched; in human form, whatever fighting skills he had would far outweigh her own. She had no choice.

"Stay back!" She shouted the order at Genevieve, who was about to try to join the fight. This challenge had to be fought one on one, or she'd lose the respect of everyone there.

Amber darted out of reach of his next attack then called on the shift. It rolled up from the bottoms of her feet, easy as an exhale. But...her feet didn't change. Neither did her hands. Or her face. Pain wrenched through her chest, and she stumbled backward.

Ito's eyes narrowed, and he lunged at her. Pressure built in her chest as she realized there was no way to dodge it this time, but the attack didn't land. Instead, her wolf collided with Ito and drove him to the ground with her jaws wrapped around his throat. Ito went still beneath the wolf, but his rage-filled eyes remained locked on Amber.

She blinked twice, staring blankly in shock at her wolf, who stood about a foot away. Her wolf was there, pinning him down, but she was still standing. Without taking her eyes off Ito, she patted her body. Still there. Definitely not a dream.

"What the hell just happened?" Genevieve demanded.

Good question, the wolf responded in her mind.

"I don't know. I didn't..." Amber shook her head, completely at a loss to explain how this had happened. "Genevieve, can you shift?"

Genevieve shut her eyes, and a moment later, her wolf burst from her chest. Everyone gathered stared at her in stunned silence. This was...not good. Tommy tried next, and sure enough, his small black wolf landed on the ground in front of him and paced back and forth, growling at the crowd that stood silent behind Amber.

"What have you done to us?" Ito demanded, his voice slipping into a growl.

"I haven't suddenly figured out the answer to that in the last five seconds," Amber snapped. Of course this was a disaster. Of course she wanted to know what the hell was going on.

"I should have killed you when I had the chance," he snarled.

Submit. Her wolf's words rumbled through the air, both audible and not. She'd spoken in Amber's mind, but this time, Amber was sure everyone present had heard the threat.

"She doesn't deserve the title of Alpha. She has corrupted us all," Ito ground out, apparently unwilling to give up so easily. "I would rather die than continue submitting to her."

Her wolf released his throat and lifted her head to meet his eyes. *Foolish child, so sure of your own understanding. Amber seeks to restore balance. Bring your wolf out and let us settle this once and for all, or I will end you and every useless pup you call pack mate.*

"No." He tried to shove her wolf away but couldn't even budge her an inch.

Amber's wolf plunged her face into his chest, but instead of the expected gore, her wolf simply dragged his out by the scruff of its neck. Ito's wolf dropped its belly to the ground in immediate submission.

They stared at each other for a long moment. Ito's wolf whimpered, as if in pain, then turned over to show his belly. Magic swelled around both wolves, then Ito's wolf vanished with a pop.

Ito cried out in pain. His eyes were wide with shock as he hugged his arms around his middle, all pretense of composure gone. "What have you done?"

Amber's wolf lifted her head, eyes blazing bright red. *He will return to you when you have proven to me you deserve him.*

"You took his wolf away?" Amber demanded.

Yes.

"You can't just do that!"

I can, and I did.

CHAPTER 10

GENEVIEVE

Genevieve stared at Amber. Then at Ito. This was a disaster of epic proportions. Worse than the apocalypse they'd accidentally caused. Worse than half the pack being missing. Not only were their wolves broken, Amber had just accidentally banished Ito's. Was he even still technically a werewolf?

Her wolf yipped, startling them all. *Her heart stopped.*

"Oh no!" Genevieve exclaimed as she raced over. Sure enough, the succubus no longer had a pulse. She flipped the frail woman over onto her back and began chest compressions. A rib cracked beneath her palms, but the succubus's heart stayed still in her chest. There was no life left in her. Genevieve sat back, her breaths as shaky as her hands. "She's dead."

Amber nodded once. "Carry her body inside."

Genevieve carefully picked up the dead succubus. She was feather-light, but her wings made her a bit awkward to hold. In the back of her mind, she realized she still had the heightened senses of a werewolf, even with her wolf outside her body. Interesting.

Her wolf trotted ahead of her, and the crowd gathered in front of the house parted before her like she was a leper. Ito's pack members were easy to pick out; they were the ones staring at her like they were trying to set her on fire with their minds. She huffed out a sigh and forced her eyes straight ahead. Once again, her pack got all the hate for someone else's screw-up. Ito had attacked Amber, and he'd suffered the consequences.

Adele met her at the door and waved her inside. "I've cleared a space in a separate room." The vampire shut the door firmly behind them then flicked her eyes toward the window. "I thought it best to keep her away from the others."

"Yeah. Good call." Her wolf stayed pressed against her leg like a comforting shadow as they walked upstairs.

Adele glanced at the succubus. "She looks like she was ill before she died."

"I had the same thought. Ill or starving."

The vampire raised an eyebrow. "I can't imagine why a succubus would starve. The angels had many admirers and therefore many willing people to feed from."

Genevieve looked back down at the succubus's gaunt face. It would be strange, but she couldn't think of another explanation. Every bone in the succubus's back was a sharp ridge against Genevieve's arms, and her cheeks were sunken in. Surely this wasn't what their race looked like with all the illusions stripped away.

"This is the room I cleared out." Adele opened the door and waved her inside.

Genevieve laid the succubus on the floor and sat back. Part of her was glad the succubus had died, but she couldn't get the woman's desperate plea for help out of her head. Maybe it had been a trick or she'd hoped to feed off Genevieve. Maybe she'd just known she was dying.

Bram appeared in the doorway. His creepy, pale eyes locked on the succubus. "There are others landing nearby. Perhaps a small group could apprehend a living prisoner?"

"Probably a good idea if we can manage it." Genevieve

smoothed the succubus's hair back then pulled the sheet up to cover her.

"I will send my people to help with any that land close by, but they cannot fight at full strength once the sun rises," Adele said, gesturing toward the east.

Everything could spin out of control in an instant. The tensions between their allies and Ito's pack were too high. They needed to know what was going on. Bram's suggestion to capture a live prisoner was a good one, but that wasn't quite enough. They needed to know how extensive the chaos was. Was it only the werewolves here that couldn't shift anymore? Or was it worldwide?

"I'll talk to Amber, but I need to make a couple of phone calls first." Genevieve pushed back up to her feet. "I have a feeling we aren't the only ones freaking out right now."

CHAPTER 11

CERI

"Well, first things first, we need to figure out where we are." Ceri put her hands on her hips and looked around. The trees were cypress. The cone-shaped "knees" that stuck out of the water all around them were unmistakable. So they probably weren't in Montana anymore. She was *pretty* sure they weren't still in the spirit realm, but the fact that she wasn't one hundred percent certain was unsettling. This place had an odd vibe.

"It smells wet." Deward stood and shook the muck off his hands. "And feels wet."

"We appear to be in some sort of swampy area with cypress trees." The water was only ankle deep here, which was lucky, but she suspected it might be deeper around them. They'd have to be careful trying to walk out.

Deward frowned. "Interesting. From what I remember, they mainly grow in the southern United States. Not Montana."

"You would be correct." Ceri took another deep breath and reached inward for the pack bond once again. It was there, yet she couldn't sense anything helpful at all. Amber and the others were distressed but not necessarily hurt. Worry was a strong emotion.

They were all alive, though, which had to be enough for now. "Can you tell how far we are from the rest of the pack?"

"No. I assume you can't, either?"

"Nope."

"I can't see through your eyes like I normally can, either." Deward slicked his wet hair back with a frustrated sigh. "And Evangeline is gone?"

"Yes. I have some vague memory of her shoving us away, but I'm not sure exactly what happened after the curse was broken. I only remember falling."

Deward turned in a circle, his hands outstretched. "There's magic hovering in the air like a fog."

"There's actual fog, too. More of a mist, actually. I think it's from our landing."

"Is your magic exhausted from the fight in the spirit realm?"

She shrugged. "I'm tired, but not as much as I expected. I have considered casting a finding spell of some sort, if that's what you're about to suggest, but wanted to get our bearings first. There's something...off."

He nodded. "I feel it, too."

"All right. Ideally, I'd get to dry ground so I can try to cast a circle, but I don't see a patch of dirt in any direction, so I'm just going to have to risk it." Ceri knelt in the water, trying not to freak out about the squish of mud under her knees and what little critters might be lurking in it. And what bigger things might be in the murky water itself.

A circle provided protection and helped focus. Simple spells could be cast without it and, of course, when fighting, she couldn't rely on one. Worry still bubbled up in the pit of her gut. There was something she was missing.

Focus, she reminded herself. *Trust the magic.* She let the water still around her until she felt the ripples of life within it, rather than caused them. *Intent.* Determine the distance between them and the rest of the pack. She inhaled and turned her face upward to the moon and whispered the spell.

Her magic flowed out. And jerked her face-first into the shallow water. Everything grew frigidly cold in an instant. A strong hand yanked her out of the water, and she took a gasping breath, but she couldn't see Deward, only snow swirling around her. She blinked, and it all vanished, leaving her in a swamp next to the troll, with one foot stuck in a frozen chunk of ice.

"What…just…happened?" she choked out. Water and gunk hung from her hair. She tried to wipe it out of her eyes, but that only served to smear it around even more.

"I'm not sure even though I could see it." Deward cocked his head to the side, thankfully still keeping one arm tight around her to hold her upright. "The spell tangled as soon as you cast it."

"Tangled?"

"Yes, there is normally a clear path for magic. It flows outward without hitting any obstacles, but this time it scrambled immediately. I've never seen anything like it." He shrugged. "Not that I have much experience seeing magic."

She wiggled her foot. The ice was melting, but not fast enough, and it was starting to hurt. "Can you break up this chunk of ice my foot is stuck in? I don't think I can bust it on my own, and I'm sure as hell not going to cast another spell in all this water."

"Oh." Deward frowned. "Of course, I didn't realize there was still ice. Which foot?"

"Right one."

He knelt down and felt out where it was. Then, with a well-placed punch, broke it in half. She pulled her foot free with a sigh of relief. The warmer water stung a bit, but with a few wiggles of her toes, she adjusted to the temperature change.

"Will you be able to walk on it, or are you injured?"

"I'm good to walk." She looked around at the seemingly endless swamp. "Though I have no idea which direction to go."

Deward thought silently for a moment then shrugged. "If we are in the southern United States, heading south would eventually lead us toward the coast. I believe most large cities are nearer the coast than the inland regions in that area."

"As good an idea as any we have right now. We should try to get as far as we can tonight. I don't want to end up having to sleep in a swamp."

"I agree. Getting somewhere dry should be a priority." He rubbed his dirty fingers together. "Locating drinkable fresh water is impossible in a place like this."

Ceri sighed. "I'd say I can purify it, but that'd just as likely set it on fire, apparently."

"Perhaps we'll get lucky and find we are at the edge of this swamp."

"Fat chance," Ceri muttered, not feeling particularly optimistic about anything at the moment. She gathered her muck-filled hair and twisted it into the best tangled bun she could manage. The mud helped it stick together at least. "I think that way is south."

"I'll have to trust your guess," Deward said with a small smile.

Ceri linked her arm in his. "It's dark enough I can't see much better than you."

"If an alligator attacks, the best defense is to attack its sensitive snout and eyes."

She glared at him, even though she knew he couldn't see it. "Are you *trying* to scare me?"

"No, sorry." He bit back a grin. "It's just that alligators hunt during both the day and night and are extremely territorial. Shouting instructions during an attack is generally ineffective, so I decided I might as well mention it now."

"Great. If I get eaten by an alligator in a swamp while unable to cast spells, I'll be *pissed*."

Deward threw back his head and laughed as they trudged forward. She didn't see what was so funny, but it was the first time she'd seen Deward laugh since he'd lost his sight. A smile tugged at the corners of her mouth.

Something moved in the water a few feet away, and she scrambled away with a shriek, half climbing up Deward to get away. He moved into a fighting stance, the laughter gone. The creature hopped into view and let out a grumpy croak.

"Dammit, it was just a frog."

Deward raised an eyebrow.

"Don't say a word," she muttered, tugging him after her. "Not. A. Single. Word."

He mimed zipping his lips shut and fell into step beside her with his lips clamped together to hide his still-obvious grin. She normally loved nature, but stumbling through a swamp in the dark was not on her list of fun activities.

For a while, the only sound was the swish of water around their legs and the incessant chirping of frogs and bugs. Every few minutes, a frog would splash into the swamp, startling her each time, but soon she was too tired to react.

Deward tightened his grip on her arm and pulled her to a stop. She let him, scanning the area in front of them. He'd heard something she hadn't. The water was still around them, but a sense of being watched grew. There was someone here. Ceri instinctively reached for the pack bond, but once again found she couldn't communicate through it.

There was a splash much too large to be caused by a frog a few feet ahead. Whoever it was had hidden behind one of the cypress trees that surrounded them. In unison, they crept closer. If they were being watched, they needed to find out by who. Or what.

It was impossible to move silently through the swamp. The swish of water had to have alerted whoever was behind the tree that they were coming, but they stayed put.

She and Deward slowed as they neared the tree. It was faint, but someone was breathing. The tree branches creaked without a breeze, and a ripple spread out in the water.

Deward pointed to the left then made a quick motion with his hand. Surprise attack it was. She moved a step ahead of him and tensed, then they lunged as one. A clump of mud smacked Ceri right in the chest. She threw her hands up to avoid another attack as she spotted who had thrown it.

A young girl, barely a teenager, if even that old, cowered at the base of the tree. Her bony arms trembled as she scrambled for something else to throw. One grime-streaked wing was tangled in the lower branches of a tree, trapping her there.

"Go away!" she shrieked.

"Wait!" Ceri pushed Deward to the side and dodged another mud clump. "We're not going to hurt you! It's a child, Deward. A young succubus."

Deward pulled Ceri behind him to shield her and held up both his hands. "Stop throwing things, please."

"Then leave!" The girl kicked water at them as she jerked hard on her wing. It didn't budge.

"You're going to hurt yourself," Ceri pleaded. In any other circumstance, she would have assumed this was some sort of trap, but if her magic wasn't working, she doubted the girl's was, either. And something about her spoke of genuine fear and desperation. "Let me get your wing free, then we'll go if you want, okay?"

The girl stilled, breaths coming in hard pants. Her eyes flicked between them and her wing. She swallowed. "I can get it out myself."

"Eventually," Ceri agreed, still keeping her hands visible. "But you'll hurt it worse."

"Fine." The girl eyed Deward warily. "Just you, though. Make him stay back."

"Okay, he'll stay back."

The girl watched her with the wariness of someone who had learned not to trust the hard way. Ceri reached for the wing, and she flinched away. The wing was badly tangled and bent. "I think it's going to hurt when I get it free."

The girl nodded once and held perfectly still, just waiting for it to be done. Ceri bent apart the branches it was wedged between and tugged on the tip of the wing. Blood seeped from a deep gash on the ridge of the wing. Several feathers had been ripped out whenever she got tangled.

"How did you get stuck in here? Was it during the fall?" Ceri asked, hoping a bit of a distraction would help this be less painful.

"Yeah. Tried to fly." The girl glanced up. "Is it broken?"

"I don't think so, but it's hard to tell." Ceri sat back on her heels and put her hands on her hips. "I can keep tugging on this, but part of the reason you're stuck is because you're practically hanging from it and wedging your wing further in the branches. Would you let my friend Deward lift you up so I can pull this free?"

The girl was quiet for a long moment then nodded. "Fine."

Deward walked over and crouched before the girl. He held out his hands. "I am blind, so it would be easier if you moved to me."

With a clenched jaw, the girl struggled to her feet and grabbed Deward's arm with shaking hands. He grabbed her waist firmly and lifted her straight up. Ceri worked quickly and was finally able to free the wing. She supported it as Deward set the girl back on her feet.

"It's definitely bleeding, and the muscle is damaged, but I don't think it broke."

Deward grimaced. "The risk of infection will be high. You need to keep it dry and as clean as possible."

The girl nodded once and curled the hurt wing around her shoulder.

Ceri rinsed the blood off her hands as she tried to figure out what to do next. It was completely unacceptable to leave the girl here, but she didn't want to have to force her to come with them and ruin the little trust they'd built up. "Would you come with us? We're going to get out of this swamp, and I bet you want to do that, too."

The girl cringed away. "You're lost, too."

"Better to be lost together, right?" Ceri asked with what she hoped was a reassuring smile. She probably looked like a crazed swamp hag right now.

"Practically speaking, yes," Deward agreed. "Less likely to be attacked by an alligator."

The girl's eyes widened. "Is that a type of demon?"

"Um, not quite. But they have teeth. And they could eat you." She shrugged. The demon comment was odd. Surely all the incubi knew demons were just fae. Had this girl never been to earth before?

"I don't want to be eaten."

Ceri nodded. "Me neither."

"I can't feed you, if that's what you want. I already did it twice this week. There's nothing left."

Deward stiffened alongside her. Feed them. It couldn't be...

"We, um, recently fed and don't need to do that at all." Ceri's mind was spinning. Were the incubi feeding on their own? Was that why the girl was so thin and frail? "I swear that neither of us will feed from you, now or ever."

The girl narrowed her eyes, somehow even more suspicious now. "Why not ever?" She stepped back. "Are you demons? Is that why he is green?"

"No! No, definitely not. It's just that there are humans here. They're much better." Ceri wanted to smack herself. This was not how she should be handling this, but she wasn't all that practiced in handling these sorts of situations. And they only had half the information. This girl didn't seem to understand anything. "And Deward was just born green."

"Fine. Guess it doesn't matter anyhow. It's not like I can run away." She pushed away from the tree and held her wing against her side with her free hand. "I'll follow you. Because of the alligators."

CHAPTER 12

GENEVIEVE

"Yep. Everyone willing to try to shift has had their wolf pop out instead of shifting." Genevieve adjusted the phone against her ear, absently scratching her wolf's head with her free hand. She was trapped under her on the couch. Not that she really wanted to move; her weight and warmth were comforting. "And we can't get them back in. They're just out there. Stuck.

Her wolf snorted. *Not stuck.*

"Well, will you go back in?"

No.

"What?" Icewind asked, confused.

"Sorry, she said she isn't stuck, but she also refuses to go back in. Stubborn butthead."

"Ah...I see. So you can still communicate with your wolf?"

She flicked her wolf's ear, which earned her another snort. "It's easier, actually."

"Glad something is," Icewind muttered. "My magic isn't working correctly. I tried to heat up my coffee and turned it into bubbles instead. Your witches wake up yet?"

"No. Any luck tracking down Jean? I'm really hoping she can help. If she *will* help."

"Yes. Velez is bringing her to you guys. She hasn't stopped crying since I located her, though, so good luck with that."

Genevieve groaned. "Great. She always seemed a little scared of everything. Vernier probably did a number on her."

"Velez should be there in two hours, then he's sticking around until things are more settled. I wanted to go with him, but it's a shitshow here, and they can't spare me right now."

"Any help you can send our way is welcome." She glanced over her shoulder to ensure she was still alone. Not that it was possible to have a truly private conversation with all these supernatural types around. "Amber kind of…accidentally…took Ito's wolf away. In her defense, her wolf did it. And Ito had attacked her. But it hasn't made things any easier with his pack."

"She can do that?" Icewind exclaimed.

"Apparently."

"How is Amber, by the way? I got your message that Kadrithan somehow took his mark away right before the curse was broken."

"She's…fine. Ish." Genevieve sighed and let her head fall back onto the couch cushions. "It'd be bad enough if it was just Kadrithan, but with Ceri and Deward gone, too, we're all just trying to pretend we aren't panicking."

Icewind was silent for a moment. "I'm sure you'll find them."

"Yeah. We will." There was no other option she'd consider. They'd all been separated before and found their way back to each other. They'd do it again.

"One sec." The conversation on the other end of the line was muffled for a moment. Icewind returned with a sigh. "The witch council is all up in arms. I gotta go."

Genevieve winced in sympathy. "Good luck."

"Tell Amber to not do anything weird for a few days so we have a chance to clean up this mess first."

"Ha. I'll let her know." She hung up and dropped her phone on the couch beside her. That was all the urgent phone calls done. Steven had been frantic, so she was glad she'd called him first. The urge to hurry back to Oregon and make sure he was really, truly safe was almost overwhelming. Knowing the trolls were with him was the only thing keeping her here. That and the fact that Amber needed her.

She stared at the ceiling as her mind whirled through all their current issues. They had discovered, at least, that they would only be randomly sucked into the spirit realm while within a certain radius of the circle Ceri had cast the spell in. Turning a powerful vampire's backyard into a portal to another realm wasn't ideal, but Adele seemed more amused than upset, at least. She currently had her clan members experimenting with walking through it to see if there was a pattern, but it seemed random so far.

Then there was the issue of the incubi. She had no idea if Saraqael knew the effects breaking the curse would have or what he had planned next. The incubi might be crippled, or they could have been expecting this and were prepared to strike back. The dead succubus upstairs still bothered her, though. She really looked like she'd been starved. If that was the case, then they had to be missing something. The incubi had been in power so long that she couldn't think of a reason any of them would go wanting.

She sighed and nudged her wolf. "We have important things to do, you know."

Rest is important.

"Who knew my wolf was lazy?" she muttered.

Alpha Greer walked into the room and froze when he spotted her. His wolf stood at his side, ears perked up in interest. "Are you...cuddling with your wolf?"

"Unwillingly. She sat on me."

He dragged a hand down his face. "I should stop expecting anything approaching normalcy from you and anyone else in your pack." He shook off the confusion and took a deep breath. "Anyhow, we have three teams ready to go. Jameson, me, and you can all lead one. Though, do you mind if I speak freely?"

She raised a brow. "This isn't the military. Just say what you have to say."

He shook his head again, with a smile this time. "I'd suggest not leaving Amber here alone."

"I wasn't planning on it, but is it that bad out there?"

"I think that, right now, everyone is too scared she could take their wolves away to do anything. But no point in giving anyone a chance to get ideas."

"Fair enough." Genevieve shoved her wolf more firmly this time, and with a grumbling growl, she finally got up. "Good grief, you shed a lot."

Her wolf shook out her fur and snorted. *Don't care.*

She rolled her eyes as she followed Greer back outside. Derek was waiting for her with one of the teams. He was even more tense than the rest of them.

"You okay?" she asked tentatively.

He stared hard at his feet, jaw clenching and unclenching. "Even as a werewolf, I couldn't do a damn thing to protect her."

She punched his arm, and he jerked his head up with a glare. "Like hell you couldn't. We held off a freaking army while she broke that curse. Don't even start on some kind of pity party now."

"Ceri is gone. How can you be so calm?"

"By staying busy. I'm doing everything I can to find her. And I trust her to keep herself alive wherever she is." Genevieve clapped a hand over his heart. "You can feel her still, too. Focus on that and keep moving."

Derek sighed. "I'll try."

"Do or do not. There is no try."

He rolled his eyes. "Don't start quoting little green men at me."

"Just saying. He had a point." She patted him on the shoulder, gentler this time. "Come on. Let's go find a living incubus to get some answers from."

CHAPTER 13

AMBER

Amber sat across from Ito and tried to muster up some pity for him. Losing his wolf after being born with a connection to it had to feel like losing a piece of his soul. However, he was making it difficult.

She set down her sandwich and met his intent gaze. After recomposing himself, he had followed her everywhere. He'd even tried to follow her into the bathroom, but she'd slammed the door in his face. "How long are you going to do this?"

Ito's glare intensified. "Until you return my wolf."

"Great." She picked up her sandwich and forced herself to take a bite. Her wolf nudged her impatiently, and she tore a piece off for her with a sigh. Having her wolf out all the time like this was like trying to care for a toddler with murderous impulses. Granted, she was way smarter than a toddler, which made it all the more difficult to keep her out of trouble. And, even worse, she kept calling Amber out.

You could make him go away. He must obey us.

As tempting as it was, she couldn't bring herself to do it. Her conscience wouldn't allow it. Taking away someone's free will was a scary prospect.

"You are an abomination."

"Yes, you've already said that," Amber said, growing increasingly weary of his mental breakdown. "I think we've established that I am evil incarnate, and you have been horribly wronged by me. However, that's really not the most important thing right now, if you can believe it."

"Of course." He laughed, though the sound was completely without humor. "You think you have to save the world again, don't you?"

She didn't bother with a response to that. It was tempting to doubt every decision she'd made. To wonder if she had done something horrible. But she knew the moment she let that kind of doubt seep in, she'd be paralyzed with fear. The curse was broken. The only thing left was figuring out what, exactly, to do next.

"Your welcoming committee could be friendlier." Velez walked into the kitchen with one hand grasped firmly around Jean Yawler's arm. The woman was practically vibrating with fear. She cradled her freshly bandaged left hand against her chest as her eyes darted between Amber and Ito.

"I'll pass your message on to management," Amber said dryly. She dusted the crumbs off her fingers and stood to greet him and the shaman. "How is your hand, Jean?"

"Fine." Jean's shoulders hunched further in, as if having the attention of the room on her was a physical weight.

"Let's head upstairs." Amber glanced back at Ito then her wolf. "Stay here with Ito."

Ito leaned back in his chair and crossed his arms but didn't argue.

Velez raised a brow as he looked between them. "You have a knack for getting yourself into interesting situations."

"Tell me about it." Amber huffed out a sigh and shook her head. "This way."

Velez followed her, keeping a tight grip on Jean's arm, which seemed strange. She didn't look like the type to run, but she doubted he would be holding onto her if it wasn't necessary.

The vampires had mostly disappeared with the sunrise. The younger ones needed the sleep, apparently, and they all needed time to feed after the battle. Adele had shown her an office that was magically soundproofed where she and her pack could have private conversations. It seemed like the perfect place for this discussion.

Amber opened the door and waved them inside. There were four chairs in a half circle in front of a desk. She took one of those and gestured for the others to sit. "Make yourself comfortable."

Velez set Jean across from Amber then dragged his chair around to sit to their left. "I haven't filled her in on anything. I only let her know you requested to see her. She's been informed of her rights. I can't make her cooperate with you, but she's also not free to leave, and we aren't making any deals for immunity or anything else until we sort out exactly how involved she was."

"Okay." Amber rested her forearms on her knees and tried to look relaxed. "We don't have a ton of time to explain everything that's going on, so I'll just get straight to it. A coven of thirteen witches broke a curse last night. The backlash from that has been... intense. One of those witches is missing, and the other twelve won't wake up. Can you help us wake them?"

Jean's fingers were in constant motion, twisting in the hem of her sweater so much she'd wear a hole if she kept it up. Finally, she swallowed and forced her eyes up to Amber's face. "Make me part of your pack."

Amber sat back in shock. "What?"

"Add me to your pack and I'll wake them up." Jean spoke a little firmer the second time, but the fear in her voice was still obvious.

"Jean, no offense, but I don't know you well enough to do that. You worked for someone that tried to kill us."

"I have to be part of a pack." Her fingers tightened in the tangle of her sweater until they began to shake.

There were many things Amber wanted to say, but she had to

be careful when dealing with something this nervous. She took a deep breath and forced back her impatience. "Why do you think that?"

Jean ground her teeth together and jutted out her jaw. "I'm weak. None of the covens would take me in, and I can't survive alone. Alpha Vernier will kill me."

Amber glanced at Velez. "Was she not arrested?"

He shook his head once. "No. She wasn't among the dead, either."

"Great." Amber dragged her hands down her face. "Regardless, the MIA will protect you, and so will we. They'll find Vernier. She won't hurt you."

"Maybe. But it's not the same, and you know it. You wouldn't fight for me as hard as someone in your pack. It's just human nature. And wolf nature." Jean's face flushed a deep red. "I may be weak, but I'm not dumb. There's a reason I've survived as long as I have."

"I can't add you to the pack. It's too…personal."

Jean hunched down in her chair. "Then the witches can stay asleep."

She'd been patient. Calm. She'd pushed down her own emotions to take care of everyone else. Right now, Amber wanted to sock Jean in the mouth. The selfishness and cowardice were infuriating. No one was asking her to save the world, just help out a little. That was it. Amber bit back her initial retort with great effort and pinned the woman down with a glare. "You're never joining my pack."

Jean's face paled, and her fingers clenched into a tight fist. "I want to leave."

"Someone might be able to come get you in a few hours." Velez pulled out his phone and typed out a quick message then looked up at Amber. "You got anywhere we can stick her until then? Don't want her running off."

"She can sit with all the dead bodies."

Velez coughed to cover a laugh. "I think I'll leave her in here instead. Can one of your pack members babysit her?"

"Yeah. Someone can. Tommy, maybe?" Amber realized she had no clue where he was or what he was doing. She'd grown so used to being able to check in on them through the pack bond that she'd forgotten to keep checking now that everything was weird. Knowing him, he was probably taking care of someone somewhere that no one else had noticed needed help.

There was a quick rap on the door, and Derek poked his head in. "Oh good, she's here. I was just coming to ask when she'd arrive."

"Yeah, well, she's refusing to help, so she's going straight back." Amber rose from her chair and headed for the door, but Derek stepped inside and blocked her exit.

"Refusing?" He shoved past her and advanced on Jean. "Why the hell are you refusing?"

Jean glanced at Velez like he'd protect her, but the agent was busy pretending to be absorbed with his phone. She swallowed nervously. "I need a pack. I'm too weak. I'll help if your pack takes me in, that's all."

"There are twelve witches laying in this house, unconscious, and you're worried about finding a new pack? You have got to be kidding me." Red crept up his neck, and Amber felt how close to losing control he was.

Jean crossed her arms. "I'm just doing what I have to so I can survive."

"This is why you're weak," Derek snapped. "Amber and the rest of the pack are strong because they do the *right* thing every time. You just slink around thinking about no one but yourself. You'll always be weak if that's all you ever do. Ceri would have helped you."

Jean tightened her arms around her waist and stared hard at the floor. "You don't know anything about me."

"You aren't willing to help the very pack you claim you want to join. That's all I need to know." Derek shook his head in disgust and turned away. "Do we have a backup plan?"

"We'll figure something out. Steven is working on a few ideas." Her phone buzzed with a text from Genevieve.

We got one alive.

Amber's hand tightened on the phone. This was their chance to get answers.

CHAPTER 14

CERI

While the sunrise had eased some of Ceri's fears, it had made nothing else easier. It was hot, humid, and miserable in whatever swampy hell they were trapped in. The endless muck had given way to strips of dry land, but the breaks were never long enough. She enjoyed the reprieves while she could, though.

But they'd found a road.

"Finally." She wrung out the hem of her dress, and a muddy puddle formed beneath her feet. "This road doesn't look like it gets a lot of traffic." It only had two lanes and no shoulder at all. She'd hoped for the comforting sound of traffic, but no luck. Everything remained silent around them.

The succubus, who had repeatedly refused to provide her name, crouched over the asphalt and prodded it with her finger as if she'd never seen anything like it. Perhaps they didn't have roads in the incubi realm.

"Are there any signs?" Deward asked.

Ceri scanned the road in both directions. "There may be something, but it's hard to tell for sure from this far away."

"We have to pick a direction regardless, so we may as well go toward the potential sign." Deward held out his arm.

She linked hers in his, and they set off. The succubus trailed behind them. She seemed more comfortable keeping a little distance between them, so they had let her. Moving was so much easier without the mud pulling at their feet and the drag of water around their legs. They still hadn't escaped the mosquitoes, though.

Ceri smacked one that landed on her arm. "Fifty-six down, fifty-six million to go." In the distance, the vague shape became clearer. She squinted, and a burst of excitement shot through her. "That is definitely a sign. Come on." They sped up to a jog, and slowly, but surely, the sign came into view. "We're on Whiskey Bay Highway."

"Unfortunately, that is not a road I am familiar with," Deward said.

Ceri deflated with a sigh. "Me neither."

"The road will lead us to people, though."

The girl's head popped up at that. "So we can feed?"

Deward looked in Ceri's direction and raised an eyebrow as if to say, *You created this problem, so you can fix it.* She was already seriously regretting the whole conversation.

"Well, not right away. We need to get to our friends first."

"Why?"

"Because we fell. You know we're no longer in the angel realm." Ceri cleared her throat and turned away. "So we shouldn't linger on this road. We just need to find a phone and they'll come get us."

"What's a phone?"

This was so much worse than she'd suspected. The girl knew *nothing* about this realm or humans. And she was hungry. For people. This was going to be tricky. "It's a device that lets us communicate with someone very far away."

The girl stood and wiped her now-black fingers on her shirt. "Are your friends going to feed on me?"

"No," Deward said before Ceri could answer her. "They will not."

"Because of the humans?" Her lips perked up into a hopeful smile. "I heard there were so many down here you could feed every day for a hundred years straight and never run out." She let out a sigh. "You could live forever."

That was odd. The incubi were already immortal. Did that many of them starve to death? She glanced at Deward, wishing more than ever they could communicate through the pack bond still.

Ceri pointed south. "We need to keep walking. It would be good to be out of this place before nightfall." And it would be even better to avoid all these questions. The girl's obsessive worry over being fed on made her stomach twist with anger, even though there was nothing she could do to change whatever had happened in her past. Still, she had to wonder how many incubi had been fed on regularly. And why.

Deward stopped abruptly, and his eyebrows pinched together as he looked up at the sky. "Interesting."

"What?"

"A storm has begun. There is lightning streaking across the sky above us. It's rather spectacular."

Ceri jerked her head up. The sky was slightly cloudy but definitely free of lightning. "Is it some kind of magical storm? I don't feel anything."

"I thought you said you were blind," the girl said, taking a hesitant step back.

"I am," Deward said, eyes still locked on the sky. "I can only see magic. It's the result of a curse."

She gasped. "A demon curse?"

"No, a witch's curse."

"Is that a type of demon?"

Ceri sighed. "Not everything is a demon. There are humans, witches, trolls, werewolves, and elves. Some of them can use magic, like curses."

The girl snorted. "Only archangels and their guardians can use magic. Everything else is demon magic."

"Who told you that?"

"Everyone knows that. It's why the archangels need us. If we don't feed them, the demons will win." She curled her injured wing tighter against her side. "It's just how it is."

"Perhaps you were lied to," Deward suggested gently.

Her eyes went wide. "They don't lie. You can't even say that! It's not allowed!"

"You fell. Things have changed," Ceri said gently.

The girl stepped back. "You're demons, aren't you? You tricked me!"

"We have not——" The rumble of a truck engine interrupted their argument. Ceri whirled around as a white truck rounded the corner. "You stay behind me and stay quiet," Ceri demanded, never taking her eyes off the truck. The girl seemed to sense the danger and slipped close behind Ceri.

The truck slowed to a stop, and a man stepped out, rifle cradled in his arms. His finger was indexed awfully close to the trigger. He wore a cowboy hat and a sleeveless shirt that displayed an army tattoo on his left bicep. "Y'all look a bit lost out here."

Ceri stepped forward from the group. "We are. Spell gone wrong. I'm guessing everyone has figured out by now that something weird is going on."

"Sure have. Angels are falling from the skies. News says they can't be trusted." His eyes flicked to the girl. "Said they can cast illusions to look like other people."

Ceri hesitated only for a moment. They only had one chance to get through this peacefully, and she was betting on honesty. "They can. Illusions and mind control, if they're strong enough." She lifted the hem of her dress to display the pack tattoo. "I'm a witch with the Hale pack. We got this tattoo to protect us from the mind control. We've been fighting them for months now."

"Is that so?"

"Yes. Considering the news, not really sure how to convince you of that, though." She smoothed her dress back into place.

"You trying to tell me that one isn't an angel?" He nodded his head toward the girl.

"No. She is an angel. We found her in the swamp, tangled up in a tree." Ceri took a deep breath. "And we rescued her."

He pursed his lips. "What for? You angling for some kind of bounty?"

"No, just trying to do the right thing. She's a kid, and she's hurt and confused."

The man tapped his finger against the rifle then looked over at Deward. "You're awfully quiet, big fella."

Deward inclined his head. "Ceridwen seemed to be covering everything that needed to be said. Do you have a question for me?"

"You claim to be fighting these angels, too?"

"Yes."

"Hell of a story."

Deward shrugged. "Simply the truth."

"We'll see." The man stepped back toward his truck and grabbed a cellphone. "I'm not much for bothering people who aren't bothering anyone else, but things aren't normal right now. I'm gonna have to let the authorities handle this one."

Ceri let out a sigh of relief. "That would be wonderful, actually. I need to get in contact with my alpha like you wouldn't believe. Don't suppose you'd let me call her while we're waiting on the police?"

The man shook his head once. "No offense, but I just plain don't trust you that much. I'm sure the police will let you have your phone call."

"Fair enough." Ceri forced herself to remain calm. They had to hope whoever came would be reasonable and listen. Without any ID, it would be easy to assume she and Deward were lying. Having an angel in tow wasn't going to help their credibility.

CHAPTER 15

TOMMY

Tommy sat back and put his head in his hands. He was exhausted even though he hadn't done nearly as much as Ithra, and somehow, she was still going. The trolls that had been injured still needed help. They'd also been keeping the unconscious witches hydrated and preparing food for hundreds of hungry werewolves. If he ever saw a sandwich again, he might scream.

His wolf bumped his arm. *Genevieve is back.*

A ripple of excitement and unrest flowed through the pack bond. Amber was worried. He couldn't blame her. Half the people here would want to rip the incubus apart. He couldn't completely blame them. After what they'd just been through, he wasn't feeling particularly positive toward any of them.

With a sigh, he forced himself to his feet. "Ithra, I have to head downstairs for a while. Genevieve is back."

The troll nodded absently, all her attention on the bandage she was changing. "Let me know if there's any news of Deward and Ceri."

"Will do." He left with his wolf close at his side. The hallways of the vampire's manor were deathly quiet. He much preferred that over the subtle sounds of feeding he'd done his best to ignore as the vampires had settled down to sleep.

Downstairs wasn't quiet at all. The different packs all huddled together in sprawling groups, both inside and out in the backyard. Ito's pack members watched him pass by with heated glares, the others with curiosity. Everyone knew his name and that he was with the Hale pack. It was weird holding a position of authority when a few months ago, most people had no idea they existed.

Derek nodded to him across the room then gestured at the hallway behind him.

Tommy picked his pace up and met Derek at the corner. "They in there?"

"Yeah. Amber asked me to wait out here and make sure no one tries anything stupid, but she wanted you in there." Derek crossed his arms and leaned back against the wall. Tension and anger radiated off him like a physical weight.

"Everything okay?"

"Jean is still refusing to help."

"Ah." Tommy rubbed the back of his neck. "Maybe she'll change her mind soon."

Derek scoffed. "Doubtful."

A door partway down the hall opened, and Genevieve stuck her head out. "Is Tommy—oh, there you are. Come on."

I'm staying with Derek.

Tommy glanced back at his wolf, then at Derek, and nodded in agreement. Derek looked like he shouldn't be left alone. He was too keyed up.

Amber, Ito, and Velez were having a quiet disagreement just inside the door, so Tommy slipped to the side to stand by Genevieve. Her wolf greeted him with a few sniffs then returned to ignoring him in favor of Genevieve. Tommy wasn't sure what he was expecting the incubus to look like, exactly, but the old man with drooping wings was certainly not it.

The incubus's closely shorn hair was streaked gray and his

hands were calloused. He sat in a chair against the far wall and kept his eyes downturned. His feet were evenly spaced with his shoulders, and his hands were relaxed despite the magic-dampening cuffs he wore. He looked…resigned.

Tommy leaned over to Genevieve. "Has he said anything?"

"Nope. When we found him in the woods, he just dropped to his knees and said, 'I am too tired to run.'" Genevieve crossed her arms. "He completely gave up."

"That's strange. Could it be some kind of trap?"

"That was my first thought, but it really doesn't seem like he's faking it." She smoothed her hair back with a sigh. "I really don't know, though."

"Why'd Amber want me here for this?" Tommy asked quietly.

Genevieve tilted her head to the side. "You're good with people, unlike Alpha Grumpy Pants. Can't hurt when we're trying to get the truth out of someone."

Velez placed a chair directly across from the incubus then sat down. He looked at the man silently for a long moment. "What's your name?"

"Linias." The incubus's voice was unexpectedly soft.

"I'm Agent Velez. My friends tell me they found you in the woods. Why were you there?"

Linias shifted his feet and hunched his shoulders further in. "Is it forbidden?"

Velez was silent for a moment. "No. We were just curious what you were doing. You looked a little lost."

"I apologize."

Amber stepped up to Velez's shoulder. "Where were you headed? Were you looking for friends?"

"I…had no plan. I was thirsty." Linias glanced up at Amber but quickly lowered his eyes. "I do not think my friends are here."

"Where are they?" Velez pressed.

Linias' hands curled into a loose fist on his knees. "I don't know. I was cast out alone."

Tommy pinched his eyebrows together. Linias looked deeply ashamed, as if he was admitting to something awful. And he thought he was alone. They were asking the wrong questions. He straightened and took a few steps forward. "Do you know where you are?"

The incubus swallowed then nodded. "In hell."

Amber stiffened and glanced back at Tommy in shock. He returned the look. While he'd suspected there was some kind of misunderstanding going on, this was not what he'd expected. But... if Linias thought he was in hell...

"Do you know what we are?" Tommy asked.

Linias froze, the color draining from his face. "Demons." He lowered his head, as if trying to bow while sitting. "I beg for your mercy. I will not fight or run."

Amber dragged a hand down her face. "Velez, you have a minute?"

"Yeah." Velez stood, shaking his head in disbelief.

"Gen, can you stay with him? Tommy, with us." Amber opened the door and waited for them. He hurried over, with a single backward glance at Linias, who still looked as defeated as ever.

Amber remained silent until they stepped inside the room next door. She turned to face them and crossed her arms. "Do either of you think he's lying?"

"No," Tommy said immediately.

Velez shrugged. "Probably not."

"I have no idea what to do here." Amber propped her hands on her hips. "Either he's lying right to our faces or random incubi have no freaking clue where they just fell to and think we're going to hurt them for some reason."

"How could they *not* know?" Tommy asked the question aloud, despite knowing neither Amber nor Velez had the answer. It was just so strange. "His appearance is strange, too."

"What do you mean?" Velez asked.

"Did you see his hands? They're super calloused. He's worked with them for decades. That's not anything like the incubi we've heard of. We're missing something." Tommy dragged his hands through his hair.

"If hundreds or thousands of incubi just fell out of the sky into what they think is hell, we're going to have a serious problem." Amber collapsed back against the wall and stared at the ceiling. "They're all going to be confused and vulnerable right as we've convinced the world the angels are a threat."

"The timing is...unfortunate," Tommy agreed.

Velez shook his head. "I'm going to make a few phone calls. We need to figure out how widespread this is. Obviously not all the angels are ignorant."

"What do we do with Linias?" Tommy glanced at the door. His wolf was still with Derek, and no one had tried to get at the incubus, but everyone was growing more and more tense as the situation dragged on. "I don't think we should leave him here."

"Definitely not," Amber agreed.

"I'll take him back with me." Velez tapped a number into his phone. "Whether he's lying or not, we can't let him go just yet." He turned away as Icewind's voice sounded on the other line but abruptly stopped and looked back. "I forgot to mention someone is here to pick up Jean. Can one of you escort her outside?"

Both Amber and Derek tensed at the mention of her name. The fury coming off Amber was, for a split-second, overwhelming.

"I'll do it," Tommy hastily volunteered. Neither of those two should get anywhere near the witch.

Amber's shoulders slumped as soon as he spoke. "Thanks, Tommy."

The room they had stashed Jean in wasn't far. One of Jameson's pack stood guard by the door. He couldn't remember her name, and wasn't actually sure they'd ever met, but he recognized her from the battles they'd fought in recent days.

"Amber sent me to grab Jean. Someone is here to pick her up."

"So you don't need me anymore?" the woman asked.

"Nope. You're good."

She nodded and jogged off. Tommy stepped inside, expecting Jean to be sitting somewhere. For a moment, his gut twisted in alarm, but he spotted her huddled up in a corner with her arms wrapped tightly around her knees.

"You okay?" he asked with a frown.

Jean picked her head up. "Did Amber change her mind?"

"No. Someone is here to take you back, like you asked."

Her face paled. "I hoped…"

"Once Amber makes up her mind about something, she doesn't really change it." Tommy felt a little pity for Jean, but he couldn't bring himself to feel really sorry for her when she was refusing to help like this. Ceri and Deward had been missing for hours now. Their absence was a constant needling worry in the back of his mind.

"She just…saves everyone. I thought she would help me."

"You're looking for someone to save you, and that's the problem." He crossed his arms. "Did you know how we became a pack?"

Jean sniffed and fidgeted with the hem of her sweater. "Rogue werewolf attack."

"Genevieve was attacked. Amber jumped in to save her. Then I tried to save Amber. Then Genevieve tried to help both of us. And in the end, we all got bit, but we were all alive. We're a pack because, when it mattered, we saved each other, and we've been doing it ever since."

"So…if I help the witches, Amber will take me in?"

"No. She turned you down, and she meant it. If you help the witches, it'll be because they need help. It's not complicated."

"But then who will help me?"

Tommy shrugged. "When I threw a rock at the back of a rogue werewolf's head, I never paused to ask myself that. Sometimes you just have to act and sort out the consequences later."

"I…" Jean stared up at him with tear-bright eyes. "I believed Tatiana would save me."

He knelt down across from her with a sigh. "She fooled us, too, for a while."

"I'll try to help your witches, but I may not be able to." Most of the tension left Jean's shoulders, and her hand stilled. "Just...I don't want an audience. I get nervous."

He considered this for a moment then nodded. "I'll see what I can do. They aren't going to let you go in there alone, though, no offense."

"Right. I wouldn't either if I were any of you." She flushed at that, as if she couldn't believe she'd said that out loud. "Not that you can't trust me, I just..."

"I know what you meant." He couldn't handle sitting there listening to her beat herself up anymore. It was exhausting. "You're going to have to tell Amber you've changed your mind, though." He stood and held out a hand.

Jean stared at it like it might bite her for a moment then accepted his help up. "I may not be able to wake them up."

"Just do your best."

CHAPTER 16

AMBER

Amber's wolf was a steadying presence against her leg. She'd had to lock Ito out in the hallway, but at least she was rid of him for a moment. Tommy was the only other person allowed in the room for this.

The twelve witches were laid out in a circle. Jean walked among them, stopping a few times to press her hands to their faces. Finally, she stopped and turned back to Amber and Tommy. "They're stuck. In the spirit realm, I think." She swallowed and picked at the bandage on her hand that covered her missing finger. "I've never seen it happen to a whole coven before."

Don't be scary. Think pleasant thoughts. Tommy had actually stepped up and threatened her to be as un-intimidating as possible so the nervous witch didn't have a complete breakdown. But it was hard because, for some reason, even the sight of her still made Amber want to punch her right in the face.

"Right. Of course. Everything is weird right now, so…" Amber forced herself to smile. Jean flinched, so she immediately dropped into a more neutral expression. "Is there anything you can do to help them get unstuck?"

"Um…" Jean glanced at Tessa and gnawed on her lip. "Maybe. I can try to go there and talk to them."

Tommy's head snapped up. "We get blips of the spirit realm in the backyard. Should we take them back there?"

"Blips?" Jean asked, her brow creased in confusion.

"Yeah. The place where the coven broke the curse has a weird effect. While you're standing there, you'll randomly vanish into the spirit realm then come back." Amber shrugged. "We brought the witches inside when they wouldn't wake up, but if you need to go to the spirit realm, Tommy is probably right."

"You took them out of their circle?" Jean dropped her hands in shock. "No wonder! They can't find their way back to themselves!"

"There were fireballs falling from the sky!" Amber threw her arms in the air in frustration. "We were trying to keep them safe."

Jean immediately shrank back. "I'm sorry, I didn't mean––"

"It's fine," Tommy interjected. "You're helping. Just tell us what to do now."

Ten minutes later, the witches were arranged back in the circle in the original positions––as well as anyone remembered, at least. Jean sat in the place Ceri had and placed her hands on her knees while she and Tommy waited at a safe distance out of the affected area. Some of Jean's nerves seemed to have subsided as she went through the ritual, which was encouraging. The last thing Amber wanted was for her to mess it up because she was too scared to think straight.

After a few moments, Jean's shoulders relaxed, and she slumped backward. The only thing they could do now was wait. Amber turned to say something to Tommy, but Jean jerked back to consciousness with a loud gasp.

"They're here." Jean's eyes were wide, and she was panting liked she'd just run a mile. "All of them."

"Then why'd you come back?" Amber asked with a frown.

"They want to talk to you. And…" Jean flushed. "They booted me out. Because they don't know me."

"All right." She'd never gone into the spirit realm without Ceri's help, but it shouldn't be that hard considering the witch's circle kept sucking people into that realm whether they wanted to or not. And she had to talk to them if it was at all possible.

"I'll keep an eye on both of you," Tommy said with a reassuring pat to her shoulder.

Amber joined Jean in the center of the circle. A shiver of magic crept up her spine. She felt a bit stupid for not realizing that *something* was still happening here and that moving the witches hadn't been the best idea. "Do I need to do--"

Snow swirled around her. Jean was no longer standing in front of her--Tessa was. Her black curls writhed in the wind. "About time you showed up. Where the hell is Ceri?"

"Missing. Her and Deward and Evangeline all vanished when the incubi did."

Tessa frowned. "The incubi vanished?"

"Yep. For a while at least. As best we can tell, they ended up falling from the sky like meteors." She dragged a hand down her face. "It's been a weird night."

"Whatever. Not important right now." Tessa waved a hand at her. "We've got a problem."

"Clearly. Why can't you wake up?"

"There's no path back. Something is way out of balance, and it has to be fixed, that's all I can figure out, and believe me, I've had a lot of time to consider the problem." Her form flickered, and for a split second, Amber could see green grass through her. "You need to find Ceri."

"I was hoping you could help us find her somehow."

Tessa shook her head, frustration clear on her face. "Can't do a damned thing from here. Why can't you use the pack bond to find her?"

"It isn't working right. Nothing is."

"Great." Tessa threw her hands in the air. "Just great."

"Do we have to leave you in this circle?"

"No. Just keep us alive." Tessa flickered again. "And find Ceri!"

"I promise!" Amber snapped back to the physical world between one blink and the next. She was on the ground, but nothing hurt, so Jean must have caught her before she fell. Pushing up onto her hands, she glanced around. Tessa still lay unmoving on the grass across from her.

"Well?" Tommy demanded impatiently.

"They can't get back. Tessa said there is no path and something is out of balance. Whatever it is, we have to fix it." Amber stood and brushed off her pants. "Can't believe I didn't think to come out here and see if we could talk to them. It was so obvious."

"It'd only be obvious to a witch," Jean said tentatively, as if afraid to say anything.

Amber held out a hand to help her up, which Jean took with wide eyes. "Thank you. For helping."

"It was…" Jean cleared her throat. "I'm glad I was able to."

Whatever Tommy had said to her clearly had more impact than the shouting she and Derek had done. Sometimes, Amber wondered why *she* was the alpha when the others were clearly better with people.

Genevieve burst out of the backdoor with Derek hot on her heels. "Ceri and Deward have been arrested."

"What?" she and Tommy asked in unison.

"Arrested!" Genevieve exclaimed again with a huge smile. "This is great. We know exactly where they are, and they're safe."

Hope and relief washed through Amber. "When can we go get them?"

CHAPTER 17

DEWARD

Everyone was tense. Deward didn't need any kind of sight to see that. Ceri was rigid where she sat on the other side of the girl, who had finally given them a name. Valiel. Something about the police had scared her into honesty, and she'd confessed everything.

Her crimes apparently involved the theft of bread *and* a handful of fruit. She'd told them everything with many tears and much shaking and asked if she had to stay in hell forever. And how many demons were going to eat her.

A door opened, and the measured footsteps of the sheriff clunked against the linoleum floors. "Got a hold of your pack, just like you said I would. I've got Amber Hale on the phone to talk to you both, privately." He set something--presumably a phone--on the table in front of them. "Y'all need anything, just knock and let Sergeant Guidry know. He'll be right outside."

Their hospitality had certainly improved, but the guard at their door was a firm reminder that they were not free to leave. Two sets of footsteps left, and the door was shut behind them.

"They gone?" Amber's voice echoed slightly in the bare room, startling Valiel.

"They are," Ceri confirmed. "Is everyone okay?"

"Yes. We're all fine. How about you two? Deward is there, too, right?"

"I am," Deward replied to reassure her. "We are both uninjured."

Valiel shifted in her seat. "Is there a demon in that shiny box?"

There was a brief pause, then Amber demanded, "Who is that?"

"We found a su--an angel. She was hung up in a tree in the swamp, and we rescued her," Ceri explained. "It's been complicated, but she's staying with us. I refuse to leave her here."

Deward snorted. Complicated was one word for it. For a moment, he'd wondered if they were going to have to fight their way out of the police station. He understood everyone's suspicions, but Valiel was nothing more than a terrified child. Interrogating a minor without their guardian present was against the law, even if that minor may or may not be part of a race out to enslave humanity. And he was starting to wonder exactly what the truth was about that.

"Ooookay." Amber didn't even argue. Of course she didn't. Deward shook his head. His alpha--something that felt less odd to think all the time--never turned away someone genuinely in need. He was living proof of that. "Velez is telling me we can be there around midnight tonight. Genevieve is talking to the Sheriff and arranging for them to put you up in a hotel for the day. Bring you food and some fresh clothes, that sort of thing. Is there anything else you need?"

"Nothing I can think of now. Has magic been acting strangely there, too?" Ceri asked.

Amber snorted out a laugh. "You have no idea. Incubi have been falling from the sky. Nothing is working right. I'd rather fill you in on all the details in person, though."

"Yeah, that's fine. Just making sure it wasn't *me*." Ceri let out a sigh of relief.

"Is my mother well?" Deward asked, the worry at the back of his mind making itself unavoidable now that he could ask.

"Yes. She and Tommy have been taking care of the injured.

There was a bit of a battle while you three were breaking the curse--" Amber stopped mid-thought. "Wait, where the hell is Evangeline?"

"We have no idea," Ceri said with a tired sigh. "We ended up in a swamp and she was nowhere in sight."

"Great." A muffled conversation followed, then Amber returned her focus to them. "This whole day is going to crap. I can't leave right now apparently, so Tommy and Derek are coming to get y'all."

"Wouldn't it be easier for them to release us so we can come to you?" Ceri asked.

Amber sighed deeply. "They won't let you go without one of the MIA agents there to pick you up. Genevieve is pissed about it."

Deward frowned. It was likely due to Valiel's presence, which certainly complicated things. A strange sense of foreboding settled in his gut. He turned his gaze upward. The magical storm still raged overhead. If anything, it had grown worse.

The incubi had fallen from their realm. All of them, most likely, based on what Amber had just said. Magic wasn't working right for anyone. It was as if the very fabric of the universe had been rattled by breaking the curse.

It was as if...

Every curse had a price. They left a mark. He had lost his sight. What, exactly, had the incubi and fae lost?

CHAPTER 18

AMBER

"The MIA is taking the lead on this, as they should." Exhaustion had eroded Amber's patience. She'd already spent *hours* meeting with the MIA, who had, justifiably, needed some answers concerning the present almost-apocalypse. Icewind and Velez *had* already been investigating the angels––who the MIA already seemed to know the true nature of. That made things much easier. Breaking a curse was in no way illegal––another point in her favor––but it had caused some serious issues. There was yelling at one point, but Amber had sworn to do everything in her power to correct those issues.

She was regretting that a little since she had no idea how to fix any of this. But, as Ito had reminded her with a sneer, she was always getting involved in things she had no idea how to fix that surely, by now, she'd become an expert at it.

Now, of course, the rest of their allies needed answers. They needed to know what was coming next. Amber wanted to know the same thing, but she had no idea. Unfortunately, she couldn't just shrug and say that. She had to have a plan. She had to lead.

"Can we trust them to do what needs to be done when they were so ineffective before?" Cadogan asked the question without any outward sign of anger, but it was obvious in the way the others gathered at the table tensed that his barb had hit the mark. "After all, it was *you* that had to scrape together an army to deal with this."

Amber bit down on the inside of her cheek to keep from snapping at him. Taking a deep breath, she leaned forward and rested her arms on the table. "They're taking the lead, not doing it alone. My pack is part of the task force, and I am not going to stop until we're *sure* the threat is over. The incubi are weakened, not defeated."

"And we're meant to simply return home and wait for further orders?" Cadogan waved a hand at the gathered vampires and werewolves.

"Actually..." Genevieve sat up straighter and pulled out a notepad. "That is something we discussed with the MIA. We're all in this fight together, and it's ridiculous to expect you all to sit around waiting for 'further orders,' as you put it. Any clan or pack still willing to help can send up to two people to assist us and help keep you in the loop. It's completely voluntary." She wiggled the notebook. "See me after to volunteer and I'll get everyone's details."

"The MIA will provide housing and transportation," Icewind–– who had been silent thus far––added. "We are hoping that this task force can help foster greater cooperation between the supernatural races, as well as humans, in addition to dealing with the current threat. Anyone willing to assist in this will be publicly recognized by the MIA for their contributions."

The mood of the room shifted a bit. Even Cadogan looked interested. Amber resisted the urge to roll her eyes. This was why she hated all the political crap. She always assumed people would be persuaded to do the right thing for its own sake, but people were more selfish than that. It was a lesson she'd failed to learn over and over again.

"Is my pack still free to leave?" Ito asked. All eyes turned to him, and a tremor of unrest moved through the group. His current predicament still had everyone unsettled, and his obvious hatred of her wasn't helping that one bit.

"As we discussed before, yes. Bram's offer to help relocate them still stands." Amber nodded toward the pale vampire who stood behind her, hovering over the meeting like the creepy bat he was.

"I am happy to discuss the particulars with you after this meeting," Bram said with a slight tone of amusement.

Ito nodded once then sat back in his chair and crossed his arms.

"Any other concerns?" Amber scanned the group, hoping with all her heart that no one else had anything to say. This had dragged on long enough. The table remained blessedly silent. A few people shook their heads. "Great." She stood with what she hoped wasn't too enthusiastic of a smile. "Come find me if you think of anything else. Our flight doesn't leave for a few hours."

Her shoulders sagged in relief as everyone dispersed. She waited for the majority of people to leave before heading toward the door herself. Just four steps from freedom, her least favorite werewolf stepped in her path.

"I need to speak with you." Ito glanced at Genevieve. "Privately."

It was on the tip of her tongue to tell him he could go suck an egg, but she simply sighed and nodded. "Fine. Gen, I'll be back in a few minutes. This shouldn't take long."

"All right. If you aren't, I'll assume he's murdered you and exact bloody vengeance." Genevieve flashed them a menacing smile then turned around and walked away.

Amber shook her head in amusement as she headed toward the sound-proofed office that had become the de facto secret meeting room. Ito followed silently, though the emotions that echoed through their new bond were loud enough to make up for it. Anger. Resentment. Fear. It gave her a headache. She threaded her hands into her wolf's fur, and the weight of them eased a little. It was easier to block when they were connected like this.

She held the door open for Ito then joined him in the room. "I've already told you I'm not going to do anything to your pack--"

"I'm going to Portland with you." He stood stiffly before her with his hands clenched in tight fists.

"What?"

"You...she," he pointed accusingly at her wolf, "took my wolf from me. I already told you I'm not letting you out of my sight until you return it. I meant that. You cannot leave me behind."

Amber ground her teeth together. The idea of Ito following her around, making snide remarks, and *judging* her every move made her want to scream. "You hate me. You hate my pack. And you are an asshole."

"You are an abo––" His mouth snapped shut, and his eyes flicked to her wolf. A tremor shook through his limbs, and he dropped to his knees. The muscles in his neck stood out as he lowered his head, seemingly against his will.

We will bring him with us when he asks his Alpha Dominus, with respect, for permission. Her wolf's words filled the air.

Amber gave her wolf the side-eye but didn't argue. She had considered bringing Ito with them somehow but had hoped he'd want to go with his pack.

"Will you...please..." He swallowed, and another shudder ran through his body. "Please take me with you, Alpha Dominus, so that I can prove myself worthy to reclaim my wolf."

Her wolf looked up at her like this had all been Amber's idea. She sighed and pinched her nose between her thumb and forefinger. "Fine. Yes." Ito's head snapped up, and the tension left his body in a rush, though he looked as shocked as she felt. "However, if you are a giant dick to me or anyone else I care about, I'll...lock you in a closet or something."

His lips thinned. "I understand."

Her wolf snorted. *Good.*

The door opened, and Bram stepped inside. His eyes landed on Ito, still kneeling before her, and he raised an eyebrow. "I'm not interrupting, am I?"

"Nope. We're done here. You two discuss...whatever."

"I will come find you when I am done with him." Bram turned his pale eyes on Ito, and his lips split wide in the most horrible smile she'd ever seen. At least it wasn't directed at her.

She spun on her heel and fled from the room. Genevieve was going to kill her. Actually, the whole pack might gang up on her and mutiny. She glared at her wolf. "This is your fault."

You are the one who agreed to it.

"You set me up!" Amber hissed.

I only made him show respect.

Amber gave up arguing. It was obvious the whole conversation was futile. She spotted Genevieve in the living room and collapsed onto the couch next to her with a sigh. "Promise not to kill me?"

Her beta looked up with narrowed eyes. "What did you agree to?"

"Ito is coming with us."

Genevieve let her head fall back with a groan. "I *knew* it! I shouldn't have let him get you alone."

"You could have warned me that was what he wanted!"

"Sometimes I wonder how you're this oblivious." Genevieve sighed dramatically. "But I knew you'd get all guilty and agree to this. So I already told Icewind he was coming."

"You could have told *me*. Butthead."

"You would have just argued with me."

"I hate you."

Genevieve's wolf huffed at that and resettled herself on Gen's feet.

"I agree." Genevieve nodded solemnly. "She treats us very badly."

"I told Ito I'd lock him in a closet if he was rude."

A laugh bubbled out of Genevieve's throat, and she clamped a hand over her mouth. "Okay, I forgive your rudeness. That's perfect."

Amber rolled her eyes but couldn't stop a smile. "At least I did that right. Have you heard anything else from Ceri and Deward? Are they in their hotel yet?"

"Yep. Fed, showered, and clothed." Genevieve showed her the texts confirming it. "Tommy, Derek, and Velez are on their way to Louisiana, and they have a return flight already arranged back to Portland."

"It's kind of surreal to think we're actually headed home." Amber threaded her fingers through her wolf's fur. Home sounded like heaven. She wanted nothing more than to be in her own bed with Captain Jack curled up on her feet and nothing more important to do than rebuild an engine. But she had no delusions there would be time for any of that, even if they did get to go back to the house. "I guess I knew we weren't going to stay here forever, but I feel like I haven't had a chance to think more than a few hours ahead at a time."

Genevieve snorted. "That's what I'm for. Speaking of..." She covered a yawn. None of them had been able to rest in days. It was a miracle they'd managed to stay conscious this long. "The coven. We're bringing them with us, too."

"Wasn't Jean concerned about taking them too far from the circle?"

"According to Ceri, since they're really, truly stuck, that isn't the problem. She's going to set up whatever protections she can once they're back in Portland and the MIA has a team of doctors that can put them on fluids and feeding tubes and all that. Ceri's hopeful that with them all reunited, she might be able to wake them up somehow."

"As long as Ceri is on board with the plan." She pursed her lips. "Is there a chance Evangeline is stuck in the spirit realm like the coven?"

"No clue. I'll add it to my Ceri list."

Amber raised a brow. "You have a list for all of us?"

"Absolutely. Yours is the longest." She lifted her notebook and tapped the first item, which had been circled *and* starred. "Icewind just confirmed there will be a big meeting with the various councils in a few days."

"Great." Amber slumped further down on the couch. "That's going to be a mess."

"Understatement of the year."

"If at all possible, before that meeting, I need to get to the Market. It was the last thing Kadrithan asked me to do." Amber rubbed her chest. "There's money to help us and some kind of records of the fae history. He had me promise to do it, so I need to go soon."

"With magic being all crazy, I wonder if it's anywhere." Genevieve tapped a finger against her chin then pulled out her phone.

Horror lashed through Amber, and she sat up straight. "Don't even say that! It has to be!"

"Calm down! I was just..." She tapped at her phone again. "It's here! Well, not *here* here, but it exists."

"Where?"

She tilted her head to the side in surprise. "Well...Portland. Um..."

"Out with it!"

"In our backyard." Genevieve turned her phone around, which displayed a picture of the Market towering over the little guest house they called home.

"While this is extremely convenient, it's super weird, right?" Amber couldn't stop staring. It was right there. Just waiting for her.

"Super freaking weird." Genevieve jerked the phone out of sight, her eyes flickering back and forth as she read something. "Also weird: no one can get in. It has a closed sign hung on the gate."

"The Market is never closed."

"And werewolves don't pop out of people's chests." Genevieve shot an accusing glare at both their wolves, who remained completely unconcerned about the situation.

Amber tried to remain calm. There was a plan in place. They'd found Ceri and Deward. They would find a way to get into the Market. And deal with all the politics. And fix magic. No big deal.

The hair on the back of her neck prickled. She followed her wolf's gaze and spotted Bram hovering in the shadows near the backdoor. With a sigh, she pushed to her feet. "Be back in a bit."

He led her further down the hall, then into a dark room she hadn't been in yet. Chills crept down her spine. Sometimes she questioned why she trusted him so much.

"You need Ito on your side," he said without preamble.

Amber crossed her arms. "He's going to be hard to win over. He hates me."

"You do not need him to *like* you, simply support you publicly. Even without his wolf, he has the respect of the others on the werewolf council. He has influence. If you are Alpha Dominus and cannot control the packs attached to you, then that position will not aid you." Bram gently traced a finger down the pulse point of her neck. "There is power inside you. Wield it."

She swallowed and stepped away from his touch. "I don't want to force anyone to do anything they don't want to do."

"Who have you ever forced to help you?" He tilted his head to the side and tapped a long finger against his chin. "The Kudzu? The vampire council? The alphas that swore allegiance to you?"

"That was…" She sighed. Bram had a way of cutting to the heart of the matter. "I don't feel qualified to lead them."

"You aren't." His fangs pressed against his bottom lip, and he grinned. "But you will be when you are done with this."

"Awfully important skill to be learning on the job," she muttered.

"If you shy away from what you *must* do, someone else will step into the role. And it will not be who you would choose." He placed his hands on her shoulders and pressed a cool kiss to her forehead. "Be fearless. It is what you do best."

Before she could respond, he vanished. The displaced air ruffled her hair around her face and left her cold. She rested her hand on her wolf's forehead. Fearless was the opposite of how she felt.

CHAPTER 19

CERI

Ceri watched Valiel explore the hotel room. Her wounded wing had been cleaned and bandaged, but she still held it close to her body with one hand. The injury hadn't hampered her curiosity one bit, though. She opened all the cabinets, turned the water in the sink off and on for a full minute, and had marveled over the mini fridge. Now, she was enthralled with the television.

"Are they inside of it?"

"No." Ceri sat down next to her. "It's just a video."

"Video," Valiel repeated in awe. "Magic."

Ceri just smiled and shook her head. Technically, they did use a little magic, and it wasn't like she knew how cameras worked anyhow. Science was a little bit magical too sometimes.

It was close to midnight. Ceri was sorely tempted to sleep, but neither she nor Deward could relax until they were back with their pack. At least she was clean now. It had taken a while for the clean clothes they'd been promised to actually arrive, so they'd sat around stinking of mud and sweat the whole afternoon.

The hotel room door opened, and Sergeant Guidry walked in with their second meal in his arms. He had turned out to be a decent person, even interacting with Valiel without cringing like the others had done. "Sorry for the wait."

"Thank you for picking it up." Ceri accepted the pizza boxes with a smile.

Deward stepped out of the bathroom, his blue hair now tamed into a tight braid that hugged his scalp. "That smells good."

"Smells weird." Valiel leaned in, her nose twitching. "What is it?"

"It's called pizza." Ceri set the box on the small desk that sat next to the television and opened it for Valiel's inspection. She'd been fascinated by lunch as well, claiming to have never heard of jelly. Or peanut butter.

Valiel poked the center of the pizza, dragging a line of melted cheese up to her mouth. She licked it tentatively then ate it with a grimace.

Ceri raised an eyebrow. "What's the verdict?"

"It's slimy."

Guidry laughed at that. "I guess it is. Never thought about it that way."

"It's cheese," Deward explained as he felt around for a plate then the pizza itself. "Cheese over a tomato sauce on bread."

Valiel grabbed a slice with a look of determination. "I like cheese. And bread."

"Here." Ceri put another slice on a plate and held it out to Valiel. "Hold them over the plate so the grease doesn't drip all over you or the bed."

Valiel's eyes flicked to the other bed, where the jelly stains from the previous meal still stood out in stark contrast to the white comforter. "Did I ruin it?"

Ceri smiled reassuringly. "No. They can wash it out."

"Your pack should be here soon. Their flight arrived earlier than expected." Sergeant Guidry took up his post by the window. There were other officers stationed outside--at least three, but maybe more.

Deward's head popped up. "How soon?"

"About fifteen minutes."

Relief flooded through Ceri. "Finally."

Deward laid his free hand on her arm in a silent request. She guided him to the bed, where he sat down across from Valiel. Once settled, she grabbed her own food and joined him.

"This is better than the jelly butter," Valiel commented as she picked up her second slice. Since they'd left the police station, she had really opened up. No more flinching every time someone spoke and no more hiding behind her wings. It was good to see.

"I'm glad you like it." Ceri took a bite of her own slice. She was hungrier than she'd realized.

"So, you think they're all gonna be..." Guidry glanced at Valiel. "Confused and relatively harmless?"

Ceri set her plate in her lap. "I really don't know. Some of them will be. Some have lived here. There's a lot we don't know."

"Your pack member, Genevieve Bisset, said the MIA was going to be picking them all up. Any that we find."

"Seems like a good plan. It's a hard situation with so many things still uncertain."

"I agree. I think they will cooperate if they are not scared by whoever finds them." Deward lifted his white eyes toward Guidry with a clear warning. "They do not understand what we are."

Guidry nodded once. "We'll do our best. We have a good sheriff. Not every parish does, mind you, but with the MIA involved, everyone will be on their best behavior."

"Good to hear." Deward lowered his eyes and focused on his pizza once again.

They finished eating their first round of pizza, got Valiel seconds, and gathered the few things Guidry had gotten them into a small suitcase. Ceri smoothed her hair back and paced the length of the small room. It felt like they'd been waiting for weeks.

A sharp rap on the hotel room door made her jump. She whipped around, and Guidry opened it. Derek stepped through the door, and Ceri didn't realize she was moving until she was in his arms. He squeezed her tight as she buried her face in his neck. She had missed him more than she wanted to admit, even to herself. All the worries she'd pushed down to the back of her mind pricked at the back of her eyes now. She had known he was alive, but seeing him here and whole was the only thing that made it feel real.

"Are you hurt?" he whispered as he threaded his fingers through her curls.

"No. I'm good. Are you?"

"Not a scratch."

She forced herself to pull back. What she wanted and needed from Derek, they couldn't have right now with an audience. And a very impressionable child who soaked up everything like a sponge. "And everyone else is good, too?"

"Yes." His eyes traveled over his face as if he were making sure she was real.

A warm nose bumped her hand. She looked down to find a familiar wolf sniffing her with interest. "Your wolf?"

"Yep. He seems to like you."

"I certainly hope so." She crouched down and pressed her forehead to the wolf's in greeting. The same warmth she felt with Derek was echoed in his wolf. They really were connected, two souls in one. She rose and stepped back, finally noticing Tommy was here, too. "Oh. Hey."

Tommy shook his head with a fond smile and pulled her into a brief hug. "Glad to see you're both in one piece."

"You too," she agreed with a grin.

Valiel crept forward, still chewing on the crust of her pizza, her eyes locked on Derek's wolf. "What's that?"

"That is my wolf." Derek knelt beside him and beckoned Valiel forward. "He is very nice if you want to pet him."

Valiel squared her shoulders and marched forward, burying her greasy fingers in thick fur. The wolf sniffed her then snatched her remaining crust. She didn't seem to care one bit. "I want one."

Tommy laughed. "Not sure if you can have one, but you could get a dog one day, I guess. They're just smaller."

"I want a big one," Valiel complained with a frown.

Derek glanced up at Ceri with a raised eyebrow. "Not what I expected of a succubus."

"Me neither. We have a lot to learn, apparently."

Velez broke away from his conversation with Guidry. "Everyone ready?"

"Yes," Deward answered for all of them. She agreed wholeheartedly. They needed to be home.

CHAPTER 20

Breaking the curse had felt personal. Despite the allies that had stepped up to help them, it had felt like their pack against the incubi. Now everyone was involved. The MIA with their task force. The councils, all freaking out over what to do. The news, reporting on every development as if it were the story of the century. And it was. This was *historic*. They had changed the world, and in ways they'd never intended.

Sometimes Genevieve sat there in the midst of everyone, and the thought settled around her shoulders like the heaviest weight.

Icewind leaned forward and smacked another file on the small table between them. Flying on the MIA's dime had its perks. The first was a private jet that was taking them straight home. "Saraqael doesn't seem to exist. We can't find any information on him. Raziel made appearances often enough to be known."

"I'm not really surprised." Genevieve picked up the folder and flipped through. The scant information Evangeline shared with them about Saraqael before she'd vanished was the extent of its contents. It was borderline useless. "They all use illusions, and he seems even more powerful than Raziel, so it was never going to be easy to find him."

"We do have information on the others that claim to be 'archangels.' There are––were––five of them. We're down one since your pack killed Raziel. The task force will be mainly focused on tracking the rest down." Icewind leaned back and crossed her legs. The dark rings around her eyes matched Genevieve's own.

"What about all the incubi that fell?"

"Local law enforcement is working with a few other groups to get all of them rounded up. We have no idea what to do with them, though." Icewind shook her head. "Most haven't done anything remotely illegal."

"Are they all as confused as Linias?"

"So far. The ones who lived here obviously know what's going on, but they've clammed up. They're more scared of talking than they are of being locked up indefinitely, which doesn't exactly reassure me."

"And…" Genevieve glanced back at Amber, but her alpha remained dead asleep, along with both their wolves who were piled on top of each other. And snoring softly. Ito sat behind her and, thankfully, hadn't uttered a word the whole flight. "None of the fae have shown up anywhere?"

"Not a single one."

The Market still baffled everyone. The MIA had swooped in and blocked off access, thankfully, but the fact that it was closed was still being blasted all over the news. Somehow, that freaked out everyone just as much as angels falling from the skies and magic going all wonky.

Icewind let out a long sigh. "I guess Amber is still worried about Kadrithan."

"We all are." And it was true. The demon-turned-fae had become one of them somehow. "We know the curse is broken, but he was in danger at the end. All the fae were."

"Your demon marks are really all gone?"

"Yep. Like they were never there." It had been a relief. Not only because it seemed like confirmation the curse was broken, but because it had been too freaking weird to be tied to Kadrithan like that. She understood why Amber had always rubbed at it. It was impossible to ignore the thing.

The pilot announced they'd be landing soon. Amber didn't stir, still snoring in her seat.

"Better go wake her up so she can put her seatbelt on." Genevieve rose with a sigh, her mind swirling with worry and frustration. There was so much still to do, and it all seemed impossible.

"There yet?" Amber mumbled before covering a wide yawn.

"Yeah. We're almost home." She couldn't help but smile at that. It had felt like an eternity.

CHAPTER 21

AMBER

Pixies swarmed Amber and her wolf as soon as they stepped out of the suburban. She didn't see Woggy or Smidge in their midst, but they all looked happy and healthy.

Steven waved from the front porch where he was surrounded by crates and boxes. "Welcome back!" One of the crates began slipping off its perch, and he scrambled to catch it. Genevieve jogged to the porch and helped him place the crate in a safer location then wrapped him up in a tight hug.

Amber shook her head with a smile. He and Gen were an odd match, but she'd grown to really like him. Ito stepped out of the suburban behind her, attracting the pixie's attention. He tried to swat one away, but she caught his arm with a scowl. "Smack one of those pixies and I will send you back to Montana without a single regret."

He drew his eyebrows together. "They're pests."

"They are part of our family." She dropped his arm.

One of the tiny pixies landed on his shoulder and stared at him. Ito stared back. It signed a demand for food. "Is that...sign language?"

"Yes. We taught them, and now they teach themselves. It's not quite American Sign Language anymore. They've added their own words and stuff." She smiled proudly at the little pixie. It wasn't one she recognized, but she was pretty sure it was from the original swarm that lived around the house. "Pretty awesome, huh?"

"What does it want?"

"Food. That's pretty much what they always want. If you have any metal you aren't attached to, you can give it to her, or you can say you don't have any. They can understand us even if they can't speak like we can."

Ito looked down at the pixie. "I have no food. Go away." The pixie plopped down and crossed its arms in a pout. He nudged it gently, but the pixie ignored him completely. Ito turned a scowl on her. "It didn't work."

She shrugged. "Oh well. Get your stuff. It's not like the pixie is heavy. She'll leave eventually."

Amber grabbed her backpack from the back. Icewind was still on a phone call, so she left her things alone. She wasn't sure where Icewind intended to stay.

Several of the pixies had gathered on her wolf's back to gather loose fluff. She hoped that might mean less shedding, but she wasn't going to hold her breath. Her wolf had endless fur.

The house's roof had been repaired while they were gone, and all the windows replaced with shiny new glass. It was good to see her put back together.

She stepped around Steven's crates and lifted her hand to open the door, but it swung inward before she could touch it. "Illya. Good to see you, too."

Pausing at the threshold, she took a deep breath. Under the scents of Steven and the trolls, it still smelled of home. Her wolf brushed past her as she finally stepped inside. The inside was clean. All traces of the fight that had occurred here right before they left were gone. The trolls had said they'd cleared everything out, but for some reason she'd half expected to walk into a dead body still laying in the living room.

Ito stopped behind her. "The door opened on its own."

"Sure did." She walked inside with a smile. Illya and the house were healing even better than they'd hoped. Not even Ito could dampen her mood right now. She was too relieved at being home to care. "We don't have any bedrooms free, so you'll have to sleep on the couch."

"I expected nothing more." Ito set his suitcase at the end of the couch. "Where is the restroom? I need to shower."

She pointed at the hallway. "On the right."

Ito nodded and pulled a smaller bag from inside his suitcase before disappearing down the hall.

Icewind walked in as she ended a call on her phone. "Do you need time to unpack or anything? I was planning on just setting up in here for now."

Amber pointed at the backpack hanging from her shoulder. "Nope. This is all I have. All the stuff we'd taken with us burned in that hotel fire in Vegas." She tossed it on the couch. "How far behind us are the others?"

"Not long. I actually expected them to beat us here."

She nodded and headed toward the kitchen. "Steven told us he stocked up the fridge yesterday. You want anything to drink? Eat?"

"I guess I'll take a beer if there are some. Can't get through the rest of this paperwork without something stronger than coffee." Icewind opened her laptop and sat back on the couch with a sigh.

"Save one for me." Genevieve waddled inside behind her wolf, arms stacked high with boxes that were taller than her head.

Amber raised an eyebrow. "What is all that?"

"Steven's research. He's working on a way to fix the no magic zones."

"I told you I'd help you carry it!" Steven complained as he shut the door behind them.

"It's fine! Just go open the bedroom door." She shuffled toward the stairs. "There's no reason to make more than one trip."

Steven rolled his eyes as he jogged up the stairs ahead of her.

"Where are Woggy, Smidge, and the babies?" Amber called after him.

He paused on the top step. "Ithra is bringing them over separately. Getting all the babies together was…difficult."

"Got it."

"Move it, slow poke, this is heavy." Genevieve nudged him.

Amber shook her head with a fond smile. It was good to be back. They'd have to make the most of tonight. She grabbed two beers from the refrigerator and popped off the lids.

She handed Icewind her beer and took a long swig of her own. It was tempting to sink into one of the leather chairs and let her eyes slip shut while they waited on the rest of the pack, but she knew she wouldn't be able to wake up again. "I feel like I need to sleep another ten hours."

"You'll learn to live off coffee." Icewind lifted her beer in a toast. "And alcohol."

Amber's wolf trotted over and pressed against her thighs. She reached down to scratch the back of her head. Having her wolf close by––preferably touching––eased the slight tension she'd felt at the separation. It wasn't something she'd noticed at first, but the longer her wolf was out, the more pronounced any kind of separation became.

She took another long drink then glanced at the back door with a sigh. There was no point putting it off any longer. Part of her wanted to avoid going out to the Market as long as possible since she knew it was still closed. But she couldn't avoid it forever. It was better to just get it over with. "I'm going out back."

Icewind nodded absently, all her attention on the laptop in front of her. "I'll let them know where you are if they get back before you're done."

"Thanks." She slipped out the back door with her wolf. The task force headed by Icewind and Velez would operate out of Thallan's mansion for the foreseeable future. Their vans were already parked outside, and guards were stationed around the property, though she hadn't seen any yet. The volunteers would be arriving tomorrow morning. The urge to take a loop to check on security herself was only drowned out by the need to get this over with.

As she rounded the back corner of the house, the Market filled the view. It had settled itself just inside the tree line in the perfect spot to be hidden from view of anyone coming up the driveway. The archway that was normally swarmed with tourists was blocked by a solid wooden gate. On the gate, a single sign hung from a nail that read CLOSED. There was nothing else. No explanation, no number to call for answers, just...*nothing*.

She stopped in front of it and pushed on the gate, just in case. A warning tingle of magic pulsed through her hands. With a frustrated sigh, she stepped back and crossed her arms. This was the one thing Kadrithan had asked of her. That she couldn't get inside and carry out his wishes made her feel sick to her stomach.

An unfamiliar car turned down the driveway, and the pack bond warmed inside her. They were here, finally. Everyone was home. She pressed a hand against the gate again. Almost everyone.

She dropped her hand and headed back toward the house. Right now, Ceri and Deward were home. That was good, even if everything was still in chaos. Her pack was back together, and nothing could take away from the rightness of that. Her wolf broke into a run, and she chased after her with a smile.

As she stepped through the backdoor, an ear-piercing scream rent the air. A tiny girl with wings was currently trying to climb Derek like a tree. Captain Jack had a mouthful of her shirt and yanked her back hard with a rumbling growl.

"Jack! No!" Genevieve grabbed him around the middle and tried to pull him away, but he still had a hold of the girl, who had a hold of Derek. The girl and the cat strung out between them like a tug-of-war. Ceri tried to help grab the girl, but a wing smacked her in the face. Deward stood by the door with two suitcases and a look of confusion. "Stop biting!"

"DEMON!" The child's terrified shrieks hurt Amber's ears.

"Get him off her, Gen!" Derek demanded as he struggled to keep hold of the wriggling child.

"I'm trying!"

Amber rolled her eyes and waded into the fray, grabbing Captain Jack by the scruff of the neck. "Let go." He released her shirt immediately with a sorrowful meow, his mangy paws still reaching for the girl. She handed him off to Gen and put her hands on her hips. "What happened?"

"De-emon," the girl sobbed from the safety of Derek's arms.

He patted her back. "Shhh, no, it's okay. Captain Jack is just a cat. Well, sort of. But he won't eat you."

"He just went for her as soon as she walked in." Genevieve rocked him back and forth like a baby as she stroked his fur. "But he wasn't trying to hurt her! He was just trying to catch her. Like a mouse or something."

"Cats eat mice!" Ceri exclaimed. That renewed the girl's wailing, and Ceri covered her face with her hands in regret.

"The only incubi he's seen have been trying to kill us. He was doing his best. And he didn't bite her." Genevieve turned slightly away, as if someone might try to take Captain Jack from her.

"You." Amber pointed at Genevieve. "Go put Captain Jack in your room. We can try to reintroduce them later." She took a deep breath. This wasn't exactly the reunion she'd imagined. "And you." She pointed at Ceri then the child. "Explain her."

"We found her in the swamp we landed in. She was hurt and confused, and we promised to help her. Her name is Valiel." Ceri crossed her arms. "And it just didn't seem right to leave her with the police. She was terrified and didn't know anyone. And she's just a kid."

"So we're...keeping her?"

"I didn't really plan that far ahead."

"She may have a family we can find," Deward suggested as he set the suitcases down to the left of the door. "Until then, I'm sure my family would be willing to care for her if we cannot. The tribe would never allow an orphan or lost child to be neglected."

Valiel's crying had slowed to sniffles. She peeked at Amber over the edge of her wing with her head on Derek's shoulder. Ceri was right; there was no way they could just hand her over to sit in a cell while the MIA figured out what to do with the incubi who didn't seem to even know where they were.

Amber sighed. "Someone will definitely have to take her in once we start working with the task force, but she can stay until then. Ito is sleeping on the couch, though."

"I can put an air mattress in my workroom," Ceri suggested with a smile.

Ito chose that moment to emerge from the hallway, his hair perfectly dried and styled. He stopped at the edge of the room, and his eyes locked onto Valiel. A muscle in his jaw jumped as he ground his teeth together, but he kept his mouth shut. The anger that radiated through their bond said it all anyhow.

"This is Valiel. We're caring for her until we can find her family or figure out a better long-term solution. She's not going to hurt you or anyone else." Amber crossed her arms. "Any questions?"

"Are you out of your mind?" Ito snapped his mouth shut as soon as the words were out.

"No." Amber turned back to the others. "What's for dinner-- wait, where is Tommy?"

"He's helping Velez unload some things." Deward gestured toward Thallan's mansion. "He said Steven put the stuff for burgers in the refrigerator and brought a grill over that should be on the back porch. And that it was Derek's turn to cook since he claimed to be a grill master."

Amber raised an eyebrow. "Derek burns everything."

"I do not!" Derek objected. "My burgers are amazing!"

"They're charcoal hockey pucks."

"Ceri, take Valiel. I'm going to make Amber eat her words. *And a* delicious burger." He handed the girl off and stomped to the refrigerator.

Valiel dragged the back of her hand across her nose and looked up at Ceri with a ridiculous pout. "Can I have my treat now? I was very scared."

Ceri sighed but couldn't hide the fond look on her face. "If you have it now, you don't get one after dinner, okay?"

"Okay." Valiel's face transformed into a smile.

Ceri pulled a little pack of powdered donuts out of her jacket pocket and let Valiel select one. "I'm going to set you down so I can help Derek. You promise not to wander off?"

"Yeah." Valiel cradled the donut like it was pure gold.

Ceri set her down and put the rest of the donuts back in her pocket. "Icewind said you were out at the Market. Is it really closed?"

"Yeah." Amber dragged a hand through her hair. "Closed and locked. It didn't much like me trying to push the doors open."

That earned her an eye roll. "You didn't do anything stupid, did you?"

"I would never," Amber said with a grin.

"Ceri, can you slice these onions for me?" Derek asked from the kitchen.

"Sure." Ceri swept her hair up into a bun as she headed over to Derek.

"I'm going to take these upstairs to Tommy's room." Deward grabbed the suitcases.

"Need help?"

"No, I think I remember the steps."

Valiel took a big bite of her donut and stared at Ito. He stared back with a carefully blank expression that Amber had come to understand meant he was very, *very* displeased. She swallowed her bite and held the other half of the donut out toward him. "Want some? Ceri says it is a do-nut. It is all sugar, which is bad for us but tastes good."

Ito's eyes flicked to the mangled donut. "No, I do not."

Valiel shrugged and stuffed the rest in her mouth then scampered into the kitchen. Amber followed her, suddenly glad she had allowed Ito to come back with them. Watching him cringe was worth it all.

CHAPTER 22

TOMMY

Tommy jogged back toward the house. Ithra had pulled into the driveway a few minutes ago, and the whole pack was gathered around her van. High-pitched squeals echoed across the yard as the babies were released.

"Tommy! Hurry up!" Genevieve waved him over with a huge grin.

He broke into a run and made it to the group a few seconds later. The babies were impossibly tiny. The six that could fly darted around amongst the pack and, no surprise, were the source of the squealing. Every new discovery resulted in another eruption of noise.

Ceri leaned over the back of the van where Woggy and Smidge stood with Woggy Jr. "And they're sure they'd rather be here?"

Smidge nodded decisively then signed something to Steven.

"She says this is their home."

Tommy's nose twitched. "Is something burning?"

Derek cussed and sprinted for the grill as the scent of charred meat grew stronger.

"We may have to order something," Amber said with a somber expression. "Derek is cursed to burn everything he grills."

Ceri put her face in her hands. "He swore he could do it."

Valiel pressed herself closer to Ceri and gnawed on her thumbnail. "Is Derek in trouble?"

Amber laughed. "No, we're just teasing him. I'll go help him in a minute and make sure there's something left for us to eat."

"Before that, introductions." Steven gestured toward the proud parents.

Smidge let out a sharp whistle. With only minimal whining, the pixies returned to the van, where she forced them to all sit in a line. They clasped their little hands around their spindly knees and gazed up at the pack. She and Woggy stood behind them and introduced each of the babies. Twiggy and Nibbles––the only set of twins––and Socket were the three girls. Koko, Tippy, Flix, and Woggy Jr. were the four boys.

"Now, we have a surprise." Steven rubbed his hands and grinned broadly. "You ready, Woggy?"

"Surprise?" Genevieve narrowed her eyes in suspicion.

"You'll see."

Woggy lugged a small box out from behind the crate and opened the clasps with a dramatic flip of his hands. He pushed the lid open, revealing two shimmery wings attached to a harness. Smidge lifted it and helped him slip his arms into the straps. With all the buckles connected, he lifted one arm, bringing the wing up with it, then the other.

"A glider?" Ceri asked in awe.

"Deward's cousin built it. The main struggle was finding light enough materials, but she did it." Steven stepped back. "Give him some room. He's still working on steering it."

Woggy approached the edge of the van and stood on the precipice, his chest puffed out in pride. Then he spread his arms wide and jumped. The shimmery wings sparkled in the sunlight as he flew forward then banked left. The babies squealed in delight, and even Smidge let out a happy whoop as she jumped into flight and joined him. One of the babies followed and hit his wing, sending Woggy into a tailspin. He hit the ground and rolled to a stop next to Amber's foot but immediately hopped up with a big grin.

"That is *awesome!*" Tommy slung an arm around Deward's shoulder. "Wish I could have shared my sight with you for that. He flew! The glider works."

"Excellent," Deward said with a fond smile.

"Oh, Ceri, we needed to talk to Illya about installing a small door the pixies can use to enter and exit at will. Ithra is pretty sure she's up for it, but you have the easiest time talking with her." Steven pulled out a small box. "Do you have time now?"

Ceri nodded. "Might as well do it before dinner."

Woggy trotted over to Deward and tapped his leg. The troll knelt and held out a hand, allowing Woggy to climb up then onto his head.

"Looks like you're still the easiest transportation method."

Deward gave him a wry smile. "And Woggy is the better guide dog."

Tommy elbowed him and tried to dart out of reach, but Deward was faster and caught him in the ribs. He rubbed it with a grimace. "Your reflexes are getting better."

"Practice makes perfect."

They all filed back into the house, and warmth filled Tommy. The house was full. Even he could feel Illya's warmth and contentment at having them back.

Things weren't exactly the same as before, of course. Ito hovered at the edges of the room, watching them with a frown. The former Alpha Dominus looked confused and somewhat disapproving. Perhaps he thought they spent their free time performing human sacrifice and plotting to take over the world.

Valiel flitted between Derek, Ceri, and Deward. She was full of curiosity and wonder over everything. Food was a constant interest, and she seemed endlessly hungry. Ceri had given her a hamburger bun to quiet her down while Derek and Amber finished grilling.

He slipped outside to help, and they made short work of the food. The grill Steven had brought over was massive. He hoped they could keep it. It would make feeding everyone so much easier, especially if the pack kept growing.

Once everything was brought inside and laid out, the pack descended on it like savages. Tommy glanced back at Ito, who was doing a good imitation of a statue by the backdoor. With a sigh, he made a second plate and steeled himself for the interaction. For so long, Ito had simply been a looming threat. It was weird beyond words to have him *here*, in their house. It was even weirder for him to look so...lost.

Tommy held out the plate. "You'll have to learn to get in there quick or all the food will be gone."

Ito eyed the plain burger with suspicion but accepted it. "I was waiting until the others had eaten their fill since I am the lowest ranked person here."

"Lowest ranked?" He pinched his eyebrows together.

"The alpha eats first, and the rest of pack in order of seniority or position." Ito frowned. "Was your pack taught absolutely none of the traditions?"

Tommy shook his head in disbelief. "If someone told Amber we had to eat in a certain order, she'd eat last in protest. Don't wait while you're here. Just eat. No one is going to get offended." He glanced at Captain Jack, who was eyeing the table. "Just watch out for him. He is a *thief*."

"How did Captain Jack get out of your room? Gen!" Amber grabbed the cat as he locked his eyes on Valiel.

"Did your pack really eat in order at every meal?" Tommy grabbed a chip and popped it in his mouth.

"Of course not. Pack members ate at home with their families most days. Those protocols were only observed at gatherings and meetings."

"Interesting. Genevieve would love to hear about all that if you ever wanted to share. Steven, too. He's a total nerd for traditions and stuff like that."

Ito's eyes strayed to Amber. "You said Amber would hate it."

"She'll hate anything too...strict. Things that might make someone feel like they're less than someone else, but she doesn't hate traditions on general principles. Besides, it's better to know when you're making some kind of statement by breaking a rule than doing it accidentally, right?"

"Your pack has never hesitated to do either."

Tommy lifted one shoulder in a shrug. "It's been confusing, but we've done our best. You asked if we were taught any of the traditions, and the answer is no. Everyone that could have was too busy threatening us." With a battle cry, Woggy leapt from the chandelier over the dining room table and swooped straight down into a bowl of guacamole. The babies swarmed him. Tommy shoved his plate at Ito, who took it in confusion, and sprinted over to the table. "Dang it, that's going to mess up your wings, Woggy!"

Sure enough, the delighted, gunky pixie's wings drooped under the weight of mashed avocado. Woggy just smiled up at him and signed, *"GOOD FOOD."*

Amber, who still had Captain Jack under her arm, shook her head with a smile. "Was it always this chaotic?"

"Probably," he replied with a grin.

CHAPTER 23

CERI

Ceri lifted the lid from the sugar dish and stared down at the two tiny pixies half-buried in the sugar. They were lucky they were cute. She nudged one aside with the spoon to dig out some hopefully not-too-tainted sugar. As tired as she was, she couldn't bring herself to care too much. The pixie rolled over and snorted in annoyance.

"They in the sugar again?" Steven scratched the back of his head and yawned widely as he walked into the kitchen.

"Yep. Do they get into it often?"

He nodded with a scowl. "Just the twins. They like sugar more than spoons. It drives Smidge crazy. She'll come looking for them in here soon."

Ceri topped off her cup of coffee then held the pot up. "Want some coffee?"

"Might as well finish that one off. Gen will be down soon, so we'll need a fresh pot."

"She's awake?" Ceri filled another mug and handed it to him.

"She was up before me. Actually woke me up talking on the phone."

"How times have changed." Ceri shook her head and took a sip of her coffee. It was heaven in a cup. She'd missed mornings in the kitchens and a reliable coffee pot and being *home*. Even if home had changed a bit. She glanced at Ito as he set his folded bedding on the floor next to the fireplace.

As if sensing her attention, he looked in her direction. "I received permission from Amber to spend the day with the task force."

"All right."

He remained there awkwardly for a moment then nodded once and left through the back door. She still questioned Amber's decision in bringing him here but was trying to remain open-minded about it. Maybe they could convince him to actually be on their side.

"Is it me or does he keep skulking around like he's afraid we're going to kick him?" Steven asked.

"He's definitely acting strange." She shrugged. "But I guess having your wolf ripped away would shake anyone's confidence."

"True."

The front door opened, and Amber jogged in, sweat beading on her forehead. Leaves dangled from her wolf's fur. "Y'all are finally up."

"Finally?" Ceri's eyebrows shot up. "It's barely half past six."

Amber shrugged. "Any coffee left?"

"I'm starting a new pot." Steven grabbed the ground coffee from the cabinet.

"What were you up doing?" Ceri asked.

Amber collapsed in one of the kitchen chairs. "We did a lap around the property. I got all...itchy not having patrolled it." She frowned at the leaves that had fallen on the floor and began picking them out of her wolf's fur. "She woke me up a couple of hours ago, and I figured I might as well get it over with. You two are working on the magic problem this morning, right?"

She nodded and took another sip of coffee. "Just as soon as I finish this."

"Gen and I will be over at Thallan's all day with the task force." Amber's lips thinned. "Still can't believe Thallan ran off like that."

"Saved us the trouble of babysitting him, at least."

"At least we knew what he was doing then. It's what we don't know about that worries me."

Ceri laughed. "At this point, the list of what we don't know is ten times longer than what we do know. Thallan's whereabouts don't even concern me at this point."

The corners of Amber's mouth lifted. "Pretty normal for us."

"True." Ceri drained her coffee and set the mug down with a sigh. "Guess it's time to work on the first thing on that list. Magic."

"Y'all have a plan?"

Steven perked up at that. "Actually, I have made a list of tests we can run. And since Deward can see magic now, we may be able to get quite a bit of information. This might even help me figure out more about the no magic zones."

"Any progress on that?" Ceri asked.

"Some." He shrugged. "Mostly just theories, but I feel like I'm close to figuring it out."

"Is Deward still asleep?"

Amber tilted her head to the side and glanced up at the ceiling. "No. He and Tommy are talking. They'll be down soon."

"We've all turned into a bunch of early birds."

A loud squeal startled them all, and Derek came barreling into the living room with Valiel on his shoulders. He laughed as he spun in a circle. Valiel clung to his shoulders, her eyes wide with fear and excitement.

"You're going too fast!" she shrieked.

"Better hold on, then!"

Something in Ceri's heart clenched while she watched them. She'd never seen him with a kid before, and he was...good with her.

Ceri slammed a mental lid on all the thoughts forming in the back of her mind. This was not the time. "I need to visit the coven before we get into the testing, I think." She set her mug down. "Want to come with me, Steven?"

"Absolutely."

Derek set Valiel down and rolled his shoulders. "Guess I'm on babysitting duty?"

"If you don't mind," Ceri said with a smile. It was obvious he didn't.

"I'll survive."

"I'm so hungry. Can I have pancakes now? You promised." Valiel tugged on Derek's hand with big puppy eyes.

He groaned. "Fine."

Ceri laughed and pushed off the counter as Deward and Tommy walked down the stairs. "Deward, you ready?"

"I am." He linked his arm in hers. "Are we doing this outside?"

"Thallan's first. I want to check in on the coven and speak with Tessa if I can. I really should have done it yesterday." She tucked a stray curl behind her ear.

Deward chuckled. "I think that was the last day of rest we'll get for a while. I suggest not regretting it too much."

Her shoulders sagged. "Good point."

The steady beep of the machines keeping the coven alive was the only sound in the dimly lit room. Ceri forced herself to walk farther inside as guilt curdled in her gut. She didn't understand why they were trapped in the spirit realm when it hadn't affected her, Deward, and Evangeline in the same way.

"They are all surrounded by tangled magic." Deward approached the closest witch and trailed his fingers through the air above her. "It's easier to see here. At the vampire's house, the area where the curse was broken was swimming with it."

"Will you be able to get to the spirit realm?" Steven asked from the doorway.

"I hope so." Ceri sat down in the center of room and pulled out her supplies. Since her magic was unreliable, she'd have to go back to the basics. A circle of salt--she poured the fine grains in a thin line around herself. Sage to cleanse the room--its bright scent filled her nose as the smoke rose from the tight bundle. And, finally, help from her spirit guide. She wrapped a hand around the totem that hung from her neck and closed her eyes.

Soft footsteps alerted her to Deward's presence as he sat down across from her inside the circle. "I can see a path."

She held out her other hand to him. "Together, then."

As their hands connected, her vision shifted, and she felt herself moving out of her body. It was different from when the spirit had helped her, but within the space of a breath, she opened her eyes to an expanse of snow.

Deward stood beside her, hand still locked with hers. "It worked."

"Don't let go of my hand. The connection is tenuous." They turned in a slow circle. In the distance, the shimmering forms of a group of people were just visible. "Tessa!" Ceri shouted.

One of the people turned and sprinted toward them. Soon, the other witch's dark curls became visible, confirming it was actually her.

They met her halfway as the rest of coven jogged up behind her. Ceri took in the haggard group. They all looked worn but hopeful. "How are you? Is everyone okay?"

"Depends. How are our bodies?"

"Safe. A medical team is taking care of you all. Fluids and food. You're with the pack and an MIA task force."

"Thank the gods." Tessa did a little happy dance. "That's all I was really concerned about. Well…sort of. The spirits have been getting very agitated." She gestured to the dark clouds that hovered on the horizon. "Storms have been coming and going more frequently with every day that passes."

"Have you spoken with any of them? Do they have any idea why we can't use magic properly?"

Tessa shook her head. "Every time we try to approach one, they flee. Sometimes they'll approach us and cry out for balance to be restored or about the destruction of the realms then vanish. But…" She clasped her hands together. "We found something you need to see."

"What is it?" Ceri hurried to keep up with her as Tessa led them down the hill.

"Some kind of wound. It has to be part of what's wrong because the spirits won't go anywhere near it. And it feels super wrong."

As the ground leveled out, a chill seeped under her skin. Snow floated down in thick clusters that made it impossible to see more than a few feet ahead. Whispers brushed against her mind, too faint to understand. She glanced over her shoulder, sure someone had to be watching them.

"You feel it, too?" Tessa asked with a shudder.

"Yes."

"It's because of that." About a yard ahead of them, a jagged, pulsing wound gashed through the snow. A humming thrummed through the air, growing deeper and deeper, until it pounded with one loud crack. A dark tendril crept further outward and buried itself into the ground, expanding the wound. It was not by much, but it was clearly growing.

"It's spreading?" Ceri asked in horror.

Tessa nodded. "More like…leeching. Or mutating. Or an infected wound that is festering and--"

"Okay, I get the idea." A chill went through Ceri as she gazed down at the pulsing blackness. "And this is what's messing up magic?"

"It's all we've found. And it's certainly not good."

"This is it." Deward stepped forward, tugging Ceri after him.

"It's a vortex." His eyes moved up toward the sky. "It reaches higher than I can see and outward, into the storms. It's tangled, just like the spells you try to cast."

"Great." Ceri stared into the darkness. "How do we fix it?"

"Good question." Tessa put her hands on her hips. "You see anything else helpful, Deward?"

"It's connected to something." He paused, his eyes flicking rapidly from side to side. "There is a path we could follow to its source."

Ceri jerked her head up. "That would be insanely risky."

"I know."

"We could get stuck."

"I know." Deward rubbed a hand over the back of his neck. "It's risky, but I'm not sure what other options we have."

"A safety line." Tessa turned back to the coven. "Get over here! We have a terrible plan!"

The others hurried over, all grimacing at their proximity to the wound. "What now?" one of them asked.

"They want to go in that." Tessa jerked her thumb over her shoulder.

"You really meant it when you said terrible," another woman muttered.

"If we form a line, all holding hands, I thiiiink we could kind of…lower you into it." Tessa beamed at Ceri. "Then we can pull you back out. Literally."

Ceri blinked in shock. "That could actually work."

Deward nodded firmly. "We should try it."

"Come on." Tessa waved everyone into a line and took Ceri's free hand, leaving Deward to enter the vortex first. "Three squeezes means it's time to come out. I'll pass it down like a game of telephone."

Ceri took a deep breath. "Right. Just like a game."

"The last time I jumped into something feet first, I ended up cursed." Deward glanced back at her. "Are we sure about this?"

"You have backup this time. But no, I'm not super confident about this plan at all." Ceri gnawed on her lip. "Just not sure how else we'll find out what we need to know."

Deward hesitated for a moment longer then seemed to steel himself. "I have this sight for a reason. Let's go."

CHAPTER 24

Ceri tightened her grip on Tessa's hand as they edged toward the vortex. The dark magic prickled along her skin and dragged at her feet like sludge. With every step, she felt heavier, as if gravity had increased.

Deward carefully set his foot in the center of the wound then the next. He glanced back at her to say something but was cut off as they were yanked into it. Crushing pressure surrounded her as they fell, spinning and twisting through the darkness. They slammed to an abrupt stop, and Ceri's hand slipped.

Tessa's nails dug into her wrist as she clung to her. "Hold on!"

Above her, Tessa dangled in the air, her other hand stretching back into darkness. Below her, Deward was suspended above a large, open ballroom. Incubi huddled against the walls, as far away from a strange pillar that dominated the center of the room as possible. No one could see them since they were only here in spirit, but Ceri couldn't shake the fear they would be spotted somehow.

"Where are we?" Deward whispered. "I can only see the magic."

"A large room. It looks fancy, like you'd see in a mansion or hotel. But I have no idea where we are exactly." Ceri searched the room for clues. Unfortunately, there were no large signs announcing the location.

"Wait a minute." Tessa wiggled around, trying to see something behind her. "I've been here before."

"You have?" She looked up in shock.

"There's a coven in the town I grew up just outside of Seattle. Their leader was old money and had this big house out in the woods with a massive ballroom with blue doors. I haven't been since I was in elementary school, but the blue doors always stuck out in my mind because they so don't match the vibe." Tessa pointed a foot at a blue door that did not, in fact, match anything else in the room. "No way there are two places like this."

"We need to get out of here. Something is taking notice of our presence." Deward's grip on her hand tightened.

"Got it." Tessa passed up the three squeezes, signaling the others to pull them out.

A moment later, a short tug lifted them a little higher. The movement made it harder to hold on. Ceri grit her teeth together and refused to let go. Tessa disappeared into the cold darkness above them, and a moment later, Ceri shivered as her arm was pulled into it as well.

That same crushing pressure surrounded her. Even though she didn't need air, she struggled to breathe. Hands wrapped around her shoulders as she was dragged over the edge into the snow. The coven pulled Deward out next and picked them all up, carrying them away from the vortex. Finally, the awful draining feeling dissipated. The woman carrying Ceri set her down on the snow and collapsed beside her, panting.

"We almost dropped you guys."

"But you didn't, and we're all still alive." Tessa pumped her fist in the air then let her arm flop back to the ground.

Ceri laughed. "I think you might be a bad influence."

Tessa grinned, unabashed. "I'll take that as a compliment."

Deward rolled over and crawled toward Ceri. "I have another bad plan."

"What now?" she groaned.

"I think I can get us all out. Tessa, you said you couldn't find a path back, right?"

Tessa bolted upright. "Yeah, that's right."

"I can see it." Deward sat in front of Ceri and crossed his legs. "If we are all connected, I think we can make it back."

Ceri took a slow breath and forced herself upright. No matter how exhausted she was, they couldn't leave the coven here any longer if it was possible to help. "Let's do this."

The coven formed a tight circle around Ceri and Deward. They all placed a hand on the shoulder of the witch next to them and other on her or Deward. Magic stuttered through the group.

"Follow," Deward breathed out.

She let the tugging in her belly draw her down toward her body. They tumbled through the darkness after Deward. It was both easier and harder this time. The way out was simpler, but after going through the vortex, even this journey was exhausting. Finally, she snapped back into her body and opened her eyes to blinding light.

Everything ached, and every beat of her heart pounded inside her skull like a hammer. All the machines were blaring out alarms. Ceri rolled onto her side with a groan. "We might have over-exerted ourselves."

"It was...worth it..." Deward gasped.

"Ceri! What the hell did y'all do?" Amber appeared over her, checking them both for injuries.

She blinked in confusion. "When did you get here?"

"An hour ago!"

"I had to call them." Steven's worried face joined Amber's. "You were both shaking and pale, and it had been ages. All the witches' heartbeats went into overdrive, too."

"Are they awake?"

"Yes. The doctors are in here now."

Relief rocked through her, and a grin spread across her face. "It worked."

Amber shook her head with a humorless laugh. "Scared the hell out of everyone, though."

She grabbed Amber's hand. "We figured out what's messing up magic."

Amber froze. "What is it?"

"The incubi. They have something. A pillar that's projecting dark magic. It's here, in the physical realm, but it's somehow wounding the spirit realm and leeching power from it." She pressed a hand to her forehead and winced as the pain of saying so much caught up to her.

"It's tangling magic. I could see it." Deward forced himself upright and grew pale from the effort. "We need to destroy it."

"Where is this pillar?" Amber asked as her wolf stepped up to her side, ears forward with interest.

"Tessa knows. She's been there before." Ceri let Amber help her sit up then leaned against her shoulder as she caught her breath. "She said it was near Seattle, but..." Her grin faded to a frown. "The house where the incubi have hidden it belongs to a coven."

Amber's face hardened. "Are they helping the incubi? Or dead?"

"Could go either way." Tessa sat up in her hospital bed as a nurse tried to get her to lay back down. She waved the woman away. "I'll cooperate in a second." The nurse threw her hands up and turned around to help the witch beside her instead. "The coven didn't have the best reputation, but I didn't see any of them in the room."

Ceri rested her arm on her knees. "Regardless of how the coven is involved, a lot of incubi were there. We will need every last bit of the task force's help to get in and destroy that thing."

"Was Saraqael there?" Amber asked.

"Not that I saw."

Amber nodded once. "I'll get Icewind. As soon as everyone is able to get up and move around, it's time for another meeting."

"We get to go with you guys, right?" Tessa asked. Another witch added on that she wanted to attend the meeting as well, then another, until the whole coven was insisting.

Amber looked down at her. "Up to you."

"They should come with us," Ceri agreed without hesitation. "We'll need their help before this is all over, and we couldn't have broken the curse without them. They deserve it."

"Damn right we do," Tessa said with a grin.

CHAPTER 25

AMBER

At the doctor's insistence, everyone had come to the coven instead of holding the meeting in one of the offices. The last member of the task force hurried inside, and Amber shut the door behind them.

Only three of the vampires had been awake. They stood in the corner of the room, eyes ringed with black circles. A werewolf from each of the packs bound to her was here as well. Ito stood away from them, hovering behind her as if he were her own personal shadow. Amber took her place between Genevieve and Ceri, who sat in front of Derek, still too exhausted to stand for longer than a few minutes. Tommy had been left on babysitting duty.

Velez powered up a large screen set on a table they'd dragged into the room and placed on the far wall. "Thanks to Ceridwen, Deward, and the coven, we have information on the whereabouts of a large group of incubi."

"Where?" Grace, Jameson's new beta, asked. She was a tall woman with dark blonde hair and sharp cheekbones. Apparently, she'd been a surprise pick but had more than earned everyone's respect in the days following Shane's death. A pang of grief cut through Amber's chest as she remembered how recently he'd been lost. In some ways, it felt like it had been years.

"Outside of Seattle." A map filled the screen, and Velez zoomed in on a satellite view of a large property with a sprawling mansion. "If Tessa is correct, they are hiding out on this property owned by the Adams Coven."

"That's not far. We could get there today." Grace straightened as if she intended to leave right that moment.

"We're not going to rush into this." Icewind stepped forward. "Deward and Ceri saw dozens of incubi there. Over the next week, we will watch them. We need to know if anyone is coming or going, or if Saraqael is there."

"There is also the matter of what's inside." Velez crossed his arms. "Ceri, I'll let you explain."

Ceri nodded. "With the coven's help, we were able to locate at least part of what we think is causing magic to react in unpredictable ways. There is a pillar inside that house that is somehow wounding the spirit realm. It's dark magic, and it's powerful."

"If there is something like that there, the incubi will most likely be protecting it." Icewind gestured for Velez to pull up the next slide and thirteen pictures filled the screen. "This is the Adams Coven. Right now, we have no idea if they're alive and working with the incubi or dead. We need to know if we're facing a full coven on top of the incubi that are there." She nodded her head toward the witches. "They need a chance to recover as well."

"Have these witches joined the task force?" one of the vampires asked. Amber was almost certain he belonged to Cadogan's clan.

"Yes," Amber replied. "They broke the curse, and they want to keep helping. They're staying."

"I'm headed to Seattle to lead the reconnaissance mission," Velez said, redirecting the conversation back to more important matters. "I can take up to four of you with me. We'll make it fair with two vampires and two werewolves. Who wants to come?" Cadogan's clan mate immediately stepped forward, along with one of the other vampires. Grace and a werewolf from Kate Ford's pack also volunteered. "All right. We'll leave at thirteen-hundred hours. Pack light."

"We need to know as much as possible ahead of the summit tomorrow. Those of us that are staying behind will still have work to do." Icewind nodded at Genevieve. "Gen and I will be heading up the research effort. Every person in the coven and all their main contacts need to be researched. If they've used a credit card or traveled anywhere in the last month, we need to know about it."

"As with everything this task force does, you are authorized to inform your alpha or clan leader, but *no one else.*" Velez gave everyone gathered a stern look. "We're relying on your discretion for not only our safety, but the success of these missions. Anyone who screws up is out, no second chances." He waited to receive a nod from each of the volunteers then dismissed the meeting.

Amber let the others leave first then trailed out after them, her mind whirling with impatience. It was strange having so much support finally, but it was slowing things down. She was so used to rushing in headfirst. This was better, though, and she knew that.

Ito followed her out of the room. "What do you intend to announce at the summit?"

Amber stopped and drew her eyebrows together as she turned to face him. "Announce?"

"Will you be taking my place on the council or not? I expected you to do me the courtesy of telling me before the summit itself, but it's becoming apparent you will not." Ito lifted his chin, as if daring her to put him in his place for speaking his mind.

"All right, we need to have a talk. You, me, and Gen." She waved down her beta as she exited the room alongside Icewind. "Emergency meeting!"

Genevieve groaned but jogged over to join them. "What now?"

She swept her hand toward Ito. "Explain what it is you are assuming I already know and should be deciding on."

Ito's frown deepened. "The extent of your pack's ignorance is alarming."

"Does that count as being a dick? Can I shove him in a closet?" Genevieve demanded.

"Maybe later." Amber gestured for him to get to the point.

He stiffened as if whatever he had to say would cause him physical pain. "Since you forced my submission, my seat on the council as Alpha Dominus is yours under every law and tradition." A muscle jumped in his jaw as he ground his teeth together. "And as Alpha Dominus, you have the right to appoint whoever you choose to certain positions within the council itself for a period after your official appointment."

"Okay." Amber crossed her arms and forced herself to think this through before she reacted. "Do I *have* to take the position?"

"No," Ito ground out.

"If I did, is it a lifelong thing, or do they have...terms? Like a president?"

"You would serve until you chose to retire, died, or were deemed incompetent by unanimous vote after a trial."

She rubbed a hand over the back of her neck. "Okay. Right." The warning Bram had given her right before they left Montana raced through her mind. If she didn't lead, someone else would. "If I didn't take the position, would someone else on the council fill it instead? Or would you keep it?"

Ito's lips thinned in displeasure. "Another alpha would be chosen."

"This is a lot to think about." She straightened her shoulders. "I have more questions, and I'm sure Gen does, too. Let's head back to the house so we can discuss this with the whole pack. This isn't something I can decide on the spot."

Ito nodded, looking like he regretted having ever brought up the topic. She was lucky he had, but it highlighted the fact that she had not been asking enough questions. Right now, for the first time ever, she had someone at her disposal that knew *everything* about werewolf politics. And he would help her because he wanted his wolf back. There was a small twinge of guilt at the idea of using someone, but she pushed it away. It was about time she found a way to level the playing field.

CHAPTER 26

AMBER

It was well past time to go to bed, but Amber couldn't face trying to sleep right now. Once again, her feet led her toward the Market. It was quickly becoming a ritual. Every quiet moment, she came here and nudged the gate, just in case.

Her wolf trotted ahead of her, taking a winding path in order to sniff different patches of grass. It wasn't as quiet out here as it used to be. Thallan's once-crumbling mansion now bustled with activity day and night. He'd hate all these people here, but she found it comforting. They'd been on their own for so long. Being surrounded by allies filled her with hope.

She and Genevieve had grilled Ito for hours. Her mind was still swirling with the new information they'd learned. The next couple of days were going to change so much, but she was more confident about it all now that they had a plan and a truce with the former Alpha Dominus.

She stopped in front of the gate and knocked once. The rap of her knuckles echoed beyond the gate, but nothing stirred inside. No footsteps. No heartbeats. Not even a hint of breathing. She lowered her hand with a sigh.

The soft pad of paws on grass notified her to Derek's approach.

His wolf reached her first, and a moment later, he stopped at her shoulder. "Weird seeing it like this. We only went once as kids, but it was such a spectacle."

"Yeah." She shoved her hands in her pockets. "I took Tommy and Gen here right after we got changed. It was in downtown Portland. He was so awed by it."

"I bet." He leaned in to inspect the sign. "Definitely locked?"

"Yep."

"Maybe a chainsaw will do the trick."

She snorted. "Ceri would string you up by your ears if you tried something that dumb."

"Only if she caught me." He bumped his shoulder into hers with a mischievous grin that faded when she couldn't return it. He slung his arm around her. "We're going to find a way in."

"I know."

"And we're going to find your demon boyfriend."

She elbowed him in the ribs. "He's not my boyfriend, butthead."

He rubbed his side, the mischievous grin back on his face. "Sure he isn't. You're just always staring at each other in a friendly way."

Amber's wolf snorted. *The fae desires you.*

She glared at the furry interloper. "Do not encourage him."

Derek burst into laughter. "Even your *wolf* noticed. This is too good."

"You're both ridiculous."

"You just don't like it when I'm right." He patted her head. "It really will be okay, little sister."

She sighed. "I hope so."

"You going to come inside and sleep or mope around out here?"

"I'm going to go for a run." She rolled her shoulders back to work out the tension. "Can't sleep right now."

Derek hesitated then nodded. "All right. Be in bed by midnight or you're grounded, though."

"I'm the alpha. You can't ground me."

"We outnumber you." He darted out of reach before she could smack him in the shoulder again. "Don't make me come find you."

Amber glared down at her wolf. "Aren't you going to put him in his place for threatening me?" Her wolf snorted and trotted off toward the woods without a response. "I get no respect around here," she muttered as she trailed after her.

Once under the cover of the trees, she broke into a run. Her legs pumped beneath her as she flew over the ground. It felt good to run like this, but she missed running in wolf form more than she expected. She missed the sense of oneness with her wolf.

With her wolf just ahead of her, they raced around the perimeter of the entire property before finally arriving back at the Market. Sweat dripped down her neck despite the cool temperature, but her body felt good and her mind had quieted. Losing herself in a run was the only thing that worked lately.

She dropped down and leaned back against a tree as she caught her breath. Her wolf laid her head on Amber's legs, tongue lolling out as she panted. "Do you like being outside me better? Getting to run whenever you want?"

Her wolf huffed. *I chose to be one with you. I would choose it again.*

Something unclenched in her chest. "Good."

But you should run more when we are rejoined, lest you grow weak and fat like a cow and become prey. We should always be strong and fast.

She laughed. "All right. Every day from now on, I promise."

A breeze brushed past her, and a scent, both familiar and strange, tickled her nose. She and her wolf picked up their heads in unison. A few feet ahead, a small white flower glowed against the dark earth. She tucked her feet under her and crept toward it. The scent grew stronger, but as soon as she was within reaching distance, the flower vanished with a tiny *plink*. Another sprouted a few feet ahead.

Without needing to speak, she and her wolf moved to the next and then the next. Every time she reached one, another sprouted up a few feet ahead of her. Part of her wondered if this was some sort of trap, but the scent was *good*. Like pure magic. Like home and earth and light.

Bit by bit, they led her to the side of the Market. Amber stopped in front of the stone wall. She and her wolf looked at each other, but neither had the slightest clue what to do next.

A slender green vine crawled up the wall, curving into an archway. The same flowers she'd followed here burst into bloom all around the vine, and the wall under the archway...vanished. She tested the air with her hand, and it passed through with ease. It wasn't an illusion. It was an opening. Without another thought, she lunged through.

CHAPTER 27

AMBER

Magic tingled over Amber's skin as she plunged into blinding light. Her foot caught on a solid object, and she slammed onto her knees, barely catching herself in time to avoid face planting on a steep set of stone stairs.

She blinked away the stars in her vision as her eyes adjusted to the dim, narrow space she found herself in. Her wolf pressed tightly against her side, ears perked up straight. She glanced over her shoulder where the opening had been and found it had returned to a solid stone wall. Fear shivered down her spine. If this was a trap, she had definitely been caught.

Warm light spilled down the stairway, and Zerestria stepped into view holding a torch. "It is very unsafe to follow strange flowers to glowing portals into magical markets."

Amber pushed up to her feet. "They smelled good. And trustworthy."

Zerestria laughed. "I've always admired werewolves' faith in their noses." Her eyes turned to Amber's wolf, and she cocked her head to the side. "So, the rumors are true. You can't shift anymore."

"None of us can. They just..." She gestured at her wolf. "Pop out."

"Interesting."

"Is Kadrithan alive?" A lump rose in her throat. She couldn't bear it if she'd lost him right as they'd finally broken the curse.

"Yes." Relief rushed through her so fast it made her dizzy. For a moment, she couldn't breathe, only blink back tears. "But he is not well. He was severely injured. That is why I broke a few rules to bring you here today. I believe he needs to see you, despite the risk the others think this may pose."

Amber's gut twisted. "Where is he?"

"This way." Zerestria stepped to the side and gestured up the stairs. "We must be quick and quiet."

She nodded and sprinted up the steps after Zerestria, who moved surprisingly quickly for an old woman.

The stairs turned once then led them out into a long hallway with a low ceiling. Dust tickled her nose as they hurried down the clearly unused corridor. This place had to be ancient, but she had no idea how something inside the Market could have been left unpopulated for so long. As far as she knew, there was nothing in the Market that was off-limits. Then again, no one actually understood how it worked.

A dozen questions about how Zerestria and Kadrithan ended up here buzzed through her mind, but now wasn't the time to ask. Nothing mattered until she could see with her own eyes that Kadrithan was alive.

Zerestria paused at a corner then waved Amber after her. They passed two doors but stopped in front of the third, which swung open immediately. Amber followed her into a small sitting room with a very nervous man. Zerestria set the torch in a sconce that hung from the wall. Its soft light illuminated the two plush chairs that sat in front of a cold fireplace. This room also seemed like it hadn't been used in a very long time, but there were recent signs of habitation. A book lay on one chair, and a discarded glass stood on a low table against the wall.

"Are you sure this is safe?" the man asked, his eyes darting back and forth between them.

"Yes, Venali. Go stand guard at the door." Zerestria beckoned her farther into the room to a narrow doorway.

Amber stepped through, and her breath caught in her throat. Kadrithan lay on a raised bed. A stark white bandage covered his otherwise bare chest. He was pale. Too pale. His breaths came in unsteady pants even though he appeared to be sleeping.

Her wolf nudged her to move, and she approached the bed with mounting fear. Bruises littered his exposed skin. She laid her hand over his, the only place she dared touch. "What happened?"

"We made our final stand as your pack broke the curse. We were outnumbered, and our defenses failed. Kadrithan..." Zerestria turned away for a moment, and when she spoke again, her voice shook. "He led those who remained into the final battle. They struck him down. He would have been killed, but the incubi vanished, and we found ourselves here, scattered throughout this haven."

"All the fae are here?"

"All that remain," Zerestria whispered.

"Can't you heal him?" The place where her demon mark had once been ached, as if it could sense he was near.

"We are trying, but his body cannot endure much magic at the moment. It is a tricky thing when someone has been as close to death as he was. We must go slowly or he could be left crippled and weak."

Amber curled her fingers around his. "But he will live?"

"He's never been one to give up." Zerestria gave her shoulder a quick squeeze. "Wake him and talk to him. He's been asking for you." She swept out of the room and shut the door behind her.

Amber's eyes trailed over his face. He looked like he always had in some ways––the same sharp, aquiline nose and firm jaw––but his hair was longer in person and his face a bit gaunter. Fine lines gathered at the corners of his eyes and mouth, as if he frowned often. There were so many details that had been blurred by their separation in different realms. But he was *here* now. Really, truly here.

She didn't want to risk hurting him by shaking him, so she leaned in and brushed his hair back. "Angel, can you hear me?" He didn't stir, so she tried again, louder this time. "Kadrithan. Wake up."

His eyes fluttered open, and he blinked up at her with a frown. "Who the hell is..." He trailed off as his eyes focused on her. "Amber?"

"The one and only." She managed a weak smile but couldn't maintain it.

"You're here." His hand tightened on hers. "Not a hallucination this time."

She raised an eyebrow. "Do you hallucinate me often?"

"Over the past few days, yes."

She cleared her throat and dropped her eyes, not really sure how to respond. "So, how do you, uh, feel? Hopefully not as bad as you look."

The corner of his mouth turned up. "That is how I know for sure you are not a hallucination. My visions of you have more tact."

A laugh bubbled up her throat. "Do you want me to pat your head and tell you that you are handsome instead?"

"And what if I did?" A full grin spread across his face.

She sat very carefully on the edge of the bed and smoothed his hair back, letting her fingers linger in the strands. His forehead was clammy despite the warmth of the room. "You are more handsome in person."

His eyes met hers. "I should ask for exactly what I want more often."

"Maybe so." She sat back and tried not to feel embarrassed. Flirting had never come naturally to her. "Zerestria said all the fae are here now."

"Yes. We created the Market long ago. I had no idea it could shelter us like this, but Zerestria didn't seem all that surprised. It brought us to the safest place it could and expanded to accommodate us." His thumb brushed across her knuckles. "At least that's the theory. They are still figuring out how, exactly, to control it."

"I've been freaking out for days trying to figure out how to get in here."

"I'm surprised Zerestria didn't fetch you sooner."

Her wolf sniffed his leg, and he jerked in surprise. "Is that...?"

"My wolf. Magic has gone...wonky. I tried to shift and she came out. It's affecting all werewolves."

"I see. But you still control her?"

"Mostly." She patted the wolf's head. "It's different, but she isn't going around biting people if that's what you're worried about."

"She has a habit of banishing me. You'll have to pardon me if I'm a bit wary."

The wolf snorted and settled at her feet. "I think you'll be okay now that the mark is gone." She flicked her eyes back to him. "You lied."

He swallowed but linked their fingers together. "I wanted to release you from the mark before the curse was broken. You were never..." He stopped, as if unsure what to say. "You deserved more than a mark trapping you."

"I never helped you because of the mark. Not after I understood."

"That made it even more important to free you. I needed to, for my own sake." He turned his head to face her fully. "I won't lie again."

"Good."

He smiled. "Is everyone in your pack safe?"

"Yes. We all made it through. Evangeline is missing, though. We think..." Amber sighed. "We think she ran away."

A muscle in his jaw jumped as he ground his teeth together. "Are you looking for her?"

"No," she answered honestly. "We have no way to while unable to use magic, and there are much bigger issues." She shook her head in frustration. "Was the fae realm really destroyed? The spirits said something about it, but we've been hoping they were wrong."

He pressed his lips into a thin line and nodded once. "Every curse has a price. We are free. That will be enough." His grip on her hand faltered, and a wet cough wracked his body. "Besides, with the Seed of Life sacrificed, there was no way to restore it."

"The incubi lost their realm as well. They all fell. We've been rounding them up all across the country––which is the main reason we haven't been able to try to look for Evangeline yet." Amber swept her free hand through her hair. "Most of them are confused and think they're in hell and we're all demons. They have no idea what happened."

Kadrithan frowned. "They're lying to you."

"We suspected the same thing at first, but they really aren't. The MIA––"

He tightened his grip on her hand. "They are. All of them. The entire race exists to deceive. As soon as the fae are recovered, we are going to wipe them out once and for all."

She stared at him, horrified. "Kadrithan, they are not all like Raziel and Saraqael. They've been feeding on their own people and using them as slaves."

"You, of all people, should know better than to believe them."

"I know exactly what they can do, and I know that the succubus child in my living room is a victim in all this. She has done nothing."

"But she *will*." He jerked his hand free. "As long as a single incubi lives, the fae are under threat. Everyone is."

An angry flush rose up her neck. "So you want to kill children now?"

"They killed ours."

"That is no excuse. I did not start helping you to become a monster."

Another cough shuddered through him, longer this time. He

gasped for breath after, his face pale and his limbs shaking. Red seeped through the bandage on his chest.

"Shit, I need to get Zerestria. You're bleeding." She rose to find her, but his hand on her wrist stopped her.

"We need your help to finish this, Amber. You cannot abandon us when we are so close to victory."

"I'm not abandoning you, but I'm also not going to abandon my morals. Genocide is not an option." She thought she'd known Kadrithan. She thought she'd understood him. As she stared at the man in the bed, she questioned every conversation and tender moment. "How could you even suggest it?"

He dropped her hand. "You will choose. Us or them."

Amber spun on her heel and walked out of the room. She hadn't thought it possible for her heart to hurt more than when she thought he might be dead. Once again, she'd been wrong. Venali jumped as she opened the sitting-room door. "Where is Zerestria? Kadrithan is bleeding."

"I'll get her." He took off at a sprint and, a moment later, returned with Zerestria and a woman in white robes.

"What happened?" the woman demanded.

"He kept coughing."

She nodded once and hurried in to attend to him, leaving Amber and Zerestria alone in the hall.

The older fae took in her expression with a frown. "The conversation didn't go well, then?"

Amber curled her fingers into her wolf's fur to steady herself. "Are the fae planning on committing genocide?"

"There are many who support it."

"What about you?" Amber held her gaze, determined to get a straight answer.

Zerestria was quiet for a moment. "Part of me would delight in it, but no. I am not one of them."

"Kadrithan is."

"I know. He is angry."

"What about the elders? Don't they make these decisions?" She stiffened as a pained grunt echoed into the hallway. Every instinct demanded she go and make sure Kadrithan was okay, but she couldn't face him again right now.

"No, our king decides now."

Something twisted in her gut. "And who is the king?"

"Until the curse was broken, we all agreed no one would sit on the throne. However, the rightful heir was crowned during our final stand."

"It was Kadrithan, wasn't it?"

Zerestria inclined her head. "I assumed he had already told you."

"No. He failed to mention it." Amber bit down on the inside of her cheek to restrain the rage pumping through her. Her wolf let out a low growl.

"If anyone can change his mind, it is you," Zerestria said softly. "He cares for you."

"He hates them more than he cares about me. Or anyone else."

"We shall see."

"The summit is tomorrow. That's not a lot of time to change his mind." She dragged a hand down her face. "The fae need to be there if we're going to get the other races to listen to us, but if some elder comes and calls for genocide..." She shook her head, frustrated at being backed into a corner by the very man she had thought was her closest ally.

"Perhaps I can convince him to send me."

"That would help."

"I can't promise anything, but I'll do my best." Zerestria glanced over her shoulder. "We shouldn't linger here."

"Why are you so concerned with sneaking me in and out?" She followed Zerestria as they headed back toward the stairs she had entered through. "If Kadrithan is king, and he wants me here, why would anyone else care?"

"Politics are always more complicated than that. As long as he is weak, he is vulnerable. There are a few people that want to reinstate the elders until he recovers."

"And that would be bad?"

"I don't entirely trust their intentions." Zerestria paused at the top of the stairs and pulled a small scroll from the pocket of her robes. "If you read this, you will know the word to access this entrance whenever you want. You will not be able to share it, though, not even with your pack."

Amber accepted the scroll and unrolled it. A strange symbol drawn in the center pulsed bright gold. Magic tingled along her scalp, then it burst into ash in her hands. She looked up in alarm. "Was it supposed to do that?"

Zerestria smiled. "Yes. It was."

"Thank you for bringing me to see him. I needed to know he was alive, even if…" She shook her head.

"Come again, as often as you can. With the demon marks gone, we have very little information about what is occurring outside these walls. Kadrithan will need you in the coming weeks."

"He told me I had to choose." Hurt and anger prickled through her as she remembered the way he'd pulled away from her.

"He's wrong more often than he realizes. Show him that." Zerestria laid a hand on her arm. "Your pack broke the curse. The fae are indebted to you forever. I will help him remember that, too."

Amber nodded once. "I have to tell the others the fae are here. We're working with the MIA."

"Tell only who you must. Secrecy is our best defense."

"I understand."

Zerestria stepped back. "When you enter through this door, I will know you have come. Wait here for me or one of my people. They will greet you if I cannot come myself. Trust no one else."

"All right."

"Your pack is looking for you, by the way. I think they're becoming alarmed."

"Crap." Amber turned and raced down the narrow stairs. The

door shimmered into existence as she approached, and she plunged through it back into the forest. A low howl sounded ahead of them, and her wolf answered.

"Amber?" Derek shouted.

"Yeah! I'm here!" She jogged away from the Market, the pack bond warming as she drew near. Derek and Ceri ran toward her, and she ended up with an armful of witch and blonde curls up her nose.

Ceri drew back and smacked her arm. "Where did you go? We all felt you vanish." Genevieve, Tommy, and Deward jogged up from their left. "You scared the hell out of us!"

"The Market."

"What?" Genevieve demanded.

"I found the fae." She pointed back at the Market. "Well, they found me is more accurate."

"Is Kadrithan...?" Tommy's face paled.

"No!" She waved her hands. "He's alive. Not well, but alive."

"Sorry, you just look like you got bad news." Tommy frowned. "And the bond, it's dampened now, but you're angry."

She took a steadying breath. "There's a lot to explain, but...some of the fae want to wipe out the incubi. Completely."

"That would be genocide," Ceri exclaimed in horror.

"Yes, it would be."

Derek searched her face. "Kadrithan wants to as well, doesn't he?"

She nodded once. "Zerestria wants me to change his mind. And uh..." She dragged her hands down her face. "Turns out he was crowned as king of the fae the night we broke the curse."

The pack stared at her in shock. And she couldn't blame them. Everything felt topsy-turvy. She'd never considered that the fae could end up being the threat. She'd thought breaking the curse would be the end of things. She'd been wrong about everything.

CHAPTER 28

Genevieve paced the length of the living room. Her wolf and Captain Jack lay in a pile on the couch next to Steven, who had fallen asleep after another long morning of poring over his research on curing the no magic zones. She wanted to join him, but she didn't have the free time to spend napping. The witch council was arriving that evening, and representatives from the other councils were already here. Even the elves had shown up. The meeting would begin just after sundown--a concession made for the comfort of the vampires.

The front door swung open, and Icewind walked through. "You ready?"

"Yep." She smoothed down her shirt. It was a button up she'd gotten for work but never worn, and the material still felt all stiff and starchy. "Do I look like a serious, no-nonsense beta?"

"You look sweet and unassuming, which is better. You'll put them off guard." Icewind tapped out a text message.

"I'm going to take that as a compliment." Genevieve mentally tugged on her wolf, who stepped off the couch into a big stretch and yawn. "Come on, sleepyhead."

"Is Ito still on board with the plan?" Icewind asked as they headed across the lawn toward Thallan's mansion––the new task force headquarters.

"He says he is." Genevieve wasn't sure how much she trusted him, but until he got his wolf back, she doubted he would make any moves to harm Amber. And he *had* given his word.

Icewind shook her head and shoved her phone back in her pocket. "He won't be our only problem. The witches are not happy, to say the least. The elves are suspicious of everyone and sprouting flowers all over the place." She pointed at a trail of blue flowers that trailed after them wherever she had stepped. "And the rest of the werewolf council has been standoffish. They want permission to run in the woods, by the way."

"I'll talk to Amber." She added a note to the running list in her phone under a section titled "Amber's Problem". The system she'd devised was working very well so far. "Did the catering finally get sorted out?"

Icewind scowled. "Yes. You know, Velez did not mention event planning when he gave me the job description. I'm not cut out for all this…" She waved a hand in a vague shape. "Entertaining."

"Good thing you have me, then, huh?"

"I count my blessings daily."

Warmth rushed around Genevieve, and a strong breeze sent delicate petals straight at her face. They swarmed around her head like bees. "Neia!"

"Sorry!" Icewind stopped and took a deep breath, and the assault finally ended.

Genevieve peeled a sticky petal off her cheek. "No more compliments."

"Just wait until we get inside. Some of the others have even less control than I do." Icewind picked a few more out of the top of her hair. "I think that's all of them."

"Great." She straightened her shirt again and took a deep breath. "Should be an absolute blast."

They wound their way through the lines of cars that now filled the front lawn. It was a good thing Thallan's mansion was as big as it was, or they'd have been forced to send half the people that had showed up to hotels. As it was, almost every room was full.

The front door stood open as a steady stream of people came and went. She followed Icewind inside, taking it all in. The foyer was dotted with smaller groups––werewolves, vampires, and the constantly flowering elves. A small rain cloud rumbled over one poor elf's head. His hair was sopping wet, and everyone that had to pass by him glared at the puddle growing under his feet, which only made his cloud rain harder.

It was interesting to see how few of the werewolves had their wolves with them. News that shifting had gone wrong must have spread fast. She hadn't expected so many to choose to not shift at all, though. Having her wolf physically by her side was odd, but not the worst. Her wolf pressed against her thigh in agreement.

Adele Damman approached and greeted her warmly. A long, semi-translucent veil covered her face and arms, reaching all the way to her knees. "Genevieve, it is good to see you again."

"You too," she replied with a genuine smile. Of all the vampires, Adele was the least creepy. Though the veil wasn't doing her any favors in that respect. "I'm surprised to see you before sunset."

"I am always willing to rise early when the occasion calls for it. It would not do to sleep while everyone else mingles."

Genevieve knew exactly how she felt. With so many powerful people here, the pack needed to figure out who was on their side and who might cause trouble. Amber, Ceri, Tommy, and Deward would be arriving soon to mingle as well. Derek was watching Valiel, whose existence was still being kept on the down low for now. "I completely agree."

"I am impressed at the speed with which your task force has uncovered such valuable information." Adele nodded toward one of the vampires that had been in the room when they'd gone over the plan for surveilling Adams Coven. "It bolsters my resolve that my support has not been misplaced."

"I'm glad to hear it." Genevieve couldn't help a little smile of relief at hearing that. She knew everyone else around them was listening, too. Adele's choice to make her support publicly known was intentional, of course, and she was tempted to hug her for it. "We couldn't have done it without your help, both now, and in Montana."

Adele inclined her head. "It seems we make an excellent team."

"Absolutely."

She felt a bit lighter after that and made an effort to speak, at least briefly, to everyone she knew by name. Her mingling took her throughout most of the lower floor. She also introduced the trolls to the packs now tied to theirs. Ithra was familiar with the alphas after the fight, but the other elders hadn't been introduced. Alpha Kate Ford and Olwen, Deward's father, hit it off immediately and ended up in a conversation about quantum physics that she didn't even attempt to follow.

Scanning the room for another person on her list, she spotted Amber. She froze, barely keeping her jaw from hitting the floor. Her alpha, without any prompting from her, was wearing something *nice*. The fitted, wine-red dress with long sleeves made her look regal, and the massive ruddy wolf at her side added a touch of "don't mess with me". No one could look at the two of them and think Amber was weak.

Her shock turned to suspicion. There was no way that had been in her closet, and they had definitely not been shopping. Genevieve made her way over and waited until Amber was done talking to Jameson to pounce.

She grabbed her elbow and dragged her to a corner then gestured at the outfit. "Explain."

Amber grimaced. "Bram. The packages were on the front porch this morning."

"Packages? As in plural?"

"Yeah..." Amber plucked at the shirt in distaste. "He keeps dressing me. That's weird, right? Should I be creeped out?"

Genevieve took in the outfit again then shook her head. "No. He's way too good at it to complain. Just be grateful."

"So it's not too much?"

"No! It's perfect!" She took Amber by the shoulders. "You look like an alpha."

"Okay." Amber let out a breath. "As long as you approve, I'll trust his taste. At least there's no cape this time." Her phone buzzed in her pocket. She pulled it out and checked the message. "All right, gotta go. Ito is here. Wish us luck."

"The plan is fool proof."

"Nothing is fool proof," Amber muttered as she stalked away.

Genevieve shook her head with a smile and slipped down the hall to find a quiet room. She needed to review her list and collect her thoughts. So far, there were no surprises. The vampire council was fairly split in their support now that the curse was broken. Cadogan and his lot were very reluctantly supportive, wanting to be only minimally involved. The only thing keeping him around was the PR boost the MIA was offering.

A small office they'd been using for research was empty. She plopped down in one of the chairs with a sigh and pulled out her phone while her wolf curled up on her feet under the table. There were a few items she was able to mark off the list and a few interesting tidbits to add to her catalogue of people.

The door opened, startling her. She hadn't heard anyone coming. Mira––leader of the Kudzu––slipped inside and closed the door behind her, holding a finger to her lips to remain silent. She pulled a small device out of her pocket and turned it on. It let out a low, steady hum. "This should minimize who can hear us. They'd have to be right outside the door to listen in."

"Useful." She set her phone down. "Velez said the Kudzu intended to stay in the shadows and not attend the meeting. Have you changed your mind?"

"No. That's not why I'm here."

"What is it, then?" She swiveled in her chair to give Mira her full attention.

"There are some rumors in the underground rings about a young girl and an old elf hunting for angels. They're recruiting anyone who wants to help."

Her heart pounded in her chest. "An elf with white hair and fire magic?"

Mira nodded. "We've got video footage of him, and it certainly looks like Thallan, but we haven't been able to get any images of the girl. I'm sure we both suspect the same person, though."

"How the hell would Evangeline have even found him?"

"Your guess is as good as mine."

Genevieve rubbed her temples. If Evangeline was off playing vigilante, she could cause a lot of issues for them. For everyone, actually. "We need to find both of them if we can."

"We're working on it, but no one is very eager to give up information on them. They seem to think they're doing a public service." Mira sighed and shook her head. "The incubi hurt a lot of people, and now that the entrancements have fallen off, those people are angry and after revenge. Can't really blame them, either."

"I'm just worried about incubi who haven't done anything paying for crimes they didn't commit. All the incubi who lived here have disappeared, so the easiest targets are the innocents."

"The MIA is rounding them up fairly quickly."

"Let's hope it's quick enough." She pressed her lips into a thin line. It was good to know this ahead of the meeting, but it was yet another complication. At least she knew now. Information was their most powerful tool right now. Amber had to stay ahead of everyone else if she was going to effectively lead this effort. They couldn't show even a hint of weakness.

CHAPTER 29

AMBER

Amber doubted this ballroom had been used in decades, perhaps longer. Moonlight filtered through the tall windows at either end of the room, but it was drowned out by the bright chandeliers that sparkled overhead. Every crystal in them looked like a flower petal--something Illya had to have chosen. Thallan would never have picked something so pretty.

The trolls had built a massive round table in just a few days for the meeting itself. Amber hadn't wanted to stand in front of everyone and give a speech. With all the egos at play, they needed this to feel collaborative.

The various council members hovered near their assigned seats. The bits of conversations she could overhear were tense and full of veiled references. Everyone was on guard, and she couldn't blame them. The paranormal races didn't work together, and they didn't trust each other.

Bram appeared at her shoulder. "You seem more confident that usual."

"It's all an act."

He laughed and rested his hand on her elbow. "I am always so pleased to see how fast of a learner you are. You really will have to allow me to paint you again soon."

She shuddered a little as she remembered his blood-splattered basement. "We'll see."

"I am very curious to see how you carry out your plans for tonight." He tapped his thumb absently along with the rhythm of her heartbeat. "You look every inch the alpha you are, at the very least."

The dress was more comfortable than it had looked, but she still felt like she was playing dress-up somehow. And it was awfully tight. "Thank you for the clothes. I suppose they are better than jeans for this sort of thing."

Bram grinned in amusement. "My sole motivation this time was the entertainment I get from making you wear clothes you don't like. You do look stunning, though."

Amber glared at him. "You are insufferable."

"And remorseless." He stepped back into a sweeping bow then glanced up to wink at her. "Good luck."

She squared her shoulders and strode toward her seat. Ceri and Ito would take the spaces on either side of her. Going counter-clockwise around the table, the vampires would be to her right, then Xenya, representing the trolls alone. Next were the elves. They had no formal leadership like some of the other races, but three influential members of the race had agreed to come to this meeting to ensure their voices were heard.

Likewise, the witches did not have a cooperative council, but the heads of the three most powerful covens made up the Witch's Conclave and had the power to speak for all the witches. They would sit directly across from Amber, and she expected them to be the most confrontational during this meeting. They had suffered the most from the backlash of the curse, after all.

The werewolves were the next group. The position Ito had previously held as Alpha Dominus put him unquestionably in charge of that council. There were four other alphas that effectively filled the role of his betas and made up the rest of the council.

Finally, Icewind would represent the MIA alone since Velez was in Seattle. Amber was grateful for her presence here. While many of the people at the meeting tonight weren't here to oppose her pack, it certainly felt like it. They were here to judge her choices and her plans to fix this disaster.

Amber stopped behind her seat. Her wolf stood next to her, giving her strength. *They will listen. We will make them.*

I hope so, she thought back. It hadn't been a lie when she'd told Bram her confidence was all an act. When in the midst of a fight, she could put her misgivings aside, but in situations like these, the doubts crept in. Less than a year ago, she'd been a human nurse; now she was trying to win a war no one had seen coming.

With a vicious mental shove, Amber pushed all the self-doubt away. She had done the *right* thing every time she'd been faced with a choice. If all of that had led her here, it must have been for a reason.

"Everyone, please take your places so we can begin." She pulled out her own chair and sat down.

Ito was the first to join her, taking his place at her right. He folded his hands in front of him on the table. Ito's demeanor was completely different here, where they had an audience, than it had been in the privacy of their home. Though he looked perfectly calm, his inner turmoil was apparent through their bond. She envied his ability to hide it so well.

After a few moments of chatter and the scrape of chairs on marble, everyone was finally seated. Their entourages spread out in segregated groups behind the representatives. Her entire pack was behind her as well, their wolves at their sides.

The table fell silent. Amber grew tense under the weight of their stares, but she leaned forward and forced a neutral expression on her face. It was time to do this. "On behalf of the task force and the MIA, I wanted to thank all of you for attending this summit. The crisis we're facing affects all of us and will take all of us to overcome." A few of the attendees sneered at her trite words, and she couldn't really blame them. It sounded good, but unless they could solve the problems they'd created, she deserved their sneers. "We will not let you down."

"Before we begin, Alpha Ito has an announcement to share." She waved a hand toward him, inviting him to speak.

Ito held his poker face firmly in place as he stood before the gathered councils. "The incubi are a threat we all ignored for far too long, trusting the snake in our midst would not reach out and strike us." His eyes lingered on the werewolf council. "In order to face an unprecedented threat, we must make bold steps toward preserving the safety of both paranormal races and humans. Amber Hale has taken on the burden of Alpha Dominus with the binding and submission of four packs." On cue, Jameson, Greer, and Kate Ford stood and took their places on either side of her amidst the gasps that rippled through not only the werewolves, but the witches and elves as well. The vampires simply nodded, already having been told about her new position. "As is tradition, those packs who have sworn fealty to her as Alpha Dominus must be presented to the council. Because of the threat we all face, it was decided this announcement should be made here, in front of all these witnesses."

Amber stood. "I will take my rightful place as Alpha Dominus on the council."

The implication of what she'd just announced exploded like a bomb on the werewolf council. One alpha leaped to his feet. "Alpha Ito, are we to understand that *you* have sworn fealty to the Hale Pack and surrendered your title to her?"

He turned his cold gaze toward the other man. "Yes."

"He hardly had a choice." Cadogan, her least favorite vampire from the council, leaned forward and rested his elbows on the table. "The...former...Alpha Dominus was entranced. Everyone at the battle in Montana was quite shocked to see it."

"Is this true?" Alpha Grey, the one other woman on the were-wolf council, demanded. They'd expected this to come out. There was simply no way to keep it under wraps.

"Yes, it is true." Ito held her gaze. "The archangel Saraqael entranced me and took control of my pack. I was forced to challenge Alpha Hale. During the course of that challenge, she forced my submission, which broke the entrancement and freed us."

Uneasy whispers continued around the table. Amber leaned against her wolf's side, using the touch to keep herself grounded. They could whisper all they wanted; there had been no other choice during that fight.

"We did away with that tradition for a reason." Alpha Grey's eyes turned to Amber. "Do you expect all of us to submit to you?"

"No, absolutely not. I would not accept it even if you wanted to." This was one thing Ito had demanded of her in exchange for his help. There was no way to undo the bonds she had already created, but she had promised him that she would not take on any more. Amber had agreed without hesitation. "I did what I had to in order to deal with a threat, but with the cooperation of everyone here, there is no need to expand my pack further."

Alpha Grey was silent for a long moment then nodded. It was impossible to tell from her expression what she thought of Amber's response. The others were clearer in their distaste.

One of the werewolves who had remained silent thus far leaned forward. "While somewhat admirable, this is still a decision that affects us all. You have been an alpha for only a year and do not have the experience necessary to act as Alpha Dominus."

"I agree." Amber nodded in acknowledgment. "That is why my first act as Alpha Dominus is to appoint Alpha Ito as my advisor. His experience and knowledge should not be wasted." Amber searched the council for any further signs of anger but found none. "I will not make any other changes at this time but reserve the right to do so."

Though the werewolves were still clearly unsettled, they seemed willing to let it be. For now, at least. She retook her seat, and the others followed suit.

Clearing her throat, she took a breath and continued the meeting. "It seems appropriate to begin this by confirming that the curse on the fae was broken. I know there have been some rumors circulating that perhaps it wasn't, but we are one hundred percent certain. I have spoken with the fae myself and confirmed this."

"Where are the fae? Shouldn't they be here since they are the reason we're all in this situation?" Helena Ashby, the leader of the second largest coven in the country, demanded. A murmur of agreement went around the table.

Amber waited for them to stop. It needed to be established early on that the fae were no one's enemy. "The incubi are responsible. They cursed the fae, not the other way around."

"Regardless, breaking *their* curse has affected us all. They cannot sit back while we clean up the mess this has left," Helena sneered.

"The fae are safe and hidden for now. On the night the curse was broken, they were attacked in their realm and suffered heavy losses."

"That is no excuse––"

"You are correct." Zerestria's voice echoed across the ballroom. Her long gray hair was swept up into an ornate style and strung with pearls. A silver dress billowed around her legs as she strode toward the gathering. Two fae flanked her, wearing formal garb with a large silver star embroidered on the chest. "I apologize for my tardiness."

Relief coursed through Amber. She hadn't been sure if Zerestria would come. "Zerestria, thank you for coming despite the risks."

"It is my honor to be included in these discussions." Zerestria turned to the rest of the table. "The King has sent me as his emissary for this meeting. I hope to address any concerns about the fae's intentions and future plans."

Bram rose and pulled out his seat for her. "Please, take my place."

Zerestria inclined her head toward him in thanks and sat to Amber's right between Ito and Adele Damman. Her guards stood behind her, hands clasped behind their backs. "I believe you were speaking of messes. Please continue."

Helena swept a hand at the elves, whose section of the table was slowly being covered in a creeping moss that occasionally sprouted purple flowers. "We have lost control of magic completely. Everyone here is affected by that. Do the *fae* have a solution for that? Or are we expected to simply accept the downfall of our entire way of life?"

"*I* have a solution for that," Amber stated, drawing the attention of the entire table back to herself. "As those involved with the task force already know, we have identified a powerful object in the incubi's possession that we believe is the cause of our inability to control magic. The MIA will be leading an assault on the location within the week."

"What do you plan on doing with this...object?" Helena asked.

"We need to destroy it," Ceri said. "It is not only affecting our ability to use magic, it has somehow wounded the spirit realm and appears to be leeching something from it."

"Where is this object?" another coven leader demanded.

"That information will not be released until after it has been destroyed," Icewind replied, leaning forward to rest her arms on the table. "Recovering this object will be dangerous. We cannot risk word reaching the incubi ahead of time."

"Are you implying there are traitors among us?" Cadogan asked, feigning offense with a hand over his heart.

Icewind stared him down. "The incubi are too well connected to rule it out."

Helena scoffed. "Yet you seem to trust the MIA and your *task force* implicitly."

"Everyone involved in the task force actively helped us break the curse and fought the incubi on more than one occasion."

Icewind leaned back in her chair and tapped her thumb absently against the table. "They've earned our trust."

"And we haven't?" Helena ground out.

"Not yet," she replied without hesitation.

"We will not be pushed out of this. My coven is staying in Portland to assist the task force. Every other race is represented." Helena swept a hand around the table.

Amber glanced at Icewind, who nodded, then returned her attention to the witches. "As long as you are willing to respect the MIA's authority, your help would be greatly appreciated. I'm sure trust can be established with time." Ceri's discomfort twisted through the pack bond, but they'd already discussed this and agreed there was no way to leave the witches out of things. "Ceridwen and her coven will coordinate with you."

"Her coven?" Nicolai Arcos, another coven leader who had been silent thus far, narrowed his eyes at Ceri. "I had understood that Ceridwen Gallagher had been rejected by her family's coven and joined your pack as a...shaman." He spat out the word with obvious distaste.

"That is correct," Ceri replied calmly. "However, with Zerestria's help, I was connected with twelve other witches who believed in our cause and not only helped us break the curse, but have decided to stay and continue helping until we have restored magic and ensured the incubi are no longer a threat."

"What is the plan for that, by the way?" Cadogan asked. "The MIA seems to be collecting as many incubi as they can, while I was under the impression we were at war."

Amber gathered her frayed patience and steeled herself to deal with this particular topic. "The MIA is continuing to investigate this. However, from what we understand now, a large portion of the incubi race were enslaved and fed on by their own people. When their realm was destroyed, they fell into this one and had no idea where they were." She folded her hands together and waited a brief moment for that to sink in for everyone. "The incubi who have gone into hiding are the real threat, along with Saraqael and the other archangels."

"So there are lost, hungry incubi who feed on...what, exactly?" Cadogan pressed, clearly delighting in stirring up a bit of drama.

Amber could almost see the tenuous thread with which everything was held together, fraying and strained. Her gaze strayed to Zerestria. If the fae came out in public support of wiping out the incubi, everyone gathered here would follow them.

"Life force," Zerestria answered, drawing the table's eager attention. "In small amounts, it is no more harmful than what a vampire would take through blood." She waved a hand to her right. "In large amounts, it is deadly. Magic offers a natural protection, which leaves humans as their only available source of sustenance."

"How much do these creatures require in order to survive?" Gouyen asked, her pitch-black eyes boring into Zerestria.

"To survive? Very little. To be immortal? Too much. If they overfeed, they can extend their lives indefinitely." Zerestria let out a harsh sigh. "That is why they sought to wipe out magic from this realm. They wanted more *cattle*."

"The archangels, like Saraqael, are behind all this," Amber added before any more objections could be raised. "They created the curse, they've fed on not only their own people, but however many humans they could get their hands on, and they intended to completely destroy magic so all of us would be vulnerable to them." She spread her hands. "That is why they are a threat to all of us."

"So your plan is to destroy these mysterious items and restore magic, then what?" Helena pressed.

"Then we hunt down the archangels."

Zerestria calmly folded her hands together. "Amber Hale has the full support of the fae as she pursues this objective."

"And now I need yours." Her wolf pressed against her leg under the table, lending her strength. "Saraqael will not go down without a fight. We cannot win this war without your help."

Gouyen was the first to agree. Something in Amber's chest

unclenched as the vampire once again pledged support. The witches, along with further demands for inclusion, also agreed. The elves were hesitant and refused to promise anything. The werewolves were the only ones left.

Alpha Grey pursed her lips. "I will respect your decision as Alpha Dominus until you give me a reason not to." It wasn't exactly rousing support, but it was better than she'd hoped for.

Amber inclined her head. "Thank you for giving me a chance to prove myself."

Bram met her eyes from where he stood behind Zerestria and grinned at her as if to say *I told you so*. It was tenuous, but they'd done it. She'd convinced them to help. Her heart hammered in her chest, but she couldn't even spare the energy to be embarrassed that everyone could hear it.

Steeling herself for this next bit, she took a deep breath. "If anyone has any further questions, I'm happy to speak with you one on one." The table exploded as everyone clamored for a chance to make their demands or concerns known.

CHAPTER 30

AMBER

Amber kicked off her heels toward her closet and swore to herself she'd burn them as soon as she'd gotten some rest. The sun was rising, which meant she'd been up dealing with people for far too long. Even worse, it was people that either hated or mistrusted her. Her mind was just as tired as her feet.

Icewind wanted to meet at two p.m. That left her six hours to sleep since she'd have to shower when she woke up. Her wolf climbed onto her bed and nosed her way under the covers. She reached for the zipper on the back of her dress but couldn't quite reach it. With a frustrated huff, she headed toward the door, intending to ask Ceri for help, but her phone rang.

She snatched it off the dresser, finger hovering over the reject button. But she froze as her eyes focused on her mother's name on the caller ID. Her mother hadn't called her in six years. She *wouldn't* call even if her life depended on it; of that much, Amber was sure. Her hand moved on its own, answering the call then raising the phone to her ear. "Who is this?"

There was a moment of silence, then an unfamiliar woman's voice responded, "My name is Taharia."

"Why do you have my mother's cellphone, Taharia?" Anger bristled through her and her wolf--whose eyes took on a deep, red glow. The entire pack had to be feeling her panic, but in that moment, she could not control it at all.

"You will not believe me now, but it is because I have done you a great favor."

She curled her free hand into a tight fist. "What, exactly, is the nature of that favor?"

"I was ordered by Saraqael to kill your families. Not just yours, but Genevieve, Ceridwen, and Tommy's as well."

Her blood ran cold. "If you so much as *touched*--"

"They are alive and unharmed in my care." Someone else spoke in the background but was quickly hushed. "I know this will upset you, since you don't fully understand my reasons for doing this. However, I want to assure you that we're after the same thing."

If they were alive, there was a chance to get them back. Amber squeezed her eyes shut and took a deep breath. "What do you want?"

"Protection. I took your families to save their lives, and in return, I need you to hear me out. It was the best way to get your attention."

"I can guarantee you it was not. I want proof our families are alive."

"Who would you like to speak to?"

"My father." He was most likely to be calm in a situation like this. She'd never seen him get flustered or angry in his life--a trait that she had come to realize was both a virtue and a flaw.

There was a shuffling noise as the phone was handed off. "Amber?" Her father's voice was wary but steady.

"Dad. You all right?"

"We're okay. They said this was because of something you're mixed up in. And about everything on the news."

Amber felt the chastisement all the way down to her core. She'd put her family in danger and hadn't even thought to protect them. They seemed so far removed from the chaos they'd been dealing with. "It is about all that. I'm sorry. Me and Derek are going to get you out, though, okay? Don't do anything brave."

"All right, kiddo. We'll be patient."

The phone was handed off once again. "I will call you back with a time and a place to meet. You won't find us before we're ready to meet, so don't bother looking."

"When will you--" A dial tone cut her off. Taharia had hung up. White-hot rage rushed through her, and the phone screen cracked under the pressure from her hand. She forced her fingers to unclench and set it back on her dresser.

Derek burst through her bedroom door. "What happened? We thought you were under attack." The pack crowded into her room. Even Ito hovered in the doorway.

Her lip trembled, and she realized absently that tears had gathered in her eyes. "They have our families."

"Who?" Derek's panic bloomed into the pack bond to match her own.

"I don't know. All she gave me was her name. Taharia. She wants to arrange a meeting."

"Our families?" Genevieve asked, fear evident in her voice.

"Yes. All of them." She swallowed down the lump in her throat. "I spoke to my father. They're alive. He said they aren't hurting them. Taharia said..." The tears threatened to spill down her cheeks. She clenched her teeth together and tilted her head backward, refusing to give into the emotions right now. "Taharia said she was ordered to kill them but took them to protect them instead. She wants something from us. She'll call back to tell me when and where to meet her."

"It has to be a trap, right?" Tommy whispered.

"Does it matter?"

No one had a response to that.

CHAPTER 31

AMBER

Amber sat at the kitchen table, barefoot, still in her red dress. She plucked out the pins holding up her French twist one at a time and tossed them in a pile. Her scalp ached from her hair being held in one position too long. Resting her forehead on the table, she massaged it away as best she could.

The back door opened, and someone approached. She didn't bother looking up to see who it was. She didn't want more bad news or more problems. Genevieve was on her way to her parents' house with Icewind, and local police were checking out each of their family's homes. They weren't going to find anything good; of that much, she was sure.

"I'm surprised to find you alone."

Amber peered up at Zerestria, not having expected it to be her who walked in. "And I'm surprised to see you here at all. You weren't sure about attending the meeting because of safety issues."

"Extenuating circumstances." Zerestria gestured at her with a raised brow. "Your family has been taken?"

She sat up and brushed her hair away from her face. "How did you even hear about that in the Market?"

"Bram texted me." Zerestria held up a phone. "Technology is helpful, especially now that I can actually use it myself."

"Oh. Of course." Her eyes drifted down to the file in front of her. It contained only one page. Information on the phone call she'd received. "And yes. They've all been taken. Someone named Taharia wants protection. Her name ring a bell?"

Zerestria frowned then shook her head. "No, but I will make inquiries. She is a succubus?"

"Yep." Amber flipped the file shut. "I imagine she is at least a little important as well since she was ordered to kill all our families. Lucky she just kidnapped them, I guess. Assuming she's telling the truth about any of it."

"Very lucky indeed." Zerestria walked over and laid a hand on her shoulder. "You are sure she has them?"

"Yes. I spoke with my dad when she called."

Zerestria gave her shoulder a squeeze then dropped her hand. "Kadrithan wants to see you. He's worried."

"Because I'm still not planning on killing all the incubi? Or because of my family?"

The old fae smirked at that. "Both, I presume. But concern for your family, first and foremost."

"I can't leave until I hear back from Gen."

"I understand." Zerestria pulled another phone from her pocket and slid it across the table. "Bram was also able to acquire this for me. It has special security measures installed. Don't ask me how they work, though." She shook her head as if exasperated by her own lack of knowledge. "However, it will unlock for you, face recognition I think, and can be used to communicate with both Kadrithan and myself." Zerestria pursed her lips then sat back with a sigh. "He is…struggling."

Amber picked up the phone. There were two numbers in the contact list and no apps or anything else installed. "Mentally or physically?"

"Both, though the wounds are beginning to heal a little quicker.

They've stopped reopening." Zerestria's fingers couldn't stay still. Though Amber didn't know her well, she didn't think it was like her to fidget like this. "The fae have lost so much. We all thought breaking the curse would free us. That it would be a new beginning."

"But you've lost your realm?" Amber's heart ached as she remembered the Seed of Life and the pain on Kadrithan's face as he'd handed it over.

"More than that." Zerestria let out a harsh sigh. "Our immortality."

"Are you sure?"

"Yes. Not everyone has realized it, but I can feel it. It is more apparent to the few of us left that were already very old."

"I'm sorry. I wish I could--" Her phone rang, and Genevieve's name flashed across the screen. "One second." Zerestria nodded as she answered the call. "What did y'all find?"

"The door was busted in. Minimal signs of a struggle." Genevieve's voice was tight with unshed tears. "Clothes were taken. My mom's cholesterol medication, too. The police say that's a good sign."

"Definitely implies they intend to keep them alive." Amber massaged her temple with her free hand. "Anything else? Fingerprints? Did your family have a security system or anything?"

"No. The police are checking for fingerprints, but if it's incubi, the odds of finding a match are very low." Genevieve let out a harsh sigh. "They're going to follow up any leads they can find, but realistically, we're stuck waiting on Taharia to call back."

"Great." Amber leaned back in her chair. "Kadrithan asked to see me again. I shouldn't be long, and *apparently*, I can receive texts inside the Market. So call me if you need me."

There was a short pause. "Don't let him talk you into anything."

"I won't."

"Text me when you're out."

"All right. Talk to you soon." Amber ended the call and stood. "Let's go."

~

Amber hesitated as she stared into Kadrithan's dimly lit room. *Us or them.* The words still filled her with anger. Her wolf walked ahead of her, clearly not sharing her reservations. With a sigh, she followed and stepped through the narrow doorway.

Kadrithan was sitting up this time. A stack of pillows stuffed behind his back supported him. He lowered the book he'd been reading and stared at her. The flickering light of the lantern by his bed highlighted the dark circles under his eyes, but some color was back in his face. His eyes traveled from her messy hair, to her dress--lingering--then to her bare feet. He slipped a bookmark into the pages and set the book aside on the bed. "Any news on your family?"

"Not really. We know they let them take clothes with them, but that's about it." She felt awkward standing so far away, but there were no chairs, and she didn't want to sit next to him like she had last time. "I'm waiting on the next phone call."

He nodded and looked away, fiddling with a loose thread on the blanket covering his legs. "It is odd how limited I feel without the marks. I hated them, yet I miss them." He shook his head with a humorless smile. "I couldn't get to you, and I couldn't sense your emotions. It's like...losing a limb."

"It's odd to not have you there." She pressed her hand to the place on her chest that still had the faded shadow of the mark. "Or here."

They were silent for a long moment. There were so many things to say and so many ways they could all turn into an argument. She didn't know how to navigate this. There was nothing to apologize for--on her part, at least--and there was no easy solution.

She cleared her throat, searching for *anything* to talk about. "Zerestria said you're healing faster."

"Yes." He pressed a hand to his stomach. "The bandages will be off soon. They're going to have me start walking tomorrow." The corner of his mouth quirked up. "All I wanted to do before all this was rest. Now I can't wait to be away from this bed."

She snorted. "I'll trade you. I don't think I've had a full night's sleep in weeks."

His face fell. "I hope to never have to see you like this. I'd rather stay in bed another month."

His sudden seriousness caught her off guard. She swallowed and shifted on her feet. "It's definitely not my favorite thing, either."

"I've been imagining you must hate me now. I wasn't sure if you would come see me at all, and I couldn't leave to find you if you refused."

She let out a sharp sigh. "No. I am...frustrated and disappointed. Though..." She shook her head. "I did consider refusing to come today. But I decided I'd never change your mind if I avoided you."

He pursed his lips. "You think I'm being unreasonable."

"I think you're angry, and you are taking that anger out on a whole race."

His lips thinned in frustration. "I am not just angry. I want--" He gave his head a harsh shake. "I *need* vengeance. They took our freedom. Our realm. Our lives. And still they are taking." He lifted his gaze to hers. "They are still trying to destroy magic. What more do they have to do for you to understand they are parasites?"

"Saraqael doesn't have to do anything more. I understand what he and all the archangels are. What every incubi that fights for them are." She looked away and dragged her hands through her hair. "But you cannot blame all of them for this. Have you forgotten Evangeline is part incubi? That there are children out there who haven't been taught to hate yet?"

He ground his teeth together. "You will see. As this war drags on, you will have no choice but to understand the truth of the matter."

"We definitely agree on that." She crossed her arms, refusing to do him the courtesy of storming off this time. If she left every time they argued, she'd never change his mind. He'd just sit there and *brood*. "Genevieve had a good suggestion. She thinks one of the fae need to join the task force. We're planning a raid soon. If you're willing and can find a volunteer, one of your people should be there."

The tension in his shoulders relaxed slightly. "I agree. That would be a good idea."

"It will be dangerous. Make sure they understand that."

"I will."

Her phone buzzed with a message from Icewind asking for her to get to the mansion as soon as possible. "I have to go."

He nodded once, finally forcing his gaze back to her. "Will you come back again when you can?"

"Yes. When I can."

"And will you answer if I call or text?"

She held his gaze for a moment then inclined her head. "When I can."

"Okay." He picked up his book, fingers tracing the embossing. "Stay safe."

"I don't think that's really an option for either of us right now." She threaded her hands into her wolf's fur and walked slowly away, reluctance dragging at her feet.

CHAPTER 32

CERI

Ceri stood in her workroom, watching the rain run in rivulets down the window. The pack was in upheaval. Their panic and fear for their families only highlighted her lack of concern. She didn't wish her family dead, exactly, but she knew she wouldn't grieve in the same way the others would if they were killed. Her family had felt like enemies for far too long for her to ever love them. Or miss them.

Derek was with the task force. He'd refused to leave until Amber got her next phone call. She knew she should be there with him, but she didn't know how to comfort him right now. Not with her mind all twisted up in guilt and resentment.

"You always used to track me down and make me stop brooding when the pack first got together." Tommy crossed his arms behind his head and stared up at the ceiling. "Guess that system only works when we aren't *both* brooding."

She laughed and shook her head. Tommy was in the same boat she was. "We're going to have to find a third person. Maybe Deward? Surely we won't all be moody at once."

"Wouldn't count on that. He's hiding with the pixies because he can't help with the research."

"Brooding it is, then." She wrapped her cardigan a little tighter around her. "It is raining, after all. We shouldn't waste a perfect brooding day."

"You make a very good point."

There was a brief knock on the door, then Ito stepped into the room. He was soaked through and dripping all over the floor. "Ceridwen, Agent Icewind sent me to retrieve you. There's been a development."

"With the Seattle situation?"

He shook his head. "No. Your family just showed up."

Her heart skipped a beat. "What?"

"They're with Icewind now. They arrived about fifteen minutes ago." He stepped aside. "She emphasized the need to hurry."

Tommy jumped up. "Let's go."

"Right." She shook off the shock and followed him out of the room. Her mind rushed through a dozen scenarios as they made their way to the mansion. It was possible her family escaped. Though that could mean the other hostages were now in more danger or injured. None of the possibilities were all that comforting. Including their decision to show up here. Her last conversation with her father had ended with him declaring her persona non grata--a formal way of disowning her from the family and the coven.

According to the rules all covens supposedly followed, they wouldn't do anything to harm the pack unless the pack made a move against them first. But, as always, the devil was in the details. If they claimed that she had put them in danger...

She ground her teeth together in frustration. They would. She knew them well enough to see that inevitability. The only thing left to discover was what they would demand.

Ito glanced at her as he opened the door to the mansion for her and Tommy. "I thought you'd be happy to hear your family was here. However, you seem...angry."

"They're kind of assholes." She shook her head. "You'll see."

Derek met them in the foyer, his face grim. "You okay?"

"I should be asking you that." She smoothed her hair back and took a deep breath. "Where are they?"

"With Amber and Icewind. I'll take you to them." He jerked his head toward the hallway.

Ito didn't follow, but Tommy and Derek walked side by side with her. The pack bond zinged between the three of them, both comforting and an echo of her own panic. She missed the easy ability to talk through it. If she could just look through Amber's eyes and gauge the situation before she had to walk in there, this would be...somewhat easier. Derek opened the door ahead of them, and her mother's angry voice sent a chill down her spine.

She ground her teeth together and forced herself to walk inside. Amber was two inches away from her mother, arms crossed, both of them glaring at each other. Her father sat across from Icewind and appeared entirely unconcerned--which meant he was pissed and in a dangerous mood.

"What a fun family reunion. Maybe we can bake a cake together later?" Ceri suggested with obvious sarcasm.

Her mother tore her glare away from Amber and turned it on her. "You should be groveling, but you never knew how to show respect, did you?"

"You never deserved it."

Her mother's hand twitched. If she'd been able to use magic, Ceri knew they'd have been in a fight that moment. Lucky for them all, she couldn't. "You know why we're here. You owe reparations."

Ceri focused on her father, ignoring her mother's demands for now. "This is a stretch, at best."

"Is it?" He tilted his head to the side. "They said we were targeted because of you. Because of your..." He glanced at Amber, and the briefest flicker of disgust passed over his face. "Pack." His gaze returned to her. "I think that qualifies as direct harm."

"Before I waste the time of everyone here arguing that point, what is it that you want?" She needed to get to the heart of this and deal with their demands first. If they aligned well enough with what the task force was after, she wasn't going to refuse out of spite. The last thing they needed right now were more enemies.

"Protection and restoration," her father stated. "Until the threat is fully eliminated, your pack will use every resource at their disposal to ensure our safety. Once that is done, your pack will repair the damage to our home."

Ceri turned to Icewind. "Damage?"

Icewind shrugged. "Some broken windows and bullet holes."

"I will speak to my alpha about your requests." Ceri turned on her heel and left the room. Amber and the rest of the pack followed, leaving Icewind alone with her parents.

They were all silent until they reached one of the recently sound-proofed rooms a few doors down. Amber shut the door firmly then turned around. "Your mother might be worse than mine. And that's saying a lot."

"We should put them in the same room one day and see if they both implode from the concentrated levels of evil." Ceri plopped down in a swivel chair. It groaned in protest and tipped ominously to one side.

"They said we owe reparations? Why would they think that?" Derek asked.

Ceri leaned her head back and stared at the ceiling. While she'd told Derek a bit about her estrangement from her family, she hadn't actually gotten into all the details. "It's a witch thing. I left the coven and weakened them, so they had a right to retaliate." She sighed. "But, on my way out, I weakened their main rival as well. They accepted the trade and called a..." She waved a hand around, searching for the best word. "Truce. A very tense truce. As long as neither of us did anything to harm the other, everything could just be left alone. The matter was settled."

"Until the incubi showed up and tried to kidnap them." Amber sighed and grabbed another chair.

"Yep." Ceri threw her hands in the air. "Now it's going to be messy."

"The protection and stuff doesn't sound too bad," Derek offered tentatively.

"'Until the threat is fully eliminated, your pack will use every resource at their disposal to ensure our safety.'" She shook her head. "That is definitely bad. We're going to have to negotiate them down or we'll need to spend all our time being their bodyguards."

"Do they expect you to negotiate? Is that a normal part of this?" Amber asked, chewing on her thumbnail.

"Yes. But they aren't going to back down on wanting some measure of protection." She pressed her lips together and shook her head. "We'll probably have to let them stay here. At least until the stuff with Taharia is resolved."

Amber dropped her hand to her lap and nodded. "And the restoration stuff?"

"We'll have to pin down the wording so we're not agreeing to anything more than paying for the literal, physical damage to the house." She shrugged. "That request is less ridiculous, which is why they included it."

"And you're sure we can trust them?" Tommy asked. "This isn't some ploy to attack us, right? Like a...parental trojan horse?"

"We can trust them like we can trust Bram. They want to survive, so they won't make trouble until the threat is gone." Ceri snorted. "And they're too arrogant to ever agree to work for anyone else. They came here out of desperation."

Amber nodded. "We'll still need to watch them."

"That I agree with."

"I'll talk to Icewind and see what we can do. We can't always have one of us here."

Ceri sat upright. "Okay. If we're all in agreement, then I need to coach you on what to say. Wording is important with all this."

Amber took a deep breath. "Okay."

She reviewed the game plan quickly, having Amber repeat her

part a few times. As long as her parents didn't argue too much, this could be settled as soon as they went back in that room. Derek watched her the whole time, his forehead creased in concern. This was not how she'd wanted to deal with the complicated topic of her family but, as usual, he was perfectly understanding. After all, his family wasn't much more functional. Just a tad bit lighter on the death threats.

Amber stood. "Let's go get this settled."

Ceri nodded, and the four of them headed back into the room. Icewind was staring at her parents impassively, arms crossed. Her mother's rage had reduced to a simmer.

She stopped by Icewind's shoulder and forced herself to look them both in the face. "Amber is the Alpha Dominus. With a position of power like that, enemies are unavoidable. We have no responsibility to protect you from every threat from now unto eternity because those enemies are too stupid to understand how little we mean to each other." Ceri's heart thumped along with the headache forming behind her eyes.

"If you try to avoid responsibility for this, I will make you regret it," her mother snapped.

"Go ahead and threaten us in front of an MIA agent. See how that turns out." Ceri planted her hands on the table and leaned in. "You are in no more danger than us right now. A mutual enemy is not our responsibility to control. Since it is in *both* our interests for you to remain safe, we are willing to offer a certain amount of protection. *Temporarily.*" She gestured toward Amber, who stepped forward.

"You are invited to stay in this house, which is protected by our pack, the MIA, and the representatives of every supernatural race until the individuals who came to your house are no longer a threat." Amber looked as pleased about this offer as she felt.

"However," Ceri added, "when you are not here, your safety cannot and will not be our responsibility. And if you threaten, harm, or provide information on anyone here or involved in the task force, you will forfeit the protection, reparations, and be held responsible for it."

Her mother started to argue, but her father laid a hand on her arm, which silenced her. He leveled a look at Ceri, as if measuring her resolve. "And the reparations your pack owes us?"

"Put what you want paid for in writing. We'll provide a third-party inspector to assess the cost and cover fifty percent."

"Eighty percent."

"Forty."

Her father's eyes hardened. "Sixty percent."

"Done." Ceri straightened. "Stay out of my way while you're here."

"Your grandmother would be disappointed that she wasted so much time on you," her mother growled, unable to let her go without one last dig.

Ceri raised an eyebrow. "I've done more than she ever dreamed and will surpass her in every way. What does the opinion of a long-dead woman matter to me?" She swept out of the room, feeling strangely lighter than she had in a long time.

CHAPTER 33

AMBER

Amber raked a grooming brush through her wolf's fur while Ceri braided her still-damp hair. The pack was gathered in the living room to wait for the next call together. Icewind and another agent with a fancy cellphone call tracker were set up in the dining room. It was quieter than usual since Ithra had volunteered to watch Valiel while they dealt with the current crisis.

Ito stood by the fireplace and watched her with a pinched expression on his face. "Is that meant for dogs?"

She glanced up. "The brush? Yeah."

His frown deepened. "That is demeaning."

"Are you feeling demeaned?" she asked her wolf, who snorted in amusement.

Our beta will groom us every day when we are rejoined.

"She says no." Amber resumed her task, pulling the fluff gathered on the brush and adding it to the pile next to her. Focusing on this was better than the alternative. It was soothing, and the more contact she had with her wolf, the less empty she felt. "Do born wolves ever groom their wolf forms? I know we never did before this. But it's kind of nice."

"No. We don't treat them like pets."

"How do you treat them, then?" She couldn't muster up her usual irritation at Ito. He was just too uptight to take seriously after a while.

"With respect. They are magnificent spirits who chose us at birth for a purpose. They are meant to guide us, not..." He swept a hand at Genevieve, who was currently asleep on the floor in a tangle with her wolf. "Cuddle."

"Maybe if you cuddled, you'd be less cranky."

Ceri collapsed in laughter behind her, barely holding onto the near-complete braid. "Imagine if there were cuddle piles instead of fights for dominance."

"I'll sign it into law." Amber grinned at Ito. "I can do that, right? As Alpha Dominus?"

He stiffened, his eyes wide with shock. "You absolutely cannot––" All the tension fled from his shoulders as he huffed out a sigh. "You're mocking me."

"Only a little." She resumed her brushing, the smile still tugging at her lips. "Even I know something like that would never work."

Genevieve lifted her head from her wolf's stomach and scowled at them. "Too noisy."

Tommy, Derek, and Deward walked in the back door. All three of the boys were slightly sweaty and smelling of grass. Derek had requested a distraction, and their solution had been wrestling, since Deward still needed to work on fighting without his sight.

"Feel better?" Amber asked.

Derek collapsed by Ceri on the couch with a groan. "Mentally, sure. Physically, much worse."

"Deward is a menace," Tommy muttered in agreement on his way to the kitchen. "Anyone else want something to drink?"

"Beer." Derek tried to wrap an arm around Ceri, but she pushed him away with a grimace.

"You're showering before you touch me."

"I don't stink!"

"You are *sticky*." Ceri tied off the braid and swung it over Amber's shoulder.

"Thanks."

"No problem." Ceri patted her head then escaped Derek's advances and joined Tommy in the kitchen.

Deward took her place on the couch to Amber's right and turned his gaze on Ito. "I've been wondering for a few days why I can always see you, when my pack is less clear to me."

"You can see Ito?" Amber asked.

"Only in this house. He has an aura." Deward leaned in. "I think it's Illya. Everywhere he goes in the house, she is watching him."

Ito frowned. "Are you referring to the house?"

Ceri nodded as she walked toward them. "Does she see him as a threat?"

"I'm not sure. Perhaps."

"You haven't fallen through the floor or anything, have you?" Ceri asked.

"No. I can assure you I would have mentioned it," Ito said dryly.

The phone rang, and in an instant, the mood in the room shifted. Amber jumped to her feet and jogged to the dining room, her heart pounding against her ribs.

"Put her on speaker," Icewind reminded her once again. "Everyone stay silent."

Amber accepted the call with a shaking finger. "You certainly took your time calling back."

Icewind groaned silently, putting her face in her hands.

"An unfortunate necessity. I understand Ceridwen's parents made their way to you."

Amber frowned. "Yes, they did."

"It was impossible to subdue them without seriously injuring them. I hope you can appreciate the choice I made in letting them go."

"Is everyone else still safe and unharmed?" Amber pressed, unwilling to praise Taharia for not hurting Ceri's parents.

"Yes."

"I want to talk to them. All of them."

"We don't have time for that. Go to Main Street in downtown Portland. I will call you again when you arrive with the next instruction. You have thirty minutes."

"I need to know--"

"I know you'll bring people with you, but you will walk in alone, without even your wolf, or the meeting is off."

Before Amber could respond or make any more demands, the call ended.

"That could have gone better." Icewind pushed up to her feet. "Should I assume you're going to this ill-advised meeting?"

"Yes."

"Genevieve, with us, the rest of you stay here." Icewind grabbed her keys and tossed Amber her cellphone. "No time to debate our options."

Amber forced herself to move past the shock and anger and hurried after Icewind to the surveillance van outside. It would be tight to make it to downtown Portland in twenty minutes. She hoped the van had police sirens.

CHAPTER 34

AMBER

The van did not have sirens, but that didn't keep Icewind from speeding like a maniac. They made it to downtown Portland in twenty minutes.

Icewind pulled into a parking spot a block away from the road Amber had to get to and turned to her. "All right, we can't have eyes on you like I want, but we will be close by." She handed her a disk with a red button on top. "Press that if there's an emergency and you're in danger. It'll broadcast your location."

"Is this one of those 'I've fallen and can't get up' things for old people?" Amber asked as she examined it.

"Yeah. It's all I could get on short notice."

Amber put it in her jacket pocket. "Okay. Anything else?"

"Try not to piss her off."

Genevieve snorted. "Unlikely."

"Y'all have no faith in me. I can be diplomatic." Amber scowled at them both.

"Sure." Icewind's expression said the opposite.

Amber rolled her eyes but hopped out of the van, eager to get to the right place before they ran out of time.

Her wolf caught the hem of her jacket in her teeth. *Remember what you are. We bend to no one*. Her wolf's message curled through her, along with a feeling of determination. She hated leaving her wolf behind like this.

I'll remember. Amber slid her hand into her wolf's fur, focusing on the comfort their bond gave her.

"Hurry up. You only have three minutes left." Icewind shooed her away.

With the phone clutched tightly in her hand, Amber jogged along the sidewalk to the appropriate crossroad. The city was a bit quieter than normal, with fewer pedestrians and a few businesses with closed signs tacked to their doors. Everyone had been shaken by the incubi falling from the skies and the chaos with magic. Only the humans seemed to be going on with business as usual.

The twenty-minute timer buzzed, and her phone rang. "What now?"

"Walk to Fifth Street." The call ended immediately.

She took a deep breath and jogged toward the next location. Icewind had warned her she'd probably be asked to move a few times before being given the final location to make it harder for anyone to follow her. No matter how logical it was, she wanted it over with. Her patience for all these games had run out months ago.

The phone rang again, and this time Taharia didn't even give her a chance to ask where to go. She simply gave her another street name and hung up. Amber jogged there. Then to the next street. And the next.

At the fifth stop, upon realizing she was almost back where she started, the last of her patience snapped. She ground her teeth together as she answered the call once again. "You're leading me in circles."

"Go into the cafe behind you. I'll text you the final instruction from there." Taharia ended the call before Amber could voice any other complaints.

She turned around, searching for a cafe, and froze when she

spotted it. The last time she'd been here, she'd ended up puking slime. But she'd also gotten Ceri and Woggy out of the fiasco with the witch that had ripped his wings off.

A wave of nostalgia washed over her as she walked toward the cafe. The help wanted sign was still in the window, just like it had been the last time she was here. It was strange to return there after so much had changed, and for a meeting where the lives of all their families hung in the balance.

The flowering canopy that covered the outdoor seating was even more colorful and dense than normal. In fact, it had grown down toward the seating. A couple of tables were so tangled in vines no one could sit in them. A small swarm of pixies peered down at her from behind the leaves as she passed underneath them.

She took a deep breath and pushed the door open. Her phone buzzed.

Take a left. Back corner booth.

She followed the instructions and walked between the happy, carefree customers that were lucky enough to be there for food instead of a hostage negotiation.

A lone woman sat at the booth. Taharia wasn't what she expected. Her long, blonde hair hung in soft waves over her shoulders. Her face was round with perfect cupid's bow lips and innocent brown eyes. She wore a simple floral dress, more suited for brunch with friends than this sort of situation. If Amber had guessed her age based on appearances alone, she'd have put her at twenty on the high end. She paused in front of the table, suddenly unsure if this was the right person.

"Amber, thank you for coming alone." Taharia gestured toward the other side of the booth. "Please, sit."

The voice was familiar. Even that didn't match her appearance, though. Her tone was all business and laced with steel, showing none of the softness her face suggested.

Amber slid into the booth and set her phone in front of her. "Interesting choice of meetup location."

"A public place is safer for both of us." Taharia leaned back, scanning her face as they took each other's measure. "I appreciate you coming alone. I have been very hopeful this meeting would be peaceful."

"I want our families back safe. Attacking you wouldn't help with that."

Taharia nodded and leaned forward, resting her arms on the table. "Well, to get right to the point, I think I should explain what I can offer first then explain what we want."

Amber nodded, itching to reach across the table and shake answers out of her.

"I am...was Saraqael's envoy. I can offer information on the archangels. I know every safe house. Every hidden account." Taharia pulled an envelope from her purse and slid it across the table. "This is a portion of that information. I'm sure the MIA can validate it for you."

She took the envelope with a nod. "So, you want to sell out the archangels. Why?"

Taharia's soft features twisted in anger. "I traded my soul for immortality." She bit off each word with barely repressed rage. "Not literally, I suppose, but it feels like it sometimes. I've lived for three hundred years, clinging so hard to this false immortality that I was willing to hurt people who didn't deserve it to maintain it." She lifted her gaze to Amber's. "I'm trying to make up for that, in whatever way I can."

"You're off to a rocky start."

"Would you really have heard me out and not slaughtered us all on the spot if I came to you?" Taharia demanded.

Amber leaned in. "Yes."

The succubus ground her teeth together in frustration. "I don't believe you."

"Can't really help you there." Amber sighed, tapping her fingers restlessly against the envelope. "What else are you offering?"

"There are fourteen of us seeking redemption. I selected them all myself." She gestured toward the envelope. "Their names are in there as well. We want to be there when Saraqael is struck down."

She pursed her lips. "That would require a lot of trust."

"Yes, it would."

"What do you want in return for all this?"

Taharia pointed at her chest, where the demon mark had been. "You have a close connection to the fae. To Kadrithan himself."

Amber's brow creased. Considering how they'd fought together, it was likely common knowledge among the incubi, but she'd never considered it. "I know him."

Taharia lifted her chin as if steeling herself. "I want protection from him and the fae for the incubi in my care."

"Why do you think you need protection from him?"

"Don't play stupid. We both know the fae want to wipe the incubi out." Taharia lowered her eyes. "I even understand their reasons. However, I can't stand by and watch it happen without at least trying to protect them."

"Who, exactly, are you protecting? We're already rounding up whatever incubi we find and don't intend to hurt them."

"I need some assurances before I explain that."

Amber dragged a hand down her face with a sigh. "Are they the other archangels or something? You have to give me a little bit to work with here. I can't go to the fae with nothing."

"No. The archangels are all corrupt." Taharia shook her head firmly. "Saraqael has gone mad. He was not the worst of them once, but he changed, and the corruption among them has festered. They are no longer simply greedy. They are willing to sacrifice everything and everyone to get what they want."

"So you simply want protection?"

Taharia nodded. "Yes. We are on the same side. I am certain that if you give us a chance, we can help each other, but until those in my care are safe, I cannot abandon them."

"And when can we get our families back?"

"As soon as you agree to the protection."

Amber ground her teeth together but nodded. "I still want to know they're all safe. I want to talk to them."

"Perhaps later today. For now, this should help." Taharia squared her shoulders. "As a show of good will, we brought one of your family members with us today. They are sleeping and unharmed."

"Where?" Amber demanded from behind gritted teeth, her body thrumming with tension.

"The location is written here." Taharia pulled a folded note from her pocket along with a cheap-looking timer that looked like it was straight from the local supermarket. "You will give me a five-minute head start. If you leave this booth before then, we will take them back." She set the note on the table right in front of her and stood. "Thank you for hearing me out."

"You left me no choice."

A joyless smile tugged at Taharia's mouth. "I know."

Taharia turned the timer to five minutes then left, winding through the tables toward the exit. Amber watched her until she turned a corner then lunged across the table and grabbed the note. Her hands shook as she unfolded it. In the center of the note were neatly written coordinates.

The timer ticked by each second at a painfully slow rate. Four minutes left...three minutes...two minutes...

Amber stared at it, willing the final seconds away. When it finally buzzed, she was already moving. She sprinted out of the restaurant, not caring about the stares her odd behavior had earned her. It took her less than a minute to run to the van. She slid to a stop, gasping with breath as the back doors swung open.

Genevieve hopped out. "What happened?"

She shoved the coordinates at her. "They're giving us one of them back."

Icewind's head jerked up. "Where are they?"

"At those coordinates. Can we put them into some kind of map?"

"Yes." Icewind grabbed the coordinates from Genevieve and typed them into her laptop. Directions popped up. She hopped over the center console to the driver's seat. "Let's go. The rest of the team is already on their way."

The coordinates led them into a neighborhood in northwest Portland. Icewind blared the horn as she careened around a corner and straight through a stop sign, slinging Genevieve and her wolf across the back of the van. There were no seats back there, leaving her with no real way to brace herself.

"Are you trying to kill me back here?" Genevieve lurched forward and wrapped her arms around the back of Amber's seat. "Icewind is never driving again."

"Shut it. I am an *excellent* driver."

Amber's wolf snorted, and she patted her on the head. "No comment."

Icewind slammed on the brakes in front of a small white house with a for sale sign planted in the front yard. "This is the place. We need to wait for--"

"No." Amber jumped out of the van, and Genevieve scrambled to follow her. It was one of their family members in there. They weren't going to wait.

She pressed an ear to the front door. There were no footsteps or hushed whispers inside. The only sound was a single heartbeat and the steady breathing of someone fast asleep. She held up a single finger, and Genevieve nodded, gesturing for her to go in.

The door handle turned easily. It was unlocked. With a deep breath, she pushed it open. No one jumped out at them. They stepped over the threshold and crept further inside.

Amber moved left toward the living room, while Genevieve went right into the dining room. Their wolves pressed ahead of them as they spread out. Icewind followed with her gun drawn and a grim expression.

Amber's wolf stopped by the couch then let out a jarringly loud yip. There was a person-shaped lump on the couch. Blonde hair poked out from under a plush blanket. "Genevieve, get in here!"

Her beta sprinted into the room and spotted the girl on the couch right away. "Susannah!" She ripped the blanket back, and her little sister blinked up at her, bleary and confused.

"Gen?" Susannah sat bolt upright, looking around in shock. "Oh my gosh, you're really here––"

Genevieve yanked her little sister into a hug, her shoulders shaking as she cried. Relief flooded through Amber. Taharia had kept her word.

CHAPTER 35

KADRITHAN

The census was complete. The remaining fae had been counted. Kadrithan pushed the report away and, very slowly, pulled himself to his feet. Even the most basic movements sent sharp pains through his chest and gut. He had a new appreciation for every muscle involved with holding himself up straight.

There were enough of the fae left to survive as a race. Barely. He understood what the numbers meant, though. They were in the human realm now, and they were mortal. People would fall in love with other races. In a few generations, the pure fae would dwindle. In ten, they'd likely be gone.

He stared out of the window overlooking the sloping hill that led toward the Market stalls. They'd given everything to break the curse and find their freedom, yet the curse had still destroyed their race. He had been too late to really save them. He had failed.

The door opened, and Zerestria swept in, holding an armful of flowers and a crystal vase. "You're not supposed to be walking around on your own."

"They said I needed exercise."

"*Supervised* exercise." She set the vase down and laid the flowers to the side. "How are you feeling?"

"Terrible." He reluctantly tore himself away from the view. "But better."

"Well enough to speak with the Market vendors? They deserve a face to face after their patience."

"Yes. I am capable of that, at least." After spending days reading, he was ready to have something truly productive to do again. Rest no longer came easily to him. "Is Amber back from her meeting yet?" His eyes strayed to the phone on his desk. He'd kept it within reach all night and all day. Waiting.

Zerestria followed his gaze with an unhappy expression but nodded. "Yes. They just returned with Genevieve's younger sister, I believe. I doubt Amber has had time to share the news."

"Yet somehow you know."

"One of my witches texted me." A fond smile tugged at her lips. "Even with the mark gone, Tessa is still willing to keep me updated. She's a savvy woman."

"I see." His fingers itched to pick up the phone and text Amber first, but he hesitated once again. Every time he thought of her, he saw the disappointed look on her face all over again. He felt an ache at the distance between them. He'd thought that once the curse was broken, she would join him here. That they could finish this together.

"Have you selected someone to send to the task force?"

He lowered himself into his chair with a grimace then nodded. "Venali."

Zerestria raised an eyebrow as she went to every window and drew the curtains open. Light spilled into the room. "Is this a passive aggressive jab at Amber?"

"Venali has nothing better to do, and I'm sick of him hovering." He sighed and pushed his hair back. His cousin was annoying and had taken to barging into his room to share every rumor he heard. Clearly, the man needed something to keep him busy. "So, I suppose it's more of a passive aggressive jab at him."

"Would you object to me choosing a second person to go with him? Every race is allowed two representatives."

He knew why she wanted to do this. To have someone loyal to *her* involved. Part of him did, in fact, object. But he couldn't bring himself to refuse her. She had done too much for him, and he was too tired to argue today. "Send whoever you want."

They were silent for a long moment as she carefully placed the colorful flowers into the vase. He recognized many of them from his time on earth. Yellow roses and daffodils, delicate purple violets, and bright red peonies. He could smell them from here.

"There is a celebration being planned that could use your input." She stepped back from her arrangement with a frown then grabbed another handful of violets.

"A celebration?"

Zerestria scowled at the flowers as she attempted to squeeze them in. "We're free. The demon marks are gone. They're surrounded by trees and life. Everyone wants to celebrate."

His hand curled into a fist. "After so many deaths, how can they even consider it?"

Zerestria's face softened as she turned to face him. "How can they not? Without clinging to these small victories, we'd all lose hope." She fiddled with the flowers until they were spread out in a splendid arrangement then moved it to his desk. "We are old, but this realm is young. It is growing and bursting at the seams with life. Don't forget that."

He stroked the soft petal of a particularly bright peony that stood out from the other flowers. "It's hard to see right now."

She laid a hand on his arm. "I know."

Pushing aside his hesitation, he grabbed his phone and opened the messages.

CHAPTER 36

GENEVIEVE

Safely back home, the knot of fear in Genevieve's chest unclenched and she took her first full breath in hours. She'd been sure someone would come and snatch Susannah back away from her somehow before they made it here.

Amber turned Steven's squeaky desk chair around and sat down across from them. She grimaced as it let out an ominous creak. "This whole time I thought it was your bed making that awful noise…" Amber let the sentence trail off and cleared her throat. "I'll get some WD-40."

A flush crept up her neck. "That'd be great. I was just going to throw the whole chair in the dumpster, but Steven will be thrilled if you can fix it." Genevieve wrapped an arm around Susannah's shoulder and turned her attention to her sister. "Now. Are you sure they didn't hurt you at all? Not even a little bruise?"

Susannah cradled the hot chocolate between her hands as she snuggled up to her side, blanketed on the other side by her wolf. "No, Gen, I *keep* telling you. They were super nice. Like…sure, they kidnapped us, but they weren't mean about it."

Genevieve groaned. "You can't kidnap someone nicely."

"They did their best." Susannah took a long sip of her drink and smacked her lips in appreciation. "They don't even get mad when Amber's mom yells at them. They just ignore her." She glanced up at Amber. "I think your dad might be getting kind of upset with her, though."

Amber winced. "They have more patience than me, then."

"Did you overhear anything they talked about?" Genevieve asked. Part of her didn't want to ask any of these questions, but Susannah had insisted. She seemed more excited about the whole situation than traumatized, for some reason.

"I guess. They weren't really trying to keep much secret. They're scared of the archangels finding them, and they're worried about keeping the *others* safe." Susannah lowered her mug and tilted her head to the side. "They kept talking about the others like they're super important. They seemed kind of secret."

"But these other people were there with you?" Genevieve frowned.

"Nope. Separate. All to protect them." Susannah shrugged and took another drink. "Oh, Mom and Dad say hi and to not fret too much, because they really think they're about as safe with the rebels as anywhere."

Genevieve rolled her eyes. "I'll fret if I want to."

"Did you ever have an idea of where you were?" Amber asked.

"Not really. It was always in some random house. Every time we had to move, we'd just suddenly be asleep and then wake up in the new place."

Genevieve tightened her arm around her sister's shoulders. "Do you know how they put you to sleep?"

"Nope. All of us hostages debated that a lot, though. Dad skipped eating and drinking for a day, but it didn't help. He didn't want to try too hard and get us in trouble." Susannah beamed at Amber. "That was your dad's input. He said you told him to not do anything brave and that we should trust you to get us all out."

"Bet that went over well," Amber muttered.

"Oh, definitely not." Susannah shook her head solemnly. "They did, uh, take your mom out of the room after that and brought her back asleep. She was out a whole day."

For some reason, Amber found that hilarious. She covered her face as she laughed hysterically. "Taharia is really growing on me."

Genevieve kicked Amber's leg. "She kidnapped our families. You're not allowed to like her."

Amber dropped her hands and stared up at the ceiling. "She saved them, too."

"Oh yeah! They said they'd been sent to *murder* us but didn't want to." Susannah announced this as if it were the best news she'd ever heard. Genevieve wondered if her sister was still under some kind of weird influence, but then again, Susannah had always lacked a sense of self-preservation.

She fought down a sigh. "Is there anything else you can think of?"

"Ummm…" Susannah tapped her fingers against the mug. "Not really? I guess I could try to describe all of them if you wanted? Like they do for police sketches."

"That might actually be helpful."

"I'll suggest it to Icewind." Genevieve turned back to her sister with a serious expression. "If you get tired or sad, you have to tell me, okay?"

Susannah's shoulders slumped a little, and she rolled her eyes. "I will." She leaned into Genevieve's arms. "I was a little scared at the beginning, too, and I wish Mom and Dad were here, but I think everyone is going to be okay. You don't need to be afraid, Gen."

She huffed out a sigh. "I'm trying to comfort you, butthead. Stop turning it around on me."

Susannah laughed. "You need it more. You're a worrier."

"Normally I'm the one accused of worrying," Amber said with a grin.

"That's because you take it to ridiculous new heights." Genevieve huffed out a sigh. "Icewind might have some more questions for you, just in case we missed anything. But she's going to wait until after dinner. So, do you want to meet Valiel now?"

"Yes! And I want to see everyone again! It's been ages!"

"All right, come on." Genevieve took her hand and led her out of the room, her wolf still plastered to Susannah's other side. The one benefit to being split like this was never having to leave her little sister's side, no matter what else she needed to do.

Susannah was almost thirteen now, but it was easy to forget she was heading into her teenage years. Looking at her now, Genevieve realized how much she'd grown since the last time she'd seen her. She was only an inch shorter and all legs. Odds were she'd take after their father and be taller than Genevieve by this time next year.

The pack was waiting downstairs with Icewind. Steven jumped up as soon as they came into view and rushed over to hug her then Susannah. "Glad to have you back, Susannah." He ruffled her hair with a fond grin.

She beamed up at him. "Mom and Dad say hi! They want to have dinner after they get rescued." The concerned expressions of everyone gathered shifted to a mixture of confusion and amusement. They'd probably expected more tears. Genevieve had, too. "Is that Valiel?" Susannah pointed at the succubus in question, who was currently half hidden behind Derek.

"Yes." Derek tugged her out of her hiding spot and nudged her forward. "Valiel, this is Susannah. She is Genevieve's younger sister."

"You can call me Susie." Susannah grinned as she thrust her hand toward Valiel. "No one does, but I think they should. Nicknames are fun."

Valiel stared at her hand with some skepticism then wrapped her fingers around Susannah's. "Susie," she repeated, sounding as if she was in a daze.

"Yeah...Su...sie..." Susannah swayed, her face growing deathly pale in an instant.

Horror rocked through Genevieve. Valiel's eyes were glowing as she tightened her grip on Susannah's hand.

"Valiel, no!" She and Derek moved in unison. Derek grabbed Valiel, while she yanked her sister away, and as soon as she was free of Valiel's touch, she collapsed. The pack moved between them, shielding Susannah and Genevieve from view.

Valiel struggled in Derek's arms, straining to reach Susannah again. "I'm still hungry!" she wailed.

Sick understanding shocked through her. Valiel was hungry. Susannah was the only human here without their pack tattoo. They should have realized the risk sooner.

"You can't feed on her, Val." Derek got a firm grip on her arms, careful not to crush her wings.

Genevieve laid Susannah down carefully and checked for a pulse, unable to breathe until she felt the steady heartbeat beneath her fingertips. "What do we do? Take her to the hospital?"

"I don't know." Ceri knelt on the other side of Susannah and placed a hand on her forehead. "She's breathing and still warm. Was she fed on before this at all?"

Genevieve started to shake her head but hesitated. "She said she wasn't, but we can't know for sure."

Susannah jerked awake with a gasp. She tried to push up into a sitting position but couldn't manage it. "Ow."

"Stop moving." Genevieve pressed her shoulders firmly down. "How do you feel?"

"Tired. Like I stayed up all night." She licked her lips. "And thirsty. Weak. And tired." She squinted at Genevieve. "Did I already mention that?"

Steven darted into the kitchen and returned with a soda. "Help her drink this."

Genevieve propped her up and held it to her lips. She downed it greedily, and some color returned to her face. "Better?"

"A little bit." She blinked rapidly and reached for the can again. "Still dizzy."

Ceri stood and joined Derek. "We'll take her outside for now. Get some more fluids in Susie."

Amber nodded. "I'll come join you in a minute."

Valiel's crying grew quiet as the door shut behind her and Ceri, leaving the pack in silence. Worry thrummed through the pack bond.

"I'm going to call Bram. They could be like vampires. They have to feed on blood and don't kill anyone doing it." Amber gnawed on her thumbnail. "We need to warn the MIA, too. If they have all the incubi..." She shook her head. "They'll have to feed them somehow, eventually."

"Yeah." Genevieve brushed a hand through Susannah's hair with shaking fingers. She'd just gotten her sister back and had almost lost her for real. "It will obviously be a problem."

Her stomach churned. This felt so beyond their ability to handle. Valiel hadn't meant to hurt anyone, but she had. With incubi still scattered across the country, how many more would stumble upon an unsuspecting human and feed on them? How many would take too much? Susannah had collapsed so fast.

CHAPTER 37

CERI

Ceri folded the last of Valiel's shirt and put it in the backpack with the rest of her clothes. She wasn't going far, just to the mansion to stay with Ithra and Olwen, who had graciously agreed to take care of her while the pack went to Seattle. They'd all agreed it was best to keep her near the task force, where it was safest, but they couldn't trust her around Gen's little sister, either.

She sighed heavily. The bubbly curiosity Valiel had shown had disappeared, and she'd reverted to the quiet and suspicious child they'd found in the swamp, not wanting to interact with anyone but herself, Derek, and Deward. Valiel spent most of her time curled up behind her wings. The only thing that could coax her out was food, but it was clear that wasn't what she really needed.

Thankfully, Susannah had perked up in the hours following the accidental feeding. A nap and some food had done wonders. The doctors that had been caring for the witches had checked her out and said there shouldn't be any lasting effects. Whatever had happened was similar to exhaustion.

The twin pixie girls, Twiggy and Nibbles, zoomed in through the open door, unusually quiet, and landed behind the backpack.

She narrowed her eyes in suspicion. Anytime they weren't making a racket, they were up to no good.

Deward walked in, his head tilted to the side as if he was listening *very* carefully for something. "Ceri?"

"I'm here."

"I'm playing hide and seek with the pixies. Are we interrupting anything?"

"No, I just finished packing." She glanced down at the twins, who had their spindly fingers clamped over their mouths as they tried to suppress giggles. "Want a hint?"

"No, I think I hear them." Deward leaned in then darted around her and tried to grab the pixies. They leapt into the air, narrowly avoiding his hand, and shrieked in victory. He shook his head with a smile. "I will catch you next time."

"Whose idea was this?" Ceri asked with a smile.

"Derek's, though I think he was joking." The twins landed on Deward's head and started tugging his hair out of its braid. "He called it ninja training."

She laughed. "And you can really hear them well enough to follow them?"

"Sometimes. It's getting easier, though..." He shook his head with a wry smile. "I know I'm still a long way from being able to actually fight or protect myself."

"You managed it once already."

"I was lucky. And Illya helped."

"Still. You might surprise yourself." She zipped up the backpack and slung it over her shoulder. "Are your parents over at the mansion?"

He nodded. "Yes, I was going to walk over with you, actually, if you don't mind. I struggle to make it across the yard. Too much empty space."

"Ah, understandable. Ready when you are."

He held out his arm, and she slipped her hand into the crook of his elbow. The pixies stayed with them until about halfway across the yard then abandoned Deward's hair nest to fly back toward the house. Smidge was probably going to read the riot act for going so far, but all the babies seemed determined to explore as much as they could.

Amber was leaving as they approached the house and jogged over to meet them. "I got another call from Taharia."

A burst of anticipation shot through her. They hadn't heard anything since the last meeting, and it had put them all on edge. "And?"

"She wants to meet again in three days." Amber shoved her hands in her pockets. "We can't put off dealing with the situation in Seattle any longer, so I didn't object."

"Agreed. Are Gen and Tommy okay with the delay?"

"As okay as they can be."

She nodded with a sigh. "And Bram? Is he willing to help?"

"Yes. We'll meet him at the warehouse at sundown." Amber's grimace mirrored her feelings on the situation exactly. "I made him promise we wouldn't have to take her down to the basement."

"That's something, I guess."

"Tessa wanted to see you, by the way."

"I can take Valiel's things to my parents, if you want," Deward offered.

Ceri cringed a little as she remembered her last parting from Valiel. She was taking the temporary separation as abandonment. To say she'd been upset was an understatement. "That'd probably be best. None of us need to go through another goodbye."

"I agree." Deward nodded as he accepted the backpack. "Amber, have you seen Tommy?"

"He's with Icewind helping pack up the stuff we have to bring with us. Want me to get him?"

"No, I'll find him in a bit." Deward nodded as he edged toward the door, using the familiar landmark to orient himself.

Ceri followed without crowding him then split off to head upstairs to the coven's room. They were all still crowded into the room with hospital beds since, even though Thallan's mansion was huge, it wasn't big enough for everyone to have their own space. None of them had objected to staying together, though.

She knocked once on the open door before stepping inside. Tessa was curled up on her bed in front of a spell book and scattered notes. "Where is everyone?"

"Outside performing useless experiments with magic." Tessa waved at the window. "It's kind of hilarious to watch."

Ceri crossed the room and peered out of the window right as a blond witch was knocked on her back and attacked by the grass. "Do they really think they can get something to work?"

"Tiffany insisted they *might* find a way to make *something* work, and since we don't have much else to do right now, they might as well try instead of sitting around inside twiddling their thumbs." She snorted. "They're going to wander back in here in about a half an hour and complain about their bruises."

"Oof. Burns, too. Celeste just electrocuted herself."

"Yep." Tessa paused for a beat then in a cheery tone added, "Your mom seems super cool, by the way!"

Ceri jerked her head around to find Tessa smirking at her. "I was really concerned for a second that you were serious."

Tessa laughed maniacally. "You're too easy sometimes."

"Did she come harass any of you? Part of the deal was that they both had to leave everyone alone." Her fingers twitched with the urge to hex her mother. If magic was functional, she'd have already been halfway down the hall.

"Nah. Just ran into her in the kitchen when I was getting a midnight snack."

"What was she doing in the kitchen at midnight?"

"She was stuck in a block of ice after--allegedly--trying to curse the food. Of course, she claimed she was simply trying to heat up her tea." A wicked grin turned up the corners of Tessa's lips. "We had a friendly little chat. Exchanged some compliments. I think we're basically best friends now."

Ceri sat heavily on the nearest bed and rubbed her temples in an attempt to stop her eye from twitching. "I'll kick her out."

"Nah." Tessa dismissed that idea with a wave of her hand. "Keep your friends close and your enemies closer. And your family *even* closer."

"I can't believe she actually tried something."

"Your dad couldn't, either. He showed up halfway through the party and didn't exactly look pleased." Tessa's smirk grew. "That man looks like a sweet potato, but he's all cayenne pepper, isn't he?"

"That is the weirdest way possible to put it, but yes. He's the one you have to watch out for." Ceri laid back with a sigh and stared up at the ceiling. "I guess we need to keep a better eye on them. For some reason, I didn't expect her to be that stupid."

"Don't worry about it. The coven is on it."

"You guys don't have to do that."

Tessa rolled her eyes. "Yes, we do. We're part of this. Also, we're a little bored."

Ceri shook her head but couldn't help a smile. "Guess I won't turn down the help."

"Finally, you say something smart."

"We're leaving tomorrow, so your boredom is about to end anyhow." Ceri pushed herself back upright. "It's going to be a messy fight without magic, though. I feel like I'm missing a limb."

"Tell me about it," Tessa groaned. "Maybe if we cast enough wonky spells we can take out the bad guys, regardless?"

"Believe me, I've considered it." And she had. She'd been turning the problem over and over in her mind without finding a solution. They couldn't risk trying to use magic only for it to backfire. Their only saving grace was that their enemy was in the same predicament. For the first time, humans would be the best prepared to fight back. They'd always had to find ways to deal with the world without the use of magic.

Her father appeared in the doorway, his mouth tight with anger. "Ceridwen. A moment?"

"Good luck," Tessa whispered with a wink.

Ceri rolled her eyes as she slid off the bed and joined her father in the hall. She crossed her arms and met his gaze, fury over her mother's actions growing every moment. "Go ahead."

He ground his teeth together. "No harmful actions were taken."

"They were attempted," she snapped.

"You have no proof."

"I'm not stupid, and neither are you." She dropped her arms and curled her hands into fists. "And you didn't come to talk to me just to claim innocence."

"Whatever you *suspect* might have happened will not occur again. Your mother sends her apologies for the appearance of her intentions." He lifted his chin. "I have counseled her to display greater caution."

"If anything else *suspicious* happens, this truce is over."

He nodded once then turned on his heel and walked away. Ceri watched him go with anger burning in her chest. Sometimes she wondered how it had taken her so long to walk away from her family. It had been so easy once she found the pack. And it was even easier now that she understood what love was really like. It wasn't obligation and shame and guilt. It was caring and understanding and hope. It was the exhaustion in Amber's eyes as she fought tooth and nail to keep them safe.

Ceri reached for the pack bond and let its warmth wash away the anger. She had found her family, and she was going to keep them safe, no matter what.

CHAPTER 38

AMBER

Amber refused to take Valiel down into the creepy, blood-splattered basement, but she had agreed to bring her to the warehouse to see Bram. It was a bit of a desperate plan, but Gen was upset, and they really did need a solution. She trusted Bram more than the other vampires.

Derek slid out of the truck with Valiel, who clung to him like she expected to be ripped out of his arms at any moment. She seemed to understand that she had royally screwed up. Both Derek and Ceri had tried to explain that feeding wasn't bad, only that she'd done it without asking. Valiel hadn't seemed able to grasp that concept, and after the conversation had dissolved into tears once again, they'd given up.

"You sure…?" Ceri let her question trail off with a wary glance at the warehouse.

"We don't have a ton of people we can ask about this."

Ceri rubbed her temples and sighed. "I know. This just feels like a bad idea."

"It's questionable." She didn't really think of Bram as the fatherly type. He was creepy on a good day and terrifying when he really wanted to be. Hopefully, this would be worth mentally scarring Valiel.

A familiar vampire wearing a red hoodie jogged over to greet them. "Welcome back," Oliver said with a toothy grin. "Bram is waiting right inside, just like you asked." He looked down at her wolf. "That's really your wolf?"

Amber edged closer to her. "Yep."

"Wicked cool. She looks like she could rip my throat right out."

Amber raised a brow. "She can."

For some reason, he found that hilarious. "Good point. Come on, don't want to keep the boss man waiting."

They followed him to the warehouse entrance. Her wolf trotted ahead of them, while Derek's stuck by Ceri in the rear. The usual scents assaulted her nose as they walked inside, but the lights were on, and there were no vampires lurking in the shadowy corners. The main room on this level appeared to be completely empty except for them. It took the place from a haunted vibe to simply in dire need of a deep clean. It was completely the opposite of the grand mansion she'd visited when she met with the vampire council. She was sure Bram had some devious purpose for hiding out here so often, but she had no intention of asking what it was.

Bram rose from a dilapidated couch and spread his arms in welcome. "Amber, I'm honored you reached out for help with this..." His pale eyes fixed on Valiel. "...delicate situation."

Valiel turned her face into Derek's chest and pulled her wings in tight. Derek rubbed her back in soothing circles, throwing a glare at Amber as if it was her fault Bram was creepy.

"Thanks for agreeing to meet on such short notice."

"It's no problem." He waved a hand in dismissal. "I'm sure you'll be willing to return the favor."

She didn't bother hiding her grimace. It was too easy to forget that while Bram was helping with the incubi problem for "free", that didn't extend to everything else. "Of course. That's what friends do," she muttered.

"Please, have a seat." He gestured at the slightly cleaner couch across from him.

Derek eyed it with suspicion. "I'll stand, thanks."

"As you wish." He stalked closer. "Now, Amber described the basics of the problem over the phone. Your little succubus tried to eat Genevieve's sister?"

"That's a bit dramatic." Ceri frowned at Amber before returning her focus to Bram. "It was just a handshake. Less than three seconds and Susannah passed out."

"Valiel has been complaining about being hungry constantly. We assumed it was malnutrition or a growth spurt or something. They didn't feed them enough in her realm," Derek added.

"I see." Bram circled around Derek to peer at Valiel, who was doing her best to keep her face hidden. "They weren't feeding you the right thing, though, were they, little one?"

Valiel shrugged, her curiosity winning as she peeked over Derek's shoulder at the vampire.

"Did you try to feed from them?"

She gnawed on her lip, a guilty blush warming her cheeks, and nodded once.

"But it didn't work?"

She shook her head then curled her wings around herself again.

Bram straightened and nodded. "I see. Very silly of your care-takers to miss all that."

"We were doing our best!" Ceri objected.

"You were treating her like a human child when she is a preda-tor." Bram's expression turned hard, and he drew back his lips to expose his fangs. "How many people buy tigers as pets, only to be shocked when they are bitten or killed? She is not like you. She is like *me*."

Ceri stiffened and ground her teeth together. "She is not some kind of dangerous wild animal."

"Until she understands how to control her impulses, yes, she is."

Bram lifted his fingers to his lips and whistled. Amber and Derek both flinched at the piercing sound.

A slender woman walked in. She appeared to be in her mid-thirties with a lean physique and the telltale scars of a feeder on her neck and wrists. There were three main reasons people volunteered to feed vampires: the money, the sex, or a chance to be turned. Amber wondered what had drawn this woman to Bram.

"Sarah, how are you?" Bram asked as he kissed her cheeks in greeting.

She smiled fondly at him. "Better than ever. What's the emergency?"

Bram stepped back and gestured at Valiel. "A risky experiment, if you're willing to help."

"Is that a succubus?"

"Yes," Derek answered. "What is this woman here for, exactly?"

"We have to attempt a feeding in a controlled environment to see what the girl is capable of." Bram placed a hand on Sarah's shoulder. "You came to mind immediately."

"It would be fascinating." Sarah's eyes lit up with interest as she stared at Valiel.

"The MIA is rounding up thousands of incubi. They will need help from leading researchers to feed them all, since it is becoming clear they do need something more than food to survive." Bram met Amber's eyes as he spoke, the message clear. Sarah's help wouldn't be free, either.

"What is your research, exactly?" Amber forced herself to ask.

Sarah's eyes flicked to her. "I've been researching *why* vampires need fresh blood. If we could design a synthetic substitute, it could improve their lives quite a bit. It is difficult for vampires to integrate with society and to control their appetites."

"And you think you could help the incubi, too?"

"Perhaps. There must be similarities. My team would be willing to work with the MIA if they could help with funding."

Amber nodded once. "I can make that happen if you can help us today. As long as you understand the risks."

Sarah waved away her concerns. "I have fed newborn vampires. The risks don't concern me."

"What's the plan, then?" Ceri crossed her arms.

"Bring the girl here."

Derek approached hesitantly, stopping a few feet away. "I don't want you scaring her."

"She's already scared. But I guarantee you that her hunger will override that. Won't it, Valiel?" Bram stepped around into her line of sight again. "Would you like to feed?"

Valiel lowered her wings and nodded shyly.

"Sarah, come." Bram positioned her just within Valiel's reach. "Valiel, look at me." He waited until she dragged her eyes away from Sarah to focus on him. "You may only take a little."

Valiel gnawed on the inside of her cheek for a moment then nodded.

"Give her your hand."

Sarah held out her hand with a gentle smile. "Here you go."

Valiel reached out hesitantly, as if worried this was all a trick, then grabbed Sarah's fingers in a death grip. Sarah nodded once in reassurance as Valiel's eyes began to glow, but her face quickly grew pale.

"Let go," Bram ordered. Valiel hissed at him and tightened her grip on Sarah's hand. He yanked Sarah away as her eyes rolled back into her head. Valiel lunged forward, and Derek was barely able to keep his grip on her. Her reaction was even worse than when they'd pulled her off Susannah.

"MORE!" Valiel shrieked, her voice full of desperation. It was awful to watch, but Amber refused to turn away. She couldn't pretend this wasn't a problem and that the incubi weren't dangerous at all. But she also didn't believe that Kadrithan was right. Valiel had never lied to them; she was just a starving child. There had to be a way to help them without sacrificing the safety of every other race.

Bram swept Sarah up into his arms. "I'll return shortly."

Derek paced in front of the couches, rocking Valiel like she was a colicky baby and not a dangerously hungry succubus. "This was a bad idea."

"No, waiting this long to figure out how to feed her was a bad idea." Ceri sat down on the edge of the couch. Derek's wolf rested his head on her lap. She threaded her fingers through his fur with a sigh. "Figuring out a solution was always going to be unpleasant."

"Maybe Sarah can help. Her research sounded promising." Amber shoved her hands in her pockets.

"Did you see her? She looks insane. I can't believe you agreed to let her help the MIA," Derek snapped.

"Bram wouldn't have brought her here if she didn't know her stuff."

"You trust him too much. We should have figured this out as a pack."

"We can't do everything on our own, Derek!" Amber threw her hands in the air, completely blindsided by how angry her brother was over this. "And you weren't offering up any genius ideas before we got here."

"If I had known you were going to let that vampire upset Valiel like this, I would have figured something out!"

Ceri stood, her eyes flashing in anger. "You know perfectly well Bram didn't do anything to hurt Val. And we *all* agreed this was our best shot at getting some decent advice."

"You can blame me if it makes you feel better," Bram said as he strode back into the room. "However, I don't think this is making it any easier on the child."

Valiel had gone quiet while they shouted at each other and curled into a ball against Derek's chest. Her wings drooped behind her, the tips of the white feathers gathering grime and dust. Guilt twisted through Amber's gut. They were screwing this all up.

Derek deflated as all the anger went out of him in a rush. "I'm sorry, kiddo. This isn't your fault."

"Don't lie to her," Bram chided him. "Set her down on the couch and let me talk to her. She needs honesty."

Derek looked at Amber in horror.

"We came to him for advice. Let him give it." Amber crossed her arms tightly across her chest and prayed this wasn't a terrible mistake. "We're clearly not handling this well."

Ceri, clearly out of patience, made a threatening gesture and pointed firmly at the couch. With a sigh, Derek finally complied. Valiel dropped her arms and let him set her down without a fuss. She looked like she expected them to leave her there.

Bram grabbed her chin and gently forced her to look up at him. "You and I are very much alike. We are both hungry all the time."

Valiel swallowed nervously but nodded.

"The difference is I can take what I need without killing the human. You can't." He dropped his hand, but she didn't look away. "Amber and her pack are worried about this because they don't want to choose between feeding you and keeping the humans safe."

Valiel picked at her fingernail. "But humans are food," she whispered. "Feeding on them makes you strong like the archangels."

"And what happens if you were to eat all the humans?"

She looked up, shock mingling with excitement on her face. "All of them?"

He nodded. "Every last one of them."

"I'd be very, very strong."

"And then what would you eat?"

She slumped back against the back of the couch. "I don't know."

"You would eat nothing." Bram clasped his hands together and regarded her very seriously. "We need humans to survive, but they don't need us. This means we must be careful to not kill them, so they stay willing to share their life force with us. You took too much from Sarah."

Valiel gnawed at her lip for a moment. "Is that why she fell over?"

"Yes."

"I'm still hungry."

Bram nodded solemnly. "I understand, but now Sarah won't want to feed you again."

Valiel let out a heavy sigh. "Maybe I just need more do-nuts. Then I won't need humans."

"That would be much easier, but I think you will have to learn how to be gentle when you feed. It was very hard for me when I first became a vampire, but I learned, and that is why I am strong today. The humans trust me, and so they come back when I need them."

She was silent for a long moment then asked, "Will Sarah be okay?"

"Probably."

Valiel slid off the couch and sidled toward Derek and Ceri. "I want to go back home."

"I believe my point has been made." Bram stood as well. "I'd like to talk to Amber privately for a moment."

Ceri took Valiel's hand and nodded then led the child and Derek outside before he could object. Amber watched them go enviously. She had a feeling she was about to receive a lecture.

Bram flicked her on the nose.

She flinched back with a scowl, unsure when he managed to get so close to her. "What was that for?"

"I was testing your reflexes. You failed." He flicked her ear this time before she could dodge the lightning-fast attack. "Go get some sleep. You are tired enough to be near useless."

She rubbed her ear and stepped well out of his reach. "Fine. Point made."

An almost fond expression softened his face for a moment. "You are doing well, you know."

"That's debatable."

"But you could be doing better."

She laughed at that. "Well, at least we agree."

"You can't be the pack's mother and their alpha. Give someone else the job of making sure everyone is fed and getting sleep."

"I...fine. I'll delegate." She took another step back, wary that he might try to emphasize that point painfully as well. "Any other life advice?"

He grinned. "Next time I have to give you advice, I get a painting in return."

She scowled. "Noted."

"Go sleep." He waved her away and headed toward the back room he'd taken Sarah to. "I need to go wake up our lovely researcher."

Amber turned to leave but hesitated. "She's good, right? I didn't just make a deal with a nutcase, did I?"

"A bit late to ask now." He winked at her then disappeared from view.

"Stupid, tricky vampires," she muttered as she headed toward the exit. Everything was always a test, and she kept failing somehow. People were frustrating. It would be so much easier if everyone was just *honest* and communicated like the adults they were.

A guilty tug on her conscience made her pause at the door. She pulled her phone out of her pocket and stared at the text Kadrithan had sent her. Every time she tried to come up with a response, it all sounded so stilted and awkward. It was ridiculous, though.

We're fine. She grimaced at the half-truth but didn't want to get into everything that had happened over text messages. *Tomorrow morning is the earliest I can meet. Need sleep.* Before she could erase any of it, she tapped send and shoved her phone back in her pocket.

Her wolf nudged her leg. *They are growing anxious.*

She nodded and forced herself to walk outside. Now that Bram had brought up how tired she clearly was, it was impossible to ignore. It was not only causing them to miss things like Valiel's obvious hunger, but it was also making them cranky. They really did need a babysitter.

CHAPTER 39

GENEVIEVE

Genevieve wanted to resent Amber for delaying their departure long enough for them to get a full night's sleep, but considering she'd not only slept last night, but until just past noon today, she had to admit her alpha had a point. The fog of exhaustion that had been throbbing behind her eyes had eased. They were all still tired, but it was manageable now.

"You ready?" Steven poked his head in the room. Amber had called an impromptu pack meeting right after they'd all woken up this morning. Apparently, it *had* to be done before they left.

"Almost." She tugged on her last shoe and nodded. "Susie still outside with the pixies?"

"Yeah. Deward's cousin is over, so she's teaching Susie sign language and letting her help with the health checks. She's having a blast."

Genevieve shook her head with a smile as she stood. "She's not going to want to go home once this is all over."

"She's already made me promise to let her come over every weekend."

"Sucker." Genevieve kissed him on the cheek. "I love that about you."

He grinned like he'd won the lottery and slipped his hand into hers as they left the room. Her wolf barreled down the stairs ahead of them. Everyone else was already crowded into the living room. Their pack had grown so much recently that they weren't going to be able to have pack meetings in here much longer.

Her nose twitched at the smell of pancakes. "Is that breakfast?"

Tommy tilted his head back to grin at her. "We ate it all. You slept too long."

"You *didn't*." She narrowed her eyes, ready to tackle him.

"Y'all are worse than me and Derek sometimes." Amber rolled her eyes. "No one has eaten yet. We were waiting for you because we are *polite*. Also meeting first, then food."

She sighed. "All right, let's get this over with."

Amber crossed her arms and stared them all down. "We're a mess."

"Can't argue with that," Ceri agreed with a yawn.

"This fight isn't over, and we really can't afford to falter now. Genevieve is swamped with planning and helping to manage the task force. I'm dealing with a new problem every half hour. Derek and Ceri have apparently adopted a dangerously hungry child. Tommy and Deward are spending every waking hour with the task force *and* trying to keep us all fed." Amber took a deep breath. "So I've decided we need a babysitter. And I'm not going to take any objections."

Derek shrugged. "A babysitter isn't a terrible idea."

"Ito is the babysitter." Amber jerked her thumb at Ito, who had been imitating a statue by the fireplace up until that point. He stepped forward and gave a sort of half bow, clearly repressing a self-satisfied grin as shock settled over the whole pack.

Genevieve crossed her arms and glared at Amber. "You have ten seconds to explain before I lead a mutiny."

"We're not sleeping, not eating well enough, and we're missing things." Amber mirrored Genevieve's posture, a little red seeping into her eyes. "He's going to make sure we get at least six hours of sleep a night, three *healthy* meals a day, and watch out for...weirdness."

"Weirdness like Valiel's little hunger issue?" Ceri asked.

"Exactly like that."

Genevieve turned her glare on Ito. "Will you really be watching out for things? You didn't seem to notice Valiel's issue, either."

Ito lifted his chin. "I avoided spending as much time as possible with your pack and especially with the succubus, so no, I didn't notice."

She raised a brow. "But you're willing to babysit us all of a sudden?"

"Amber suggested it would impress her wolf if I was successful in helping your pack with this." A grimace twisted at his lips. "I can assure you I will enjoy it as little as any of you will."

Derek snorted. "Understatement of the year."

"Why couldn't one of us have been the babysitter?" Tommy asked, looking particularly put out by the announcement.

"I need all of you focused on the task force. And..." Amber sighed, a guilty expression crossing her face. "Ito is the most experienced werewolf here. We could probably...learn something from him."

They all looked at her in shock. Ito included.

"I mean...I guess that's true," Genevieve admitted reluctantly.

"Of course it's true." Ito narrowed his eyes at Amber. "But I didn't expect you to acknowledge it."

"Smug babysitters will end up *demoted*," Amber threatened. "And I already said all of this when we formed our truce."

"You only admitted I understood more about werewolf politics, not the day-to-day needs of a pack."

Amber rolled her eyes. "Well, now I am. Happy?"

"Is that emotion permitted, or is it too close to smug?" Ito deadpanned.

Tommy snorted out a laugh then clapped his hand over his mouth with a guilty flush. "Just, uh, coughed. Allergies."

Amber glared at him, but there was no real heat behind it. "You're not gonna be laughing when he makes you eat something other than pizza."

"I'm actually getting kind of sick of pizza," Tommy admitted.

"Ditto." Even the thought of grease and cheese made Genevieve throw up a little in the back of her mouth. "What do we get instead?"

Ito grinned at them, a truly terrifying sight. "Vegetables."

"But we're werewolves!" Derek objected, his eyes wide with horror.

"Your bodies remain, unfortunately, very human. Werewolves need a balanced diet, just like everyone else." Ito shook his head in disapproval. "It's amazing any of you are still able to shift with how little quality protein you eat."

"I agree with Ito," Deward said with a nod. "I have lost muscle mass since spending most of my time with the pack."

"Well, maybe this won't be so bad." Genevieve plastered on a smile. Amber was delegating. This was a positive thing they should support. Even if she had delegated to Ito.

"This is going to be weird and miserable," Derek muttered, earning a smack on his arm from Ceri.

Amber rolled her eyes. "I'm going to go collect our fae volunteers. Y'all better all behave while I'm gone. And save me a plate of pancakes."

Venali had to be some sort of punishment Kadrithan was inflicting on them. Genevieve was sure of it. She'd never met anyone both so entitled and nervous in her entire life. It was a seriously unfortunate combination of character traits.

The only reason he hadn't ended up stuffed in someone's suitcase was because he had *finally* fallen asleep. And was, of course, taking up two seats on the plane even though they reclined. And snoring.

The other fae Amber had brought back was the exact opposite. Leena was older, though her exact age was impossible to tell, and radiated a calm determination that had everyone sitting up a bit straighter. Even Ito treated her with genuine respect. Genevieve wanted to be exactly like her when she grew up.

The plane landed on the narrow runway with a gentle bump. Venali snorted awake and looked around, blinking in confusion. "We're there already?"

Genevieve's eye twitched. "After two hours of you snoring."

Venali huffed and threw back the blanket covering him. "I don't snore."

Leena tossed Venali's bag at him, nearly bowling him over with it. "Yes, you do."

He flushed a deep red and slung his bag over his shoulder, trying to look like he wasn't embarrassed. "I'm sure it can't be that loud."

Icewind snorted and shook her head. "Pretty sure all of Seattle heard you when we flew over the city."

Genevieve pressed her lips together to keep from laughing aloud as she grabbed her things. She *almost* felt sorry for the poor guy, but he really needed to drop the pompous act.

"Amber, you're driving the second suburban with your pack. Leena and Venali, you two are with me." Icewind hurried them off the plane and into the waiting caravan.

The small, private airport they'd landed at was a decent distance from Seattle itself, and their drive took them even farther from the city. The two-lane highway wound through a brilliantly green forest. Dense underbrush and mossy trees softened the evening light around them. Halfway there, a rainstorm washed over them, pouring down so hard Genevieve wasn't sure how Amber managed to stay in her lane, then passed just as quickly.

Finally, after nearly an hour of driving, their caravan turned down a gravel road then took a left onto the narrow driveway toward the cabin where Velez and the rest of the task force had been staying.

Amber parked directly behind Icewind. "This place reminds me of summer camp."

She snorted. "Too bad we're here for a fight instead of canoeing and horseback riding."

"We deserve a vacation when all this is over." Amber tapped a finger against her chin and pursed her lips. "Maybe to the Bahamas."

Ceri leaned in between the two front seats with a grin. "We should do a cruise! The mermaid-run cruise lines have some great shows."

"I've never been on a cruise. That would be awesome," Tommy added from the very back.

Amber nodded decisively. "I'll make Kadrithan pay for it."

"Ha. Even better." Genevieve hopped out and slung her backpack over one shoulder. Their home base for this mission consisted of a little log cabin and two large, canvas tents on either side of it where they would sleep. Three ominously grungy portable toilets loomed in the shade of the trees a few yards from the tents.

Velez stepped out of the cabin and nodded his head in greeting. "Welcome, everyone, to our five-star resort."

"There better be a real toilet in that cabin," Icewind threatened.

"There is," Velez reassured her. "But only one."

"Great."

"Everyone can put their luggage in their assigned tent. Meeting in five minutes." Venali shooed them to hurry. "Let's hustle, people."

As they dispersed to unload all their luggage and the extra equipment they'd brought with them, Genevieve took stock of who had come. She was pleased to see Kate Ford was already there. Jameson and Greer's pack had sent volunteers but hadn't been able to personally join them this time. Kate had brought half her pack—— all volunteers——and had insisted on joining the fight herself as well.

They'd all flown in the day before while Amber had been forcing her pack to rest.

The ordered five minutes turned into ten, but soon enough they were all crammed into the cabin with an impatient Velez. It was standing room only. Genevieve was squished between Ceri and Tommy. Her wolf sat right on top of her feet, also squished between her pack mate's wolves. They were lucky it was pretty cool this time of year.

Velez pulled up a map on the large computer screen they'd set on top of a box so everyone could see it. "This is the outline of the property we've been surveilling. The green block is the coven house. There is only one driveway here on the west side of the property. However, there is no fence, so it may be possible to move in on foot." He flipped to the next picture, which was the same map, but the black property border had been replaced by several colorful lines that overlapped all around the property and the house. "This is the bigger problem. Wards."

"They're still active?" Ceri asked.

He nodded. "Any magic or spells cast before the curse was broken have stayed active and potent. Which, unfortunately for us, includes these wards."

"Normally, I could break them without too much effort, but with magic not working..." Ceri shook her head. "It could be a problem."

Tessa wormed her way out of the midst of the coven. "Could you strengthen them?"

"The wards?" Ceri asked with a frown.

"Yes."

"Why would we want--" Ceri's eyes lit up. "Destabilization. Yes! That could work!"

"Because new magic would totally screw it up." Tessa did a little dance.

"That is perfect. It could backfire, of course, but it's our best shot. It's going to screw those wards up big time. Hopefully in a way that lets us get past them." Ceri turned back to Velez. "If the coven is there, they're going to know we've messed with them, though."

Velez pursed his lips but nodded. "We'll go with that for now and anticipate not having the element of surprise." He flipped to a satellite view of the property with red and orange heat signatures. The highest density was in the house, with a few dotting the surrounding acreage. "Which brings me to my next point. This mission has two goals. One, get the relic. Two, *arrest* the incubi hiding out here. The MIA has a responsibility to offer every person in there a chance to surrender peacefully. Does everyone here understand that?"

Leena shook her head. "They won't surrender. They never do."

"Things have changed. Maybe they will this time," Amber said firmly.

"I'll follow your rules, but don't be surprised when I'm right." Leena gave a short bow to Amber.

Genevieve gnawed on the inside of her cheek. She wanted to believe Leena was wrong and that her fae prejudice was showing, but they couldn't just disregard what she was saying. The fae had been fighting them for centuries.

"Noted." Velez tapped on the screen. "We've counted eleven people moving around the property. Heat signatures show there are at least twice that many more inside that haven't left since our surveillance began."

"So many?" Genevieve asked, a sinking feeling settling in the pit of her stomach.

Velez nodded. "This is going to be difficult."

"How badly are we outnumbered?" one of the vampires asked.

"With the addition of Alpha Ford's pack, not by much." Velez nodded toward Kate. "However, we will have to split our forces. We will have two squads taking point and attacking the house and one squad holding the perimeter and watching our backs." He flipped to the final picture. "After this, we're dividing up to go over the plans for those individual squads. We'll go over the final plan one last time before we do this."

Icewind stepped forward. "We only have one day to prepare for this. Our plans will be solidified tonight, and tomorrow we have to get what sleep we can during the daylight hours. As soon as the sun sets, we're moving out."

Genevieve squared her shoulders and took a deep breath. Planning was her thing. And honestly, a day was more time than they normally had. This *was* going to be hard and risky, but they weren't alone. They had allies and more information than they'd ever had access to before. Outnumbered or not, they were going to make this happen.

CHAPTER 40

TOMMY

Tommy crouched next to a tree behind his squad. The distance between him and his wolf made his chest tight. It was the part of the plan he liked the least, but with no other way of keeping an eye on the rest of his pack, he hadn't objected.

He checked that the safety on the pistol hanging from his hip was still on for the fifth time, sure that it had somehow spontaneously switched to fire. It was an awkward weight against his side. He hadn't packed a belt, so the holster kept tugging down the waistband of his pants. Having a gun at all was weird. He'd never really fought outside of wolf form. That was also why he was on the B team along with Genevieve that would be holding the perimeter. Amber and Derek knew how to shoot at least, so they were taking on the riskier part of this mission.

I will watch their backs. No one will touch our alpha or pack mate. Tommy's wolf mentally bared his teeth. *We are still strong enough to protect them.*

I know, he thought back, fingers tapping out a nervous rhythm against the edge of the holster. *Still gonna worry.*

Trust your instincts while we are separated.

I'll do my best. The light on the communicator strapped to his

237

arm still showed a steady red. He shifted his feet, anxious to get started. If Ceri couldn't get through the wards, they were kind of screwed.

Their target was a patrol that should be in this area based on the surveillance the scouting team had done. If possible, they needed to intercept them and prevent them from flanking Team One as they surrounded the house. Their squad, along with the other perimeter squads, were also tasked with preventing anyone that might flee the house from escaping the property.

The vampire on his squad––a woman named Penelope––stood, her body tensed. "Do you hear that?"

"Hear what––" A faint but deep rumbling became apparent, growing louder every moment. The trees around them trembled and the ground beneath his feet swayed. It was an odd feeling, as if he was on a boat.

"An earthquake?" Venali hissed, his eyes wide with fear.

"No." The familiar scent of Ceri's magic permeated the air. "Ceri is breaking the wards. I think it's working."

Ben, the MIA agent leading their team of four, edged closer to the wards. "Everyone, get ready to move. The witches said we may not have long to get through if this works at all."

They moved into position alongside him. The scent of magic in the air grew stronger every moment. Their wrist communicators all flashed green at the same time. Phase two had begun.

Ben was the first to move. He lunged over the invisible line. A strange whistling noise was the only warning as a large tree to their left bent at its middle and swung down toward him. Penelope slammed into Ben's back, and her momentum knocked them out of the way a split second before the tree impacted the ground.

Tommy sprinted forward as fast as he could. The surrounding trees groaned as they thrashed. A low-hanging branch swung at his head like a bat. He ducked and rolled, narrowly dodging a large pine that smacked into the ground less than a foot behind him.

The ground sucked at his hands as he pushed back to his feet.

His left leg sank knee deep before he could jerk free. The forest floor had turned to quicksand. All those movies he'd watched as a kid were right. Quicksand really was a threat.

He tried to dig his leg out, but the dirt flowed back into place like water. It was impossible to shovel away fast enough, and the harder he tugged against its grip, the more tightly it held on. Panic started to build in his chest. Penelope and Ben were too far ahead and still moving. They couldn't see him. There was nothing within reach that wasn't trying to kill him. He was actually, fully stuck.

"Crap." With renewed urgency, Tommy attempted to crawl forward, clawing at the ground in an attempt to get some kind of leverage. But the dirt was too soft. Nothing was working.

A piercing shriek startled him into whipping his head around as Venali barreled into him. The fae continued screaming as he grabbed Tommy's arms and yanked him free of the quicksand with a frantic tug that almost dislocated his shoulder.

"Run!" Venali shouted in a panic as he attempted to drag Tommy after him.

"I am! You can let go now!" His left shoe was still lost somewhere underground, but he wasn't about to go back for it.

He dodged tree after tree as he raced after his squad and wondered if Ceri had accidentally set off the whole forest. The wards had *not* been this big before.

A resounding crack that made his ears ring echoed through the forest. It took a couple of seconds before he realized that everything had gone still. He slowed to a stop and turned in a circle, still wary of the dormant trees around him.

"Is it over?" Venali gasped out.

"Can't assume it is," Ben warned as he motioned for them to move forward. "Keep going, and don't forget the real threat is ahead of us."

"Velez mentioned it might get a little crazy, but I wasn't expecting this," Penelope muttered as she followed Ben. Somehow, she moved in complete silence. Tommy wasn't sure he'd be able to hear her coming even if he was in wolf form. It was one of the creepiest things about vampires.

Venali stuck as close to him as he could without tripping over each other's feet. It was on the tip of his tongue to tell the guy to back off, but Venali *had* dragged him out of the quicksand. That earned him a little respect.

Ben held up a closed fist, which signaled for them to stop, then gestured for them to spread out. This was the place they expected to cross paths with the patrol. With the ruckus getting through the wards had caused, Tommy had no doubt someone would come investigate.

Penelope climbed up a tree and disappeared into the shadowy branches. With no heartbeat and very little need to breathe, it would have been impossible to spot her up there. Venali, however, seemed incapable of staying silent. He was crouched next to a tree but every few seconds found a need to adjust something. His gun belt. His feet. His hair. Even Ben, who was human, was managing to stay quieter.

Tommy suppressed a sigh and pushed his senses outward. His ears had finally stopped ringing, and he could hear the crack of gunfire in the distance. He had no idea who was doing the shooting, but as long as it was going on, it meant his pack mates were still alive to fight back.

As he strained to hear any sign of approach, the hair on the back of his neck stood on end. They were being watched. He could feel it.

He glanced at Ben, once again frustrated he couldn't just telepathically let him know what was coming. If they ever got it back, he'd never take the pack bond for granted again. Ben must have sensed something as well, though, because he met Tommy's eyes and held up a closed fist. *Wait.*

Tension thrummed through his muscles. Whoever was watching them had to be close, but he couldn't hear a thing. They were as quiet as Penelope up in the tree... He froze. The incubi could fly. They were *above* them.

Tommy launched himself backward. "Above us!"

Ben moved a split second after he did, and an arrow struck the ground where he'd just been standing. Penelope leaped straight upward and collided with one of the incubi circling silently above them. They tumbled into the trees out of sight as the other two dove toward him and Venali.

He dodged the initial attack and ducked beneath the arrow that followed. It slammed into the tree behind him with a dull thunk.

"Police! Hands up!" Ben aimed his pistol at the incubi with steady hands.

The succubus leading the group drew her sword with a sneer. "You have no authority over us."

"Like hell I don't. You're in our realm now." Ben tightened his grip on the gun. "Drop it."

Tommy glanced at Venali as he took a step back and drew his gun as well. The fae was shaking, but he had his weapon clutched in his hands, ready for a fight.

"We will never surrender," the succubus hissed. "Not to *mortals.*" She spat out the word like a slur then launched into motion.

Ben fired twice before her feet left the ground. The bullets struck her chest dead center, but an arrow struck him as well, going clean through his leg. Venali charged forward with a shout. Tommy swung his pistol toward the remaining incubus and pulled the trigger. The shot went wide, but it startled his target just enough to give Venali an opening. The swing of the fae's sword sliced through the incubus's bow.

With a snarl, the incubus tossed the useless weapon aside and drew his own sword in time to block Venali's second attack. He never saw Penelope coming. Tommy didn't, either. Just her hand bursting through the incubus's chest, heart clasped between bloody fingers.

She jerked her arm free, and the incubus toppled over. "You don't mind if I feed, do you? Seems like such a waste."

"Do whatever you need." Tommy tried to put his pistol away but missed the holster three times before finally managing to get it in. He rushed to Ben's side. "You okay?"

Ben had his hands clamped around the wound and his teeth clenched tight against the pain. "Help me tourniquet this."

"First aid--" Pain seared across his ribs. Tommy jerked to his feet in surprise and whirled around, expecting someone to be standing there, but there was no one.

Penelope dropped her snack and tensed. "Where are they?"

"I--" His leg gave out, and he collapsed onto his knees. Warmth spread across his side. He lifted his arm and found blood had seeped through his shirt. "Blood," he choked out, barely able to think as stars danced across his vision. He fell forward as consciousness slipped away.

CHAPTER 41

Amber knew she'd been stupid getting separated from the group like this, but she'd been so angry. They wouldn't surrender. They wouldn't listen. The first incubus that had gone to his knees and raised his hands had been killed by the incubus standing next to him.

She slid to a stop by Tommy's wolf as her own rushed past and attacked the last remaining incubus. Stupidly, she'd thought the incubus she'd chased down was alone. She'd managed to kill the two others with him, but being outnumbered and caught off guard, she hadn't seen the final attack coming. Only heard the horrible yelp of pain. Smelled the blood. Tommy's wolf had thrown himself in the path of the strike meant for her.

A loud shot cracked through the air and struck the incubus's head. Ito stopped beside her. "Are you hurt?"

"Tommy's wolf, not me." She pulled back and found her shirt was drenched in blood. In Tommy's blood. It smelled like him––the source didn't matter, it was *his*––a scent she was too familiar with.

"Carry him. Keep moving." Ito hovered between them and the door, but he couldn't protect them indefinitely. She knew this logically, but her body was frozen. "*Amber. Get up.*"

The sharp command gave her the strength she needed. Grinding her teeth together, she scooped up the wolf's horribly limp body and stood. He was alive. The heartbeat thrumming beneath her fingers was proof of that. Her wolf pressed against her right side and Ito against her left.

"Bet you never guessed you'd end up my bodyguard." It was surreal to be walking along with him and trusting him with her life with no hesitation. She had no idea when she'd stopped hating him. Perhaps when he'd agreed to the truce. Maybe before even that.

Ito glanced at her with a furrowed brow. "No, I expected to end up killing you."

"Awkward."

He almost smiled but shook his head and moved into position at the door, a mask of concentration covering whatever amusement he might have felt. "Stay close."

She didn't argue. It was lucky that Tommy's wolf had followed her and even luckier Ito had come, too. They crept back up the narrow staircase, pausing only briefly on the landing, before jogging down the hall. It was worryingly quiet all around them. The crack of gunfire had been almost constant since they'd approached the house and demanded surrender.

Her wolf moved in front of Ito, forcing both of them to stop, and focused on the hallway ahead of them. *Someone is coming. Five or more.*

She couldn't fight with Tommy's wolf in her arms like this. As gently as she could, she laid him down against the wall and swung her rifle back around to the front. The footsteps, barely audible, stopped.

"Hale, that you?" Velez shouted.

Relief flooded through her at the sound of his voice. "Yes!"

His wolf rounded the corner first, followed closely by Velez himself. "We've been looking for you. Glad to see Ito found you first." He paused when he spotted Tommy's wolf. "Alive?"

She nodded once. "Hurt bad, though."

"Have we secured the house?" Ito asked.

"For now. We have three teams doing a final sweep. The medical teams are already on their way." Velez motioned for one of his men. "Escort them back the way we came." He turned back to Amber. "The archangel got away. We're working on tracking him down, but his route of escape isn't clear. Don't let your guard down."

"We won't," Ito replied as she picked Tommy's wolf up again.

The wolf's body was limp, the heartbeat growing more thready by the minute. "We need to hurry. He's losing too much blood."

Ito frowned. "He should be healing quickly enough to prevent that."

"Nothing is working as intended right now."

The MIA agent led them back through the house to a side exit. Bodies lined the halls. Blood soaked the carpet and was splattered against the walls. Amber tightened her grip on Tommy's wolf and fought against the urge to let her eyes linger. It wouldn't help. She didn't need any more fuel for her nightmares.

There were very few people she regretted killing. The pack in Vegas still weighed heavily on her, especially after forcing Ito to submit. She might have been able to save them. The incubi here had already been added to the list. They'd fought so desperately. Arresting them had never been an option.

Ito's grip on her arm startled her. His eyes bored into her own, an indecipherable emotion in his gaze. "You're falling behind." He pushed her ahead of him. She let him guide her. Focused on putting one foot in front of the other. For Tommy, she had to hurry.

The cool rush of air upon exiting the house cleared the stench of death from her nose. It helped. The smell of blood was always the worst part for her. Sometimes she was glad she hadn't stayed working as nurse just because of the blood. Other times she longed to be saving lives again instead of taking them.

Venali sprinted toward them, waving his arms and shouting her name. His shirt was covered in blood just like hers was. "Tommy collapsed!"

She tightened her hold on his wolf and ran after him. Cots were lined up outside. The medical team had moved fast. Ceri was already by Tommy, her hands clenched tightly around his. Two doctors were working on him. His shirt had been ripped open to gain easy access to his injury.

Tears blurred Amber's vision, but she could still see that the wounds matched his wolf's exactly.

"The wolves are inextricably joined to us," Ito whispered, reverence mingling with horror on his face. "Whatever happens to the wolf happens to the human, just as if Tommy had shifted properly."

Amber shoved past the doctors and, operating on instinct, laid Tommy's wolf right next to him. As soon as they touched, their heartbeats steadied in unison. She *felt* their strength increase through the bond. Separating from their wolves was so much riskier than she could have possibly conceived.

"He's healing. Finally." Ceri sat back in relief, tears coursing down her cheeks. "They couldn't figure out what was wrong."

Amber placed a hand on each of their heads, giving them what strength she could. The gash had already begun to knit back together. He'd be conscious again soon.

Ito watched with a furrowed brow. "You cannot separate from your wolves again."

"I wholeheartedly agree."

CHAPTER 42

AMBER

The chaos had settled. Every nook and cranny had been searched. The fight was officially over. Amber couldn't get her heartbeat to slow down, though. Even her wolf remained restless and kept going from pack mate to pack mate, just to make sure they were still safe.

Tommy was with the medics. He and his wolf's wounds were already healing, but the fact that an injury to his wolf affected his human body as well had unsettled everyone. That neither had begun healing until they were reunited even more so.

She shot off a quick text to Kadrithan as she walked toward the back of the house where Velez was waiting for her.

We all survived. Can't say more over the phone.

Before she could lock the phone, her message changed from delivered to read. He must have been waiting with the phone in his hand to see it so soon. Without waiting to see if he'd respond, she put her phone away. There was too much to do to chat with him right now.

Amber stopped a few yards from Velez. There was a wide circle of dirt in front of him that had been recently disturbed, and the stench of death was overwhelming. A single, pale face had been uncovered. "The coven?"

He nodded once. "Smells like they've been dead for over a week. The incubi probably killed them the night the curse was broken."

"You can tell just from the smell?" she asked, barely processing her own words as she stared at the corpse in the dirt. There was something especially horrible about seeing a corpse abandoned with so little care. In the heat of battle, there was no time to focus on the empty look in a dead person's eyes. But a week-old corpse had already started to decay, and the horror of their death was impossible to avoid.

"Smell enough of them and you start to notice the nuance between a day and a week." He smiled at her over his shoulder, but it didn't reach his eyes. "Just one of the perks of being a werewolf in law enforcement."

She swallowed down any further questions. "Right."

They also had sixty-four dead incubi. Only five of them had surrendered. *Five*. Bile rose up the back of Amber's throat, and the urge to vomit was so strong for a moment that she had to hold her breath and shut her eyes. This was exactly the kind of slaughter she hadn't wanted. The entire plan for taking this place had revolved around allowing as many of the incubi to surrender as possible, but it had all been for nothing.

The few that had surrendered seemed completely shell-shocked. None of them were talking. One had tried to drain the succubus sitting next to him, forcing them to keep the prisoners six feet apart to prevent any more attacks.

"If the smell is getting to you, there's no shame in getting some fresh air." He startled her with a gentle touch to her shoulder. She hadn't even heard him approach.

"No. It's…" She shook her head in frustration. "I thought more would surrender."

"Me too. But now we know for next time." He clapped her on

the shoulder and nudged her toward the house. "No point in lingering out here. Our crime scene unit will get them out of the ground and identified."

They walked back in silence.

Genevieve met them at the door. Her face was pale, but she had her usual look of determination. "They're still working on analyzing the relic, but the succubus who was attacked has decided she's willing to talk to us."

Amber's lips thinned, but she nodded. "Guess her friend attacking her used up the last of her loyalty."

"Sounds like it," Genevieve agreed. "We can go see her now."

The few prisoners had been placed in police vans for transport. Their potential informant was alone in one. The succubus stared straight ahead, her eyes wide as if she was shocked any of this had happened. Her long, strawberry blond hair was falling out the complicated braid it had been in.

Amber sat down on the cold, metal bench opposite her. "You wanted to talk to us?"

The succubus started at the sound of Amber's voice but nodded. "The holy relic. That's what you're here for, isn't it?"

"You mean that pillar?"

A slow blink was the succubus's only response for a moment. "Yes. The holy relics. The heart of the temples." Tears glistened in her eyes. "And now it is lost. We will be so weak."

"What does it do?" Amber prompted, but the glazed expression on the succubus's face made it clear that her words were hardly being registered.

"We were supposed to live forever. But now they're all dead."

"Why did no one surrender?" Amber asked, keeping her tone as gentle as possible.

"I'm going to die now. Just like Uriel said." Tears spilled unheeded down her pale cheeks.

Amber glanced at Genevieve, whose frown matched her own. "Why do you think you're going to die?"

The succubus's bottom lip trembled. "The demons are going to win. We'll never be able to feed enough to live forever."

Amber bit back the angry tirade she wanted to launch at the succubus and forced herself to stay calm instead. "That's why they wouldn't surrender?"

The succubus's whole body began to shake with little tremors. "Are you going to give me to the demons?"

"What?" Amber sat back in confusion.

"No prisoners. That's what he said. The demons never take prisoners. They hate us."

Amber took a steadying breath. "There are no demons. We offered you a chance to surrender peacefully and meant it. No one is going to hurt you or feed on you. You. Are. Safe."

The succubus shook her head. "You're lying."

"I'm not--"

"LIAR!" the succubus shrieked, a wild panic burning in her eyes. She yanked at the chains that linked her handcuffs to the floor between her legs hard enough to bruise her wrists. "Get away from me!"

So much for talking. Amber slid out of the van. Her presence was only upsetting the succubus at this point. A doctor hovered nearby, clearly prepared to sedate the succubus if she didn't calm down.

"That was enlightening and frustrating," Genevieve commented with a sigh.

"Mostly frustrating." Amber crossed her arms. "If they all think like this, how are we going to convince any of them to trust us?" Her eyes strayed to the body bags piling up on the lawn. "Especially after the number of deaths here today."

Genevieve was silent for a long moment. "I don't know."

"This was a disaster."

"We have the pillar. Ceri is going to figure out what it is and how to destroy it. Therefore, this was a success." Genevieve crossed her arms stubbornly. "A messy one, but a success nonetheless."

Amber let out a huff of frustration. "Keep saying that until I can believe it."

Her phone buzzed, and she glanced at the screen. Another text from Kadrithan. She put it back in her pocket. That was another messy success she didn't have the energy for right now.

CHAPTER 43

CERI

Ceri stood as far away from the pillar as she could while still being in the room. It was, unfortunately, not far enough to avoid the sickening stench of dark magic that permeated every breath she took.

The pillar––some sort of "holy" relic according to the succubus Amber had spoken with––stood about ten feet high. At first, they weren't sure what it was made of, but Velez had sniffed it. To their horror, he announced it was somehow made of bone. Human bone.

"This is creepy, and I hate it," Ceri muttered.

"It's not really any creepier than those crypts in France that are made of skulls." Tessa leaned in, somehow completely unaffected by the thing's aura.

"Those people died of natural causes, not human sacrifice or whatever awful ritual made this abomination." Ceri waved an accusing hand at the relic.

"*Obviously*, but if you just don't think about it like that, it becomes less creepy. Geez." Tessa rolled her eyes in exasperation then jabbed a finger at one of the ornate runes carved into the border that wrapped around the base of the relic. "Does that look familiar to you? I swear I've seen it before."

She reluctantly walked over and crouched down to take a closer look. There was something familiar about it, but like Tessa, she couldn't quite place it. "It's like someone carved these runes in cursive. They're all...swirly and overdone." A thought tickled the back of her mind, and before she could second-guess it, she grabbed the edge of the border and yanked hard.

"DON'T—" Tessa's shriek died in her throat as the border tore away. Behind it, there were more runes. Real ones. "How did you even think to do that?"

"Illusions. The incubi are always hiding things. Why not the real runes, too?" She tossed the chunk she'd ripped off behind her. "There was no way those could do anything anyhow. They're too distorted."

Tessa shook her head with an admiring smile. "I should have thought of that."

Ceri's eyes jumped from rune to rune. Surprisingly, there were hardly any protections built into the magic. Its purpose was clear. And simple. This so-called relic was a parasite. The original target was designated with an unfamiliar rune, but she could guess that, too. "I think this drew energy...life...from the fae realm."

Tessa's smile faded into a frown. "That shouldn't even be possible."

"Neither should cursing an entire race. It would take an insane amount of power." She stared at the runes in frustration. "With the fae realm *and* the incubi realm destroyed, it simply shifted its target. That's all that makes sense."

"To the spirit realm." Tessa stood and brushed off her knees. "That certainly lines up with what we felt in there. The tangled magic and the awful pull of the dark magic." She put her hands on her hips. "How do we destroy it? We have no magic."

"Explosives."

"What?"

"This only protects against one thing—magical interference. Saraqael is arrogant enough to discount anything remotely human as a threat." She gestured toward a series of runes. "We'd need a huge coven and a week of hard work to break through this if magic was even an option. *But*, in the physical sense, this thing is completely vulnerable."

Tessa's jaw dropped, and she spent a long moment imitating a fish then threw up her hands in exasperation. "I can't even argue with your logic, but I feel like I should."

A grin spread across her face. "Don't worry, it's going to freak Amber out, too."

Tessa turned in a slow circle then asked, "We're not going to blow it up in here, are we?"

"I'm not sure how much choice we have. It won't exactly fit through the door." Ceri tilted her head to the side. "I wonder how they got it in here."

A frown creased Tessa's forehead. "Maybe it just appeared here when they fell?"

"Awfully convenient." Ceri circled the relic and inspected the runes again. "Aha. There it is."

"What?" Tessa leaned in close to inspect the rune she'd found.

"This relic is tied to..." Ceri paused as shock settled in. "To someone. One of the archangels, I think." She stood abruptly. "He was able to summon it here."

"Could he do it again? Snatch it out of here right under our noses?"

Her heart jumped into overdrive. "We have to assume he could."

Tessa jerked upright. "How fast can we get explosives?"

The answer to that turned out to be approximately five minutes. Ceri paced as the bomb tech carefully placed a series of explosives on the pillar.

"And you're sure this is the only way?" Velez asked again, oddly reluctant to blow the thing up. "We were hoping for more time to search this place."

"If I'm interpreting these runes correctly, one of the archangels could summon this to a new location at any moment. We can't risk losing it." She gnawed on her thumb nail then shook her head. "This is our only chance."

Amber jogged in, her face pale and drawn. The stress of this fight had taken a large toll on her. "Tommy's awake so they're getting him out of here. I sent Derek with him."

"Good." She relaxed a fraction. Knowing Derek was with Tommy was a relief. She didn't want him left alone while still so vulnerable.

"The demolition almost ready to go?"

Velez nodded. "Should be."

The bomb tech stood and headed toward them. "Everyone needs to clear out of here and get behind the vehicles."

Velez immediately got on his walkie talkie and gave the order. The majority of the task force had already moved a safe distance away. Ceri fell into step beside Amber and Tessa as they hurried out of the house.

"This is so much cooler than I expected when I signed up for this," Tessa said with an excited grin. "Witches never get to explode things normally!"

Amber shook her head, but a faint smile of amusement tilted up the corners of her mouth. "It is kind of satisfying."

Velez barked out orders, and within a minute, the remainder of the task force was safely hidden behind the line of vehicles at a minimally safe distance. The bomb tech would have preferred farther, but they really didn't have the time.

There was no countdown. No drawn-out anticipation. The bomb tech simply checked that everyone was in place then pushed the button. Ceri pressed her shoulder to Amber's and tensed. Before she could take a breath, a thunderous explosion shook the ground and knocked her off balance. Tessa kept her from falling over.

A hot burst of wind smacked into them, startling her all over again. For a moment, she was sure they'd been too close, and she'd managed to kill everyone, but it vanished as quickly as it had come. She blinked against the shock as she finally caught her breath. She hadn't expected it to be so intense.

At a sign from the bomb tech, Velez poked his head up. "Should be safe to check if it worked now."

Glass rained down on the lawn with soft thunks as the smoke cleared. The house hadn't taken as much damage as she'd expected––intentional on the part of the bomb tech. She had no idea how any of it worked, but he'd been able to minimize the collateral damage with the same techniques they used to bring buildings straight down instead of toppling them over when they needed to be demolished.

Ceri nodded, but before she could take a single step forward, magic flared bright and warm. It swirled through the surrounding air and settled on her skin. As it sank in, she felt something akin to a sigh of relief flood through the earth beneath her feet.

Tessa's eyes grew wide. "You feel that, too?"

Ceri nodded as she knelt and pressed her hands to the dirt. With a slow exhale, she pushed her magic outward. It stuttered as a faint circle formed around her. The line was squiggly and didn't connect in one place, but it was there.

Hope burst in her chest as she looked up at Amber. "We were right. The relics are what has broken magic, and we can *fix it.*"

CHAPTER 44

TOMMY

Tommy peeled back the bandage. He was supposed to wait for Amber to come check on him this morning, but the medicine made his nose sting and, as he'd suspected, the wound had faded to a pink scar.

His wolf rolled over and stuck his feet in the air. *Healed but still weak.*

"You aren't supposed to be messing with that." Deward lifted his head from his pillow and glared blearily across the room at him. They'd managed to squeeze Deward's twin bed from home in here since he'd joined the pack and never left anyhow.

"It's healed. I don't need it anymore."

Deward shook his head in disapproval as he sat up and swung his pajama-clad legs over the side of the bed. "You still feel *off.*"

He sighed but didn't try to deny it. "Yeah. I shouldn't even have a mark left on me at this point. Normally, it would have healed completely, but I'm still tired. And achy." He poked at the scar and winced. Definitely achy.

There were footsteps on the stairs––a steady, measured cadence that could only be Ito.

"I'll get the door." Deward opened it as Ito appeared at the top of the stairs with a tray covered in food that drowned out the sharp scent of antiseptics.

"Breakfast for the rest of the pack is downstairs," Ito said as he set the first plate in front of Tommy's wolf then pulled down the little legs on the tray and placed it over Tommy's lap. "Protein for healing and carbohydrates for energy. Eat it all."

"This smells awesome." Tommy grabbed a fork as his wolf sniffed at the raw steak and chicken. "Look good, buddy?"

Would prefer to hunt it, but this will do.

"I appreciate it." Tommy grinned up at the still stoic Ito. "I'm normally doing the cooking, not getting breakfast in bed."

Ito narrowed his eyes, as if he suspected he was being mocked. "Amber made my duties clear."

"Doesn't mean I can't thank you."

"I suppose not." Ito glanced around the room, lingering on Deward's bed, which partially blocked the closet, forcing them to leave the door open. "Are there no other rooms free?"

"I guess Derek's is effectively free now that he spends all his time in Ceri's room." Tommy shrugged. "You wanna move out, Deward?"

"No. Sharing a room is excellent for bonding. I consider Tommy a brother, so the experience is enjoyable." Deward gestured toward the closet. "Besides, I still have trouble picking out my own clothes. The marks we've added to the tags haven't worked out. They're too hard to distinguish."

"I see."

Amber jogged up the stairs. There were still dark circles under her eyes, but it looked like she had slept. "I see you already took it off."

Tommy held the bandage out for her. "It stinks."

"Can't argue with that." She took the bandage and tied it up in a small trash bag that she set on the end of his bed. "Let me see it."

He moved the tray to the side and lifted his arm to give her better access to the wound. She poked and prodded, frowning when he winced, then inspected his wolf's wounds as well. His wolf curled his lip and snarled in protest as she palpated the area around the wound.

She straightened after a moment, her eyebrows drawn together in concern. "It hurts both of you that bad?"

"Yeah. Surprised me, too."

With a sigh, she crossed her arms and looked to Ito. "You ever seen anything like this? Or should we blame the wonky magic for this, too?"

Ito raised an eyebrow, apparently surprised to be asked. Every time they treated him like a person, it seemed to throw him for a loop. "I've never seen a failure to heal without poison or silver involved."

"I didn't even think about poison. We'd be able to smell the silver." Amber tapped her fingers against her arms as she glared at the scar on his side. "We should get a blood sample, just in case. You can walk, right?"

Tommy nodded. "I'm not that bad off. Just sore and tired."

"All right. Go see the MIA doctors after breakfast." Amber stole a piece of bacon off his plate and shoved it in her mouth before he could object. "Take Deward with you. I don't want you alone until you're completely healed."

"I agree." Deward nodded solemnly in acceptance of his appointment as babysitter.

Tommy rolled his eyes but didn't protest. He really didn't feel great. "All right."

CHAPTER 45

CERI

Ceri offered Valiel another game, but the succubus turned her back on it and plopped down in the window seat.

"I don't *want* another game. I want to go somewhere else. This is *boring.*"

She really couldn't blame her. Being cooped up in there would wear on anyone, and she was just a kid. "Deward is going to bring the pixies to visit you tomorrow."

Valiel just sighed and rested her chin on her knees. "They're too small to play with me."

Ithra tapped Ceri's shoulder and jerked her head toward the door. She followed the troll silently, leaving Valiel to her brooding. Once they were outside, Ithra turned to her. "Until she can leave, I think these visits only frustrate her."

She pushed her hands through her curls. "I just don't want her to think she's been abandoned."

Ithra gave her shoulder a squeeze. "She's resilient. All her complaints lately have centered around boredom. Give her a few days. Perhaps we can coordinate some supervised time outside in the evenings."

"Whatever you think is best." Ceri shoved her hands in her cardigan pockets. "I'm really not any good with kids."

"Don't be so hard on yourself. You've done great."

Tessa appeared at the end of the hall. "You ready, Ceri?"

"Yeah, sorry to keep you waiting!" She turned back to Ithra. "Thanks again for agreeing to watch her."

"I'm happy to help my son's pack however I can."

She hurried to join Tessa, and they made their way out to the forest line where Amber, Deward, and the coven awaited them. They needed to be as far from the house as possible for today's activities, but she hadn't wanted to be in the forest itself. Just in case something ended up on fire.

Tommy—who she hadn't expected to be here—stood in front of Woggy Jr. "This little escape artist has added theft to his list of crimes." He crossed his arms and stared down Woggy Jr., who didn't look the least bit sorry.

In fact, Amber would go as far as to say he was *smug*. It was impressive that he'd somehow not only gotten out of the house but had also stolen Woggy's flying harness and dragged it halfway to the forest line.

"Well, he's got his dad's determination," Amber said with a grin tugging at the corner of her mouth.

"Smidge is going to lose it."

Amber knelt in front of him and signed, "Not allowed."

Woggy Jr. tightened his grip on the harness and signed back a stubborn *yes*. Repeatedly.

"It's too big, buddy." Amber's fingers stumbled over the signs, but the tiny pixie seemed to understand what she meant. And he wasn't happy about it.

Tommy shook his head and scooped him up. "I'll take him back inside."

"Maybe we can make him a harness that fits," Amber said as she followed Tommy.

"Okay. Time to get down to business." Tessa clapped her hands together with an eager grin. "This is so going to work."

Ceri gave her a skeptical look. "We'll see."

A half hour later, Tessa's confidence proved to be well-placed. Ceri knelt and pressed her palms against the grass. This was the third time she'd tested creating a circle today, and every time, she was convinced *this* would be the time it failed.

With a gentle nudge to her magic, it flowed outward into the ground, and a wobbly, half-finished circle formed around her. Just like it had with every previous attempt. The whole coven had gathered to watch, and a few whooped in excitement.

"Well, it's not getting worse." Tessa paced around her, inspecting the circle for herself.

"Definitely not." Ceri nodded in satisfaction. "Destroying the relic made a difference."

"The flow of magic is much clearer now." Deward traced something she couldn't see in the air around her. "I want to try something."

"I'm up for anything."

Deward beckoned for her to join him. "I want to try to guide you while you form the circle. The interference has lessened, so I may be able to help you avoid the worst of it in the same way I found the path to the spirit realm."

"You could try the candle again." Tessa wiggled it at her. She'd tried to light it twice now, but while she could cast a circle, that had failed.

"Might as well." She accepted the candle and placed it between herself and Deward as they settled into place across from each other and joined hands.

This time, when she nudged her magic toward the candle, the pack bond tugged on it. She didn't resist its pull. As soon as her magic connected with it, warmth poured into her. Her awareness of Deward grew clearer––almost as clear as it had been before magic had been corrupted.

"Cast the spell," he whispered, the words echoing inaudibly through her mind.

Her magic pushed outward, but before the spell could tangle, the warmth of the pack bond stretched toward it. The world seemed to spin on its axis, and it took all her remaining control to stay upright. The dizziness increased, and nausea churned in her stomach. Then, with a snap, the magic disconnected from her. She opened her eyes with gasp, but instead of mayhem, the candle sat between them burning merrily.

Deward grinned. "It worked, didn't it?"

"It did." She hovered her fingers over the flame to reassure herself by its warmth that it was real. "I almost threw up, but it *worked*."

Tessa plopped down to her left. "You think you can do it with someone who isn't pack, Deward?"

His grin widened. "Only one way to find out."

CHAPTER 46

AMBER

With breakfast long gone and only a sandwich for lunch, Amber's stomach growled in anticipation of dinner. The meeting had gone well. Icewind and Genevieve had managed to connect everyone that had been at the summit to a video chat so Ceri could share the success from the most recent mission.

The witch's conclave was pleased––except for Helena, who seemed pathologically incapable of it––that magic had partially stabilized. It sparked a bit of hope for everyone involved, herself included. The lingering worry that she'd somehow permanently broken magic by ending the curse had been draining.

Tomorrow, she would meet with Taharia again. The pack had the beginnings of a plan to resolve the hostage situation, but she forced it out of her mind. There were too many issues to spend energy worrying about the things she had the least control over.

As soon as she walked into the house, Captain Jack wound through her legs with a purr like a diesel engine. She squatted down to pet him, her wariness having given way to affection. After all, he had eaten a few bad guys and none of them. And they fed him quite a bit. "Miss us, you little monster?"

He meowed, which she took as an affirmative.

Amber straightened with a smile then headed toward the kitchen. She hovered at the edge of the room as Ito pulled ingredients for dinner from the refrigerator. It was still weird seeing him doing such normal things. "So, how'd I do? Any feedback?"

He set the chicken aside and leaned against the counter as he considered her question. "Your distaste for these meetings is obvious."

She grimaced. "I thought I was hiding it pretty well."

"Your eyes bleed red every time there's a delay, your shoulders are tense, and you tap your fingers against the table. For anyone who's learned to pay attention, it's obvious." He shook his head. "And they have all learned to pay attention. It's why they're in the positions they are in."

"Right." She shoved her hands in her pockets. "I'll work on that."

Ito pursed his lips then sighed. "The success of the first mission has earned you a bit of their respect."

"You make that sound like a bad thing."

He shook his head. "Like all people, they're fickle. You have their respect today, but now you have to keep it." His face was a mask of indifference. She understood it a little better now. In a world where emotion was taken as weakness, he had to be cold. Unassailable.

"I will do what is right, to the best of my abilities, today and forever. That will have to be enough."

"And if it isn't?"

She lifted her chin. "Then I'll carry on without them."

He held her gaze for a moment then turned back to the chicken. "Dinner should only take an hour to prepare."

"Okay. Thanks." She took a step back then turned and headed out the back door with her wolf pressed to her thigh. No matter how confidently she'd spoken, the idea of losing all the allies she'd gained left her feeling cold. This was exactly why she'd never wanted to be a leader. But there was no turning back.

She stopped in the backyard and stared at the Market. It had been easy to make excuses to avoid this call since their return, but it was beginning to feel petty. Kadrithan still cared about her and the pack, even if they weren't on the best terms.

Forcing down the lingering hesitation, she found his number on the contacts and hit call.

Kadrithan answered on the second ring. "Amber?"

"Yes. Hello." She bit the inside of her cheek in frustration. There was no reason to be so awkward after everything they'd been through.

A sigh of relief puffed over the receiver. "You said you're all alive, but was anyone injured?"

"Tommy." It was her turn to sigh. "We learned that any injury our wolves receive are mirrored on our bodies. Even though we're separated, we're still one entity somehow."

"Is he recovering?"

"Sort of. He started healing once we put him back in physical contact with his wolf, but it's slower than it should be."

There was an extended beat of silence. "Are you all right? Of course, you're worried. But hopefully you're well other than that." There was as rustle of clothes and his shoes tapped against marble, which she took to mean he'd stood and was now pacing. "It's very disconcerting to no longer have access to your stronger emotions."

"I'm worried and angry and frustrated." She paused again, chewing on her lip as she hesitated to continue. But if this was going to work––any of it––she had to be able to be honest. "They wouldn't surrender, Kadrithan. They thought we were going to hurt them or kill them no matter what we said, and they fought to the death." The lump in her throat forced her to pause again. "A few did surrender, but they were terrified. It was awful."

He didn't respond. The seconds stretching into an unbearable silence. "I should go. Zerestria needs me."

Anger flashed through her, but she didn't argue. "Okay."

She hung up before he could say anything else to piss her off and shoved the phone in her pocket. The urge to find him and shake him until he saw sense almost overwhelmed the reasonable part of her brain. It wouldn't work. His resentment ran too deep. If he was ever going to overcome the bitterness, it had to be his choice.

CHAPTER 47

AMBER

Amber tugged the hood of the rain jacket farther down, but it was no use. The rain was coming down sideways. Her shirt was half soaked through, and the short hairs around her face were dripping.

The phone buzzed--no making her wait this time--and she answered it before the second ring. "Please tell me I don't have to go in circles for the next hour in this weather."

Taharia laughed. "Come to the cafe. Same booth. I'll be waiting."

The call ended abruptly, as always. Amber lowered the phone with a frown. Part of her insisted it was some kind of trick, but what would be the point? Taharia had no reason to try to kill her at this point.

She hesitated for a moment and glanced back at the parking lot where Icewind and Genevieve were waiting with a small task force. If she wanted, it might be possible to send them some kind of signal. They could arrest Taharia. With a sigh, Amber shoved her phone into her pocket and headed toward the cafe. This wasn't a trick, but it might be a test. Capturing Taharia wouldn't guarantee their families would be returned. It wasn't worth the risk.

A particularly loud burst of thunder reminded her that she

needed to get out of the weather. Holding her jacket's hood in place, she jogged to the cafe.

Other customers were huddled around the door waiting to leave. She slipped through the mass of people then tugged off her rain jacket. Her shirt was worse off than she thought, and the air conditioning sent goose bumps prickling over her skin.

She ducked past the hostess and spotted Taharia in the back corner, exactly like last time. They probably looked like two old friends meeting for lunch.

Amber slid into the booth across from Taharia. "I appreciate not being led around in circles this time."

"Another extension of trust that I hope you can return." Taharia pushed two plates toward her. One with chocolate pie and the other with blueberry. "I wasn't sure which you would prefer."

She raised an eyebrow but dragged the chocolate pie toward her with a nod. "Hard to beat chocolate."

Taharia took the other plate and picked up her fork. "I have yet to find a pie I don't like, personally."

Amber took a few bites, relishing in the sugar, before setting her fork down. "The task force and MIA are willing to accept your request for protection."

Taharia's eyes flicked up. "But?"

"We can't control the fae."

"I see." Taharia twirled her fork between her fingers. "I'll have to consider whether that will be enough."

Amber bit down on the urge to beg and nodded. "I actually have two requests for you as well."

"Oh?"

"The first is that there is a young succubus we are caring for. She..." Amber took a deep breath. "Fed on Susannah and hurt her. We're trying to work with her, but nothing has helped so far."

Taharia nodded in understanding. "The child was never taught control. The way they feed them..." She shook her head. "An older incubus will allow the children to feed then forcibly remove them when they've had enough to keep them minimally healthy. Eventually, control is beaten into them, but they are never truly taught like they should be."

"That's horrible."

"Yes, it is. It keeps them slaves to their instincts. Saraqael is a master of control, and he designed every aspect of our society to force the lower-ranked incubi into dependency and desperation." Taharia's fingers curled into her palm in a tight fist. "When someone is chosen for promotion, it's as if the gates of heaven have opened. The relief of feeding regularly is intoxicating and addictive. It was many years before I thought beyond my next meal."

"That's how you were raised?"

"Yes. It's the same for all of us going back centuries. Saraqael took control before the fae were cursed. He quashed every rebellion and killed anyone with enough morals to object to his plans." She pressed her lips into a thin line. "It was a bloody time."

"Is there a way to teach Valiel how to feed without hurting someone?"

"With the trauma she has already endured, it will be difficult. You will have to control her physical contact with whoever she is feeding from. Only allow her to feed in short bursts but do it six or seven times a day. Talk to her and reassure her she *will* be fed. You'll have to pardon the analogy, but right now she's reacting like a starving dog would to a pile of meat. She will gorge herself given the opportunity until the desperation is overcome." Taharia shook her head. "It's going to be very difficult."

"And there are hundreds or thousands more just like her, aren't there? More children who will need to be taught."

Taharia's expression grew grim. "You're beginning to understand. Now, what is your second request?"

Amber steeled herself for the next question. It was something she hadn't discussed with the pack, unsure if she should ask at all. But she had to try. It was the only thing she could think of that might convince Kadrithan to hear the incubi rebels out. "Do you know who killed Kadrithan's sister?"

Taharia was quiet for a moment then replied, "Yes."

"I'm hoping that if I can find the person responsible, it could help convince Kadrithan, and all the fae, to help. I wasn't lying when I said we can't control them. He needs to realize that it was Saraqael and the archangels who hurt him, not all the incubi." She pushed her hands through her hair. "I don't want..." She shook her head, still unsettled by the whole plan. "I don't want to just deliver their head on a silver platter or something. But maybe he needs justice for that, at least. He loved his sister."

"If there is a chance it can change the fae's mind, consider it done." Taharia's fingers traced the grain of the table, a distant look in her eyes. "Can you arrange a meeting between us? Tonight?"

Amber was stunned. "That soon?"

"I know who killed Faylen. If he will meet with me to learn the name of the person responsible, I do not want to delay."

Her utter shock rendered her silent for a moment longer, but she nodded. "I can try. I think he'll be willing. How can I contact you if he agrees?"

"I'll call you every hour until you have an answer." Taharia stood, abandoning her pie. "Give me a five-minute head start like last time. I'll trust you to time it yourself." She swept away, practically running out of the cafe.

Amber watched her go as if frozen in place. The suggestion had been a gamble. She'd been sure Taharia would refuse or simply have no idea who killed Kadrithan's sister. She curled her fingers into her palm as hope pounded in her chest.

CHAPTER 48

KADRITHAN

Kadrithan drained the pain-relieving potion. It spread throughout his gut like a cool wave and removed the lingering aches. He still had to be careful--it was only the pain, not the injury that the potion relieved--but he could have this meeting with a clearer mind.

His phone finally buzzed with Amber's response to a question he'd asked almost an hour ago.

No, I'm not coming. Taharia insisted on meeting with you alone. She said it had been too long since an incubi and a fae sat down and spoke peacefully. Said it should be a private moment.

His lip curled in derision. *Perhaps she's worried you'll interfere in her assassination attempt.*

This would be the most convoluted plot in all of history if that was the end goal.

Though he couldn't see her face, he knew she was rolling her eyes right now.

Have you searched her for weapons? Or is your trust in the incubi now so complete that you haven't even bothered?

She's been searched by no less than five people. And I'm sure you're going to do the same. Stop being an ass.

His fingers itched to send a retort, but he forced himself to set his phone down instead. He wanted her to understand, not be angry with him. Though she would likely be angry with him after this meeting regardless. The only reason he was even considering letting the succubus leave the meeting alive was out of worry for Amber and her pack's families. The temptation to kill her remained strong.

A brief knock announced Zerestria's arrival. She swept into the room in her formal attire, her silver dress flaring out behind her like a cape. "The rebel is here. They are almost finished searching her." She scanned his face. "Are you ready for this?"

"I've been waiting years to find out who killed my sister." He stood and adjusted the hem of his jacket. The material was stiff and unforgiving. "Of course I'm ready."

Zerestria looked unconvinced but didn't press the issue. "I see. Walk with me, then."

He joined her, and they stepped out into the hall where a ridiculously large contingent of guards fell into place around them. The elders' message was loud and clear with their insistence that he remain protected while he was still "weak and injured." Some of them seemed to regret their moment of sentimentality that led them to crown him as king when they thought they were all going to die.

"Is Alpha Hale doing well?" Zerestria asked, as if she didn't know better than he did how Amber was doing.

"She seems to be from our brief conversations." He regretted leaving his phone behind already, but it was for the best. Amber would only be a distraction during this particular meeting. He was still surprised Taharia hadn't insisted on her presence. Surely the succubus had to realize how strong an influence Amber had on him since she was using Amber as a way to get his attention.

"Perhaps you can visit her soon."

He glanced at her, surprised she would suggest that at all, much less with so many listening in. "Perhaps."

"We will not hide in this place forever, and you are healing quickly." Zerestria nodded as if it was decided. "I'm sure the MIA agents would be happy to meet with you as well."

"I'm sure they would." Finally, they reached the throne room. It was nothing like the one his parents had ruled from. The room was open to the outside with sweeping patterns of inlaid glass on the walls and ceiling that captured the sunlight in a glittering spectacle. Motes of light seemed to dance through the air as the lush leaves of the ferns that hung from the pillars of the balconies waved in the breeze.

The throne itself was a twisting mixture of emerald and wood, all twisted together as if they had grown up from the marble dais it clung to. And perhaps it had. His ancestors' wild magic had been capable of that and more before the curse.

His guards spread out around the room. Their tabards bore the symbol of his house in gold and red thread. Kadrithan forced himself to walk up the two short steps to the throne and take his seat there. Zerestria stood to his right as his closest advisor. He had forbidden the other elders from attending this meeting––an unpopular decision that he had refused to back down on despite multiple attempts to change his mind.

The chief guard strode into the room, crossed both arms in a salute, and bowed low before straightening. "Your Majesty, the succubus is clear of any weapons or magic. We can bring her in whenever you command it."

Kadrithan nodded once. "Bring her now. There is no reason to delay this any further."

The guard bowed once again and gestured toward his men near the door. It swung inward, and Taharia was led inside between five fae. She looked like a child with a round face and wide blue eyes, not the envoy of an archangel. Appearances could be deceiving, though, and he could feel the power that coursed through her from here. This was not someone to underestimate.

Kadrithan gestured toward the chair that sat a few feet from him. "Have a seat."

The guards parted, allowing her to do as requested, and formed a half circle around her. Taharia sat and crossed her legs, resting her hands on her knees. "Thank you."

He tapped a finger against the cool wood under his palm as he observed her. Her shoulders were relaxed, her hands still, and her breathing even. It took a strong will to walk into the midst of your enemies without showing a single tremor of fear. "Amber told me that you want protection from *me* for the incubi in your care."

"You and all the fae," Taharia replied without hesitation. "It is no secret that many of your people would prefer the incubi wiped out completely."

"Why shouldn't we?"

"Because many of the incubi are innocent. They are as much a victim of the archangels as the fae."

The guards stirred at her bold claim, exchanging looks amongst each other. There wasn't a single fae that believed that--not even Zerestria who had not stopped campaigning for mercy since the curse was broken.

"As you can see," he swept a hand at the room, "everyone here is shocked you have the audacity to say that."

Taharia tilted her head to the side and considered him with curiosity. "Yet, it is true. The archangels take children away as soon as they are born. Anyone who has not been recruited into an archangel's service is fed on. They are all slaves, not to a curse like the fae, but afflicted by the same evil nonetheless. Saraqael and the others are not kind rulers."

He ground his teeth together as his conscience warred with his heart. The niggling doubt that she was not lying bloomed into a problem he could no longer ignore. If it was true... "Amber said you knew who killed my sister."

"I do."

"I want their name."

"I can give you more than a name. I can give the person responsible to you."

He had to take a steadying breath before he was able to reply. "But you will not unless I meet your demands."

She nodded, her expression unrepentant.

"State them."

"They are the same I asked of Amber Hale. If I deliver the one who wielded the blade that killed her to you, do you swear to end your vendetta against the incubi? Will you protect the innocents?"

His fingers tightened on the arm of the throne as he struggled to think amidst the overwhelming rage pounding in his skull. He had a duty to protect the fae, but all he had wanted for so long was to avenge his sister's death. Faylen deserved it. "How, exactly, should we sort out the innocent from the guilty?"

Taharia tensed, finally showing a bit of emotion. "The children and slaves are innocent in every way." She swallowed. "The others...I gave Amber a list of names. They are all I could convince to fight back against the archangels. We have all taken fae lives. All I can ask for them is mercy and a chance for redemption. The incubi will need to be taken care of and taught control in feeding. They can do that." She took another breath and lifted her chin. "Those still in service to an archangel will either surrender or they will fight to the death. I cannot ask anything of you, other than to show mercy if they surrender, but I will not demand it."

Kadrithan turned to Zerestria. "Does that satisfy your need to show mercy to our enemies?"

She held his gaze, her eyes filled with sorrow. "It is a start."

"The children and slaves, if they truly are slaves, will be given to the MIA and human governments. Your rebels will not be killed, but they may be imprisoned under human laws if there is proof of any murders they may have committed." He hesitated over the last point, but Amber's disappointed face flashed through his mind, her accusations of his hate the very voice of his conscience. "If any incubi surrender, we will hand them over to the human governments to do with as they see fit."

A look of pure relief washed over Taharia's face. "Do you swear it?"

"As King, you have my word." His heart thumped with fury and anticipation. "I want the name now."

Taharia stood, the abrupt movement startling the guards into drawing their weapons. She stepped forward calmly, never taking her eyes off of him, and knelt. "It was me. On Saraqael's orders, I killed your sister Faylen." She lifted her chin. "I will accept any punishment, but do not forget what you have sworn."

His sword flared to life in his right hand before the intention to summon it could become a coherent thought. The flames churned in eagerness as he stood. For so long, this was all he had wanted.

Zerestria turned away as if she could not bear to watch. He descended the three short steps to stand in front of the succubus. Faylen deserved vengeance. He met Taharia's eyes as he lifted the sword, wrapping both hands around the hilt. She held his gaze without fear or hesitation. A shout of fury tore from his throat as he swung the sword toward her neck.

CHAPTER 49

AMBER

Amber's heart was in her throat as she followed Zerestria through the glittering halls. Any other time, she'd have admired what was around her, but she couldn't right now. All Zerestria had been willing to say was that Taharia had been the one to kill Kadrithan's sister. Amber dug her nails into her palm, doing her best to stay calm.

Zerestria paused near the door that led into the throne room and looked back at her. "Be gentle with him."

A deep sense of foreboding settled in her gut. "I'll do my best."

With a final nod, Zerestria pulled the door open and waved her inside. The throne itself was empty, and the room appeared to be as well. She stepped over the threshold with a frown as she searched for Kadrithan. Her footsteps echoed off the marble floors as she walked farther inside.

Kadrithan stood at the edge of the room, his arms braced on the balcony railing, partially obscured by a particularly leafy fern. He didn't move as she approached.

"You asked for me," she prompted.

"Zerestria told you what Taharia confessed." His voice was thick with grief, and every muscle in his body was tensed.

"Yes."

"She walked in here today expecting to die." His hands tightened even further on the railing.

Amber shifted uncomfortably on her feet. "Yeah, it seems she did."

"Did you know when you arranged this meeting?"

Her head jerked up in shock. "No! I would have told you. I wouldn't--couldn't--have kept something like that from you."

He let out a sigh and nodded then pushed himself upright. In slow motion, as if it pained him to do so, he finally turned and met her eyes. "And would you hate me if I said I killed her?"

A dozen thoughts and emotions swept through her, but she'd already decided her answer to that question before she walked in the room. She hated his choice, but she couldn't hate him. Not for this. She held his gaze as she shook her head. "No, I don't hate you."

He moved closer and reached out with a shaking hand to trace the scars on her cheek. The warmth of his touch sent goose bumps down her spine, but the moment was over too soon. He dropped his hand and stepped back. "Taharia is waiting for you in the next room. She'll take you to your family."

Shock stole her ability to speak for a long moment. "What?"

"I didn't kill her. I agreed to all her demands." A muscle in his jaw twitched as he ground his teeth together. "Go retrieve your pack's families. We'll talk about the rest later."

"You didn't--why?"

"I wanted to, but when I swung the sword at her neck, the look in her eyes reminded me of you." He took another step back, as if he couldn't bear to be close to her. "And I couldn't do it."

She swallowed down the lump in her throat, at a loss for how to respond. "I...I'm sorry."

Kadrithan laughed once, the burst of noise seemingly startled out of him. "I've finally relented, and now you're apologizing. Every time I think I understand you, I discover I'm wrong." He shook his head and turned completely away.

She hesitated for a moment, her desire to *fix* whatever this was between them warring with Kadrithan's obvious need for space. "I'll text you. Later, after we get them all back."

He nodded, his shoulders stiff with tension, then strode away. His footsteps receded until she was left alone in the silent throne room, completely unsure how to feel.

CHAPTER 50

AMBER

Amber hesitated at the door. There was a muted conversation barely audible through the thick door, but she had no idea who was in there with Taharia. A guard, at the very least. Kadrithan wouldn't have left a succubus alone in the midst of the fae. Whoever it was, they weren't shouting and didn't sound angry. Lifting her hand to open the door was still one of the hardest things she'd ever done.

Taharia wasn't in chains, bloodied, or bruised like she'd expected. Instead, she was having what looked like the fae version of high tea with Zerestria and Leena. There were cakes in the shape of flowers, small crystal cups with no handles, and a steaming teapot that smelled of citrus and sunshine.

Zerestria stood, a wary crease between her eyebrows that dulled her smile. "I apologize for the suspense. It was something Kadrithan deserved a chance to share with you himself."

Amber nodded. "I understand."

Zerestria motioned toward Leena, who immediately stood. "I can't escort you back, unfortunately, but Leena will guard you and Taharia while you retrieve your and your pack's families."

"Right." Amber shifted her weight from one foot to the other. "I guess we can just head out, then? Nothing else to do?"

"No. Nothing else." Zerestria approached and placed a hand on her shoulder, giving it a quick squeeze, then exited out the same door Amber had entered through.

"I need to make a phone call whenever it's convenient." Taharia smoothed a nonexistent wrinkle out of her shirt. "I, ah, had assumed that one of my people would need to make contact this evening to deal with the return of your families."

"Because you came here today expecting to die so you could save them." Amber didn't bother making it a question. Everyone in the room knew it was true.

"Yes. It was a reasonable expectation of how that confession would go." Taharia lifted her chin a bit. "And deserved. There is no justification for what I did."

Amber rubbed her fingers across her forehead. "We should go. You can make a call once we get back to the task force. I'm sure Icewind will want to listen in or something."

Leena gestured for Taharia to walk in front of her, and the three of them filed out of the room. Amber knew the way well enough at this point to get back to the corridor that led to the secret exit. All pretense of having to stay hidden from the other fae was over now, thankfully. She'd hated skulking around like a teenager sneaking in to see her boyfriend.

Amber's body seemed incapable of relaxing between her anticipation about being reunited with her family--which was sure to be *interesting*--and her conflicted feelings over the conversation with Kadrithan. His abrupt change of heart had left her reeling. She'd thought she'd be happy, but there was only a strange sense of loss. As if he'd sacrificed yet another thing for the sake of this bloody conflict.

Leena and Taharia kept up a conversation as they made their way to the house. Amber caught a few snippets but couldn't focus on it. It all seemed friendly, which surprised her even further. Leena *was* someone Zerestria trusted, so she'd always assumed Leena was less prejudiced against incubi than perhaps the average fae, but those kinds of beliefs were always tested when you were face to face with someone that you'd likely fought against before. That may have killed your friends or family.

The pack was waiting right outside the Market. Tommy jumped to his feet as soon as they exited, his eyes locked on Taharia. "Is it done?"

"Yes. Kadrithan has made a deal with her." Amber slipped her hand into her wolf's fur, relieved to be reunited. "Icewind, Taharia said she needs to contact her people so we can meet and get our families back. I figured I'd let you handle that."

Icewind nodded. "We're set up for that in the dining room."

"Leena, can you go with her? I want to talk to my pack."

"As you wish." Leena gave her a short bow then gestured for Taharia to walk in front of her once again.

Amber waited for the three of them to be out of earshot before returning her attention to her pack. "The fae should be fully on our side from here on out. Now that Kadrithan has...softened his position."

"This is good," Ceri said gently, her eyebrows drawn together in concern. "But you look like you got bad news or something."

"No, I just..." She exhaled sharply. "Kadrithan is upset. She, um..." Amber shoved her hands in her pockets and forced herself to stop dancing around the issue. "Taharia is the one who killed his sister. Evangeline's mom."

"If she went in there to confess that, then she knew..." Genevieve paused, her mouth forming a round *oh* of surprise. "She thought he'd accept the trade of her life for his help."

"Yeah."

"And he *didn't* kill her?" Tommy blurted out, immediately looking as though he regretted it. "Not that I wanted him to have killed her, he just always seemed like he had a temper. You remember how he reacted when your wolf banished him right before we rescued Evangeline, right? He completely lost it."

"I think his decision surprised him, too."

"All right, well, it's done. And it's working out much better than anticipated for once." Genevieve nodded as if that settled the matter. "Do we have a plan for getting our families back, or has Taharia not made that clear yet?"

"Didn't get a chance to ask her. We should do that, though. I just wanted to explain privately."

Genevieve nodded. "I'll handle it." She swept toward the house, and the rest of the pack moved to follow, except for Tommy.

He seemed frozen in place, alternating between staring at her and the ground.

Amber stopped and let the others pull away. "What is it?"

"I'm not going with you guys to get them. Someone from the pack should probably stay here, anyhow, and I don't want to go." Tommy's fingers were clenched in tight fists under his crossed arms.

It was on the tip of her tongue to argue, but she bit back the impulse. He had run away from home for a reason. Besides, it's not like she didn't understand having a bad relationship with a parent. If she could avoid seeing her mother today, she would. Hell, it was tempting to stay behind with him, but as alpha, she just couldn't. "Okay. I think you're right. It is best to leave someone behind, just in case this is a trap."

He nodded, and his fingers relaxed a fraction. "And I don't want…" Tommy hesitated. "Even if he asks for me, which he *won't*, I don't want to see him."

"Understood. You won't have to." She tugged him into a brief hug then stepped back. "I promise."

He nodded once. "Thanks."

CHAPTER 51

AMBER

At Velez's insistence, the task force would be moving into position for the hostage recovery in waves. He wanted it kept subtle--with a few groups of agents going to different locations--under the assumption that they were being watched by people loyal to Saraqael.

Because of this, Amber was currently laying shoulder to shoulder with Taharia in Icewind's trunk. Ceri, Derek, and Genevieve were similarly hidden in different vehicles that were taking a slightly different route to the coordinates Taharia had provided them.

She tried not to fidget, but every minute that passed, her anxiety increased. Taharia had been extremely cooperative. She'd made no demands on how many people they could bring. In every way, she seemed determined to prove that her and her rebels were on their side. That they could work together. It felt too good to be true with the luck they'd had lately.

The smooth hum of the highway gave way to a less well-maintained road with bumps that would have been hardly noticeable sitting in the car but were accentuated by the tight space and lack of padding in the trunk. The weight of her wolf on her legs only made the whole thing more claustrophobic.

"Today has turned out pretty weird," Amber said, breaking the awkward silence that had started when they climbed in the trunk.

"Indeed." Taharia shifted a little, her elbow smacking into something metal. "This was not something I envisioned, and I have a talent for predicting all possible outcomes. Somehow, a ride in a trunk didn't make the list."

Amber snorted. "Didn't make my list, either."

Taharia shifted again then turned to peer at her in the dark. "I know I said before that kidnapping your family was to protect them, but I know it was scary for you. I'm sorry for that part of it."

"It's...well, it's not okay, exactly, but I appreciate that you kept them alive."

The car's tires hit the rumble strip on the side of the road as it moved to the right and slowed. Amber's teeth rattled in her skull as she clamped her hands over her ears. Those things were obnoxiously loud on a good day, much less in the trunk. The other set of tires hit it as well, and the car bumped along a gravel road for a moment then stopped.

The trunk popped open a moment later, and Amber glared up at Icewind, who grinned down at them in amusement. "Ready to ride up front?"

"You have no idea." Amber's wolf hopped out first. She swung her legs over the lip of the trunk and slid out. Icewind had turned down a narrow, gravel road that led deeper into the forest. An old, wooden sign that read *Camp Beacon Hill* hung over a sagging metal gate. "Wait...is this a summer camp?"

A smirk tugged at the corner of Taharia's lips as she headed toward the gate. "It's been abandoned for about five years. A half-senile old man owns it. I've used it for a few...projects. No one ever comes here or checks on it. And if they did, we, of course, have forged documents proving we own it. It would buy us enough time to disappear."

Amber shook her head. "That's genius."

She climbed into the front seat of the car alongside Icewind. Taharia undid the lock and pushed the gate inward then closed—but didn't lock—it behind them. They moved far enough down the driveway to be hidden from the road then waited a few minutes for the rest of the pack to catch up. It wasn't long, but it felt like an eternity.

Finally, their small caravan headed into the heart of the camp. It looked as if it had been frozen in time. The paint on the buildings was faded, and the signs hanging in the windows announcing signups for the next year were at least five years out of date. An old truck had been parked by the office and forgotten. All its tires were flat and cracked from the sun.

A group of incubi emerged from the largest building, their hands raised to reassure everyone they had no weapons. Icewind parked in the middle of the open yard between the buildings and glanced back at Taharia. "You need to talk to them first?"

"No. Everything is settled. They'll cooperate."

"Time to go say hello to our new allies, then." Icewind opened her door and climbed out. Amber followed her and Taharia, heart pounding in her chest like a drum.

An incubus moved to the front of the group to greet Icewind. After a moment's hesitation, he held out his hand. "My name is Pravil. I have assumed command of our group at Taharia's request and am pleased to welcome you here."

"Agent Icewind." She shook his hand firmly. "I appreciate your cooperation and the warm welcome."

Pravil inclined his head. "We are honored to join your cause."

The rest of the pack—excluding Tommy and Deward, who had both elected to stay behind—tumbled out of the other vehicles. Genevieve jogged over and stopped at Amber's shoulder. She was practically shaking in anticipation. Derek and Ceri stopped at her other shoulder, and her brother wrapped an arm around her.

"There is much to discuss, but I'm sure you are eager to see your families." Pravil stepped to the side and gestured toward the double doors that led into the building. "They are waiting for you in the cafeteria."

"Go ahead." Icewind stepped aside as well. "We can deal with the practical stuff in a bit."

None of them needed any further prompting. Without even registering that she'd moved, Amber found herself in front of the door. It swung inward, and Amber's heart clenched in her chest. Her entire family was here, gathered with the others at a long table, eating burgers. It was such a bizarrely normal thing for them to be doing that her brain couldn't quite reconcile the sight of them. Part of her was sure this had to be a dream.

Derek rushed past her, spurring her to cross the threshold. Her eldest brother met him halfway and pulled him into a back-slapping hug.

"About time y'all swooped in for the rescue!" Jackson grinned wide. "Though I was hoping for something a little more exciting."

Derek snorted. "We've had enough 'exciting' to last a decade. I'm glad we managed this with no bloodshed."

Amber stopped a couple of feet away, not sure what to do with her hands or her face. The last visit home had been so messy, with hurt feelings all around, and she wasn't eager to repeat any of it. And they might blame her for this. They should.

Jackson turned his grin on her and crossed the distance between them without hesitation, pulling her into a wonderfully tight hug. "Don't have to look like you're walking to your execution, little sister."

She tucked her face down into his shoulder. "Are y'all mad at me?"

He pulled back and ruffled the hair on the top of her head like he'd always done when she was little. "No. We've seen the news. We know you're mixed up in something big." He shrugged. "Not exactly my favorite type of vacation, but you came for us, just like you promised. That's good enough for me."

"Thanks." She took a step back and realized her father was standing right behind him.

Without hesitation, he pulled her into a hug as well, his strong arms squeezing hard enough she thought he might leave bruises. "I knew we could count on you, kiddo." An unexpected burst of emotion put a lump in her throat. She couldn't respond, but she squeezed back. When he let her go, he jerked his thumb over his shoulder. "Your mother is, eh, taking a bit of a nap. I reckon we should get her out of here before she wakes back up."

Amber grimaced. "That bad?"

"She's been...struggling," her father replied diplomatically.

"Understatement of the year." Jacob, her second oldest brother, stepped up for his hug. He'd grown his hair out since the last time she'd seen him and had it tied up in a bun on top of his head. "I think she's finally cracked."

"She cracked seven years ago when Dylan died." Derek had spoken quietly, but with the effect it had on them all, it felt like he'd shouted it. It was something they just didn't mention out loud, especially not around her. "We all know it. Don't look like I just announced some big, shocking secret."

Jacob shoved his hands in his pockets and nodded. "Nah, you're right. We do all know it."

Amber wanted to disappear into a crack in the floor. She was not really prepared to deal with this whole issue here in front of the incubi and everyone else.

Ceri, who had been hovering at the edge of their group thus far, stepped up to Amber's shoulder and stuck her hand out toward Jacob with a grin. "Hi, I'm Ceri, and I'm dating your brother."

The tension fled as her family's attention turned to Ceri and Derek with shrieks of dismay, shock, and loving insults about how there's no way Derek could convince such a pretty woman to put up with him. Much less a *witch*. Amber gave Ceri's hand a quick squeeze then escaped with a muttered excuse about checking on the others that no one paid any attention to.

She tripped over her wolf in her haste to get away. *You did that on purpose.*

You're fleeing with your tail between your legs. It's pathetic. Her wolf trailed behind her as if embarrassed to be seen hurrying away with her.

I'm not fleeing. I just have more important things to do than reminisce. You can't lie to me.

She picked up her pace. It was easier to ignore her wolf when she was just inside her head. Searching for a distraction, she spotted Genevieve and her family. They were all crying and hugging, which was just as bad, if not worse, than what she'd just escaped from.

Stopping in the middle of the room, she frantically searched for a way out. A man she assumed was Tommy's father was slumped at the table, still eating and reeking of beer even from a few yards away. Also not someone she wanted to talk to.

Icewind stepped inside with Taharia and nodded for her to join them. She let out an audible sigh of relief and jogged over to join them.

"If I can pull you away from your family reunion for a bit," Icewind raised an eyebrow with a pointed glance at her family, who she was obviously nowhere near, "Taharia and Pravil said they need to introduce us to the incubi they've been protecting and explain a few things."

"Sounds great." Amber tried not to sound too enthusiastic, but based on the way Icewind's eyebrow rose another inch, it seemed she'd failed.

Genevieve's mother spotted them and waved at Taharia with a big grin then hurried over. "I'm so pleased you didn't end up killed." She pulled Taharia into a tight hug. The succubus looked as shocked as everyone else and went stiff in her arms. After a moment, she pulled back and patted Taharia on the cheek. "You are a brave woman, and I know this has been a little tense, but I think it's worth acknowledging your good intentions."

Taharia's eyes managed to get even wider. "Um, thank you."

She nodded in satisfaction. "I'll let you all get back to it. Good to see you again, Amber."

"You too," Amber replied, still stunned. It was clear where Susannah got her optimism and easy acceptance from. She had no idea how Genevieve had ended up so opposite both of them. Though maybe that was for the best. Someone needed to have the capacity to be mad about *literally being kidnapped*.

Taharia edged toward the door. "That was, uh…something." She cleared her throat. "We really shouldn't keep Pravil waiting."

The three of them hurried out of the cafeteria before anyone else could waylay them, all in a bit of a daze from the unexpected gesture. That mood quickly lifted as they crossed the open yard toward the cabins that were situated down the hill from the main buildings. It appeared they'd been patched up recently--a few shiny new windows, a patch of shingles that weren't darkened from the constant rain, and freshly swept steps.

Pravil waited for them by the center cabin and nodded in greeting. "They're excited to meet the werewolf and the elf."

A small face peeped out the window then disappeared behind the curtain. Amber's brows pinched together in confusion. That had been a child. She wasn't sure who she'd expected they were protecting, but for some reason, children hadn't made the list.

Pravil opened the cabin door, and about ten children filed out. They all looked to be under twelve. A few might have been young teenagers, but it was hard to tell when they were that age. A similarly sized group of children emerged from each of the cabins until they filled the yard. These kids were the "others" Susannah had heard the rebels talking about who had to be protected at all costs. Who Taharia was willing to die for.

"I expected…" Amber shook her head. "I guess more rebels. Maybe families. Are they all orphans or something?"

"They're the children of the archangels."

Amber laughed; she couldn't help it. "All of them? There's got to be fifty of them. That would be crazy."

Taharia didn't laugh. None of the rebels did. "The archangels are anything but sane."

Swallowing down the embarrassment, her eyes slid back to the children. "And they've all just been abandoned?"

"They were cared for. In a sense. You have to feed your soldiers, after all." Taharia's shoulders tensed, and she clasped her hands in front of her. "However, they *were* abandoned when the curse was broken. We were able to get to them before they were separated by the fall. Those of us with enough strength were able to direct our path down to this realm."

Icewind took a deep breath. "How have you been feeding them?"

"We feed them with our spare energy." Pravil crossed his arms and stared her down, as if daring any of them to object.

"And who feeds you?" Amber asked. If they were going to work together and trust each other, she had to ask these questions. She couldn't turn a blind eye to their needs just because it was awkward to press them on it.

Pravil glanced at Taharia, who nodded. He dropped his arms and pushed a hand through his blond hair. "No one right now. We were *lucky*," he spat out the word with venom, "and were able to feed often before the fall. We have enough energy to spare."

"For now," Taharia added with a sad smile. "And only because we've been able to avoid fighting or using magic."

"Using magic drains you?" Amber asked.

They both nodded, and Pravil added, "Quickly enough that it would make it hard to feed the children and fight. Though..." He hesitated again but continued after another nod from Taharia. "Being in this realm helps. It's a slow trickle, but once well-fed, we think our need would be greatly reduced. Even the air in this realm is dense with energy."

"The vampires have never failed to find willing donors." Icewind squared her shoulders. "I'm sure there will be a viable long-term solution for the incubi as well. And for now, if your people can continue feeding the children, we'll do everything in our power to prevent you needing to use up your energy fighting."

"Where will you house them?" Taharia asked.

"My gut is telling me not to move the kids right now. If your people are willing to stay and continue caring for them, I think they'll be happier and safer here." Some leaves fluttered around Icewind's head as she gnawed on her thumbnail with a furrowed brow. "No, I'm sure of it. Moving them is a terrible idea. The incubi we do have in custody have to be kept separate because we've had various attacks, which makes sense now with your explanations of how they've all been feeding for so long. Any objections, Amber?"

"Not that I can think of right now." She shrugged. "We can always reevaluate later."

Pravil appeared stunned for a moment, his eyes flicking between Taharia, Amber, and Icewind. "You trust us that much?"

Taharia huffed out a sigh. "Are you trying to talk them out of it?"

"No, but we all expected there to be more ill will."

"If our families had been anything other than perfectly unharmed, I would have ripped your throats out." Amber smiled, red bleeding across her vision at the thought of it.

Pravil took a half-step back and swallowed audibly. "I see."

"But everyone was fine." She pulled her dominance back with some difficulty and brushed her fingers through her wolf's fur to steady herself. "And you are both clearly motivated to protect these children. I agree with Icewind. Moving them seems risky. We've had enough trouble trying to take care of one kid."

"The child you asked my advice on?" Taharia asked.

She nodded. "Valiel. She's still struggling."

"Bring her to us. We can care for her along with the others," Pravil suggested.

Amber hesitated. "I'll talk to Ceri. She found Valiel, and I'm not sure how she'll feel about sending her away."

Derek hollered her name and waved toward the waiting vans. It was time to get their families home. Finally.

Icewind nodded her head toward the pack with a smile. "You get back. I'll stay here and work out the details."

"You sure?"

"This is actually my job, believe it or not."

"Good point." Amber said a quick goodbye then jogged over to rejoin her pack, only slightly jealous that Icewind had an excuse to stay behind. As much as she wanted to avoid dealing with this reunion, she *had* been worried about her family. She needed at least one afternoon to make sure they were all really okay.

CHAPTER 52

TOMMY

Tommy focused on the burn in his muscles. He hadn't pushed himself this hard in ages. It felt good.

"Down and hold." Ito stopped at the bottom of the pushup and held himself less than an inch above the ground.

Tommy did the same and glanced over at Deward. Unlike him, neither of them were trembling. He forced himself to slow his breathing. That helped a little, but it wasn't going to buy him much time. He was going to fall first. Again. A moment later, his arms buckled, and he dropped face first into the grass.

"That's enough." Ito pushed back up with ease and shifted into a sitting position. "You still haven't completely recovered, have you, Tommy?"

He rolled onto his back and pressed a shaking hand to the scar that was still a shiny pink on his side. His wolf laid on his legs, and the contact immediately eased some of his exhaustion. "Not quite. And every minute I'm not touching my wolf, I feel...wrong."

"It's very unsettling." Ito stared unseeing into the distance for a moment before bringing his attention back to the present. "This separation is unnatural. You should touch your wolf as much as possible for now. It's obviously affecting your healing."

"Crazy how bad it is even after they destroyed that relic. Kinda glad no one got hurt before that." He grimaced as he pushed upright.

"It was extremely fortunate," Deward agreed.

His wolf lifted his head. *They're back.*

Tommy's heart dropped into his stomach, and he had a sudden urge to run and hide. He didn't want to see his father––perhaps sperm donor was a better term since the man had failed at anything resembling parenthood.

Before he could decide which direction to flee, the first car screeched to a halt and the back passenger side door was flung open. A tall woman with red hair the same shade as Amber's stormed out. "We're not staying here! I want to go *home.*"

Derek stumbled out after her. "Mom, come on. It's not safe."

"Because of her!" the woman spat out.

Another man about a half-inch shorter than Derek and lacking the thick beard held up his hands. "That's not really true, and you know it."

"You're all taking her side!" The woman, apparently Amber's mother, pointed accusingly at Amber herself, who now stood by the driver's seat with a blank expression. Her emotions were anything but blank as the shouting continued. Tommy could feel the roiling mix of anger, embarrassment, and hurt from here.

Ito watched the spectacle with a tight frown. "Who is that woman? Amber should not allow anyone to speak to her like that."

"Amber's mother." Tommy cringed as the argument grew even more heated as Amber's mother started to threaten them all for keeping her there against her will.

Ito rose and wiped the grass off his knees. "I see."

Tommy shook his head and stood as well. "She's actually worse than I'd imagined."

"Likewise." Deward's mouth was turned down into a severe frown. "Her effect on Amber, even muted through the pack bond, is extreme."

"This is a good opportunity for another lesson on how a pack should operate." Ito motioned for them to follow.

Tommy scrambled after him, half-eager and half-terrified Ito was about to sock her mother in the jaw or something crazy. He was ninety percent sure you couldn't just challenge a human to a fight, but werewolves had a lot of weird traditions.

The rest of the caravan arrived, and Genevieve's family stepped out of one, followed by his...parental relation. Tommy didn't have long to fret over the man's presence before Ito stepped between Amber's mother and the rest of her family.

"What are you--" Derek's objection was cut off with a wave of Ito's hand.

"This spectacle has gone on long enough. What is your name?" All the chatter was silenced.

Amber's mother appraised him with pursed lips, the red flush on her cheeks deepening. "Miranda."

"What accusation do you lay at the feet of the Alpha Dominus? I will hear your challenge and accept it in her stead."

Miranda's eyes narrowed. "What the hell are you talking about? This is a family matter. It's none of your damn business."

"Incorrect. Amber Hale is my Alpha Dominus--a tie closer than the bonds of family. It is my duty and privilege to protect her from all threats. *You* have threatened her, and I will hear your accusation, or I will remove you from pack lands."

Tommy glanced at Amber and found her staring at Ito's back with eyes the size of saucers. But she wasn't stopping him. In fact, her wolf looked extremely pleased with the whole thing. Ito had said this was a lesson. And he was protecting Amber while the rest of them had just been standing around watching.

With a mental kick in the butt, Tommy forced himself to move and walked over to stand at Ito's shoulder. He crossed his arms and shut out the awareness that his father was here, watching him. Or, worse, still unaware of his existence. His wolf pressed against his legs, and he forced himself to speak. "You've been shouting at everyone since you arrived. Why go quiet now?"

Miranda's hateful gaze snapped to him. "She killed Dylan. My youngest boy." Her voice began to shake. "It's her fault."

"Like hell it is--" Derek stopped when Ito held up his hand once again, but he didn't look happy about it.

"Let her explain herself without interruption." Ito motioned for her to continue. "How did she kill him?"

"She took him to some *pack* and let them *bite* him! He died right in front of her!" Miranda jabbed a finger at Amber, her eyes wild with hate and grief. "She should have stopped him from going!"

"Before an alpha may gift a human the bite that could change them into a werewolf, they must interview the human. Both the alpha and the human must sign a contract and a waiver--"

"Don't give me that crap," Miranda spat.

"You had your chance to speak, and now I will have mine," Ito snapped, the cool and unconcerned mask slipping as anger seeped into his voice. "Your son, Dylan, would have been informed of the risks. He would have agreed to them and would not have been given the bite without a waiting period in which he could change his mind. The only person responsible for his death is *him*. He chose to accept the risk and paid the consequences." Ito took a step forward into her space. "Why would you blame your living daughter?"

"She should have stopped him!" Miranda shrieked. "She always took care of him! Always!"

"That is not a sister's job. A parent's, perhaps, but your son would have been a man by the time he could have been given the bite, and the only person to blame for a man's actions is the man himself." Ito shook his head. "Your accusation is without merit, and your challenge will not be honored."

Miranda spent a moment imitating a fish before gathering herself up and glaring at Ito. "You have no right to do any of this."

Ito, ignoring her completely, turned his attention to Amber.

"Will you allow this woman to stay here under the pack's protection, or do I have your permission to remove her from the property?"

Amber remained silent as all eyes turned toward her. She stared at her mother, and Tommy had a moment of rage as Miranda refused to acknowledge her daughter even now, when Amber held her fate in her hands. "She stays."

Miranda stiffened. "I don't want to stay."

Ito nodded in acknowledgment. "I'll escort her to her room." He flicked his gaze to Miranda. "Where she will remain, under guard."

"No." An older man with graying hair Tommy assumed to be Amber's father stepped into view. "No, this part is my job. Should have handled it years ago, if we're being honest."

"I'll show you the way, then." Ito stepped back and waved a hand toward Thallan's mansion.

For a moment, Tommy was sure Miranda was going to dig her heels in and refuse, but when Carl placed a hand on her elbow, she went with him and Ito.

The whole pack and their families stared at one another, unsure how to break the awkwardness that came with witnessing someone else's family argument.

"Well…" Amber shoved her hands in her pockets and shifted on her feet. "I guess I should introduce everyone." Discomfort still pulsed through the pack bond so strongly he had the urge to tuck his nonexistent tail between his legs.

Lesson learned, Tommy stepped forward. He could do this for Amber. "I'm Tommy." He pointed at the rest of the pack and introduced them in order. "This is Genevieve, Amber's beta. Ceri, our shaman, who I guess you have already met. And this is Deward. He's blind, so don't try to toss him anything, I guess."

Deward rolled his eyes. "I think that goes without saying."

"Jackson. Amber's older brother." Jackson waved at the pack. "And everyone already met our dear, old mother and our dad, Carl.

And Derek. Guess that just leaves Jacob." He patted the man with sandy blond hair standing to his left on the shoulder.

"Nice to meet the infamous pack," Jacob said with a grin. "Derek has kept us updated, but he did leave out the part where he was *dating* one of you."

"Because y'all are nosy as hell," Derek muttered.

Amber laughed. "One of you would have shown up on our front porch if he'd told you that."

"Speaking of…" Genevieve waved at Susie and Steven, who were jogging toward them. Susie broke into a sprint and ran straight into her parents' arms, all smiles and happiness.

Tommy's gaze was drawn unwillingly to his own father, who hadn't moved from his spot near the van he'd arrived in. He was smoking and not paying the least bit of attention to what was going on. His skin was sallow, and he'd gained weight. Unsurprising considering how much beer he'd been drinking when Tommy left.

"Well, what now?" Jackson asked.

"We have rooms set up for everyone in that mansion. You'll have to share, though. Sorry," Genevieve apologized with a shrug. "We're seriously out of space at this point with the task force and stuff."

"And we definitely need to stay for a while?" Genevieve's mother asked.

"Yes. Until Saraqael is no longer a threat," Amber answered firmly. "He may try to hurt y'all again. We just can't risk it."

Jacob stepped forward. "We want to help, though, if we can."

"We're ready to fight. Do whatever it takes." Jackson crossed his arms and pushed his shoulders back. "I know we aren't pack, but we're still family."

Amber was quick in her refusal, but as they dissolved into arguments about who could and couldn't risk their lives, Tommy wondered if it would be good if they helped. It would be ridiculous to give Susie a gun and tell her to have at it, but Amber's older brothers were just as well-equipped to deal with this as they were––which was to say not at all. None of them had the experience or training to go to war or run around with MIA agents, but they were doing it anyhow. He let them argue uninterrupted, though. It was always easier to convince Amber of these things one-on-one.

What followed was a whirlwind. The arguing dissolved into laughter and teasing. Amber's brothers ribbed her and Derek equally. Genevieve's mom seemed to find a reason to hug everyone. He did his best to focus on the good and ignore the man that stayed at a distance, apparently more interested in smoking than anything else.

Ito returned before they managed to get everyone's luggage out of the various vehicles. He paused by Tommy. "I could use help cooking this time."

"Absolutely. Let's go start." It didn't count as fleeing if there was a perfectly good reason to leave. Ito clearly needed his assistance, and he was the best cook in the pack. Definitely not eager to help for any other reason. It was *logical*.

CHAPTER 53

CERI

Ceri had attempted to slip away unnoticed while everyone was eating, but she hadn't made it ten feet out the back door before Derek had caught up. His announcement that he was going with her hadn't even annoyed her. It just felt...nice.

They stepped inside Thallan's mansion, the silence strangely heavy after the joyful chaos of the house, and Ceri tightened her hold on Derek's hand.

He squeezed back. "Talking to them could wait until tomorrow."

"I want it over with. Having them here is like an itch between my shoulder blades I can't scratch."

"If magic wasn't wonky, I'd ask if your mom had somehow managed to curse you."

She snorted. "We'd have never made it past that first talk if we could use magic."

"True." He shook his head. "I really thought her and Amber were going to end up in a fistfight before you got there."

"I'd have only been sad because I would have missed it."

He grinned. "It would have been epic."

As they passed the kitchen, the familiar scent of herbal tea wafted toward her, and she slowed to a stop. That tea was her father's favorite. He'd had a cup every evening as long as she could remember.

"What?" Derek asked, his brow creased in confusion.

"Looks like my father is in there. I'll be just a minute. Wait here for me?"

Derek nodded once. "If that's what you want."

She squeezed his hand with a smile before untangling their fingers. A mess of anxiety and sorrow churned in her gut as she went to face her father. A tiny part of her missed the trust she'd had in him as a child before she'd seen how flawed he was. How flawed they all were.

Her father was alone in the kitchen. Waiting. His eyes flicked to hers, and he leaned forward to rest his elbows on the table. "You retrieved the other families."

"Yes. It's over." She crossed her arms. "The individuals who attempted to kidnap you are no longer a threat. Saraqael and the incubi still aligned with him are. Stay or go, it's your choice."

"We will be leaving."

Something about the weight of his words caught her attention. He didn't mean just that they were leaving the house but that they were *leaving*. The city. The state. Perhaps the country. The question hung on the tip of her tongue for a moment, but she realized she didn't want to know where they'd go. She let that thought settle in her gut until it no longer stung. It was a relief, and that was okay.

"Do you need transportation?"

"No. We drove here."

With a final nod, Ceri turned and walked toward the tug of the pack bond. Away from the lingering bitter resentment for her twisted family. Away from shame and into acceptance. Derek was where she'd left him in the hallway.

He tangled their hands together as he fell into step beside her. "What did he decide?"

"They're leaving." A contented smile pulled at her lips. "Leaving the state, I think, and not coming back."

"You're okay with that."

It wasn't a question, but she nodded regardless and gave his hand a squeeze. "I am. Really okay."

He smiled in return. "Good."

CHAPTER 54

AMBER

Amber sat across from Kadrithan and fiddled with her cup of fae tea. It was the same sunshine-scented blend Taharia and Zerestria had been drinking, and it tasted just as good as it smelled. There were little sandwiches and cakes, too, but her stomach was twisted up in too many knots to even consider eating them.

Kadrithan stared into his own cup like it might hold all the secrets of the universe. Or like he was avoiding looking at her directly at all costs. Finally, he cleared his throat and pushed the cup away. "Your families are settled and recovering?"

"Not much to recover from, honestly. But yes, they're mostly settled." She turned her cup in another circle. The half-drank tea had gone cold. "We've decided not to risk letting anyone go home until Saraqael is dealt with, but we're running out of room in Thallan's mansion since we're hosting the task force as well. Some members of the task force have been stuck sleeping in tents."

Kadrithan finally looked at her. "There are rooms here they could stay in."

She drew her eyebrows together. "In the Market?"

"Yes. I would be happy to provide a place for your families to stay, and there is nowhere safer at the moment."

"That would be amazing. Thank you."

They fell silent again, but it was slightly more comfortable now. She took the opportunity to look around the room, something she'd been too anxious to do up until now. Tall windows flooded the space with early morning sunlight. A shelf stuffed with books took up one wall while their small table and a single leather chair stuffed in the corner took up the remaining room.

"Do you read in here a lot?" She gestured toward a book with a cloth bookmark balanced on the arm of the chair.

"Recently, yes. It's been ages since I've been trapped in such a small space for this long. I'm probably going to try out every sitting room in the tower at this rate." A hint of a smile tugged at the corner of his mouth. "I miss getting to barge in on you at will."

She rubbed the still-aching place on her chest where his mark had been. "I miss that part, too. It was easier than sneaking in here at least."

"It was." He stood abruptly, and his chair nearly toppled over from the force of the motion. "Would you like to go for a walk?"

"Sure." She downed the last of her tea in a large gulp and stood as well. "Where to?"

"Anywhere," he replied, already striding toward the door, leaving her to hurry after him before she was left behind. "There are libraries and sitting rooms and gardens." He paused and glanced back at her. "The gardens on the balconies near the top of the tower have some excellent views."

"Sounds good. Lead the way." She followed him, often having to almost jog to keep up with his long strides. They spiraled up the tower in a winding path that led them through an ever-changing series of rooms and hallways. Every few levels, the theme of the decor changed drastically. Large windows were fairly common, but a few floors were almost completely closed off from the sunlight with cool blues and grays that made her feel like she was underground.

Kadrithan stopped ahead of her on the stairs and pressed a hand to his chest. His heart was beating hard--harder than it should have been--and his skin was pale. She'd been so distracted looking around she hadn't noticed.

"You shouldn't be walking this much, should you?" She moved up two steps to face him.

"They told me I needed exercise."

"And I'm sure they told you to stop when it started aching, too." She tugged at his arm. "Are you bleeding through the bandages?"

"No. I just need to catch my breath."

"Are you sure? I could carry you--"

"Absolutely not!" Sheer horror crossed his face. He pushed off the wall and began making his way--very, very slowly--up the stairs.

"You're being ridiculous!"

"I am not. I simply don't need to be carried like a *child* up the stairs. This is not going to kill me."

She rolled her eyes. "Men are so dramatic sometimes."

He threw a glare over his shoulder. "You wouldn't let me carry you up the stairs if you were hurt, either."

"I would, actually, because I am reasonable." She stepped up beside him and slipped her arm around him. "Stop looking at me like I just ruined your whole day and let me help you this much at least."

He huffed in annoyance but leaned into her support nonetheless. "I could have made it."

"I'm sure."

They hobbled up the stairs together. Kadrithan leaned more heavily against her with every few steps until she was supporting nearly his entire weight. The idiot may have been able to make it to the top, but he would have collapsed when he got there. Amber bit her tongue to keep from yelling at him about it some more, but only because she knew it would only serve to make him *more* stubborn.

They finally reached the last step and stumbled their way into the garden. It was beautiful, but she didn't care about the view or anything else right now.

"Bench." She steered him to the right, and he followed without argument.

A hiss of pain escaped his lips as she lowered him down to the seat. "See? I'm fine." He leaned back and place a hand over his eyes. "Perfectly fine."

She plopped down next to him. "Never felt better, I'm sure."

He dropped his hand and stared up at the vines that wound through the rafters. "I had all these grand plans for when we finally met in person. I intended to sweep you off your feet." He turned his gaze on her as she sat frozen next to him, her heart racing in her chest once again. "It's been very frustrating to be not only crippled, but to have pushed you away every time we've spoken."

She lowered her eyes and fiddled with a loose thread on the outer seam of her jeans. "I...well, I'm still here."

"As grateful as I am for that fact, I have no idea why." His hand settled on her arm, and he swept his fingers across her skin in a caress that left goosebumps everywhere he'd touched.

She watched his fingers move. Before, he'd always been hazy and just out of reach, even when he made himself "solid." The detail had never been there. The lines on his knuckles, the curve of short nails, the ink stain on the edge of his palm. The imperfections were what proved he was real.

As a blush warmed her cheeks, she laid her hand over his. "I had faith you would do the right thing in the end." She swallowed down the lump in her throat. "And I couldn't bear the idea of never seeing you again, not even when I was furious."

"I still hate them," he whispered as he turned his palm to interlace their fingers.

"I know."

He leaned forward, keeping his grip on her hand. "The fae are hosting a celebration tomorrow evening. I would like you and your pack to come as my guests. And your families, as well, of course. We can get them moved in today."

"A celebration?" she asked, drawing her eyebrows together.

"It was Zerestria's idea, but she was right to suggest it. Even though the conflict is not over, we need to celebrate the breaking of the curse." He lifted his eyes to hers. "And honor the pack that made it possible."

She groaned and sat back. "You're going to make me stand up in front of everyone, aren't you?"

He laughed and sat back with her, pressing their shoulders together. "I tell you that I want to honor you in front of all the fae, and you are concerned about stage fright."

"I'm not trying to be ungrateful, I just--I'm not..."

He shook his head with a fond smile. "Neither of us are well-suited for the spotlight. Come suffer through the ceremonies with me, please. No speeches, I promise."

She sighed and slumped further down. "Only because you said please."

CHAPTER 55

TOMMY

Tommy circled Deward with quiet care. No matter how carefully he placed his feet, the troll's eyes flicked to his location as he listened for Tommy's movements.

Between one step and another, Tommy shifted his momentum and swung the padded stick straight at his head. Deward ducked beneath it then shot up and grabbed his wrist. Tommy tossed his weapon to his free hand and swung again, but Deward twisted into him and took the blow on the shoulder where it was too weak to do any harm.

Tommy stepped back with a grin as Deward released his hold. "You're getting more consistent."

"We've done this enough you're starting to become predictable." Deward smoothed a hand over the stray hair that had escaped from his tight braid.

"I think I'm vaguely insulted by that." Tommy twirled the stick in his hand as he narrowed his eyes.

Deward rolled his shoulders, irritation pouring off him in waves. "This is just all so pointless––"

Tommy lunged forward and smacked the padded stick against Deward's thigh with a resounding *thwack*. Then he struck again.

Deward blocked the worst of that blow with the back of his arm, but the tip of the stick grazed his jaw. With a frustrated growl, Deward kicked Tommy in the gut. The force of it knocked him back a few steps, but Tommy moved in again without hesitation and swiped at Deward again from another angle.

Their play-fight grew in intensity as Tommy rained a flurry of strikes down on Deward with increasing power. Deward couldn't block them all, but the troll kept moving and avoided more than he'd done all afternoon. Tommy ignored the growing ache in his side. Moving and really *pushing* both of them was too satisfying.

A particularly hard strike caught Deward across the jaw. Tommy only hesitated for a second, but it was enough. Deward tackled him with a shout. They hit the ground hard, and Deward planted his forearm in Tommy's throat.

"I give!" Tommy wheezed.

Deward rolled off him and collapsed in the grass, panting just as hard. "That hurt."

"What? You didn't *predict* that?" Tommy asked with a grin.

The scowl Deward turned on him was truly impressive, but the hum of amusement through the pack bond took all the heat out of it. "If that had been a real fight, I would have lost."

"Yeah, but it wasn't. And you *are* getting better."

"Better, but still not good enough to go with the pack when they face Saraqael. Not good enough to be left without a babysitter. Not good enough to…" Deward stopped, grinding his teeth together. "I don't see how it will ever be enough."

Tommy pushed himself upright. "Good enough to lead Ceri through the spirit realm. Save the lives of an entire coven. Help us break a curse."

"You're determined to be optimistic, aren't you?" Deward muttered, though some of the tension had left his shoulders.

"You can blame Ceri for that. She never lets me brood, either."

Deward snorted and sat up. "Maybe I'll trip her next time we're in the spirit realm in revenge."

Tommy laughed aloud. "I bet Tessa would help. She strikes me as the mischievous type." He grabbed his phone to check the time and realized he should have been back at the mansion ten minutes ago. "Crap. I didn't think we'd been out here so long."

"Time to feed the dragon?" Deward asked with a smirk.

"Yep."

Deward let Tommy haul him to his feet. They headed inside where the mouth-watering smell of fajitas greeted them. As much as Tommy loved cooking, he'd decided he liked Ito being in charge of the menu even more.

Tommy grabbed a few plastic containers out of the cabinet and loaded them up with meat, veggies, and other toppings. Everyone made their tacos different, and the last thing he wanted was Miranda claiming she couldn't eat it. "Hey, Gen, can you grab two water bottles for me?"

"I'm still surprised you aren't just letting Ito deal with this." Genevieve tossed him both the water bottles he'd requested.

"Someone has to make sure they have what they need. Ito could but..." Tommy tucked the bottles under his arm then picked up the stack of containers. "I don't know, it just feels like it should be one of us, and I have the most free time."

Genevieve gnawed on her lip. "Yeah. I already feel like crap for not getting in the middle of that argument with her mom."

Tommy lifted one shoulder in a shrug. "Ito said it's because we're still trying to apply human thinking to pack dynamics. Maybe if we weren't tied together so closely, it'd be better not to get in the middle of someone else's family drama. But it's *our* family drama now."

"At least Gen's parents are nice," Ceri said with a grin as she stacked three tortillas on her plate. "You think they'd adopt us all?"

"Ugh, don't tempt them. My mom would be here with paperwork before you could *blink*." Genevieve buried her head in her hands. "She's still wearing the *Bitten = Born* glitter shirt everywhere."

"I like it!" Tommy exclaimed. "She's the only person who has ever been enthusiastic about it. Literally, the only one. Even we were all just freaked out at the beginning."

Genevieve opened her mouth to object then snapped it shut with a frown. "Never thought about it that way."

"We sound so tragic," Ceri said with a wry grin and a shake of her head.

Tommy snorted. "Guess that's why we all fit together so well."

He double-checked he had everything then hurried over to the headquarters. Amber's parents had been moved to the same rooms Ceri's parents had stayed in since they were more isolated. Miranda refused to see or speak to anyone but Carl--which suited everyone just fine. Amber's brothers had lost all patience for their mother's behavior and were spending most of their time either with Amber or the trolls.

Eager to get his delivery over with, Tommy left his pack to argue over who should adopt who and whose family was worse. That was one contest he didn't even want to try to win. He preferred ignoring his father's existence just like he was ignored. It was easier that way.

The headquarters was teeming with activity, as per usual. He ducked inside and hurried upstairs. A few of the people he passed acknowledged him with a nod and a wary glance at the wolf pressed to his side, but no one attempted to stop him or talk to him. Most of their allies gave him and his pack a wide berth. A mix of prejudice and fear kept everyone from treating them with anything approaching friendliness. Overall, he was fine with it. Socializing was the last thing on his mind in the midst of this conflict.

Tommy rapped once on the door then waited as Carl's heavy footsteps approached. The older man opened the door a crack at first but pulled it wider when he saw who it was.

"Fajitas today. I brought a bit of everything." Tommy handed the still-warm containers over. "Need anything else?"

Carl hesitated for a moment. "One thing. Let me set all this down. I'll be right back."

Tommy nodded, and Carl disappeared back into the room for a brief moment before rejoining him in the hall. "What did you need?"

A look of concern mingled with determination on Carl's face as he struggled to find words for whatever he wanted to say. "I've never been good at saying what needs to be said. So, I suppose this whole..." Carl waved his hand at their general location. "I suppose it's been good for me. Made me sit with some things I'd gotten too good at ignoring."

With some effort, Tommy bit back what he *wanted* to say and nodded. "Okay, but I'm not really sure where you're going with this. We don't really even know each other."

"I..." Carl hesitated again, and for a moment, Tommy thought he might give up on whatever grand speech he'd worked himself up to, but he pushed out his chin and kept going. "I let Amber and my wife down when Dylan died. Spent so much time grieving that Miranda had no damn support, and I never bothered to check on Amber. He was her twin. Don't know if she told y'all that." Carl stared hard at his shoes, hands clasped tightly together behind his back.

"She did." Tommy wasn't sure how much to say or why Amber's father was telling *him* all this and not her. "She still wears Dylan's jacket sometimes. It got torn when she was bitten. I patched it for her."

Carl was quiet for a long moment. "Didn't realize she kept it."

"No offense, but I don't think I'm the one that needs to hear all this. Amber is."

"I'm planning on telling her, but I've just spent nearly a week with your father and had an inkling you might need to hear a little of this, too."

Tommy stiffened. "You here to tell me I should forgive him or some crap?"

"No. He let you down and hasn't even tried to fix things. Maybe he will one day, maybe he won't." Carl took a deep breath and stood up straighter. "When Amber first left, I thought she was just running away. Punishing us, maybe." He shook his head. "But she was right to leave, and she was right to stay away. We were hurting her, and no one, not even family, has a right to do that. Especially not family." Carl's shoulders hunched in, and he cleared his throat uncomfortably. "You deserved to be treated better. Your mother's death wasn't your fault any more than Dylan's was Amber's. It's one of life's greatest tragedies that becoming a parent doesn't make us better people. We keep all the same flaws, and our children pay the price." Carl shoved his hands in his pockets, and for a moment, the resemblance to Amber was overwhelming. "Do you hate him?"

"Are you asking if Amber hates you?"

Carl sighed. "I suppose I am."

Tommy picked at the hem of his shirt as he thought about his answer. "To be honest, she never talks about you. She's mentioned her brothers, and her mother once, but never you."

Even without a bond to tie them together, the pain in Carl's face was obvious. "All right." He nodded and took a deep breath. "You, uh…thank you. Amber is lucky with the pack she found. The family."

"We'd never have survived without her."

Carl held his gaze for a moment then nodded. "I'm glad you did. Survive. I hope you have a chance to live, too."

Tommy stood frozen in the hallway, fingers gripped tight in his wolf's fur as Carl walked back into his room and shut the door. The conversation thrummed under his skin, old wounds and the ever-present bitterness he ignored so well feeling raw once again. But not as raw as he'd expected. Carl was right; he and Amber both deserved better. And they'd found better with each other.

Nothing would ever take away the pain of a father who'd abandoned him, but one man's failure didn't mean he would never have a family or know unconditional love. Becoming a werewolf was a gift, and he would never take it for granted. Family was the most valuable thing in this world--real family. The kind you choose and would choose again, not the miserable luck of shared genes.

Tommy took a deep breath and turned away, following the pack bond back home.

CHAPTER 56

Ceri had a tight grip on Valiel's hand as they hopped out of the car and approached the main hall of the camp. Unlike her, Valiel wasn't even remotely nervous. The little succubus was thrilled to be out of the room she'd been staying in with Ithra. To be fair, she had been cooped up there long enough to make anyone a little stir-crazy.

"If you get scared, or don't like staying here, you *can* come back to the house, okay?"

Valiel rolled her eyes. "Pravil promised me do-nuts. I will be okay."

Deward chuckled and shook his head. "I miss the days when everything was that simple."

"You and me both." Derek, who had Valiel's other hand, shook his head in commiseration. "Though donuts do still make a bad day better."

Valiel nodded with a serious expression. "Even though they are not humans."

Pravil, the promiser of donuts, emerged from the cafeteria to greet them. He bowed slightly then knelt in front of Valiel. "Welcome. The others are excited to meet you."

"I smell lunch." She tried to peek around him, but the doors were closed.

Pravil stood with a smile. "They're just waiting on you for it to be served." He turned his attention to Ceri. "Whenever you're ready."

She took a deep breath and forced herself to nod. This was the best option for Valiel. They couldn't take care of her like she needed, and they clearly couldn't keep her hunger satiated. It hurt, though. She'd become very fond of the little succubus since finding her in that swamp.

They followed Pravil into the cafeteria, where dozens of tiny, curious faces turned to stare at them. The incubi children sat in neat rows at the long tables, the plates in front of them heaped with burgers and chips. One particularly eager girl waved at Valiel.

"Astrea volunteered to show Valiel around the camp and share a bunk with her." Pravil gestured at the girl. "You can sit next to her, Valiel."

Valiel didn't even hesitate. She dropped Ceri and Derek's hands and bounded over to her new friend, where she slipped onto the bench. The two succubi immediately began chattering, and the kids descended on their food.

"Well, that's good. She's not scared at all." Ceri put her hands on her hips and nodded decisively. "Very good."

Derek wrapped an arm around her shoulders. "You can stop repeating that now and be sad if you want."

"Shut it. I'm fine. This is good." She pressed her lips firmly together to prevent herself from saying that for a fourth time. Derek, blessedly, kept his mouth shut about it.

"We will keep her safe, and the pack is always welcome to visit the children."

"Once Saraqael is gone," Ceri reminded him. After this visit, no one else was coming near the camp to ensure it would stay safely hidden.

"I can update you whenever I see you, and she knows she can talk to any of us if she wishes to leave."

"I know. And that would be good." She sighed. "Just feels like I'm abandoning her, I guess."

"She will do better with people who can teach her control." Deward patted her elbow. "And she is safer here."

"She looks happy." And she did. Valiel was back to grinning, finally. After the whole debacle with Susannah, she'd wondered if they'd scarred the poor kid for life. This really was the best option. These kids all understood her struggle. They were dealing with it right alongside her, and they could help her.

"Perhaps we should leave while she is distracted," Deward suggested gently.

Ceri nodded. "Good point."

They slipped back out of the cafeteria, and Pravil reiterated his promises to keep them updated. Relief mixed with guilt as they drove away. Sometimes, the right choice felt pretty crappy.

CHAPTER 57

Genevieve mentally reviewed the checklist one last time as their group walked toward the Market. Deward's family had brought over their golf cart to transport all the luggage since a car couldn't make it back into the woods. Everyone was accounted for. Their families would be even safer––and it was a huge relief to have them out of Thallan's mansion. Even though it was the safest place for them, the headquarters was a target for their enemies. The Market, on the other hand, was the safest place in the world right now.

Her mom jogged up and linked their arms together. "You look lost in your thoughts."

"Just making sure we haven't forgotten anything." She glanced back. "Where is Susannah?"

"With Deward's cousin and the pixies, of course." Her mother shook her head with a fond smile. "They're plotting a way to reach out to the swarm near our house."

"I thought she'd want to see the Market over pixies."

"Apparently, she'll have *plenty* of time for that later, but the esteemed cousin will only be here for the afternoon."

"Well, I can't wait to see inside. Only Amber has been inside since the fae took over, and she said the palace is awesome."

Zerestria stood outside the secret entrance with Amber and was greeting each person before they entered.

"Where is Dad?" Genevieve asked as she glanced back over her shoulder.

"He got held up in the back somewhere with Derek. They were talking about cars."

She raised an eyebrow. "Dad doesn't even know how to change the oil."

"I think that may have been the issue at hand. Derek was rattling off instructions about something."

Amber's mother was the first to enter. She walked past Amber without so much as a glance and strode straight through the portal. Her father paused to pat Amber's shoulder before he followed his wife inside.

They were next up. Genevieve linked her arm with her mother and stepped through the portal with an excited grin. A blinding flash of light hit her like a gut punch. She found herself sprawled out on the grass blinking up at a whirl of branches and sky with spots dancing across her vision. The whole world was spinning like she was on a tilt-a-whirl.

Her wolf looked down at her. *We're banned from the Market.*

"Ah crap." She pushed upright and glared at the pack who were all *laughing hysterically* at her. The traitors. "It's not funny!"

"It's a little funny." Her mother sat up beside her and picked some leaves out of her hair. "Are you banned, too?"

"Too? I thought you got kicked back because we were connected. Why are you banned?"

Her mother threw her hands in the air. "All I did was throw a turkey leg at a man's head. He was being *very* rude to one of the vendors. It was way out of line."

"You can't just throw turkey legs at people!"

"Well, what did you do?" Her mother crossed her arms.

"I tried to punch a werewolf that had been stalking us and called me a very rude name." She stood and dusted more leaves off her butt. "I didn't waste a turkey leg."

"That werewolf did have it coming," Amber agreed with a grin as she helped Genevieve's mother back to her feet. "But the turkey leg attack sounds pretty spectacular, too."

Her mother bowed with a dramatic sweep of her arms. "Thank you. Glad someone appreciates me."

Genevieve rolled her eyes. "You're ridiculous."

"Though this is a bit of a complication." Amber pursed her lips. "Obviously you can stay in the house, or something, at the very least."

Zerestria strolled up, an amused twinkle in her eyes. "I believe our benevolent king has the power to pardon their crimes and allow them entrance."

"Oh, thank goodness." Genevieve breathed out a sigh of relief. "I don't suppose he's free?"

"I'm sure he can spare a moment for this."

Sure enough, less than ten minutes later, Kadrithan had arrived in his fancy clothes. It was weird seeing him real and solid. She generally pictured him as the ridiculous red devil form he'd often taken, so it was easy to forget he was an actual person.

An absurd number of guards had spread out around him, effectively blocking them from view. Which was also extremely odd to see. He'd always just been their own, personal demon. She really couldn't wrap her head around his royal status.

He stopped beside Amber and smirked at her. There was the annoying demon she was so familiar with. Turning to her mother, he plastered on a much more polite expression. "I hope you didn't bang your head when you were tossed out."

Her mother waved away his concerns. "Honestly, it was kind of fun."

Kadrithan's polite smile widened into genuine amusement. "I'm sorry I missed it." He straightened and assumed spread his arms imperiously. "You are both pardoned for the violent actions you took within the protected realm of the fae. Please, enter and be at peace."

Genevieve lifted her chin and stuck a foot over the threshold, just to test it. Nothing happened. She let out a sigh of relief and took a decisive step into the Market. Magic tingled over her, but it felt accepting.

"Oh. Expected it to be a bit brighter in here, to be honest." Her mother moved up a few steps and looked around the dank stairwell with open curiosity.

A lovely fae woman appeared above them with a torch. "Sorry to leave you waiting. You can follow me."

They followed her upstairs as the others filed in through the portal. No one else got booted out, since they were all such saints apparently. Kadrithan had set aside a whole floor just for their families, complete with grand rooms, libraries, gardens, and a cozy kitchen and dining room. It was everything she'd hoped for and more.

"Susannah is going to adore this place," her mother declared as she twirled around in the kitchen.

Her father laughed. "Perhaps not as much as you."

"It's like a fairytale! I mean, who would have imagined we'd be invited by a *king* to hide out in a golden palace never before seen by human eyes?"

"Well, when you put it like *that*," Genevieve agreed with a grin.

Amber's oldest brother Jackson opened the refrigerator and pulled out several bottles of fancy-looking wine to the delight of everyone there. "You think fae drinks have more alcohol or less?"

"Only one way to find out!" Derek grabbed a bottle and set about searching for a way to open it.

Tommy hovered at the edge of the group, his eyes locked on his father's back. Anger crawled down Genevieve's spine. The man hadn't even *attempted* to talk to Tommy, yet he had the audacity to hang around eyeing the wine like it was manna from heaven. It was ridiculous and unforgivable for him to not even try. And no matter how much Tommy said he didn't want to see or talk to his father, she knew it still hurt to be ignored. Shame, anger, resentment, and a lingering sadness all pulsed through the pack bond despite his best attempts to suppress it.

Her dad clapped a hand on Tommy's shoulder, startling him. "Genevieve tells me you're studying for your GED. You thought much about college?"

She smiled as Tommy fumbled through an answer. It was good to have family closer. She needed to make more time to see them in the future.

CHAPTER 58

KADRITHAN

The narrow streets of the Market were full. Kadrithan leaned against the balcony railing as he swept his gaze over the gathering. Long banners undulated in the steady breeze, their bright colors reflecting the mood of the fae. He had been caught off-guard by the level of excitement. Zerestria, of course, was smug at being right once again. His people had needed this. Needed to celebrate and feel alive. An abundance of music, wine, and food certainly seemed to help, as well.

He moved away from the balcony to mingle with his guests before the food was served. His eyes caught on Amber, and for a moment, he could not look away. She wore the same dress he'd first seen her in at the werewolves' conference. The sleek gold and black gown was no less entrancing with familiarity. He forced his gaze away. People would notice if he stared. His every move was under scrutiny tonight. And not everyone watching wished him well.

Inviting the incubi that had defected from Saraqael's rule had been a risk. Perhaps even stupid. Every time he caught sight of them, his hand twitched toward his sword. He felt pinned between his former enemies and the elders whose suspicious gazes crawled over his skin.

Zerestria approached and handed him a goblet of wine, which he accepted with a nod. "The celebration is going well," she commented.

"For now. They're circling like vultures."

"Less of them than I expected, though." Zerestria gestured toward two of the elders that had remained neutral thus far but were now introducing themselves to Amber and Genevieve. He hadn't wanted the crown, but it still rankled that so many of the elders had only been willing to acknowledge his birthright when they expected him to die.

"I suppose you want me to celebrate this small victory as well?" He knew he sounded as petulant.

"I want you to drink your wine, eat good food, and speak to the guests you invited." She took a drink from her own glass and gave him a placid smile. "You are perfectly welcome to be miserable while you do it."

He ground his teeth together. "I don't know why I bother listening to you at all anymore."

Zerestria simply laughed and walked away, abandoning him to his fate. He drained the goblet and set it aside. If he lingered here any longer, all alone, there really would be gossip. And he'd end up drunk before the first course was served.

Steeling himself, he strode himself into the fray. While all eyes flicked to him as if magnetized, the people parted with bows as he crossed the room. It was strange to be the focus of so much attention after working in the shadows for so long.

Amber, the only one here who didn't care at all about his status, met him halfway there. Her wolf stayed pressed to her side, though the wolf's red eyes were locked on him. "Mind if I join you?"

"Not at all. I'd appreciate it, in fact." He glanced uneasily at her wolf. After the banishing incident, he'd never felt entirely safe around her.

"I figured." She pressed her lips together, as if holding back a smile. "You looked a bit like you'd swallowed a lemon."

A smile tugged at the corner of his mouth. "My expressions were easier to control when I was projecting. I'm out of practice."

"Don't feel bad. Apparently, I suck at controlling my face, too. Ito said I fidget."

"He's not wrong."

Amber scowled at him, but there was no heat behind it. "You could have warned me I was so obvious."

"Then I'd have an even harder time figuring out what you're thinking." He turned his attention to the incubi while Amber grumbled about *untrustworthy demons* and *stupid men* under her breath. Only three of the incubi had come, one man and two women.

The man stepped forward as they approached and bowed. "Alpha Hale, it is good to see you again."

"You too, Pravil," Amber replied with an awkward half-bow, half-curtsey, as if she wasn't quite sure what to do with herself. "This is Kadrithan--King--" She stopped trying and huffed out a sigh. "Just introduce yourself. I don't know the rules for all this formal stuff yet."

Pravil's face paled in a mixture of horror and disbelief, and he bowed again, as if that could make up for whatever faux pas he feared he'd stumbled into.

Kadrithan held back the laughter threatening to bubble out of him, but only just. "Considering the three of them know exactly who I am, it's fine to simply introduce Pravil then allow him to introduce his companions."

Amber nodded. "Right. Of course. Kadrithan, this is Pravil. He is our liaison and has been very helpful."

Pravil, still nervous, managed to recover and introduce his companions--Yvas and Briada--and make it through the niceties that these sorts of formal events generally required. Throughout the entire thing, Kadrithan could feel the eyes on his back. Some of his guests were bold enough to point or direct a scowl toward their group.

"Your invitation was unexpected but much appreciated," Yvas

said, holding her chin high as the unhappy whispers around them grew audible. "Those of us who are eager for this useless war to end were not sure if our races could be friendly, though I know I have hoped it would be possible."

Kadrithan inclined his head in agreement. "I'm sure it will take time, but I am happy to provide the opportunity for reconciliation."

Anger still simmered in his gut, but the more he said it, the closer he came to believing his own words. He *did* want peace. And unnecessary bloodshed wouldn't bring them that. These incubi had risked their lives to challenge Saraqael even though they would have benefitted from staying neutral at the very least.

He watched Amber from the corner of his eye. She was practically beaming as they spoke with the incubi, unaware or uncaring that so many were disgusted with them for even having this conversation. As usual, he envied her resolve. She always made it seem so easy to do whatever she deemed *right*.

CHAPTER 59

GENEVIEVE

The cheery dance music that echoed into the quiet hallway was jarring. Genevieve tightened her grip on the phone as horror flooded through her. "How many dead?"

"At least five hundred. Maybe more. They haven't finished counting." Icewind's voice was flat, reciting the numbers like she was relaying the weather. "The NYC location was completely wiped out."

"And you're sure..." She took a deep breath and swallowed down the lump in her throat. "You're sure it was Saraqael?"

"He left a note for Amber."

Genevieve slid down the wall and pulled her knees to her chest. "What does it say?"

Icewind cleared her throat. "Amber, I have paid sorely for my mistakes. You made clear to me my weaknesses, and now it is time I return the favor.'"

"He's off to a damn good start." Her hand shook as she pressed it to her eyes. They'd expected an attack on the fae or the house. They'd never considered that Saraqael would kill his own people.

"What he did today isn't just for us. He's sending a message to the incubi as well. They're not going to go with police peacefully anymore. Not when it's a death sentence."

Her mind spun into a list of worst-case scenarios. Saraqael had shown how much damage he could inflict and how horribly willing he was to do it. "We have to find him."

"I don't think he's trying to hide anymore." Icewind sighed into the receiver. "We were already able to trace the incubi who carried out the attack back to a place nearby in New York City––the Woolworth Building. The trail they left feels...intentional."

"That can't be a good sign. He hasn't been stupid up to this point, so if he's just broadcasting where he is, it's because he thinks he's untouchable, right?"

"Pretty much," Icewind agreed, frustration clear in her voice. "We need to meet, but we also need to keep this under wraps as long as possible so we don't have a panicky public on our hands, too. We'll have maybe a day before it gets out. Don't interrupt the fae's celebration."

"Got it. I'll find Amber and Kadrithan. Tell them what happened and that we have to keep it quiet."

"I'll call you again in a few hours. Don't plan on sleeping any time soon."

"Yeah. I figured."

They ended the call, but it was a long moment before Genevieve found the strength to push back up to her feet. The whole world seemed to have tilted on its axis. They'd fought many battles at this point but never against someone like this. Someone willing to burn down the whole world out of spite.

She plastered a smile on her face as she waded back into the revelries. Amber met her eyes across the room, and Genevieve knew she could feel that something was wrong. The whole pack had to be feeling it at this point. Her heart was trying to beat its way out of her chest. She dug her fingers into her wolf's fur and gave Amber a slight shake of her head to indicate the need to be subtle.

This had changed everything. What little time they thought they had to find Saraqael or plan for a fight was gone. Once again, they were fighting on his terms.

CHAPTER 60

EVANGELINE

Evangeline retched into the toilet. Every time she caught her breath, the nausea rolled through her again.

Someone banged on the door. "I need to pee! Hurry up!"

"Go outside!" she shouted back before vomiting again. Her fingers clenched around the rim of the toilet seat until it stopped and she could finally breathe again.

"Just get out!" The banging resumed with renewed fervor.

Evangeline wiped her mouth with the back of her hand and stood on wobbly legs. Inhale, one, two, three. Exhale. Her now-empty stomach churned, but she managed to hold back the nausea. For now.

The constant pounding was only adding to her headache. She yanked the door open, and the jerk on the other side almost toppled over. It was Samantha, one of their newest "recruits" and a complete pain in the ass so far.

Samantha blinked at her, eyes glassy from drugs or alcohol. Maybe both. "Oh, it's you. Sorry. I didn't--"

"Yeah, I'm sure." Evangeline shoved past her. The abandoned theater they were hiding out in had been built in the 1920s. It had shut down sometime in the 1970s and *clearly* hadn't been cleaned since.

She wove through the dusty seats in the concert hall. Most of their group slept in here on cushions they'd ripped out of the chairs on top of the petrified popcorn and discarded ticket stubs from the final show that still littered the floor. The creepy cherubic statues that dotted the walls loomed overhead like chubby gargoyles. She swore they were watching everyone, which was part of the reason she spent as little time in there as possible.

One thing the time with Katarina and Charlie had taught her was how to sleep in uncomfortable places. She made do with a sleeping bag in a more secure part of the theater, uninterested in the late-night conversations everyone else seemed to thrive on. The stench of cigarettes and other things they smoked made her nose burn––though she couldn't get away from that anywhere in the theater.

She paused in front of the door to the storage room and pressed a hand to her stomach. *Stop thinking about it.* As usual, her brain didn't listen to her. The incubus's unseeing eyes were staring back at her every time she shut her eyes. She'd killed before with Katarina, Charlie, and her mother. But it hadn't been like this. She hadn't *felt* the last of their soul slip out of their bodies. She hadn't known how awful it would be for someone to die while she fed.

With a frustrated sigh, she shoved the door open and stalked inside. She needed to get the taste of bile out of her mouth.

Thallan glanced up from his makeshift throne––quite a few of the theater's chairs had donated their cushions for his master-piece––and eyed her with suspicion. "You look unwell."

"So do you."

He snorted. "Of course *I* do. I'm dying. You, however, just fed. There's no excuse."

She shrugged then tilted her head to the side. "Can you get food poisoning from bad people?"

Thallan chuffed out a laugh. "Perhaps." He extended his half-smoked cigarette toward her and waved a hand at the stack of liquor bottles. "That should get the taste of vomit out of your mouth."

She rolled her eyes and grabbed the last can of warm soda from the now-empty carton instead. "One of us needs to be sober. And cigarettes stink."

He took a long puff before looking back up at her. "You never complain when I smoke."

"Would it stop you?"

He exhaled a long plume of smoke from his nostrils. "No."

"Waste of time and energy to ask then, isn't it?"

"I suppose so." He twirled the cigarette between his fingers and watched the smoke go up in jagged spirals. "Saraqael made his move earlier tonight."

She froze. "Why are you telling me just now?"

"Because I only found out a few minutes ago." He swung his legs off the side of the cushions and stubbed out the cigarette. "The MIA is trying to keep it a secret. I only know thanks to my informant."

A frown tugged at her lips. "Why would they do that? It's not like people are unaware of what's going on."

"Because it makes them look bad. Out of control." He poured himself a glass of cheap scotch. "Saraqael wiped out one of their little refugee camps. Killed everyone there. Agents and incubi alike."

Her heart froze in her chest then leaped into overdrive. "He killed the incubi?"

Thallan nodded once. "And left the head of an archangel on a stake in the midst of all the carnage. Apparently, he considers them all traitors for accepting the help of *humans*." He smirked. "Saved us a bit of trouble, though."

Part of her agreed, but something in her gut twisted at the news. The incubi were the enemy. *Saraqael* was the enemy. "He was stupid to kill them."

"Every mistake he makes only helps us." Thallan swallowed

down the scotch and looked at her, his eyes searching her face with intent. "Are you sure this is still what you want to do?"

She crushed the now-empty soda can and tossed it in the growing pile by the defunct popcorn machine. "You going to ask me that every day?"

He tilted his head to the side. "Yes."

"Why? I thought we'd already established asking pointless questions is a waste of time and energy." Magic—useless and unruly—tingled at the tips of her fingers as anger rushed through her. She was tired of the prodding and doubting. She had found *him* after all. Recruited *him*.

"I'm not the one vomiting in the bathroom every time I kill someone."

She ground her teeth together. "Having the energy of some disgusting parasite in me makes me nauseous. My conscience is just fine."

"Of course. My mistake."

The door banged open, and Camus strode in, fury clear on his face. "This King has betrayed us."

"What?" Evangeline knew now that her dear, old uncle was actually king of the fae.

Camus had joined them after the curse had been broken, dissatisfied with the fae's decision to stay huddled in the Market like scared children instead of striking when their enemy was at their weakest.

"He hosted a *celebration*," Camus spat out the word, "for the breaking of the curse and invited some incubi that claim to have defected. He *dined* with them."

Anger rippled through Evangeline. After everything that had happened, she'd never imagined that Kadrithan would do this. That he'd accept them. She curled her fingers into a fist. "Have you found that group of incubi we suspected were hiding out in Manhattan?"

Camus's eyes snapped to her. "Yes."

"We go tonight."

CHAPTER 61

Amber dragged the brush through her wolf's dense fur just to give her hands something to do. As soon as they'd been able to slip away from the celebration, they'd met Icewind at their house only to find out there'd been another attack already. Another slaughter. No note or head left on a stake this time, but the message was still loud and clear. Saraqael would keep killing until he was stopped.

"These incubi weren't in MIA custody." Icewind pushed the file away in frustration and slumped back in her chair. The dining room had been claimed for an impromptu meeting once again. Leena and Venali were here along with the whole pack. And Tessa, who Amber was starting to suspect was magically tethered to Ceri. "If they were another rebel group, there's no evidence of it. None of Taharia's group recognized them."

Leena pulled one of the crime scene photos toward her. "It is odd."

"Do you recognize any of them?"

"No, but if I can bring the footage back to Zerestria, someone might."

"Worth a try." Icewind pushed her hands through her hair. "This one has already hit the news, which means we have even less time than I thought before the first massacre is out."

Amber stood and tossed the brush aside. "We know he's sitting in the Woolworth Building. How long do we wait before we just kick down the door?" Her anger was clear in her voice, but Icewind seemed to understand it wasn't directed at her.

"I don't know. Velez wants to go now; I'm more wary." Icewind's eyes strayed to the crime scene photos. "But delaying may not help us at all. It may be what Saraqael wants."

"What about the surveillance? Has the MIA gotten *any* information from it?" She hated waiting. There was no outlet for the anger, only the sick anticipation of the coming fight.

"Only that there are a large number of incubi there."

"We need to find the other relics," Ceri interjected. All eyes turned to her. "Magic has stabilized a bit, but the whole pack is at risk fighting like this." She gestured at Amber's wolf.

"Going back to the spirit realm is a risk." Deward nodded his head toward Tessa. "And we got lucky identifying the location last time."

Ceri chewed on her lip for a moment. "Since we destroyed one relic, it should be less of a risk to go back this time."

"That's true," Deward agreed.

"If there's a chance we can locate them, we should probably take it." Amber tapped her fingers against her crossed arms. "But I'll leave it up to the two of you since you're the ones that would have to do it."

Deward lifted his chin. "I am willing to try."

"Me too." Ceri straightened her shoulders and put her hands on her hips. "The coven should be able to help, too. Anchor us. We were able to cast some spells as a coven with Deward's help; this should be no different."

Amber took a steadying breath. "All right. We'll wait for that then, at least. Find the relics, then make a decision."

Icewind nodded in agreement. "That's a good start."

"I need to get some fresh air. Call me if you need me." She did her best to walk toward the back door calmly, but all she wanted to do was run. The urge to shift crawled over her skin despite her complete inability to do so. It was infuriating.

Halfway across the yard, Ito spotted her and jogged over to catch up with her. "Where are you going?"

"To run. I have to do something before I punch a hole in a wall."

"I'll run with you. Trying to keep up with me should help burn off your nerves."

"Trying to keep up? There's no way you're that much fa––" She was forced to scramble after him as he took off in a sprint. "Cheater!"

His only response was to speed up. She ground her teeth together and pushed herself to *move*. Trees flew past as she raced through the forest. Her wolf kept pace with her easily and could have outstripped Ito in a second but stayed by her side instead.

Ito took a winding path and made sudden turns, as if he was trying to lose her. He was right that she could think of nothing else while chasing him, which only made her more determined to catch him. The constant mantra of *prey prey prey* echoing through her mind from her wolf sent a thrill through her. There was nothing that compared to the blissful freedom of a run since she'd become a werewolf. Every instinct rejoiced in it.

As the miles passed, her legs began to shake, and her lungs struggled to keep up. She ignored it all and forced herself to go even faster. Ito was close. Only an arm's length ahead of her. If she just...

Her foot caught on a stick, and she pitched forward, fingers scraping the back of Ito's shirt but unable to catch him. She hit the ground hard, all the breath forced from her lungs, and slid in the leaves. Embarrassment burned at her cheeks, but she was too tired to really care. Running without being able to shift was significantly more tiring. When she was a wolf, it always felt like she could go on forever.

She rolled onto her back and blinked up at the leaves as she tried to catch her breath. That had hurt. Ito walked back and stopped by her head. Sweat dripped from his brow, but he didn't even seem to be breathing hard as he grinned down at her, smug as ever.

"How are you not dying?" she wheezed.

He raised an eyebrow. "I've stayed in excellent shape my entire life. You don't exercise in human form enough. It's common with bitten wolves. The added strength they develop from their transformation fools them into thinking they are truly fit."

She straightened with a groan. "I *am* in way better shape than I was as a human."

"And yet you are average, at best, as a werewolf. I could see it when we fought. You were tiring too quickly. If I hadn't been struggling against the influence of the archangel, I would have..." He looked away without finishing the thought. But he was right. He would have killed her if there hadn't been interference. "Your pack's power and your dominance has made up for your weaknesses, but those things shouldn't be relied on."

She snorted and pushed back the short hairs that were stuck to her forehead.

"You disagree?" he asked sharply.

"Not at all. We just haven't had a ton of downtime to work on the rest. It's been one fight after another."

He pressed his lips into a thin line. "Of course." Deep lines creased his forehead, and he clasped his hands behind his back. "I hadn't fully grasped how tumultuous your transition to alpha was until I was forced to stay with your pack."

Amber glanced at her wolf, who looked particularly pleased with herself. "I suppose that was part of her plan."

Ito's lips twisted, half-grimace and half-smile. "I'm sure."

"It's not the first time she's done something like this. She banished Kadrithan somehow when I had the demon mark." Amber ran her fingers through her wolf's thick fur. "Is that...normal? Or is it another bitten wolf struggle?"

"I've never encountered a dynamic such as yours before, so I suppose I can't blame it on you not being a born werewolf." He nodded toward her wolf. "She would be the only one with a chance of explaining it."

"Figures."

Ito shifted on his feet then let out a harsh sigh, as if he'd been holding back whatever he had to say for far too long. "Do you intend to attack Saraqael soon?"

Amber's hand stilled on her wolf's head, and she lifted her gaze to Ito. "What would you do?"

He leaned his shoulder against the tree beside him and crossed his arms as he took a moment to contemplate her question. "I don't like the position you have put us all in, and I blamed you for all of it for a long time, but it would be naive to claim we could have avoided this conflict. Saraqael has shown a single-minded pursuit of his goals. I have reviewed the evidence the MIA has on the no-magic zones and their growth. From what I understand, if the curse had not been broken before the incubi succeeded in spreading those zones around the world, there were prophecies saying it would never be broken?"

Amber nodded once. "That's correct."

"You were not prepared for the scale of this conflict." His eyes bored into her own as if he thought he could drag the answers he sought out of her with sheer determination.

"Also correct, and I won't pretend otherwise." She gave him a flat smile as she pushed up to her feet. Her legs shook, but she didn't fall back over. "I feel completely out of my depth most days."

"But you did all of this, regardless of the risk, because you believed it was the right thing to do?"

"It was the right choice. Even with all the chaos, I still believe that."

He dropped his eyes finally and shook his head. "I believed I was powerful enough that the incubi would not make a move against me. I believed we could bargain with them, and I let them enter pack lands. I spoke with the archangel believing I was untouchable." A muscle in his jaw jumped as he ground his teeth together. "And my free will was stripped from me, endangering my entire pack and the rest of the world."

Amber wasn't sure what to say to that. It was true, and he didn't seem like the sort to want platitudes about how he couldn't have known. He *should* have seen and listened, but his pride blinded him. "You're helping us now," she said instead, even those words feeling empty.

"I stopped hindering you, but that is a far cry from helping." He pushed off the tree. "If I were in your position, I would not give Saraqael any more time to prepare. I would reach out to every potential ally and gather as many as were willing to help. The sooner he is put down, the better. Waiting seems to provide us no better chance of winning, but it may help him in some way we do not see."

She sucked in a shaky breath. So many had died in the battle with Raziel. If they marched against Saraqael, even a victory would not ensure they didn't lose anyone. "Do you think they will all be willing to fight again? It's already cost so much."

"I cannot speak for them, but I can speak for my pack." He stepped forward and dropped to one knee. "My pack has seen the need of the Alpha Dominus. Your enemy is our enemy. Your battle is our battle." He lifted his gaze to hers. "I had no choice but to submit when we fought, but today, I choose to support you willingly. Will you accept my offer?"

A thrum of magic that she'd only felt once before when she'd taken her oath before the Alpha Trials shivered through her. Ito was offering her something more than the forced submission that tied them together currently. This would change the bond.

"Why now?" she asked, hesitant to accept this without understanding his change of heart.

"Because I finally understand that it *is* the right thing to do. And I trust you."

Acting on instinct, Amber placed her hand on his shoulder. "I accept you as a brother and trusted advisor. I will protect your pack as my own."

He held her gaze as he rose to his feet. "I——"

The wind picked up around them. Wind and magic and something feral that made Amber want to sling her head back and howl even in human form. The ache to shift thrummed under her skin, torturously out of reach.

Ito's eyes were locked on her wolf. He trembled, his breaths turning to gasps. The bond between them tightened and expanded in a rush of warmth, then Ito's wolf appeared next to her own.

Finally, you understand. Her wolf's words echoed through the air around them.

Ito fell to his knees and buried his hands in his wolf's fur. They stayed there, heads pressed together, for a long, quiet moment. Finally, he lifted his gaze. "Thank you." He stood but stayed pressed against his wolf. "I need to call my pack and bring them here."

She nodded once, tightening her fingers in her wolf's fur. "And I need to talk to mine about making the first move against Saraqael."

"You have doubts."

"Every moment of every day."

"As do I. Yet, here we are, resolved to fight together." He lifted his chin. "We will win."

She glanced over her shoulder toward the house, though she couldn't see it this far into the woods she could sense her pack. "I hope so."

CHAPTER 62

KADRITHAN

Sometimes, Kadrithan wondered if he'd ever made a good decision or if he'd been stumbling blind through his life for centuries and had arrived in his current situation by sheer dumb luck. After all, he hadn't chosen Amber; she'd fallen into his life. He'd been unable to break the curse on his own. And he was clearly incapable of keeping his niece safe and happy.

The door opened, admitting Katarina and Charlie. He hadn't been sure if they would show up today.

"Thank you for coming." Kadrithan waved a hand at the chairs in front of his desk.

"We almost didn't." Katarina leveled a resentful look at him as they sat. "But you offered a lot of money."

He deserved that. The magic of the demon marks had required an even exchange, so while he hadn't technically asked more of them than was allowed, he had pushed very close to the limit. And he hadn't cared one bit for their safety as long as his niece survived.

Charlie took the toothpick out of his mouth. "And Evangeline grew on us a bit. She's a mess, but she's a good kid."

"And if you're an overbearing ass, I can sock you on the jaw now." A smug grin spread across Katarina's face, and she looked very much like she was considering it.

He sat back in his chair, barely suppressing a matching smile. "Perhaps I shouldn't have dismissed the guards so readily."

Charlie snorted and stuck the toothpick back between his lips. "As if that would stop her."

"What's the deal with Evangeline? I know she went missing, but I assumed Amber would have tracked her down for you by now."

He shook his head. "We've only recently found any sign of her. I'll show you."

One of the benefits of residing in this realm was the easy access to technology. He pulled out the laptop, video ready to go, and turned the screen at an angle so Katarina and Charlie could see. There was not much to see. One incubus fled the building and was struck down by a sword thrown in his back. Inside, flashes of magic and fire illuminated the windows.

"It wasn't Saraqael." Kadrithan watched the footage along with them and only felt more resolved this was the right choice. The bright flames were unmistakable. Evangeline had been behind the slaughter in Manhattan.

"She cut off their avenues of escape just like you taught her." Charlie nodded his head toward Katarina. "You sure they didn't deserve it?"

Old resentment twisted in Kadrithan's gut at the question. "They probably did, but I'm not concerned with their deaths, only the risk she's taking."

Katarina shook her head with a sneer. "We spent *months* on the run. Fighting and killing dozens of people. She's aware of the *risk* and can handle herself."

"I'm trying to keep her alive." Kadrithan managed to keep his voice level, but it was a close thing.

"Sure you're not just worried she'll be a PR problem? Since you've apparently decided to make nice with the incubi."

He stiffened. "I'm doing what is *right*. For the fae *and* for Evangeline. Or have you forgotten she's half succubus? Because I have not." Forcing his fingers to unclench from the arms of his chair, he sat back once again. "The rebels defected from Saraqael and have given us every bit of information they had. I'm surprised you expect me to kill them regardless of all that."

Katarina looked away, her jaw tight as she ground her teeth together. "Bit hard to trust them."

"Understatement." Charlie shook his head.

"Besides, genocide is fairly universally frowned upon," Kadrithan said.

Katarina snorted at that. "I suppose it is."

"Which leaves us with only one option: peace with whoever surrenders." He pushed a hand through his hair and sighed. "If Evangeline isn't stopped, she will end up dead or in prison."

"And who's to blame for that?" Katarina asked, leveling a hard stare at him.

"I am. I dragged a child into a war, and now she's lashing out in violence." Kadrithan curled his fingers into his palm as he fought against the urge to break something. He'd made so many mistakes in his pursuit of vengeance and justice. Even now, some seemed unavoidable. Evangeline's involvement was necessary to break the curse. Despite knowing that, all he could feel was regret that he hadn't protected her from the burden. "I've never protected her well enough."

Katarina was silent for a long moment then shook her head with a heavy sigh. "And now you think kidnapping her is the best option? She will hate you for this. More than she already does."

"Better me than herself." He leaned forward and braced his elbows on the desk. "There are some mistakes I can't allow her to make. All I can do is keep her out of this war. When it's over, and she is *safe*, she can hate me all she wants."

CHAPTER 63

CERI

The hair on Ceri's arms stood on end as lightning cracked through the sky overhead. She'd expected things to be better in the spirit realm, not worse. And definitely not this much worse.

Wind buffeted them relentlessly. Deward's tight grip on her hand was the only thing keeping her upright.

"You can feel it, can't you? The tangled magic around us?" Deward shouted.

"It's awful!" she shouted back. And it was. At first, she'd assumed it was the storm, but it was more than that. A sense of wrongness prickled over her skin and tugged at the magic within her. It was chaos—and something more twisted. Something hungry.

"At least we won't have trouble finding the vortex," Tessa shouted right before a crack of thunder made them all flinch.

That much was true. They couldn't see it from where they were, but the source of the darkness came from their right.

"Let's get this over with."

Ceri linked hands with Tessa, who grabbed hold of the witch next to her. The entire coven trailed through the storm after Deward. Fear twisted through Ceri as they walked. The amount of power it must have taken to damage the spirit realm was nearly inconceivable. She knew Saraqael hadn't done all this alone, but the fact that the incubi had done *any* of this was terrifying.

Sometimes, at the back of her mind, she questioned if he was truly killable. It had taken everything they had to kill Raziel, and according to Taharia, he had been the weakest of the archangels by far.

Deward stopped abruptly at the top of the hill, his eyes locked on the valley below them. "Can you see it?"

She tightened her grip on his hand. "Yes."

There wasn't a single vortex this time. There were four. The nauseating weight of their pull made it hard to breathe as she stayed frozen in horror. They seemed to feed on each other, or perhaps this was how the first one would have looked if they hadn't destroyed it when they did.

"How close do we have to get?" Ceri asked, fighting the urge to turn around and demand Deward lead them out of the spirit realm right then.

"Closer than is entirely safe." He pushed his shoulders back and tightened his grip on her hand. "Stay close and move quickly."

They edged toward the nearest vortex. With every step, the dark magic clung to them and weighed them down even more. An involuntary shudder rushed through her as Deward stepped into the wound. She didn't want to follow, but she had no choice as they were yanked into it just like last time.

Pressure and darkness surrounded her as they spun and twisted. This time, she was prepared for the harsh stop. Her nails dug into Deward's wrist as they jerked to a halt, dangling in the center of a dimly lit apartment. The relic stood in front of the couch like it was just another piece of furniture.

"They're all here. Close by," Deward whispered.

"The relics?" Ceri blinked, eyes still adjusting to the lack of light.

"Yes. I can see them through the walls. One below us, the other two above us."

Ceri hung there, heart racing. She had no idea if Saraqael had

had them all along or if he had summoned them here after the first was destroyed, but he must have decided keeping them close was safest.

"You recognize this place?" Tessa asked.

"Nope. We have to be pretty high up based on the view out the window, though." She squinted, hoping to spot something out the window that would make it obvious where they were, but all she could see was a generic skyscraper.

They knew Saraqael was in New York, and while the view seemed to confirm that, it could be one of any number of different cities. Chicago. Houston. Even Los Angeles.

"Don't suppose they left any mail laying around with an address on it?" Tessa muttered.

Deward snorted. "That would certainly make this easier."

Ceri gnawed on her lip. "Maybe we should try letting me down so I can do a quick search––"

"No." Deward tightened his grip on her hand. "Absolutely not. That...every instinct I have says that would be a very bad idea."

"I just don't want to leave without anything that can help us pin down the relic's location. Especially with all of them here."

"Normally, I'm down for bending the rules, but if Deward is super against it, I'm siding with him," Tessa said without her usual levity. "Just saying."

Deward tensed as his gaze jerked toward the door. "We have to go, now. Someone is coming. Someone powerful."

"Crap. Pull!" Tessa shouted.

They moved upward in halting increments. Ceri's heart pounded against her ribs as she watched the door Deward was staring at. They were moving too slow.

Less than a foot from their entry point, the door swung inward, and an archangel strode into the room. It wasn't Saraqael, but Ceri could still feel the power emanating from him. Dark brown hair hung artfully around his face, and he wore a sleek suit. He was a picture of perfection, just like they always were.

His piercing gray eyes lifted to her own even though they should have been invisible. "You won't be able to stop him. It's too late."

Ceri had no idea if he'd be able to hear her, but she found herself unable to stay silent. "It's never too late."

Darkness enveloped her as they were pulled back up into the vortex.

CHAPTER 64

CERI

"He not only saw you guys, he *spoke* to you?" Icewind planted her hands on the table. Her eyes were ringed in dark circles, and she was on her third cup of coffee. Even the unruly magic she still couldn't completely control was droopy--it was faint, but Ceri was pretty sure the blue flowers circling her head were snoring.

"Yep," Ceri confirmed before stifling a yawn of her own. "He looked right at us."

Amber's eyebrows were pinched tightly together as she tapped her fingers in a haphazard rhythm against the table. "He said it was too late to stop Saraqael, but nothing else? No threats?"

"No threats, just that."

"If it were anyone else, I'd say it was a plea for help." Amber sat back in her chair with a sigh. "But it's probably just a taunt or a ploy to make us think they're not united and draw us into the trap."

Deward cocked his head to the side. "The statement felt honest, but the incubi layer illusions on top of illusions, so it's impossible to know what his intentions were in telling us that."

Ceri glanced at Kadrithan, but he was staring blankly at the wall. She wasn't sure if he was even listening. The whole thing had clearly disturbed him.

"He might hate Saraqael and *still* not be on our side. Not like he can't try to play both sides. Make us hesitate or screw with our heads." Derek shrugged and gestured at the room with a wide sweep of his arm. "We've spent a half hour analyzing his parting comment instead of looking into anything else."

Amber groaned. "Well, when you put it like that."

"Back to the relic's location, then." Ceri steepled her fingers and pursed her lips. "We don't have a ton to go off of. It could have been any living room in any condo in any major city."

"It was really nice. Expensive furniture, probably a good view if we could have gotten close enough to the window to see it properly." Tessa leaned in and shuffled through some pictures she'd swiped from the file in front of Ceri.

"And it had to have been fairly high up." Deward leaned back in his chair and crossed his arms as he stared blankly at the ceiling. "The relic I sensed below us wasn't close. Neither was the one above us. At least ten stories in either direction, I'd guess."

"Definitely some kind of skyscraper, then." Ceri frowned at the itemized list on the stack of pictures that Tessa had now tugged into the space between them. "These are all condos we know the archangels own?"

"The ones you have there we can prove belonged to the incubi." Icewind slid another file across the table. It was even thicker than the first. "These are off Taharia's list. They could be outdated, but she said they owned them all at some point."

"These are all in the Woolworth Building?" Ceri asked as she scanned the list.

Icewind nodded as she took another long drink of her coffee. "Yep."

Amber stared at the list in Ceri's hands for a long moment then turned to Kadrithan. "That's the same building the MIA tracked Saraqael back to after the first massacre. You think he'd keep the relics with him like that?"

"Bold choice to keep them with him," Tessa muttered.

"Or he believes he's invincible." Kadrithan's statement settled over the room like a physical weight.

The archangel's warning flashed through Ceri's mind again. Maybe he was right. Maybe Saraqael had accumulated too much power to really be stopped.

"He's not," Amber insisted. "No one is."

Kadrithan turned to face the table. "I would not be surprised in the least that he would be bold enough, as Tessa so eloquently put it, to keep the relics with him. He has never truly seen us as a threat."

"Not even after we broke the curse?" Amber asked with a frown.

"That didn't scare him. It *annoyed* him." Kadrithan lifted one shoulder in a shrug. "But Taharia would know him better, as his former envoy."

Amber's fingers tapped restlessly against the arm of her chair. "Maybe I should ask her then?"

Kadrithan stilled for a moment then took a deep breath and nodded. "I can arrange that."

"Maybe she can identify the archangel that spoke to us as well," Ceri suggested. "It'd be nice to know who he was."

"I'll ask about that, too."

Leena stepped into the room and waved the two incubi she'd been escorting ahead of her. Pravil and Briada nodded in greeting to everyone and took the two free seats on Tessa's right.

Kadrithan rose, obvious tension thrumming through him. "If you'll excuse me, I should go take care of Amber's request."

No one called him out as he fled the room. The fact that he could tolerate his life-long enemies in his home was impressive enough. She wasn't sure she'd be able to remain so calm if she was in his place.

Tessa raised a brow. "Well, that was awkward."

Amber snorted as Pravil paled. "Yes, thank you for pointing that out, Tessa."

"Better to acknowledge it than sit around all stiff and weird for hours." Tessa pulled a stack of pictures out of her bag and smacked them on the table. Everyone jumped, and a wicked grin spread across her face. "Since our lovely rebels are here, we should go over the relic again. See if we can figure out the runes a bit better."

They'd hesitated over bringing the incubi rebels into this discussion but had decided the night before that they should accept any help they could get. And if they trusted them enough to fight beside them whenever they finally faced Saraqael, they should trust them with this. Especially if there was even the slightest chance they could help.

Pravil stiffened as he looked at the pictures. "You've seen one of the relics?"

"We blew one up," Tessa announced, her grin growing wider as the incubus's jaws dropped open in shock.

"Blew up..." Pravil gaped at them. "You just..."

Ceri leaned forward and tried––somewhat unsuccessfully––not to grin at them like Tessa. "Seemed like the most straightforward solution. And it worked."

Briada shook her head and laughed. "Such a simple solution all of us would have overlooked. We've spent too many years scheming to think straight."

"Shocked me, too, to be honest." Tessa leaned back and slung an arm around Ceri's chair. "But Ceri is great at thinking outside the box."

"What do you know about the relics?" Amber's question burst the light-hearted atmosphere like a bubble. Her alpha's gaze stayed on the rebels as their smiles faded into twin pictures of wariness. This was a test, and they all knew it.

"The holy relics were a closely guarded secret. We knew they existed, of course, but their purpose was never shared beyond the archangels themselves. Even Taharia could only guess," Pravil said quietly, his hands curled into white-knuckled fists on the table.

"But we always assumed it was part of what made them so much more powerful than other incubi," Briada added with a nervous glance around the table. "None of us are born with innate power like what they wield, and no matter how much you..." She lowered her gaze as a blush crept up her neck. "No matter how much we feed, no one has ever approached their levels of power."

Ceri pursed her lips as she considered their theories. "The relics are screwing with magic ever since the curse was broken and the realms destroyed, but we know that wasn't their original purpose."

"If they are what keeps the archangels powerful, then I can kinda see why Saraqael planted that guy's head on a stake." Tessa shrugged. "Probably thought he should have fought to the death to prevent the relic from being destroyed."

Pravil froze in his chair. "Who was killed?"

"Over five hundred people, including MIA agents and most of the incubi we've collected from the east coast. But the person Tessa was referring to is an archangel." Icewind slid a closed folder toward them. "We don't know which of the archangels he was. I won't make you look, but we were going to ask one of you to identify him if you could."

With a nod, Pravil dragged the folder toward him and opened it. He didn't linger over the gruesome picture, but no hint of grief passed over his features. "Uriel. After Raziel, he was the weakest of the archangels and has long been at odds with the others. He had no hunger for war and was...merciful. In comparison to the others, at least." He slid the folder back to Icewind. "Saraqael has been looking for an excuse to kill him for centuries."

Amber sat forward with interest. "Any other tension between the archangels?"

Briada snorted then looked embarrassed for her reaction. "There is nothing *but* tension between them. After so many centuries, it is impossible for creatures with so much power--too much--to truly trust each other."

"I'm surprised they've stayed loyal to Saraqael, then," Icewind said, her eyes searching the two of them for any hint of dishonesty.

Pravil nodded in agreement. "He has some kind of hold over them, but they never speak of it."

Ceri plucked at the hem of her sleeve. If Saraqael had a hold over the other archangels, then maybe the archangel they saw was looking for help. Or trying to warn them. She tuned back into the conversation as Tessa finished describing the archangel they'd seen in great and dramatic detail.

Briada and Pravil exchanged a look before he leaned forward and rested his elbows on the table. "If they were able to access their magic, I would caution you not to trust what you saw, but…" He sat back and shook his head. "Based on your description, that would be Haniel, his second in command."

"Any chance he's had a change of heart and would help us?" Amber asked with a weary smile.

"I could believe he wanted Saraqael dead, but I would not trust him. He is second in command for a reason. His thirst for power matches Saraqael's." Pravil looked disturbed by the whole interaction, which only increased Ceri's own unease. He returned his attention to the pictures of the relic that Tessa had given him. "This is the relic you destroyed?"

"Yes," Ceri confirmed with a nod. "You can see in that first set of pictures how it looked untouched and in the next set the runes we found hidden underneath the decorative base."

Briada sat forward with interest, her eyes flicking from picture to picture as Pravil slowly flipped through them. "Have you determined their meanings?"

"I'm fairly certain we interpreted the basics correctly." She pointed to the one unknown rune. "As far as we can tell, the relic had a target it was draining of power. I can't say with a hundred percent certainty, but I believe it originally targeted the fae realm. Once that realm was destroyed, it latched onto the spirit realm."

"Or was purposefully shifted to target a new place." Briada's gaze rose to hers. "That rune doesn't indicate a certain place. It's a rune that ties two things together." She pointed to the outer edge of the rune. "This is the target, as you called it, but this inner part," she tapped the center of the rune, "is the *recipient*. Whoever is getting the power would have the same rune somewhere on their body for it to work properly."

"The target is not fixed," Pravil added with a frown. "It is chosen through the will of the recipient."

Ceri's heart clenched in her chest. "If that's true, and all the power that was drained from the fae realm went to one person..." She sat back in her chair and stared blankly at the wall across from her. "Saraqael is receiving all the power. There's no way he'd have maintained control of the incubi otherwise."

"And that's why the other archangel said it's too late to stop him." Amber ground her teeth together, and red bled into her eyes.

"And the other archangels must be dependent on him to share his power with them." Pravil shoved the photos of the relic away with a grimace. "They would be as weak as any of us without him."

Briada's fingers curled into her palms. "He feeds them like we feed the children. Enough to keep them strong enough, but never so strong they could challenge us. Never sharing enough to weaken ourselves."

"This is a fight we may not win," Ceri whispered.

Amber met her gaze. "But it is yet another one we have no choice but to walk into."

She nodded in agreement, but fear had wormed its way into her heart. The power they would be facing was more than she could even imagine. Saraqael was a parasite fat with centuries worth of stolen magic. This was more than a trap; they were trying to kill a god.

CHAPTER 65

AMBER

The lingering worry that Kadrithan had Taharia chained up in a dank cell where she was being subjected to various unspeakable tortures vanished as Amber walked into the room. It was, unmistakably, a prison, but it was comfortable.

Taharia's cell was closer to a studio apartment than anything Amber had imagined. A bathroom was visible through a half-open door on the back wall. A small kitchenette sat below a picturesque window with a view of a garden, and across from that a canopied bed and a snug leather chair in front of a fireplace. The only reminder that this wasn't a vacation spot was the magical barrier that prevented the prisoner from leaving. Or Amber from entering.

Amber's wolf trotted ahead of her and sniffed at the barrier. Taharia looked up, her eyebrows raised in surprise as she realized who was visiting, and set aside her book. Her hair hung around her face in soft curls. She looked even younger in here dressed in casual clothes. Sometimes it was hard to remember how dangerous she had been and the lives she had taken.

"I might ask Kadrithan to put me in there with you after this is all over so I can get some sleep," Amber said with an awkward half-smile. They'd never been friends, exactly, but she respected the sacrifices Taharia had made to save her people and do the right thing after so long of doing the opposite. That sort of change was hard––impossible for most people.

Taharia unfurled from the chair she was curled up in and laughed. "I didn't expect to see you, but I'm sure I have you to thank for all of this, so I'm glad you're here."

Amber waved her comment away. "I didn't have anything to do with this. I'm surprised as you are that you aren't stuck somewhere...less pleasant."

Taharia's face softened. "Whether you realize it or not, this is your influence." Seeming to sense Amber's growing discomfort, she walked closer, stopping just short of the barrier, and tilted her head to the side. "But you aren't here for compliments. What do you need to know?"

"What do you know about the holy relics?" Amber's gut twisted with a mix of anger and fear. They'd been lucky to destroy the first one before realizing just how important the things really were.

Taharia drew her eyebrows together, the last of her smile fading into a frown. "Their purpose was never clear. Each of the archangels protected one. I wondered for a while if Saraqael was somehow using the relics to control the other archangels, but even as his envoy, I was never able to get close enough to confirm my suspicions." She shrugged. "I even wondered if they were part of the curse. That's when they were built, so it was a possibility."

"So you never suspected the relics are what made Saraqael so powerful? That he was using them to drain the life and magic from the fae realm all this time?" She ground her teeth together. "He shared some of the power with his archangels. Just enough to keep them dependent on him."

Taharia's face drained of color, and she stepped back, stunned. "No." Her voice came out a whisper, only audible because of Amber's enhanced hearing. "I knew they were important and their power was obvious if you got anywhere near them, but...I never suspected they were the key to his power. I would have destroyed them long ago if I'd known."

"You really never suspected?" Amber remained tense, frustrated at how long Saraqael had been allowed to do so many awful things unchecked. With no one to truly challenge him.

Taharia shook her head, face still pale. "They were so closely guarded, and I had bigger problems. But that, as with all my excuses, it's not good enough, is it?" A wan smile tugged at her lips, but it never reached her eyes.

She is telling the truth. Amber's wolf looked back at her. *And she will punish herself for this along with her other crimes.*

Amber squeezed her eyes shut and took a deep breath. She knew Taharia wasn't lying even before her wolf had said it. The succubus had done too much to help them to withhold something that could help them like this.

"We need to destroy the relics to have a chance at killing Saraqael, and we think we know where they are, but we aren't sure. Can't be sure." She took a deep breath and forced her gaze back to Taharia's face. "We need to know anything you can tell us about him. How he thinks, how he'll respond when backed into a corner, and just how crazy he actually is." Amber crossed her arms. "We're taking a risk assuming the relics are with him."

Taharia pushed her shoulders back. "Saraqael believes not only that he is smarter than everyone around him, and that his superiority justifies his actions, he also believes that he is destined to rule. That every victory he's ever had over the fae is further proof that what he's doing is as much fate as a result of his power." She took a deep breath before continuing, "He is insane, but not in the way you might think. He's been alive for too long and unchecked for too long. At this point, he genuinely believes his own lies. He thinks he is something more than an incubus--a god, perhaps. If those relics are the key to his power, then yes, I think he'd keep them nearby."

"And the other archangels? Will they support him to the end?"

"If what you're saying about the relics is true, then I don't know.

There is no love or loyalty among them, but they may be more dependent on him than I ever suspected."

Amber nodded. This was not going to be easy. Even though Saraqael was delusional, he had more power than any living thing should ever wield. A false god with real power. "If you think of anything else we should know, send a message. And..." Amber forced herself to take a breath. "Thank you for your help."

"It's the least I can do," Taharia replied in a whisper.

She turned to leave, but Taharia stopped her.

"Wait! I--" The succubus hesitated for a moment but finally straightened. "I have one last request, though I have no right to ask anything of you."

"What is it?" Amber asked with a frown.

"I could help you fight him. I know him best, and if anyone should take on that risk, it should be me. Will you ask Kadrithan? If the request comes from you..." Taharia let the sentence trail off.

She tapped her fingers against her thigh, mulling over the request. "I'll ask, but I won't try to persuade him."

Taharia nodded in thanks. "I understand."

CHAPTER 66

The dining room was full. Amber's pack was spread out around her, and Icewind sat at the other end of the table. She longed for a time when they could gather together like this without a threat hanging over their heads, but she knew that was impossible until this war was over. It was the reason they all kept going even while they were exhausted and wrung out.

She forced her attention back to their current debate. They'd decided to have this conversation privately first. There was too much to discuss to navigate politics on top of it all.

"We have to destroy the relics during the course of the fight to have a chance of defeating him. These relics not only corrupt magic, we've discovered they are also channeling power to Saraqael." Ceri waved a hand at the pictures of the relics spread on the table. "Pravil confirmed our translations."

"There are four relics left." Amber straightened. "Genevieve, Tommy, Derek, and Ceri could each find and destroy one while I face Saraqael."

Ito hesitated then shook his head. "That's a terrible idea."

Genevieve bristled, but Amber lifted a hand to ask her to wait and turned her full attention to Ito. "Why?"

"Your pack is strongest together. Splitting up makes each of you more vulnerable. It's my opinion that your pack should face Saraqael *together,* alongside the fae, and the destruction of the relics should be delegated to other groups." He held his poker face firmly in place, but Amber could feel the tension within him. And the unwavering belief that he was correct.

She pursed her lips. "Gen, what do you think?"

Her beta huffed out a sigh. "He has a good point. I don't like the idea of splitting up, either."

"Everyone else agree?" She looked at each of her pack mates in turn, and they all nodded. "I do, as well." Taking a deep breath, she squared her shoulders. "It's decided, then. We'll have to look for volunteers for the relic missions. Maybe the packs tied to me can be in charge of that."

Ceri twisted the sleeve of her cardigan around her fingers. "We have no chance if even one of them is left standing."

Amber nodded. "We'll have to trust the teams to do their part." She met Ceri's gaze for a moment and gave her a reassuring smile. "I hate it, too."

"Nothing we plan can guarantee us victory," Ito said solemnly.

"I know." Ceri sighed. "Just not used to depending on anyone else to help us."

"Everyone helped us break the curse. They're not going to back out now." Tommy rarely spoke up in these sorts of meetings, and she could feel his nerves snaking through the bond, so she appreciated the effort even more.

Ceri nodded once. "That's true. Saraqael is a threat to everyone."

"Just to be clear, I won't take this plan to the councils until we're all in agreement. The last thing we need is to end up arguing in front of everyone else. So, if something bothers you, speak up." Amber leaned forward and braced her arms on the table. "If Saraqael and the relics are in the Woolworth Building, we're going to have a hell of a time getting to them."

"How many floors is it?" Derek asked.

"Fifty-three." Icewind rubbed her temples. "It's going to be a nightmare to get into, much less clear. We're going to have to work our way from the bottom to the top."

"Climbing up fifty-three stories sounds miserable. Fighting our way up that far is going to be rough." Genevieve leaned forward and chewed on her thumbnail. "Is there no way we could somehow enter higher up?"

Icewind shook her head. "Nothing practical."

"Then we enter through the first floor." Amber dragged the floor plan to her. "There are multiple entrances at least. Maybe we can send a scout in first? See where their guards are?"

"I could go," Tommy volunteered without hesitation. "I'm good at sneaking––"

"You're already hurt," she objected, her protective instincts bristling at the thought of one of her pack mates in there alone.

Tommy rolled his eyes. "I'm not *that* hurt."

Amber glanced at Ito, hoping he'd back her up on this as well, but he looked like he was considering it. "If one of us is seriously injured, or taken captive, our pack will be weakened. I don't think we can risk it."

"Then I'll go," Ito said, his face tensed with determination as he pressed against his wolf. "I have the most training out of all of us. I know how to hunt prey." A hint of red filtered into his eyes as he spoke, and she felt a thrill of eagerness through the bond that connected them.

Hesitation still churned in her gut, but she knew they wouldn't win this fight without risk. "Okay." She exhaled sharply. "Do we have a safe way of getting him in and out, Neia?"

The elf pursed her lips, and the snoozing flowers floating around her head perked up, shedding tiny blue petals around her like raindrops. "There is an entrance here," she pointed to a door in the narrow alley between the Woolworth Building and a neighboring building, "used to bring in food and other deliveries. We have surveillance on it, and it hasn't been used. The incubi have stuck to the normal entrances, either hoping to hide their comings and goings with the regular visitors or simply because they aren't trying to hide anything."

"Could we get him in disguised as a delivery person?"

A sharp rap on the door startled them all, but she calmed when it was Leena that peeked her head in the door. "Do you have a moment, Amber?"

She was hesitant to step away from the meeting but knew Leena wouldn't ask if it wasn't important. "Sure. Y'all can fill me in when I get back."

Genevieve nodded. "Will do."

Amber met Leena at the back door. "What's up?"

Leena simply nodded her head toward the backyard and waited until they were outside and a decent distance from the house to speak again. "I apologize for pulling you away from the meeting, but it is important." She gestured behind them.

Amber turned and froze when she saw Kadrithan standing at the edge of the same garden they'd first spoken in. Leena bowed then disappeared into the garden, likely still close enough to guard Kadrithan but giving them at least the illusion of privacy.

Amber's heart pounded in her chest as she gazed at Kadrithan. "What are you doing here?"

"I decided it was time I stopped hiding." He slipped his hands in his pockets. "And we need to talk. You said you were planning the attack."

"Yes. And I'm glad you came, just surprised."

The corner of his mouth twitched upward. "I do miss startling you."

She rolled her eyes. "*That* is no surprise at all."

His smile faded, and he took a deep breath. "Why now? Is the retaliation for the slaughter at the MIA safehouse?"

"No. That makes the decision a bit easier, I guess, but it's because there's nothing to be gained in waiting. We know he has the relics, and every moment he's connected to them, he only grows more powerful. And he may be planning something else. Something worse." She shrugged. "At some point, we simply have to stop waiting and act."

Kadrithan inclined his head in agreement. "I see."

"Do you think this is a terrible idea?"

"No. I had been planning on convincing you of this myself, but it seems we came to the same conclusion." He lowered his gaze and rocked back on his feet. "Which leaves me with only one thing to convince you of."

She narrowed her eyes. "And what is that?"

"You need to get into that building to face Saraqael, but it will be difficult. Icewind sent me the layout. Fifty-three floors."

Her suspicion was growing as he spoke, but she nodded. "Yes, it's going to be very difficult. We're going to try to get Ito in to scout the place out."

"I have a better idea."

"Oh?" She raised an eyebrow.

"The Market can go wherever the fae will it. Even straight into the Woolworth Building." He lifted his eyes to meet her own as her heart plummeted into her stomach.

"That is an insane risk," Amber hissed. "Our families are in there. Your people are in there!"

Kadrithan ground his teeth together. "I understand the risk of doing *nothing* as well. Saraqael has barricaded himself in a veritable fortress. This is the only way past those defenses. Using the Market will save lives."

She curled her hands into fists. "Unless we fail."

"If we fail, then we're all dead anyhow."

Most of her wanted to refuse outright, but she knew it was idiotic. She was just so angry that, once again, Saraqael was forcing the fae to sacrifice something so important. There was a chance, of course, that they would win. That the Market would not be damaged or destroyed. But she still hated it with every fiber of her being.

Swallowing down all the objections she wanted to shout at him, she finally managed a nod. "It's your choice."

"I hate it, too," he whispered. "But it will be worth it to end this war."

"Can...would it be possible for someone else to relocate the Market as soon as we're inside? To take it somewhere safe while we fight?"

He was quiet for a long moment then finally nodded. "We will have no escape route if they do."

"Do you really think we'll turn back when we finally have a chance to destroy Saraqael?"

"No."

"Then I want to give the fae a chance to survive this, even if we don't."

He stepped in close and cradled her face in his hands then pressed a kiss to her forehead. "Then we will give them that chance."

She turned her face into his palm and pressed a kiss of her own there. With that settled, there was only one question left. "Taharia wants to fight with us. She asked me to ask you, but I told her I wouldn't try to persuade you."

He was quiet as he searched her face. "Trusting her is a risk."

"That's why I'm leaving the decision to you."

"I'll consider it."

"Let me know what you decide."

They had the beginnings of a plan--a damn good one if they could use the Market to take them straight to one of the relics. Now all they needed to do was convince everyone to help. Again.

CHAPTER 67

GENEVIEVE

The witches wanted to help because they, more than anyone else, needed those relics gone. Helena hadn't even given them a hard time about it, just insisted on being involved. Amber had accepted their offer without hesitation and had insisted after the meeting they were self-interested enough to be trusted with that, at least. Genevieve supposed she was right, but she didn't like it.

She hadn't been sure of the vampires, but Gouyen had said, "Yes, we will fight," and the others hadn't argued. Much like the vampires, the werewolves had simply accepted their new Alpha Dominus' choice––though everyone at the meeting had known it was because Ito had been standing right beside Amber backing her up. Ito's entire pack had arrived in the middle of the night, each of them with a wolf at their sides, ready to go to war.

The trolls and the fae had always been a sure thing. Surprisingly, it was the elves who had only sent a few to help. Volunteers, all of them. To be fair, they weren't exactly known for their prowess in battle, and their magic *had* been especially wonky.

Everyone had looked at the fae with a new level of respect once the plan to bust into the Woolworth Building like an uninvited trojan horse had been explained. They'd also been intrigued to see the mysterious fae king for the first time—though she had a hard time thinking of him as anything but the annoying little red demon that used to follow Amber around like a gnat. She snorted to herself. No matter how fancy he was now, she'd never be able to shake that image from her head.

Her nerves jangled with apprehension as she tightened the laces on her boots. She'd never had to worry about how she was dressed when going into a fight before. It was odd to even think about facing what was to come on two feet instead of four, yet here she was, stuck in human form. Maybe the elves had a point.

Her wolf huffed in offense at her doubts. *We will win. Being separated hasn't made us that weak.*

"No other option but to win," she muttered aloud.

"Are you talking to me or her?" Steven asked, nodding his head toward her wolf.

"Both. But mostly myself."

He sat down beside her, his leg bouncing with the same nerves she felt. "I'm not going to ask you to stay behind, but I wish I could."

She tangled her fingers in his. "I wish I could, too. I know you'll be with Ithra, but…" She let her thought trail off as a lump formed in her throat. "I knew those trolls were going to talk you into something dangerous when they started teaching you how to fight."

"I can't stay behind while you go fight anymore," he whispered, returning her squeeze. "And if there was ever a time for me take the risk, it's now."

Forcing herself to breathe, she nodded firmly. "I know. And it all makes sense logically, but I still hate it."

"So do I. After this is all over, I'm going to lock us both in a library somewhere and never leave." He gave her a tremulous smile. "Tommy can slip food under the door."

A hysterical laugh bubbled out of her throat. "That sounds like heaven."

"I'm sure our kids will love it, too."

Her head jerked up, and she stared at him in shock, but he was staring determinedly at their linked hands. "Kids?"

He squared his shoulders and finally lifted his eyes, determination blazing in them. "Yeah, I want to have kids. With you. One day. When you're ready. I'm not trying to rush you, I just--"

She cut him off with a kiss, tangling her fingers in his hair and pouring all her love and affection into it. This could be the last time they ever touched--though she pushed that thought away as soon as it entered her head, she still couldn't waste the opportunity. Finally, when she really needed to breathe, she pulled back and gazed into his eyes. "Yeah. Kids. That could be a thing we do."

A loud rap on the door followed by Derek's shout to "stop boning and get ready to fight" sent a mixture of embarrassment and nerves spiraling through her.

"We're not boning!" she shouted back, though it *had* been a tempting thought what with the impending death and all that.

They walked hand in hand down to the main hall amidst a rush of fae and their other allies. Her eyes widened as she took it all in. Everyone that had gathered to fight spilled out of the hall and into the road in front of the palace. It was an army. There was no other way to put it.

Every supernatural creature was represented--even the incubi. The rebels had insisted on helping. They would be going after the relics. One of them had stayed behind with the children, but the others were all here. Pravil caught her eye and gave her a solemn nod, which she returned.

Amber and Kadrithan stood on a balcony above the chaos, engaged in a quiet conversation. She paused as she stared up at them, Amber's fiery braid contrasting sharply with Kadrithan's dark hair and clothes. Even so, they looked...well-matched. The perfect pairing of fire and shadow.

As she tore her gaze away, she noticed fae staring up at them with hope and awe in their eyes. The same way you'd look at a hero. And, to them, that's exactly what Amber was. She'd broken their curse and had gathered all these people here to fight for them.

Genevieve's heart swelled in her chest. She knew exactly what they were feeling. When Amber had thrown herself in front of a rogue werewolf to save her, she'd known then and there that Amber was more than just a good person––she was something special. After all, no one else at that concert had done anything to help. Except for their pack.

Ithra joined them, greeting them with a warm hug. "It is time to move into position. Are you ready?"

Steven adjusted the MIA-issued vest and gun belt and nodded, his mouth set in a thin line of determination. "I am."

"Be safe," Genevieve whispered.

Ithra laid a hand on her shoulder. "I will watch his back as I know you will watch over Deward."

She gave the troll's hand a squeeze. "Always."

It had been a source of a lot of tension, but in the end, they'd decided they couldn't leave Deward behind, not with his ability to see the relics in a way no one else could. As soon as they arrived, he would direct the teams toward them from a––hopefully––safe location. Though they all knew there was nowhere truly safe in the midst of the coming fight. Ito would stay with him as a guard and escort while the rest of their pack focused on killing Saraqael.

It still filled her with fear, but as Ito kept saying, they *were* stronger together. And as soon as the relics fell and their pack bond was fully restored, Deward would be able to see through their eyes. He'd have a chance. She clung to that hope stubbornly. They *would* do this. And they would *all* survive.

The remaining preparations were a whirlwind of activity. Genevieve rejoined her pack at their designated spot. Each squad was clustered together by the new exits Kadrithan had created. One-way exits. When the Market arrived and they walked out, there was no going back. They were already taking such a huge risk, and there were too many innocent people still inside. Including their families.

Each squad that would be taking down a relic included a coven of the witches––at their insistence, of course––vampires, five of Ito's pack members, a fae, an incubus or succubus, and a couple of MIA agents. Greer, Jameson, and Ford would be leading them.

Amber's brothers were both on teams, as well. They'd refused to be left out of this, and in the end, Amber had been outnumbered. It was as well-rounded a group as they could manage considering they had no idea what sort of resistance they'd be facing. For a rushed night of planning, it was impressive.

Tommy stopped beside her, and his wolf licked her fingers in greeting. "It feels so weird to know we're going into this unable to shift."

"Tell me about it." She rubbed a hand over his wolf's head. It was never something she really expected, but she missed the sheer joy of running on four legs. "But we have these. We'll make it work." She patted the electric baton at her side. They had a button that, when pressed, caused the baton to shoot out to full length and another that allowed them to administer a seriously powerful zap to whoever it was in contact with. Icewind had spent about ten minutes lecturing them on how much it would hurt if they were still in contact with the person when they zapped them.

Tommy nodded, but the worry didn't leave his eyes. "Still doesn't beat biting things."

Deward snorted in amusement as he approached with Ito. "I thought guide dogs were trained not to bite?"

"I've gone feral," Tommy replied with a wide grin.

Ito shook his head, but the normal disapproval wasn't there. He'd gotten used to them finally. "Ceri and Amber will be here soon. Does everyone remember the plan?"

They each nodded, and Genevieve forced herself to take a deep breath. There was no way the incubi would see this coming. Hell, *she* hadn't seen it coming. Using the Market as a trojan horse wasn't just outside the box thinking, it was...outside all common-sense thinking. Especially after the effort the fae had put into staying hidden for so long after the curse was broken.

Finally, Amber, Ceri, and Kadrithan joined them, as well as Kadrithan's royal guard. Leena was the only one she recognized, but the other two were fae that Zerestria had hand-selected for this mission, so they were trustworthy. And likely skilled enough to take off her head.

Amber's eyes were already tinted red, and her wolf paced restlessly by her side. "Everyone ready?" They all nodded their assent. "All right. Kadrithan, go ahead and make the announcement."

The fae king had put on some kind of sleek, leather armor since she'd seen him on that balcony. A sword hung from his hip that thrummed with magic and black leather embroidered with some kind of emblem hugged his chest. He looked ready for war.

With a tense nod, he turned to the crowd. "If anyone has doubts about this upcoming fight, now is your last chance to change your mind." All eyes turned to him, and he stepped forward to be more easily seen. "Once we go through these doors, the only way out is through Saraqael and the enemy incubi. There will be no way to retreat, no one to swoop in and save us at the last moment." He squared his shoulders and let his warning sink in. "However, we will not need to retreat. With the curse on the fae broken, the centuries of suffering we have experienced at the hands of our enemies will be avenged. The monster who seeks to make slaves of everyone in this realm will be killed. We will not stop until we are truly free."

A deafening cheer went up, sending a shiver of anticipation down Genevieve's spine. More than anything, she wanted to finally finish this and be free. It was time to end it all.

CHAPTER 68

EVANGELINE

There was a scuffle in the hallway, then Camus tumbled through the door, hands bound behind his back and a gag tied around his mouth.

Evangeline jerked upright but froze when Katarina walked through the door. The curse had been broken, which meant her uncle no longer held their marks. There was no reason for them to be here. So, she asked the only question she could think of through the shock of seeing them again. "How did you find me?"

Camus tried to shout some accusation through the gag, his eyes full of hate. Katarina gave him a look, and he went silent. She didn't blame him; the elf could be very scary when she wanted to be.

"Your uncle tracked you down."

"And? You plan on dragging me kicking and screaming back to him? Because I can guarantee I won't be going peacefully." Magic stuttered to her fingertips, but she had other ways to defend herself now. The others would help. They wouldn't let Katarina and Charlie just take her.

"No, I owe Kadrithan nothing, and he can no longer control me, so I will give you the choice that should have been offered to you all along. They've found Saraqael, and they're attacking tonight. Now." A thrill went through her. This was it. Finally. "Do you want to fight, or will you let them protect you? You could, you know." Katarina crossed her arms. "Your uncle would do anything to keep you safe at this point, including hiring us to kidnap you."

"Further proof he's a dick who doesn't care about me," Evangeline spat.

Charlie had the audacity to roll his eyes. "Proof he does, really. He cares. He's just got no clue how to go about showing it." He shook his head and slipped a toothpick between his lips. "And lord knows the two of you have never had a civil conversation."

"Because he doesn't *listen*," she snapped.

"That I can't argue with." Katarina lifted one shoulder in a shrug. "However, I do, which is why I'm giving you a choice, even though I think your uncle is right to try to keep you out of this. This isn't your fight."

"Saraqael made it my fight when he killed my mother." She curled her nails into her palm and let the pain distract her from the lump in her throat. "Both of them."

"If that's your final decision, then so be it." Katarina curled her lip in displeasure as she glanced at Camus, who was still struggling against his bonds. "Do you intend on bringing any of your...friends?"

"Not if the MIA are in on this fight. I don't want to risk any of them getting in trouble." Or dying. She couldn't be responsible for another innocent death. The last mission had been risky enough, and not everyone had made it back. This time, she was risking only one life––her own.

"What about Thallan?" Charlie asked with a casual drawl.

"He didn't kidnap me, you know. It was my idea to do this." She crossed her arms.

Charlie snorted. "Sure. The grown man just followed the teen girl, no questions asked."

"He wants the same thing I want. Don't make it sound gross."

"Is he here?"

"Yes." She hesitated. "He might come with us. To finish this."

Katarina stepped out of the doorway and nodded for her to go ahead. "Talk to him and get whatever you need, then we'll leave."

She hurried down the hall and found Thallan waiting for her.

"They're here for you?"

She nodded. "Amber and Kadrithan are attacking Saraqael."

"I see."

"Are you coming?"

Thallan shook his head. "I'd be nothing more than a hindrance at this point." He had grown even more gaunt in the past week as he continued to refuse treatment. The constant smoking probably didn't help.

She gnawed on the inside of her cheek. "They might be able to help you."

"I don't want help." He glanced up at her, his eyes reflecting the dull glow of his cigarette. "This is about penance."

"I know that," she snapped. He had no right to question her resolve, not after everything she'd done to make up for her mistakes. "That's why I have to kill him."

"And that's why I'll die without making myself a burden on people who have already done enough on my behalf." He sat back and dragged a bottle of whisky toward him. "Go fight. I'm done."

"You don't have to be--"

"I am *done*," he growled. "You don't need me for this. I did my part. Kept you alive while you were screwing around. Go let someone else babysit you."

She turned and left. His decision made no sense to her, but she couldn't waste any more time trying to change his mind. After the fight, if she made it, she'd tell Icewind where he was and let her deal with it. That was all she could do.

Amber would find a way to change his mind. The stray thought sent a surge of anger spiraling through her. She wasn't Amber. Not everyone could spend all their time saving people who didn't want to be saved. Gritting her teeth, she rejoined Katarina and Charlie. There was nothing here she needed to bring with her. All that mattered was killing her father.

CHAPTER 69

AMBER

Amber tightened her grip on her baton. Her heart crashed against her ribs with every beat, and her blood roared in her ears. The connection to every werewolf in the packs tied to her crawled under her skin. Being aware of so many other people was overwhelming. Her wolf stayed tense beside her, not leaving her even for a moment since she'd woken from her fitful rest just before the sun set.

Bram caught her gaze and grinned at her, his cheeks already warm from feeding ahead of the battle to be at full strength. At least *someone* was looking forward to this fight.

Kadrithan stepped closer to her and pressed their shoulders together. "You broke the curse. This will be no different. We will win."

She choked back the doubts on the tip of her tongue and nodded, as much to convince herself as him that she was confident about this battle. "I'm ready to finish this. We all are." Of that fact, she *was* confident. The nerves twisting through the pack bond were inevitable, but along with them was a clear determination. Her pack was strong, and they were ready.

Kadrithan held her gaze for a moment then stepped away and

nodded to the elder that had been entrusted with guiding the Market to its new, temporary location. A hum started that raised the hair on the back of her neck. As it grew, the ground trembled beneath their feet. The unease amongst her packs pressed against her skin, and her wolf let out a low growl. Even the mermaids that swam in the enchanted tanks above them were restless.

Being inside the Market while it moved was nothing like she expected and so much weirder than she could have imagined. She could *feel* that they were moving, but without a visual reference for how fast they were traveling, it only made her dizzy.

The hum pulsed louder and faster, sounds twining together until it almost sounded like a song. Old magic swelled up around her, wild and bright and smelling of rain and growing things. It reminded her of her short time in the fae realm, though this was much stronger than any scent she'd caught there.

The abrupt cessation of movement startled her. Derek bumped into her shoulder, and a few other stumbled around them, disoriented as well. Red bled across her vision as she tensed.

After days and weeks of waiting, the gates opened in a flash of blinding light that briefly illuminated the unnaturally dark room ahead of them. Each group poured out into the heart of the enemy's stronghold, weapons ready, and were met with...silence. The hall ahead of them was pitch black, impenetrable even by her eyes.

The Market had landed in the center of the Woolworth Building as planned, which had expanded around it, a single hallway stretched out into a massive chamber. As she scanned the area ahead of them, she knew something was staring back. They were being watched, and whatever it was, it was waiting for them to step into its trap.

She reached back and tapped Ceri's arm, signaling for her to handle this. This darkness wasn't natural; even she could feel that.

Ceri stepped out ahead of her, the coven and Deward following close behind, and knelt to place one hand on the ground. The coven had only been able to manage simple spells with Deward's help, but she held out hope it would give them an unexpected edge over their enemy. Amber's eyes flicked from shadow to shadow as she scanned for movement or any hint of a threat.

The coven began a soft chant. Even this close, she could barely make out the words, not that she'd understand what they were saying even if she could hear them clearly. A trickle of magic crept around them, then with a crack, the coven's spell sliced through the darkness.

Ceri glanced back, her expression grim. "They shrouded the whole building in darkness somehow. If they can do that..."

"Then we aren't the only ones that can use a little magic." Tessa finished for her as she shifted uneasily, eyes flitting around the room. "If Deward hadn't been with us, we would have been stuck in the darkness."

"And it'll be obvious we're here now." Ceri's fingers curled into a fist.

"Stick to the plan." Her gaze flicked to the troll in the center of the coven. "Deward?"

He nodded. "Two are below us, one near the ground floor, another only five floors down at a guess." He paused and turned his gaze upward. "The final relic is about ten floors above us."

The message was passed on, and the squads that would destroy the relics moved out, following the blueprints to the nearest stairwells. They'd all take a different route. If one team failed, it was up to the nearest team to finish what they started.

Deward's gaze focused above them. "Saraqael is at the top of the building, assuming he's the darkness up there. It looks similar to the relics, only more...concentrated."

Taharia shook her head with a sneer. "I have no doubt he's waiting at the top of this place. He loves nothing more than to tower over everyone else."

"Then he can die up there as well." Amber pressed forward, catching Icewind's eye and nodding. It was time to get off this level before their enemy stumbled onto their location.

Icewind lifted one hand and gave the signal to move forward. The last of their group stepped free of the Market, and it vanished without a single sound or flash of light. One moment it had been towering behind them, now the ceiling felt too close and their squad was packed into the narrow hall. It was suffocating.

The group after the relic took the west stairwell, leaving the east for them. As quietly as possible, they made their way to it. Icewind and Velez had point, followed by Amber and her pack. Ito and Deward were protected in the center, while the coven and the other MIA agents took up the rear.

As they walked, Amber took in the details of the building she hadn't noticed during the adrenaline rush of their arrival. There was no wood; everything was marble and metal with a Gothic flourish. This looked like exactly the sort of place Bram might live.

They'd landed on the twenty-eighth floor, not wanting to burst into some innocent person's condo and give them a heart attack. This was the final floor that held offices––and thankfully they were all empty thus far, as they'd expected this late in the evening. All the doors stayed closed, with no lurking heartbeats to indicate an enemy or innocent human might be hiding within them.

She strained to listen and keep from panting as they jogged up the stairs. They had a long way to go, and she appreciated Ito's point that they had to keep in better shape quite a bit right now. Her legs were already burning.

Four stories up, Tommy grabbed her shoulder and beckoned for the others to stop on the stairs. He pressed an ear to the door. Now that they had stopped, she could hear it, too. The heartbeats were faint, but there were at least ten people in the condo on the other side of the wall.

Icewind motioned toward the exit she stood in front of that would let them out in the hallway then pressed a finger to her lips to remind them to stay silent. As slowly and quietly as possible, she pressed the door open, and they filed after her into the hallway.

Tommy slipped past them and crept down the hallway, pausing

by each of the other five doors. Once he reached the end of the hall, he gave the all-clear signal. Only one condo was occupied.

Icewind drew her gun and moved to the left of the doorway. Velez moved in front of the doorway and checked everyone's positions then held up fingers, counting down from three.

If we have to enter a room, don't stop moving. Hug a wall and kill anything that moves. Icewind's advice pounded through her mind. As soon as they breached the door, there was no room for hesitation. Even a moment's indecision could get then all killed.

Velez dropped his last finger then kicked the door in. Icewind lunged through the doorway as a shocked yell from inside the condo shattered the tense silence. She fired first, three quick raps that echoed off the marble in the hallway. Amber's earplugs dampened the sound, but it was still loud enough to make her eardrums ache.

Already firing as well, Velez and his wolf charged in, moving in the opposite direction of his partner to cover more of the room. Amber's wolf lunged through the doorway, followed closely by Genevieve's.

Don't hesitate. Amber grit her teeth as she raced inside and zeroed in on the incubus fighting her wolf. With an enraged shout, she brought her baton down on the incubus's shoulder and pressed the button with her thumb. There was a crack as the electric shock coursed through him. All his muscles seized and the sword slipped from his fingers. Her wolf didn't hesitate. Amber barely had time to release the button before her wolf's jaws clamped over his throat and separated it from his body.

She whirled around and swung at the next enemy, forcing him back into Derek's range. Her brother's baton dented the incubus's head with the force of the impact. He dropped like a bag of rocks and didn't so much as twitch.

Though tensed and ready to continue fighting, she realized their attackers had already been subdued. There hadn't been very many. Definitely not enough to really slow them down. Either they'd caught the incubi completely unprepared, or the bulk of Saraqael's forces were with him at the top of the building.

Amber smoothed back the flyaways that had come free of her braid during the fight and tried to catch her breath. This reprieve wouldn't last. They had to get out of this hallway, and soon.

Icewind wiped a smear of blood off her chin. "Someone probably heard that. Gunfire tends to echo."

"Then we need to move faster." Kadrithan sheathed his sword.

"Unexpected resistance at Relic One. Assistance requested." The agent's voice was barely audible through Icewind's earpiece, but his cry for help had come through clear enough to make Amber's stomach twist with fear. That was Jameson's team.

Icewind's lips thinned. She looked to Amber, asking her to make the decision. "This will slow us down."

"The relics *must* fall," Ceri insisted, stepping out of the group. "There's no point reaching Saraqael if he can still draw on their power. He'll slaughter us."

Amber glanced at Kadrithan. The tension she saw in him matched her own. But there was no other choice; they had to help the other team. "We're helping them. How far away are they?"

"Three floors up." Icewind was already in motion. "Take the stairwell. We'll try to catch the incubi guarding the relic between us and the other squad."

Don't hesitate, her wolf reminded her as she pressed against Amber's leg. And she was right. They didn't have time to debate every decision, and the relics had to fall. Pushing down the doubt, she ran after Icewind.

CHAPTER 70

AMBER

They wound up the stairs at a punishing pace. With every step, the sounds of the fight above them grew louder. A second call for help spurred them to move even faster.

Velez slid to a halt in front of the stairwell exit, waiting only for Icewind to take her position on the other side of the door before slamming through it, gun raised. The hallway was filled with carnage. Amber's stomach nearly rebelled as the scent of blood and worse things washed over her.

Red bled into her vision, and she charged in after Icewind and Velez. The incubi guarding the relic had pushed the team back to the other stairwell, spilling out of the one of the two condos on this floor. Velez fired in quick bursts into the unsuspecting group of incubi. When the third one fell, they finally realized they were being attacked from both directions.

A group swung around to deal with them, swords drawn, sneers on their too-perfect faces. The pack's wolves charged ahead and forced the incubi back. The incubi couldn't fend off the wolves and avoid the attacks from their squad. One of the incubi let out a sharp whistle, and those who remained fell back into the condo.

"Don't let them regroup!" Velez shouted, sprinting for the door.

Her pack and the MIA agents rushed after him, but the coven stayed put.

"Buy me two minutes!" Ceri shouted as she knelt in the hallway, her jaw tight with determination.

Amber nodded and returned her attention to Velez as he fired into the room. His wolf yanked him back by his belt as an arrow whizzed past his head, missing its mark by less than an inch. Getting through the chokepoint looked like a suicide mission at this point. Ceri would have all the time she wanted and then some.

One of the MIA agents had made it over to the original relic team and was bandaging up a woman with a nasty gash on her arm. Bram stepped out of the shadows of the stairwell behind them, startling her. He winked, his irreverent attitude not dampened by their current circumstances, apparently.

An alarm blared through the hallway and echoed off the marble. The sprinklers overhead sputtered to life, dousing them all in a torrent of water. Amber whirled around in shock and spotted Tessa balanced on Derek's shoulders with a lighter under a sprinkler, pleased as punch. She scrambled down from Derek's shoulders and slid into her spot within the coven's circle.

"Be ready!" Ceri began a chant, hands sweeping over the growing puddle around her.

The water from the sprinklers rushed through the doorway in a wave, turning into thin shards of ice then exploding outward. This distraction would only give them a moment to act. Amber plunged through the doorway after Velez and barreled into a group of three incubi as she lost traction on the ice-covered marble floor.

Her wolf took down one of the three, and she thrust her baton toward the second like a sword. It struck him hard in the gut, but the third incubus slammed his fist into the side of her head. Stars danced across her vision as she kicked out, catching him in the balls with the toe of her boot. His howl of pain was cut short as her wolf's jaws clamped over his throat.

Amber swung again at the second incubus, this time managing

to hit the button as her baton made contact with his shoulder. His muscles seized, and he dropped. She struck again twice, slamming the metal against his temple, and he went still. Blood pooled around his head. She forced herself to keep moving as bile rose up in the back of her throat.

Don't hesitate. Don't stop.

The ice was already melting, which helped her footing, but the puddles weren't much better. Her only saving grace was that her enemy was struggling right along with her, but her wolf was doing just fine. The pack bond pounded in her chest as they fought.

Every few moments she caught a glimpse of one of her pack mates. Genevieve kicking a succubus toward Tommy, who caught her wrist with his baton, knocking her sword out of her grip. Derek standing guard at the door as Ceri and the coven cast the few spells they could to help. Ito and his wolf moving like a shadow through the fight, dropping incubi with quick strikes she could barely see.

Amber ducked under the swing of a sword and lunged forward, tackling the succubus that had attacked her. Her wolf struck from the side where she couldn't defend and tore out her throat in a spray of blood that nearly blinded her. She shoved the body away and stumbled back, wiping the mess from her eyes with the sleeve of her shirt.

Bram grabbed her hand and spun her around like they were dancing, his bloodstained fangs on full display as he grinned at her. Bram was splattered in blood, but his expression was exultant. He *loved* this. All the violence and blood and death. "You look good in red."

"Don't be disgusting," she snarled.

He spun her once more then shoved her at a succubus that was charging them both, sword raised high. Amber ducked low and swung her baton at the succubus's leg, but her attack went wide as the succubus leaped over the strike. Dodging that didn't save her, though. Bram, moving too fast to see, snaked past the swing of her sword and trapped her in his deadly embrace. His fangs sank in deep. The succubus thrashed, panic taking over as she dropped her sword and battered him with hands and wings.

Her struggles didn't last long, and Bram dropped her body with a contented sigh. He returned his gaze to Amber and flicked a lazy finger toward her. "Behind you."

She shook herself out of her daze and rolled just in time to avoid the sword coming at her. Her wolf bit her attacker's ankles, giving her a moment to jump back to her feet.

It felt like they'd been battling for what felt like hours, but she knew logically it had only been a few minutes, if even that long. Bram stayed near her, seeming to take great amusement in shoving varying incubi toward her as if this was all some game and the fate of the world didn't rest on their success or failure.

When the final incubus fell, it was a shock. A sudden end to a fight that had felt endless. She stood amongst the littered corpses, her lungs aching with every breath and her fingers numb where they grasped the baton in a tight grip. They'd killed them all. The bodies of both enemy and ally lay strewn around the relic like a bloody sacrifice.

Kadrithan caught her eye from across the room where he knelt over a fallen fae. His expression was perfectly blank, but she knew he grieved. Had already lost too much to see more fae dead.

A rumbling of the explosion shook the entire building. She tensed, but the swelling of magic in the air made it unmistakable--a relic had fallen. The pack bond zinged with renewed power. Her wolf's vision overlaid her own for a disorienting moment.

"Let's not waste any time before destroying this one as well," Ceri said as she stepped cautiously into the room.

Icewind rolled up to her feet. "Everyone, clear out. Smith and Peterson, you two get the injured to a condo and barricade the door." She waited until everyone still able to fight was in the hall and surveyed the group with a critical eye. "Jameson, will your team be able to head downstairs toward the final relic and backup that team?"

Jameson glanced around and, after receiving tired nods, confirmed they would be able to. The team immediately left, filing back into the stairwell they'd nearly been slaughtered in. The only one who stayed behind was the vampire that was currently licking his fingers clean like a cat.

"You aren't going with them?" Amber asked.

"And miss all the fun you're sure to have?" Bram shook his head with a mock scowl. "Don't be ridiculous."

Velez stepped forward. He looked just as gory as she felt. Fighting up close and personal like this was a messy affair. "Everyone ready? We need to get at least one floor up before they blow this thing."

With murmurs of consent, they jogged to the stairwell and up another level. The explosion was immediate and much more forceful this close. Amber stumbled and distantly noted the rest of the werewolves seemed similarly affected.

For a terrifying moment, she found herself on four legs looking back at her human body, where her wolf stared back at her. A rumbling yelp burst from her chest, but before she could really freak out, she was back in her body and Kadrithan was shouting her name.

"Did anyone else..." She gasped for breath as she patted herself down. "Anyone else switch with their wolf?"

"Yep," Genevieve wheezed as she rolled onto her stomach. "Being stuck separate is bad enough, I do *not* want to switch bodies."

Icewind hovered over them about five steps up. "Are you going to end up like this when the last relic falls?"

Ceri met her troubled gaze and gnawed on her lip. "There's no way to know. This isn't exactly something any of us have seen before."

"We'll just have to be prepared for the backlash next time. We can't sit in this stairwell and give Saraqael even more time to prepare." Amber forced herself back to her feet with Kadrithan's help.

"Better to attack when he's at his weakest than when we are," he objected before dropping his hands from her waist.

"Saraqael has to understand we're destroying the relics by now." Taharia stepped forward, eyes flicking nervously to Kadrithan. "If we don't go attack now, he may send more reinforcements to the relic and prevent its destruction entirely. We can't give him a chance to interfere."

Kadrithan ground his teeth together but nodded. "It's a risk, but she's right."

"All we can do is keep moving now that we know something odd might happen when the last relic falls. For all we know, it may hurt Saraqael just as much, if not more, since he's drawing on their power." Amber rolled her shoulders back to work out the soreness. "Everyone ready?"

"I was born ready," Tessa declared with a grin and dramatic hair toss.

Derek snorted and tried to hide his laugh with a cough, but based on Tessa's glare, he was unsuccessful.

"How many more floors?" Amber asked, staring up the narrow space that reached to a dizzyingly far height above them.

"You don't want to know," Icewind muttered. "Just keep moving and keep your ears peeled. We still need to make sure we don't get pinched between Saraqael's forces and a group hidden behind us."

CHAPTER 71

AMBER

"You can feel it, can't you?" Ceri asked as she fell into step beside Amber.

She nodded. The pack bond purred under her skin. It hadn't felt this right since before the curse was broken, and she had missed it. "I almost feel like I could shift."

"The storm hasn't dimmed," Deward said, his gaze turned upward. "Saraqael is doing something."

"Any idea what?" Tommy asked with a frown.

"I can't be certain, but the final relic is reacting to whatever it is. Perhaps he's drawing on its power?" Deward shook his head. "Or it could be malfunctioning."

"Whatever he's doing isn't going to be good for us." Amber let out a little sigh of relief as they passed onto the fifty-second floor. Saraqael was only one floor above them now. The adrenaline from the previous fight had waned just enough for her to feel the exhaustion tugging at her limbs.

Use the pack bond. You must be at full strength for this confrontation.

She glanced at her wolf. *I'm not the only one fighting. I can't just use the others like that.*

You must. This is a fight we cannot lose.

Biting back further arguments, she tentatively tugged at the pack bond. An awareness of the hundreds of werewolves connected to her as Alpha Dominus surged through her mind. She stumbled over a step, but Kadrithan caught her arm and helped her back upright.

"Are you injured?"

"No, just distracted. I'm not used to this Alpha Dominus stuff." She shook her head in an attempt to clear the disorientation. "Plus the bond still isn't quite back to normal."

"Are you sure? Perhaps we should stop and check--"

She rolled her eyes. "Stop fussing. If I was hurt, I'd tell you. I'm not that much of a martyr."

Genevieve snorted from behind them. "Even if she was, I'd feel it and tattle on her." She tapped her temple with a smirk. "Pack bond is almost back to normal."

Velez paused in front of them, causing the whole group to stop. "Do you smell that?"

Tommy sniffed the air and grimaced. "It's faint, but it smells like death."

Silence fell over the group as they picked their way up the final few steps. The sickening reek of rotting flesh grew stronger and stronger until even the humans among them were gagging at it.

Amber stopped a few feet from the doorway just behind Icewind and Velez. The stairwell door was already open. Severed heads lined the hallway. Each of them was displayed with care on ornate stone pedestals, as if they were flower arrangements and not the gruesome fear tactic she knew them to be. Her eyes skipped over the faces. She couldn't look at them. If she did, the rage would overwhelm her. She had to stay in control of herself and not let the bastard get to her.

Ceri stepped forward and lifted her hands. A breeze swirled past them, taking the overwhelming scent of decay with it. "That's all I can do for now."

Velez looked back at her and nodded once, pain clear in his eyes. "Thank you."

"Do we just...walk in?" Genevieve whispered.

The entryway opened into an open room. No one was visible from here, but Amber could sense something--someone--waiting for them just around the corner.

"We have our invitation." Amber swept her hand at the hallway. "So yeah, I think we do just walk right in." She ground her teeth together as she forced her feet to move. Every part of her screamed at her to run, to not get any closer to the evil in this room, but running wasn't an option. It never was. Kadrithan moved up to her right side and Genevieve to her left. At the very least, she wouldn't have to face this alone.

Saraqael was waiting for them on a raised dais in front of floor-to-ceiling windows, arms spread as if he was welcoming old friends. His wings were flared out behind him, and he was bathed in brilliant light. He looked every inch an angel. Glorious. Beautiful. Dangerous. The two remaining archangels stood on either side of him, just as beautiful and false.

The drained husks of dozens of incubi were strewn across the floor below them. The archangels must have fed on them, deeming them more valuable as a food source than as guards.

"Amber." Saraqael whispered her name like it was a caress. He smiled, eyes twinkling with joy and insanity. "Welcome to my home."

CHAPTER 72

KADRITHAN

Rage and grief warred inside of Kadrithan, though after so many years of struggling against the incubi, the two emotions were beginning to feel the same. As he met Saraqael's eyes across the room, the rage won out. This *creature* had caused so much suffering. Taken so many lives. And now he stood in front of them grinning as if it had all been a grand joke.

"I must say, I didn't expect you to arrive this evening." Saraqael took a single step forward, and his wings relaxed behind him, but the glaring light didn't fade. "But I knew you would come soon, and I have been ready."

"I'll give you this one chance to surrender peacefully." Amber spoke calmly, as if she was facing down nothing more than a common criminal. He had no idea how she did it. "I won't pretend you won't be executed after, but we can prevent this from being a bloodbath if you cooperate."

Saraqael's smile stuttered, then he pressed a hand to his chest and *laughed*. The archangel to his left glanced back at him with a frown, but neither joined him in his hysterical cackling. Finally, he pulled himself together and beamed at Amber. "It has been so long since anyone has been so bold. I'd forgotten how amusing it could be."

"Your relics are gone," Amber continued as if he'd never interrupted her. "And soon you will be, too."

"It's too late to stop me," Saraqael said, shaking his head fondly. "Far too late."

Amber's eyes flicked to Haniel, who stiffened almost imperceptibly. "It's never too late."

"Isn't it?" Saraqael whispered. "Faylen is dead. The fae are dying." The ground shifted under Kadrithan's feet, and the white marble of the condo gave way to a clearing of skeletal trees. He stepped back, but blood still soaked through the soles of his shoes. Faylen's blood. It was exactly like he remembered. Her body, lifeless. She wouldn't stay hidden like he'd commanded.

"The Seed of Life has been sacrificed, and for what?" Saraqael's pale eyes met his across the clearing as he walked toward Faylen's body, dragging a bloody sword behind him. "So you can watch another person you love die?"

This wasn't real, and Kadrithan knew that, but the familiar heat of the orange sun and the dryness of the air *felt* real. This was more than a simple illusion.

Kadrithan. The voice that whispered through his mind sounded like Amber, but he couldn't trust anything he saw or heard in this place.

"The only person that will die today is you," Kadrithan bit out from behind clenched teeth.

Kadrithan!

"I will let you choose who dies first and who dies last." Saraqael swept his hand in a lazy wave, and the pack appeared between them, kneeling with their hands bound.

Amber, tears streaming down her pale cheeks, looked up at him. "Kill me first. I'm not afraid."

Angel, please, I need you.

His eyes shot open with a gasp. Pain throbbed through his shoulder as he blinked up at Tommy's wolf. "What--"

Move!

He rolled to his right as the searing heat of white flames scorched the marble where he'd fallen and nearly singed his arm. Scrambling to his feet, he drew his sword as he searched for Amber amidst the chaos. He had to see her. Had to confirm she was still alive.

Tommy grabbed his arm and yanked him back as another stray bolt of fire hit less than a foot in front of them. "Don't just stand there!"

The archangel Khamael bore down on Tommy and Genevieve, but Derek's wolf forced the incubus to change directions to avoid losing a chunk of his leg. He had no idea how long Saraqael had held him in the illusion, but every second he'd spent laying on the floor instead of helping them fight could have gotten someone killed.

"Where is Amber?" The air reeked of magic and smoke. A white couch near the wall had caught fire, and the black smoke that poured from it was slowly filling the room.

"Fighting Haniel!" Tommy flung his arm toward the front of the room.

Saraqael stood by the windows watching the fight play out like a mad conductor. The bastard was enjoying this. The coven stood between him and the rest of the room. Ceri lifted her hands as the coven's chants grew. A gust of wind slammed into Saraqael. It barely moved him, but the windows exploded outward in a dazzling shower of glass.

An enraged howl from the other end of the room echoed over the cacophony of the fight. Velez lay prone in a growing pool of blood as his wolf staggered toward him, bleeding from the same wound. Amber's wolf charged Haniel from the left as Taharia launched herself into the air and dove toward the archangel, sword thrust forward like a spear.

Haniel kicked Amber's wolf and batted away Taharia's attack with a lazy wave of his sword. Amber charged in, baton raised high, and managed to slip under the first swing of Haniel's sword, but a well-timed kick knocked her off her feet and sent her rolling toward Icewind, who also appeared to be wounded.

Fear squeezed Kadrithan's heart like a vice as he sprinted toward Amber. They were outmatched. Even with three relics destroyed, the archangels weren't weakened at all. They were being toyed with.

The vampire appeared from the shadows behind Haniel. Daggers flashed through the air as he managed to slice open the archangel's arm. That small victory was all he managed. Haniel lifted one hand and blasted Bram with blinding light. The vampire let out a pained shriek as his skin caught fire in the conjured sunlight.

Amber let out a panicked shout and tried to crawl toward the rest of her pack where they fought Khamael. Kadrithan whipped around in time to see Derek flying through the air. He hit one of the marble pillars that stood between the entryway and the living room, and his head snapped back against the solid marble with a sickening crack. Kadrithan's heart dropped into his stomach as Derek fell limp to the floor and his wolf dropped to the ground a few yards away. With an enraged shout, Tommy and his wolf charged Khamael.

Unable to watch Amber's pack be slaughtered right in front of him, Kadrithan summoned what power he could and raced back. His magic stuttered and twisted, and it took longer than it should for the horns to push out from his skull and the fiery wings to explode from his back, but it was enough.

Launching into the air, he shot up with a hard flap of his wings then dove down at Khamael. He swung at the archangel's head with a vicious strike, forcing him to go on the defensive.

Khamael threw himself back with a snarl. "This resistance is pointless, and you know it, *King*," the archangel taunted as he regained his footing.

"I'll take satisfaction in knowing you die with me, then." Kadrithan charged again. Their swords clashed in a shower of sparks as he drove Khamael back. Tommy and his wolf circled around behind Khamael, boxing in their prey.

"Derek!" Amber's pained shout spurred him to attack.

He let out all the anger he'd been forced to hold back for so long. Magic lashed out of him, barely controlled. The final relic prevented him from putting the power he wanted into his attacks, but it was enough to see Khamael forced to finally fight back.

A wave of flames swept out from his blade as he swung at Khamael, but the magic fizzled out before it reached its target. Kadrithan ground his teeth together and attacked again. And again. And again. Tommy and Genevieve moved in and out, their wolves snapping at Khamael's legs as they tried to get in close enough to do some damage, but Khamael managed avoid every attempt as Kadrithan pressed him back toward the shattered windows.

"I'm surprised you can move this well after your injury." Khamael waved a hand at Kadrithan's side. "We were convinced for a while it had been a mortal wound since you disappeared without a trace."

The pain of the deep wound was constant after the day's fighting, but he knew better than to favor it and show how vulnerable it truly made him. "I'm not so easily killed."

"We'll see." Khamael lunged at him, and they clashed amidst the growing smoke.

Ceri and her coven were still attacking Saraqael. He had lost track of Amber once again, but out of the corner of his eye, he could see that Taharia at least still fought Haniel. His ally's losses were growing, and they had not done more than scratch one of the archangels. It wasn't enough.

Kadrithan twisted as he thrust his blade forward. His sword slid past Khamael's defenses and pierced the archangel's side in almost the exact same place where his own wound lay.

Before he could press his advantage, Khamael shot into the air and flew back to Saraqael, where he collapsed with a hand pressed to the growing wound on his side. "Saraqael, enough! You've had your fun!"

Saraqael dropped his hands and turned a scowl on Khamael. "Are you so weak that you could not last a few minutes more?"

"If he is weak, then it is your doing," Haniel retorted, anger leaking into his voice as he batted away another of Taharia's attacks.

For a tense moment, Saraqael remained silent as he stared at Haniel. Then, with a sneer, he relented and placed a hand on the pendant that hung around his neck. Ceri shouted some instruction to the coven, but it was too late. It glowed beneath Saraqael's palm as he whispered an incantation then exploded outward in a wave of darkness that swept through the room. There was no avoiding it. No running away.

Kadrithan stumbled back in shock. His wings were gone. The flames had died at his fingertips. There was nothing. No magic. He was *empty*. His sword slipped from his hand and clattered to the floor. Amber's scream split the air as she cried out for her wolf. A few paces ahead of him, Tommy dropped to his knees, hands clamped around his head as if he was in pain.

A sickening grin spread across Saraqael's face as he took in their reactions. "It seems you all forgot how easily I can make you human." He stalked forward, eyes sweeping over them as if selecting from a buffet. "Humans are a surprisingly resilient race but still so weak." He crouched in front of Icewind and grabbed her chin to force her gaze up to his. "How does it feel? It must be strange for an elf after having grown up so connected to nature."

She spat in his face.

Saraqael's smile never faltered as he tightened his grip on her jaw. "I wonder how much I can take before you die?"

Every instinct Kadrithan had screamed at him to pick his sword back up and do *something*. Anything but stand there and watch another person die. Yet his feet were frozen in place as he watched Amber struggle to her feet. She picked up her baton and walked toward Saraqael, entirely human and entirely defenseless. It was brave. She was always, always brave, but there was no point to this. They had lost.

He had lost...everything.

CHAPTER 73

AMBER

Amber's body ached, and everything in her screamed at the loss of her wolf, but she didn't dare stop moving. She couldn't simply lay down and die. They'd come too far to give up now.

"Get your hands off of her!" She lunged at Saraqael and swung her baton, electricity crackling along the metal, but he simply caught it and wrenched it from her grasp. The abrupt movement jerked her forward, and her knees slammed against the hard step that led up to the raised platform he stood on.

Before she could recover from the fall, he backhanded her hard enough to send stars dancing across her vision. She fell back, only just catching herself and preventing her head from cracking against the marble.

Saraqael grabbed her supporting arm and yanked her forward, driving the baton through the flesh of her bicep and into the marble below, pinning her in place. The pain didn't register right away. It was the shock that hit her first. She was effectively human within the no magic zone and wouldn't heal from this. Facts on blood loss swam through her mind as she scrambled to put pressure on the wound.

He shook his head, feigning disappointment. "Be patient. I can't give everyone my attention all at once."

Kadrithan's enraged shout echoed through the room. She wanted to scream at him to get whatever was left of her pack and just *run*, but he was already racing past her to attack Saraqael. Taharia charged the archangel from the other direction, but Saraqael sidestepped both attacks, still able to move inhumanly fast.

Taharia fell first. Saraqael wrenched her blade from her grasp and smacked the hilt of it into her head with a crack. She crumpled to the floor and remained still. Kadrithan attempted to use the distraction to move in.

Saraqael caught him by the throat, stripped the sword from his hands, and tossed it aside. "I didn't realize you had so much fight left in you." He dropped Kadrithan then kicked him, sending the fae tumbling back across the open space toward Amber.

Kadrithan gasped in pain, his arms wrapped around the wound he'd received from the previous battle weeks ago. "Despite your best efforts, the fae are free."

"Free to die, just like their king," Saraqael said as he stalked toward Kadrithan.

Panic flooded Amber's body as she tried to pull the baton free, but it wouldn't budge. She couldn't watch Kadrithan die. Frantic, she looked around the room, hoping *someone* could help, but Haniel had cornered her pack and the coven and taken their weapons. The only person missing was Deward. She swept her gaze around the room again, terrified she'd find his body somewhere, but he wasn't anywhere.

Before she could process his absence, the building shook with the force of the several explosions, one after another. Hope surged in her chest and was extinguished equally quickly. The no magic zone stayed in place. Whatever Saraqael had used to create it was unaffected by the fall of the final relic.

Khamael grabbed the wall and pulled himself back to his feet.

"They've taken the last relic, something you *swore* was impossible. You must share from your reserves. I can't heal without it."

Saraqael ignored him as he circled Kadrithan with a sick grin. Her heart pounded in her chest as she watched, still pinned to the floor like a bug. There was nothing she could do to stop him from hurting Kadrithan or any of the others.

Haniel's eyes locked onto the back of Saraqael's head. Anger twisted his mouth into a scowl. "You made a promise. To us. To *me*."

Saraqael froze at the interruption and whirled around, blue eyes crackling with rage. "To you? *You* are an ant. A pawn that I will use however I see fit. I am your god!" Saraqael spread his arms wide.

Haniel stepped back, and his fingers twitched toward the sword at his side. "When did you start believing your own lies, Saraqael?"

"Lies? Look around you!" Saraqael's eyes were wide with fanatical zeal. "I cannot be touched. I control magic itself. What am I if not a god?"

Haniel glanced back at Amber as if to say, *I told you so.*

With as much determination as she could muster, she met his gaze. "It's never too late. *Never.*"

She didn't see him move. One moment, Haniel was by the coven, the next his sword was slicing through the air toward Saraqael. With an enraged snarl, Saraqael ducked beneath the attack and drew his own sword--the first time he'd been forced to truly defend himself since the fight had begun.

It was impossible to track their movements as they danced back and forth across the room in a blur of fire and glinting blades. Khamael hung back near the shattered windows, his eyes flicking between the fight and the exit as if he was considering running.

A soft touch on Amber's shoulder nearly started a scream out of her, but she bit it back when she saw Genevieve and Tommy hovering over her.

"Can I pull it out? Or will it make the bleeding worse?" Genevieve's face paled as she gestured at the baton.

"It would make the bleeding worse. Maybe if..." Amber took a deep breath as a wave of nausea hit her. She had to stay focused and not think too hard about the fact that it was *her* arm they were discussing or she'd lose it. "Maybe we can get it out of the floor but leave it in my arm?"

Tommy moved around to her other side. "Come on. They won't be fighting forever. Wrap your hands around her arm and hold onto the baton. I'll try to get it out of the floor."

"Okay. I can do this." Genevieve took a deep breath and nodded her head firmly. Her face paled further as she wrapped her hands around the wound. "I. Can. Do. This."

Amber glued her eyes to the fight, needing a distraction. The tip of Haniel's blade caught Saraqael's cheek. Blood dripped down the bastard's perfect face onto his white shirt.

"It seems you *can* be touched," Haniel taunted.

The wound closed as if it had never been there. Saraqael glared at Haniel. "A scratch means nothing."

"Then I'll drive my blade deeper next time." Haniel flung himself into the fight once again.

"Now!" Tommy yanked the baton upward.

Amber bit down on the inside of her cheek to keep from crying out as pain shocked through her arm. Gray swam at the edges of her vision, but Tommy grabbed the back of her neck and shook her, forcing her back to consciousness.

"Stay awake. Come on. You have to be able to run."

"Run?" She blinked, and the pain returned full force, barely muted by the adrenaline coursing through her.

"While they're fighting. It's our only chance." Genevieve tugged her upright.

"The others..." Amber spotted Icewind laying on the ground where Saraqael had left her, leg bent at an unnatural angle. Velez in a pool of blood. Bram huddled in a corner, his flesh still smoking. Taharia was still, possibly killed by the blow to her head. And Kadrithan...crawling to his sword. She tried to push Genevieve away and stand, but her legs weren't functioning. "Stop him! You have to stop him!"

Tommy's head jerked up. "Shit. I'll try to get him. Gen, get her out of here."

"We can't just leave them behind!" She struggled against Genevieve's hold on her, but her beta still managed to start dragging her away.

"We can't do anything as long as we're stuck in this no magic zone. *Think*, Amber. You have to heal."

She slumped back against Genevieve as a sob filled her throat. "They're hurt, and we're just leaving them to die."

"We're not. We're coming back, we just have to--"

Saraqael let out an enraged shout as Haniel's sword sank into his thigh. He dropped his own weapon and stared down at the wound in shock.

"Do it now!" Haniel forced Saraqael back toward the other archangel.

Khamael lunged toward them, but a blast of blinding light threw him back and obscured Amber's view as she blinked the spots out of her eyes.

"No..." Genevieve's horrified whisper registered before the scene in front of her did.

Saraqael had both hands around Haniel's throat, the sword in his leg apparently forgotten as he *squeezed*. "Impudent, foolish, and arrogant! I knew I couldn't trust any of you!" Haniel's shaking body went limp as something in his neck cracked and broke. Flames surged from Saraqael's fingertips and consumed Haniel. He flung the now dead and charred husk of the archangel aside and whirled around to face the last of his mutinous allies. The pendant he wore must have allowed him to use magic when no one else could.

Khamael dropped his sword and held up his hands in surrender. "Please, I will serve--" White flames swept over Khamael and ended his pleas for mercy. Saraqael didn't stop until even the ashes of his body had burned away.

When Saraqael turned back to her, Amber saw in his eyes that whatever sanity had remained was now gone. He spread his arms wide. "They couldn't understand the truth, but it's so obvious, isn't it?" He leaned his head back and laughed. "I am all powerful. I *deserve* to rule." The sword remained in his leg, and blood from the wound had soaked through his pant leg down to his foot. He left bloody footprints behind as he paraded around in front of the shattered windows amidst the carnage. His gaze locked onto Tommy and Kadrithan, who had just reclaimed his sword. "And you have long deserved to die."

"No!" Amber struggled to her feet. She had to get to them. Had to stop Saraqael.

The door to the condo slammed open, and...Steven ran in. He looked terrified, but he sprinted straight for them. Genevieve tensed behind her, but before either of them could react, Steven slid to a halt, threw his shoulders back, and let out a long, warbling yell.

Saraqael stared at the human, appearing to be just as confused as the rest of them at the interruption. "Was that meant to accomplish something?"

"Your hair looks like a toupee!" Steven clenched his hands into fists. There was a bandage on his arm with a fresh spot of blood seeping through the white cotton. "And...and you have a sword in your leg!"

Genevieve's eyes flicked between Saraqael and her boyfriend. "Steven, what the fu--"

A waterfall of blood came out of nowhere and splashed down over Saraqael. The runed necklace sizzled and sparked as the blood drenched it. Amber looked up in shock as the swarm of pixies dropped the plastic bucket they'd somehow managed to carry all the way across the room and darted out of the broken window to safety.

Steven swallowed nervously and took a step back, his eyes darting around the room like he expected something to happen. "Ummm..."

Saraqael stood on the dais, covered in blood, his breath coming in short pants. "You *pathetic* creature. I will rip out your throat for your *insolence*." Before he could take a single step, the necklace exploded. He ripped it free with a snarl.

Amber watched it fall in slow motion as power and *magic* swept through her. Real, pure, untangled magic. Her soul cried out in relief as the familiar warmth of her wolf returned. A ripple of awareness of her pack, and all the packs connected to her, surged through her mind as the rest of their allies burst through the door with Ithra and Deward leading the charge.

CHAPTER 74

AMBER

Amber rose and ripped the baton out of her arm. The pain nearly dropped her again, but she pushed it aside as finally, *finally* the shift rolled up from the bottoms of her feet. Somehow, Deward had brought back help, and Steven's experiments with the no magic zones had paid off. He'd found a way to break them after all.

Her wolf howled in her mind, enraged at their temporary separation but jubilant at being reunited. Red bled across her vision as she landed on four feet. Though she couldn't see herself, she knew she was much larger than normal. Larger than when she'd fought either Carter or Ito. The power of being a true Alpha Dominus roiled inside of her as the alphas connected with her freely shared their power. The wound on her arm filled in, and the pain receded.

A series of piercing shrieks preceded the pixie swarm as they rushed back in through the broken windows. The glint of a shimmery glider sweeping over the crowd had her heart plummeting into her stomach. Woggy. He shouldn't be here, none of the pixies should be, but a dozen of them were zooming overhead, being chased by as many incubi.

Tommy was dragging Kadrithan back from the chaos, but there

was no way they'd make it to safety before being overwhelmed. Saraqael's eyes met hers across the room, then he looked at Kadrithan and she *knew*. He would kill Kadrithan just to punish her.

Her claws scraped against the marble as she raced toward them, a warning howl bursting from her throat. Tommy's panicked mind brushed against hers through the pack bond as he threw Kadrithan over his shoulder and ran. Amber poured strength into him. She had to reach them before Saraqael. There was no other option.

A thick fog rolled in through the open windows and swept over the attacking incubi and Saraqael, bringing with it the fresh scent of Ceri's magic. The fog obscured her vision, but with the pack bond's connection, she knew exactly where Tommy was, and the thick scent of Saraqael's blood left little doubt as to his location.

Tommy changed directions abruptly and ran straight toward her. She pushed herself to move faster. Her front leg ached from the still-healing wound, but she was too enraged for a little pain to slow her down. Kadrithan's fingers brushed along her side as she flew past him and Tommy. It was a brief touch, but it spurred her on. Saraqael had to pay for all the pain he'd caused.

She felt the weight of Saraqael's magic as a warning prickle down her spine that stood all her fur on end. On instinct, she crouched low and lunged to the side. A white-hot ball of fire slammed into the marble where she'd been. The heat of it had burned a tunnel through the fog, giving her a brief glimpse of Saraqael. His eyes were wide with fury and his teeth were bared like an animal. The illusion of his perfect, supernatural beauty was shattered. He finally looked as mad on the outside as he was on the inside.

We're with you now, Genevieve said through the bond. *All of us.*

Derek pulsed with determination and only a little fogginess as he continued healing from his injury. Relief flooded her. She couldn't do this alone, but with her pack's help, they had a chance.

Kadrithan is with the coven. He's safe, Tommy added as he drew close behind her. *Let's finish this.*

Get ready. I'm putting up a barrier. No one in or out until this bastard is dead. Ceri's fearless resolve filled the pack bond.

"*Claustra!*" Ceri's voice cracked through the air. The fog swirled around them, growing even thicker, as a strange, electric buzz filled the air.

Amber pushed her awareness out to locate each of her pack members and found it was not just her pack there to fight, but also the alphas that had sworn allegiance to her—Jameson, Greer, Ford, and Ito. They were all circling Saraqael. Ceri, Deward, and the coven were close behind her near the edge of the magical barrier she could sense through her connection to her shaman.

And...her nose twitched as Captain Jack's familiar scent drifted past her. He shouldn't be here anymore than the pixies should. Part of her wanted to find a way to get the not-cat to safety, but she had a feeling he was just as capable of defending himself as any of them, if not more so.

"Enough! Do you intend to hide in this fog forever?" Saraqael demanded.

Now. Amber pushed the command out as she raced toward Saraqael. It was both strange and exhilarating to be so connected to her pack once again. She could *feel* their locations within the barrier, and they all moved as one, perfectly coordinated.

Her teeth closed around Saraqael's ankle. His pant leg was already soaked in blood, and he nearly toppled over as she ripped her teeth free.

Fire seared through the air as he whirled around with a bellow of pain, slinging his magic without a target or clear purpose. It hit Ceri's barrier with jarring force that even Amber felt through the bond, but the coven held firm.

Her pack moved in and out, never staying still, as they struck at Saraqael over and over. Smoke mingled with the fog as his magic burned into the marble floor, leaving dangerous molten-hot traps all around them.

"Amber?" Kadrithan's voice was quiet against the chaotic backdrop, but he was close enough for her to pick it out.

She edged toward him, furious he hadn't stayed put. He was hurt. She could smell his blood through the smoke. Finally, she bumped against him, and he leaned heavily on her, twining his fingers in her fur.

"He is weak."

Her lip curled as she growled at him, hoping he understood what she couldn't say aloud: *So are you.*

"I can't just sit back while your pack fights for me. I need to finish this." He straightened and drew his sword from the sheath, the metal ringing against the leather. "Can you draw his attention?"

She nudged him to show her agreement then crept forward as she shared the plan with the pack. They'd worn Saraqael down and needed to strike while he was still disoriented--Kadrithan was right about that at least, no matter how much she wanted to stash him somewhere safe until the fight was over.

Ito charged in first. Amber followed, leaving Kadrithan to circle around behind Saraqael as they darted in and out, forcing the archangel to focus on them.

Amber jumped over a molten pit in the floor and attempted to get a grip on the sword still stuck in Saraqael's leg, but he jerked back too quickly for her to follow and sent a blast of fire right at her. She lunged to the left to avoid it, but the flames still singed her fur.

She couldn't see what happened next from where she was, but she smelled the fresh blood and heard something hit the floor with a fleshy *thunk*.

"NOOO!" Magic pulsed out from Saraqael as he let out a scream full of rage and desperation.

Get back! Ceri's desperate plea through the bond came just in time. The pack scattered as Saraqael's magic exploded in a fiery wave. Kadrithan dove on top of Amber and drove her to the floor, but he couldn't completely shield her from the searing heat as the barrier shattered and Saraqael's magic swept through the room. The fog vanished with the barrier, leaving the pack exposed as a furious Saraqael staggered in the center of the room.

His left arm lay on the floor, severed close to the shoulder. He stared at in shock then slowly lifted his gaze to Kadrithan. "You have ruined *everything*." A whirlwind of white flames started at his feet and spiraled up around his body until he was hidden behind them.

A tendril of fire lashed up and hit the ceiling like a whip. Smoldering plaster rained down on the incubi still battling their allies. Another lashed out, then another. Half her pack was forced to retreat behind the coven. At this rate, the flames would consume everything. Saraqael had either lost control or decided to take them all down with him.

The incubi took this as their cue to ramp up their attacks. A group of them launched into the air and headed straight for the coven. Jackson swung his rifle around and fired. The lead incubus crumpled midair and fell. He fired twice more, and two others dropped, but the final two dove down in a sharp descent toward their goal. But they never made it.

A gray blur streaked through the air and slammed into both incubi with a roar that shook the air. Captain Jack ripped into the two incubi before they could fight back, ending their lives with terrifying efficiency.

Woggy gave a fierce battle cry from Captain Jack's back. This was nothing like the time the pixie had ridden into battle with the tuna can armor. Captain Jack's muzzle was soaked in blood, and he was three times his normal size, with large spines jutting out from his back. The vulnerable, wingless pixie was here to fight, and with Jack's help, they were doing some serious damage.

Amber pushed up to her feet and supported Kadrithan as he did the same, his bloody sword clutched in his hand.

"We have to get through those flames before he wrecks this place." Kadrithan leaned heavily on her as he spoke, and she could smell fresh blood beneath his clothes, but nothing she could say would convince him to hold back.

Ceri and Deward pushed to the front, pressed together shoulder to shoulder, and lifted their hands. The coven's chants grew behind them. Ceri flicked her hand down then curled it into a fist. The marble floor in a wide swath ahead of her shattered like glass. She raised her other hand, and the jagged pieces rose into the air. At her command, wind swept over the last of the incubi.

Amber nearly lost her footing, but Kadrithan caught her shoulder with his free hand. The wind swept up the bits of marble, turning them into deadly shrapnel that slammed into the incubi charging them. It pierced their light armor easily, and they dropped with cries of pain, causing whoever was behind them to stumble.

The remaining incubi began to retreat, but as Amber scanned the room, she realized how many of their allies had been injured in the fight while they'd been inside the barrier. Saraqael's magic was only growing more erratic. The heat from the flames had sweat dripping down Kadrithan's face.

She shifted even as the terror that it would somehow separate her from her wolf again made her heart pound. But, back on two feet, she could still feel her wolf inside her mind, right where she should be.

Kadrithan steadied her with a hand to her elbow. "You have a plan?"

"Nope. You?"

"Stay alive long enough to kill Saraqael."

She snorted. "That's the bare minimum requirement for success, *not* a plan." Still shaking her head, she jogged over to Ceri and the coven. They looked exhausted. "Anything you can do to stop this?"

Ceri's lips thinned. "Maybe, but it's going to be messy. I can't erect another barrier. We're running on magical fumes over here."

"We have to get the injured out of here, then. Everyone but the pack needs to retreat."

Derek, who had just joined them along with Tommy, frowned. "Going to be hard to get Jackson and Jacob to leave."

"I'll drag them out myself if I have to."

"We have to move quickly. Do whatever you have to now and give us a little time to––" Ceri gaze was focused on the window where a lone owl flew in and circled above Saraqael, seemingly unaffected by the heat. "Change of plans."

"We never had a plan to begin with," Kadrithan muttered.

"Get everyone out now." Ceri stepped forward, her eyes still locked on the owl. "I think we're going to get a little help."

Amber pushed out a mental command to Jameson, Greer, and Ford to force everyone out. The other alphas shifted back to human form and ran to organize the retreat. Amber spotted Icewind in Ford's arms. Her face was pale and her leg was...not okay, but she was still alive. That was all that mattered at this point.

Taharia limped toward them, blood matted in her blond hair and smeared down the side of her face. "I'm not leaving. I can still fight."

A particularly large flare of fire hit the ceiling and sent a crack splintering all the way to the far wall. Dust rained down as the crack continued spreading.

"Get back!" Derek yelled.

The pack and coven scrambled to dodge as half the ceiling caved in and collapsed, cutting them off from their remaining allies with a wall of dust and smoke. There had been injured people still laying where the ceiling had fallen. Amber wanted to scream at the horror of it all, but there was no time to have a breakdown. Saraqael's magic was only growing more erratic.

"Whatever you're going to do, do it now." Amber ran toward Saraqael, shifting as she went. The pack sprinted after her as Ceri linked hands with Deward in the center of the coven. Even now that magic was working properly again, they were more powerful together.

The pack bond swelled as Ceri drew on its power. Amber reached out to the other alphas and through them to their packs. Strength poured in, and she swelled with it, sharing it freely amongst each of her pack members.

She slid to a halt across from Saraqael and met his eyes through the flames. He reached for her, and the white fire followed his arm and flared toward her liked a clawed hand. She darted out of reach, mentally begging Ceri to hurry. The flames that surrounded Saraqael had reached so high they were burning a hole in what was left of the ceiling, and the floor around him was nothing more than a moat of lava.

Ceri drew hard on the pack bond, and a rush of fresh air swept into the room through the broken windows. The owl dove toward Saraqael, and reality itself split open above him. Light poured out, and at first, it appeared to be a solid stream, but Amber realized it was *hundreds* of spirits all pouring out of the portal at once. Thunder echoed throughout the room, and lightning cracked down amidst the spirits, striking the floor in a blinding flash as they swarmed Saraqael. He screamed.

The heat of the flames vanished, and the whirlwind of fire was snuffed out. Saraqael stumbled out of the midst of the spirits and ripped the sword from his thigh with a shout. He swung the blade at them, but it passed through their transparent bodies without any effect.

This was it. This was their chance. She howled, and the pack charged. Taharia and Kadrithan shot into the air and dove down at Saraqael alongside the spirits. Bram, his burned flesh still blackened, sprinted in from behind.

The vampire reached him first and bit a chunk out of his remaining arm before slipping back out of reach. Amber snapped at his injured leg but was forced back by an awkward swing of his sword. The distraction was enough, though. Kadrithan thrust his sword ahead of himself. The point slid along Saraqael's side and ripped open a jagged wound beneath his severed arm. The archangel staggered back as Taharia knocked the sword free from his grip.

Amber saw her chance and took it. Red bled into her vision as she lunged, jaws open wide, and bit down on his exposed throat. Blood filled her mouth, and for a moment, a fierce triumph surged within her, but it was cut short by an explosion of fire and pain.

Absently, she noted that she was flying through the air, but her mind was fuzzy, and the pain overwhelmed everything. Screams echoed through the room, pounding inside her already aching head. She blinked, but the gray haze covering her vision remained.

Someone was touching her.

Amber.

The room spun as if she were at the center of a hurricane. Flashes of sound and light served only to confuse her more, but she could feel the pack. They were alive, at least.

Amber! It was Tommy this time, his voice panicked. Was he hurt? Did they need her?

She struggled to move, but something was holding her down. Her legs were pinned. When had she shifted? Her wolf...she reached out in a panic, but she was there. She hadn't left her again.

Dark eyes looked down at her, and something brushed against her lips. Her face was wet. Someone's hands were brushing the wetness away.

The pack bond stuttered to life in her chest and swelled. There was love and fear and anger, but most of all determination. A hand slipped into hers as the magic burned through her, almost too intense to bear. The pain receded, not completely, but enough to take a deep breath. She nearly choked as oxygen flooded her lungs; her throat was raw, and her entire chest felt too tight and too tender. She wondered if her ribs were broken as stabbing pain nearly sent her back into unconsciousness.

"Amber, please wake up." Genevieve's broken plea broke through the humming that filled her ears.

She tried to open her eyes, but they felt too heavy.

"We have to get her to a hospital. We've done all we can."

There was the sensation of movement and the pain surged again. Everything went dark.

CHAPTER 75

TOMMY

Tommy's eyes were drawn to what was left of Saraqael as Kadrithan lifted Amber from the floor. They'd killed him. Torn him apart, really, but the damage had already been done. The explosion had thrown them all back, but Amber had been at the center of it. The flames had consumed her, and for a terrifying moment, their connection had flickered out.

His heart still pounded in his chest, and he couldn't get his muscles to relax. The fight had ended so abruptly it didn't feel real.

Deward's hand landed on his shoulder. "It's over, Tommy. Breathe."

He forced himself to take a breath as instructed, but he couldn't slow his heartbeat. "Amber's hurt bad."

"I know."

"She can't…we can't…" He couldn't finish the sentence. But losing the family he'd found was too much to consider. He needed Amber. They all did.

"Amber is strong, and she has us. She'll make it, I––"

Shouting interrupted them, and Tommy whirled around as Evangeline forced her way into the room, followed closely by Katarina and Charlie. "Where is he? Don't try to stop me!"

Derek shook his head and stepped aside. "Go see for yourself since you're so damn determined."

Evangeline clambered over the debris from the ceiling and ran toward her father's corpse. She stopped less than a foot away and stared in disbelief. "I...I missed it. I was too late."

Tommy started to take a step toward her, but he knew he couldn't make her feel better. Couldn't take this pain away or offer some platitude to make it all okay. Her father had hurt her in ways he hoped to never experience, and her hate for him and everyone that had tried to control her had driven a wedge between her and the pack that may never be repaired. The least they could do was give her the space to grieve over the revenge she was denied.

"We should go with Amber," Deward prompted. "Can you lead the way?"

"Yeah. Sorry." Tommy held out his arm, which Deward took, and they picked their way over to the exit. Kadrithan had transferred Amber to a stretcher, which Derek and Genevieve lifted from the floor. Kadrithan had injuries of his own, and no matter how much he argued the point, there was no way he was making it all the way to the bottom floor carrying *anything*.

Ito joined the pack in the elevator and placed a hand on Amber's leg as he continued to share whatever energy he could with her. Together, they'd managed to pull her back from the brink, but her injuries were extensive and were taking too long to heal.

Ceri put an arm around his shoulders. Tears streamed down her face, and she shook with exhaustion. "It's over, but it doesn't feel like it, does it?"

"It will when Amber is back on her feet." Genevieve lifted her chin. "And she will be. She's going to be okay."

Kadrithan remained silent at her side, his eyes rimmed in red. One hand was clenched in a tight fist at his side, and the other gripped hers like he was afraid she might vanish if he let go. He couldn't blame him--they were all afraid of that as they huddled around her in the elevator.

CHAPTER 76

AMBER

Her mouth was dry as a desert and tasted vaguely of roadkill. She groaned and tried to lift her hand, but it was tangled in something.

"Stop moving, or you'll yank out the IV." Kadrithan pressed her arm back down to the bed as he stared down at her, brow creased with worry. There were dark circles under his eyes, and he was still covered in soot and blood.

"Is he--"

"Dead. We made sure of it. Ceri went back and burned his remains just to be sure after we got you to the hospital."

"Buried the ashes in salt, too." Ceri leaned in and smoothed back the hair that had been bothering her. "We're not taking *any* chances."

"Everyone...here?" Amber asked haltingly. Her throat still ached.

"As if we'd leave you in the hospital all alone," Genevieve scoffed from the end of her bed with a tap on her foot. She managed to lift her head enough to look around and saw them all there. Tommy and Deward stood by Ceri. Steven had an arm wrapped around Genevieve, and Amber's brothers were jockeying for position with

Derek. Her dad gave her a nod from behind them. He looked just as tired as she felt.

"They had to clear out a whole suite since none of us would leave," Tommy added with a grin. "The nurses weren't happy, but Icewind--from her room across the hall, by the way--got the MIA to order VIP treatment for you. Since you're a hero and all."

She tried to laugh, but it came out a wheeze, which hurt even worse than talking.

"Get her water!" Ceri demanded, waving an imperious hand at Kadrithan.

He jumped up and grabbed a cup of water from the tray behind him. It even had one of the little bendy straws, which he helpfully guided to her mouth so she didn't have to put any effort out. The icy water was bliss on her throat.

"Thanks," she whispered when he finally lowered the cup. Memories of those final moments fighting Saraqael were hazy, but she remembered the explosion and the pain. "I felt y'all. Heard y'all calling my name. What happened?"

Kadrithan sat back and looked away, his face paling.

Ceri took her hand and squeezed it tight. "When Saraqael unleashed that final explosion, I was able to shield the pack from the worst of it, but you were too close. You were *on* him." She paused and cleared her throat as if choking back tears. "You were broken. Burned."

Amber's eyes flicked to her hands, but they looked normal. None of her skin hurt like it should if she'd been burned as bad as Ceri was implying.

"It's healed. The pack...we..." Ceri took another breath. "We gave you all the strength we had left, and it was just enough to bring you back from the brink. If the spirits hadn't... They helped. Ito and the other alphas helped, too. We were lucky to have them nearby."

"You've been healing faster and faster since we got you out of there, but the doctor said your ribs are still cracked, and even though you're a werewolf, you're going to be exhausted for a couple of weeks." Tommy pinned her with a serious expression. "You're going to have to *rest*."

At that moment, she didn't even have the energy to argue. Rest sounded wonderful. Blissful, even. "Okay."

Genevieve's jaw dropped. "Oh god, she's dying, isn't she?"

"She's not dying," Kadrithan snapped.

"I was being sarcastic, you overly dramatic *dork*." Genevieve rolled her eyes then turned a skeptical look toward her. "But I am a little worried at the calm acceptance."

Amber shook her head. Gently. "I'll argue tomorrow after I've had a full night's rest."

Derek raised an eyebrow. "You've been asleep for eighteen hours already."

"What? That long?"

"It's been a tense wait for you to wake up," Deward acknowledged quietly.

Weariness was already tugging at her eyelids again, but she couldn't pass out again just yet. Especially not after the pack had been so worried. She could feel it now, a constant thrum under her skin. "Who else was hurt?"

"Velez lost a lot of blood, but since the relic team managed to take down the final relic in time, his werewolf healing saved him. He's actually back on his feet already," Genevieve explained. "Umm, Taharia has seen better days, but she didn't need to stay in the hospital, either."

"People died, mostly on the relic teams," Ceri admitted with a grim expression. "We'll have some funerals to attend once the chaos dies down."

"Ito is taking care of the packs that lost members while you're recovering, and I'm doing what I can to help with all that." Tommy shoved his hands in his pockets. "Not much to say to those grieving, though."

"Or Evangeline," Derek muttered.

"Evangeline?" Amber drew her eyebrows together and turned to Kadrithan. "You found her?"

He wrapped a hand around the back of his neck and grimaced. "Katarina and Charlie were supposed to get her to safety ahead of our confrontation with Saraqael, but instead, they brought her straight to the fight." He sighed and shook his head. "They arrived moments after the fight was over, thankfully."

"Could have been helpful to have her there," Ceri insisted as she crossed her arms.

"I think she's been through enough without adding killing her own father to mix," Kadrithan shot back with a scowl. "They should have taken her somewhere safe like we agreed."

"Katarina was right. Asking them to kidnap her was *stupid*."

Amber rolled her eyes. She had a feeling these two would always find something to argue about, and she was too tired to deal with any of it right now. "What's done is done. I'm assuming we have bigger problems now."

"Eh...they're mostly handled." Genevieve patted her foot in reassurance. "The councils are stepping up finally and helping deal with the fallout."

"Where's Bram?"

Ceri frowned. "I haven't seen him since the fight. I assumed he disappeared somewhere to feed and recover."

Sudden panic shot through her. "And Woggy? And Captain Jack?" She struggled to sit up. "I saw them there! At the end. They shouldn't have even--"

"Chill out." Ceri pushed her back down. "They're fine. All the pixies are. Even though they have been *thoroughly* lectured about the insanely stupid risk they took, it did kind of save us all." She shook her head. "No one bothered to lecture Captain Jack, though. We just gave him his own pizza."

Amber's gaze snapped to Steven, who was already blushing. "You told Saraqael his hair looked like a toupee."

He covered his face with his hands as everyone cracked up in laughter. "I'm never going to hear the end of that, am I?"

"Never," Derek cackled, reaching over to slap him on the shoulder.

"It was all I could think of in the moment! He was terrifying!" Steven protested.

She grinned at him. "I hope he died knowing he was having a bad hair day. He was prissy enough that probably bothered him." Unexpected tears pricked at her eyes, and Kadrithan slipped his hand into hers. She turned her gaze to him. "It's really over?"

"Yes," he whispered, hope clear in his eyes despite his obvious exhaustion. "We're finally free."

CHAPTER 77

KADRITHAN

"Let me just——"

"No, I can do it." Amber batted his hands away as she staggered out of the car.

He stepped back with a scowl. She was hurting even though she claimed she was fine. Her calm acceptance of the doctor-ordered rest had lasted all of one day. "You said you would let me carry you if you were ever hurt. It appears that was a *lie*."

"I'm not trying to climb five flights of stairs. It's like a hundred feet to the front door!" She flung her hand toward the house, which was indeed fairly close. That didn't mean she could make it without tiring herself out.

Ceri, who had driven them back from the hospital, had to pinch her lips together to keep from laughing. She shook her head and left them behind to continue their argument.

"You broke a centuries old curse *and* killed the bastard that ruined my life. Will you let me do *something*, dammit? Please?" He threw his hands in the air in exasperation.

Amber stared at him in shock. "I…you helped with all of that!"

With a sigh, he dragged his hands down his face. "Helped while you took on all the risk and were nearly killed. Just…" He took advantage of her confusion and swept her up. His side still ached, but it was healing well, and this wouldn't tire him out like it would her. "Just let me do this."

She crossed her arms but didn't demand to be put down as he carried her toward the house. "I could have made it."

"Has anyone told you that you become extremely grumpy when you're hurt?"

"Might have been mentioned a few dozen times," she muttered.

He nudged the door Ceri had left cracked for them fully open and stepped inside. "Couch or bed?"

"I don't know, do I get actually get a choice?"

He didn't grace that particular complaint with a response, just raised an eyebrow and waited for her to pick.

She only managed to hold her glare for a moment then rolled her eyes and waved at the couch. "I'm sick of laying in beds. At least I'll be sitting up in here."

He set her down as carefully as he could but still noticed she stopped breathing for a moment to avoid a hiss of pain. "I'll get you some water." He tugged the blanket off the back of the couch and laid it over her lap while she glared at him. Captain Jack was appreciative at least and climbed into her lap with a rumbling purr. "Are you hungry?"

"I can--"

"I'm making her a plate already," Tommy yelled from the kitchen, cutting off her objections.

Kadrithan crossed his arms as he mentally thanked her pack for not listening to anything she'd said since she'd ended up in the hospital. "Want a foot stool?"

"Offer me one more thing and I'll *tackle* you. Ribs be damned." She scowled as she petted Captain Jack. "Or maybe sic Jack on you."

"That second option is actually a little scary."

Tommy grabbed a tray table with his free hand as he delivered the promised food. "Ito taught me how to make ramen. You're going to love it."

His phone buzzed with *another* text from Zerestria. He had promised to return to the Market and handle some urgent business once Amber was safely back at home, but he had hoped to delay the inevitable a bit longer. Unfortunately, that wasn't an option.

With a sigh, he nodded farewell to Tommy. "Don't let her run off while I'm gone."

"Where are you going?" Amber immediately demanded.

"Duty calls."

"Fine." She stabbed her spoon into the bowl. "Go do important things while I watch TV. See if I care."

He didn't want to leave, but she had her pack. She didn't need him there as much as he needed to be near her. And no matter how much he resented it, he *did* have other responsibilities still. The Market was reopening in a week--and relocating, though not far. They had decided to direct it out of the pack's backyard so visitors wouldn't wandering through pack lands to access it.

"I'll be back this evening. Soon as I can." He suppressed the urge to lean down and give her a kiss goodbye. It wasn't entirely clear where they stood, and that sort of thing was…just not something he could do on a whim.

She shooed him away. "Go handle your *duties*."

Tommy shook his head with an amused smile. "I'll watch our invalid alpha, don't worry."

With great effort, Kadrithan forced himself to nod and walk out the back door. The entire way back to the Market was a miserable effort of wills as he fought the urge to turn back and check on her. Make sure she hadn't somehow disappeared.

When the explosion had happened, he thought she'd been killed. She'd been so still and so very hurt. The memory still sent a spike of fear through him.

Zerestria was waiting in his office when he walked in and took in his appearance with an unimpressed expression. "You need sleep."

"I've been sleeping."

"In a hospital chair."

He tugged off his jacket and tossed it on the chair by the fireplace as he strode toward his desk. "Amber is back home. I'll take their couch tonight, instead."

"Not her bed?"

He rolled his eyes. "We haven't had five minutes alone. I'm not..." He sighed. "There hasn't been time to discuss that...sort of thing."

Zerestria scoffed. "Put it off too long, and she'll start to think you've lost interest."

A familiar pit of uncertainty churned in his gut. "I'm not putting it off. She just needs rest." He cleared his throat. "Now, I left so I could deal with whatever urgent matters you texted me about, not for a lecture on my..." He waved a hand in a vague gesture. "What did you really need?"

Zerestria looked entirely unconvinced by his arguments but sat down and pulled out her list regardless. "The first issue is reintegration."

He nodded, having expected this conversation, and settled in for a long, boring, but entirely necessary conversation. The elders all had their own opinion on the matter, but the ultimate decision was his, and it wasn't an easy one. Part of him was eager to renounce his position, let the fae become US citizens, and move on with his life as no one important, but he'd found he couldn't do it. They had already lost so much. He wasn't willing to give up what little remained of their kingdom as well.

And so, it seemed he was destined to be King of the Market. The final preserve of true fae magic and power.

CHAPTER 78

EVANGELINE

Evangeline lay in the middle of the library and stared up at the ceiling, the book she'd tried to read abandoned beside her. She didn't know why she'd agreed to come here. After seeing her father's body, everything was a big blank. Leena--some fae guard they pretended hadn't been assigned as her babysitter--said they'd burned his body to ash.

Her purpose had been stripped from her. The incubi had surrendered, and with her father's death, the burning hatred for their kind had simply been snuffed out. Her chest felt empty without it.

The door opened, and quiet footsteps led into the room. She knew who it would be without looking. Her uncle. He visited every morning and every evening and talked at her. She never responded.

"Thallan is in hospice. Icewind is with him."

Silence.

"Katarina spent another half hour yelling at me over breakfast this morning." He cleared his throat awkwardly. "I've been told that in addition to my previous apologies, I should add my sincerest regrets that I didn't get you birthday presents as a child. Apparently, this oversight would have added to your feeling of being used, since I didn't dote on you like a loving uncle should."

Even though she knew she'd regret it, the apologies were getting increasingly ridiculous. "I think Katarina is just making things up at this point."

He shrugged. "Does that mean you don't want presents?"

"I don't want anything from you." The more she said it, the less she meant it, but there was too much resentment built up over too many years for her to accept things from him. "I want to leave."

The silence stretched into discomfort before he finally responded. "Okay."

She sat up and looked back at him for the first time. "That's it? Okay?"

He stared at her uneasily. "Should I be arguing with you? I'm trying to…let you decide things."

"It's just weird. You always argue." She curled her arms around her legs and rested her chin on her knees. She'd said she wanted to leave, but she didn't actually know what she wanted. That was the problem.

"I'm trying very hard to be better. To listen." He crossed his arms and took a deep breath. "Where would you like to go? Or…do you want to keep that information private?"

"You really mean it? You'd let me just walk out?"

He lifted his chin, as if accepting a challenge. "Yes."

She shook her head in disbelief. "Katarina must be very scary."

"She is."

Picking at her jeans, she mulled over her options. Maybe leaving was a good idea. She needed space from all of this--her uncle, her past, the pack, and the memories of everyone she'd lost. "I'll tell you, I guess. I don't care if you know. Maybe…" She hesitated for a moment before forcing the words out. "Maybe you could pay for college or something."

"Of course. Do you have a school in mind?"

She gnawed on her lip. "Maybe somewhere with a beach. Hawaii? I haven't really looked yet."

"Wherever you want."

The silence stretched between them again, and the question that had been gnawing at the back of her mind for weeks rose up to the forefront again. It had felt too awkward to ask him before, but he *had* spent days apologizing for every single transgression, both real and imagined. Maybe it was finally time.

"Can you tell me about my mom? About Faylen." A lump filled her throat as soon as she'd forced the words out, and she turned her face away from her uncle.

He walked over to the chair by the fireplace and sat down. "Yes, I can. I'll tell you everything I remember."

CHAPTER 79

GENEVIEVE

Genevieve pulled her feet up onto the couch and tucked them under Steven's shoulder. He was snoring, as was Derek where he was sprawled out with his head in Ceri's lap.

The news was muted, but the images of the Woolworth Building said it all anyhow. Talk of their fight there was the biggest news of the week along with the restoration of magic. The councils and the MIA were handling how the information was shared with the general public, but there wasn't much to hide. The details of the relics, of course, were being kept under wraps. They did *not* need any copycats.

The "cure" for the no magic zones, however, had been blasted everywhere. Steven's discovery was so simple but so brilliant. Apparently, a willing donation of human blood was enough to break the dark magic. She smiled down at his sleeping head. The last of the zones was being fixed today, a week after the fateful battle with Saraqael.

Their pack and so many others still struggled with the lingering wounds of that fight--both physical and mental. Amber's healing had sped up, but healing such serious injuries had left her sleeping ten to eleven hours a night. Ito, Tommy, and Deward spent most of their time planning funerals and finding ways to support those who had lost family members in the battle. Her time was swamped reviewing press releases and staying in touch with Icewind, who unfortunately couldn't heal nearly as quickly as any of them. Her broken leg had required surgery.

Ceri had been forced to work much more closely with the Witch's Conclave than any of them wanted, but efforts to prevent anyone from trying to copycat the no magic zones was too important for petty grudges.

With all the chaos, it had actually felt so much longer than a week, yet it hadn't. They were still pulling bodies from the Woolworth Building.

Captain Jack prowled into the room with Woggy on his back. He meowed plaintively as he paced in front of the couch.

"We *just* fed you an *hour* ago," Gen groaned as she uncurled from the couch and shuffled to the kitchen. "There's no way you're hungry."

Ceri snorted in amusement. "Amber bought extra treats. We're taking no chances."

"I knowwww, he's just so demanding. I swear Woggy is training him somehow." She eyed the pixie, who was trying way too hard to look nonchalant as she pulled the bag of jerky pet treats out of the pantry. It was meant for large breed dogs, but Captain Jack liked it better than the cat treats, and considering he wasn't actually a cat, no one was too worried.

She pulled out a treat, but it vanished from her hand in a blur of gray wings and squeaks. The twins got two feet before the weight of their stolen goods dragged them to the floor. Woggy's high-pitched chastisement sent the twins scampering beneath the cabinets as Jack waddled over and settled in for a snack, unconcerned at its near loss.

"Those little *menaces* are getting way too crafty." She tossed the treats back into the pantry and closed the door. Pretty soon they'd figure out how to open doorknobs, and not even that would be enough to keep them out.

She couldn't help but smile at the thought. Today, pixies in the pantry was her biggest problem. Sure, there was still crap to deal with, but it was annoying, not life-threatening. The pack was home. They were...okay. Everything was good. And as normal as it would ever get for them.

"Hey, Ceri?"

"Yeah?" Ceri glanced back at her with a worried frown.

"Want to go get our nails done tomorrow?"

Ceri blinked, then a grin spread across her face. "That would be amazing."

CHAPTER 80

Tommy yawned over breakfast. He'd slept in today, finally. He and Ito had done all they could for the packs that had lost people, and now all that remained were the funerals, which wouldn't be held until next week.

Deward approached and smacked down a stack of brochures on the table in front of him, startling him into nearly dropping his bacon.

He stared at the brochures. "Um, what's all this?"

"College. I...want to go."

His eyes snapped up to Deward's face. "Really? You're actually willing to do it?" He'd been bugging Deward about this for *ages,* and the troll had refused to commit to anything. Until now, apparently.

"Only if we go together. First of all, I don't like the idea of living without at least one other pack member. Second of all––"

Tommy dropped his bacon and tackled him in a bear hug, cutting off his completely unnecessary list of stipulations. "Of course we're going together! No way I'd room with some stranger." He stepped back and smacked Deward's shoulder. "Plus, I'm your guide dog."

Deward smirked at him. "I'll remember that when I need someone to read out my homework to me."

"Psh, we're past all that. You can just tap into the bond and use my eyes."

"I have to learn to function *without* that. Becoming even more dependent on the pack is a terrible idea, and you know it."

Tommy sighed but didn't argue. Deward *was* right, after all. "I know, but it's still an option every now and then. Can't let the pack bond get all rusty with disuse just because we aren't fighting for our lives every week."

Amber strolled in with her own plate of leftover breakfast food. She had finally stopped limping, and the undercurrent of pain and tension had faded from the bond. She eyed the brochures with a mix of excitement and hesitation. "Colleges?"

"Yep," Tommy confirmed with a grin.

"Y'all will pick something within driving distance, right?" She hesitated. "Not that you have to. I just...it'll be weird. And something could...happen."

"There is a brochure for Oxford in there, but I doubt we'll choose that one." Deward managed to say it with a straight face, but he knew him well enough to see how amused he was at Amber's reaction.

Her head snapped up, and she paled. "Oxford? As in England? Across an *ocean*?!"

Tommy busted out laughing.

Deward joined him for a moment but took pity on Amber and clarified their plans. "We're not going to Oxford, Amber. These are all colleges in Washington and Oregon."

Amber closed her jaw with a click and glared at them. "This is what I get for not making my pack treat their alpha with respect."

"What's this about respect?" Genevieve asked as she strolled in with three pixies dangling from the buns on top of her head.

"Deward was just trying to give me a heart attack," Amber muttered.

Tommy shook his head and held up a brochure. "We're sorting through our college options."

"Oooh, gimme." Genevieve snatched up a few of the brochures and immediately tossed two aside. "No party schools allowed. If I had to suffer through a lame and purely educational college experience, so do you."

"Hey! We're choosing, not you!" Tommy tried to wrestle the brochures back, but Genevieve danced away and led him on a chase into the living room and around the couch. Even though she was tiny, she was quick and managed to keep them just out of reach no matter how close he got. "Deward! A little help, man?"

"I'm blind. I can't *possibly* see how I could help," Deward said with a smirk. "Amber, want to go over the ones they aren't fighting over like a bunch of children?"

Genevieve gasped in mock offense. "I am a responsible adult!"

Amber snorted and shook her head, but she was smiling. "I don't interfere with fights for dominance. Gotta let the wolves sort it out amongst themselves."

He perked up. "So, if I get the brochures back, I get to be beta?"

"Sure." Amber shrugged.

"Don't even think about it!" Genevieve warned, backing away with the brochures still tucked safely against her chest.

Tommy grinned. "Time to get myself a promotion."

Genevieve shrieked as he lunged, and the fight was on.

CHAPTER 81

CERI

Sunshine streamed in through the large garage roll-up doors as Ceri and Derek entered the mechanic shop. They'd come alone today, but in a few days the whole pack intended to come for a big cleaning day to knock out whatever they couldn't get done this afternoon.

"I'm basically starting from scratch." He nudged a dust-covered toolbox with his foot.

Ceri turned in place and took it all in. The place *was* a mess, and they hadn't entirely repaired the damage from the attack by the golems. It was weird to see. It seemed like it had been years since that attack, but it hadn't been all that long ago. Still, the place wasn't a disaster. They could work with this.

"Not entirely from scratch." She cast a quick dust-removal spell, which left the toolbox sparkling. "Everyone is going to want to go to the mechanic that saved the world. You have free advertising."

He rolled his eyes, but some of the tension in his shoulders relaxed. "Might still be a while before I can pay my own bills again. Spent most of my savings to get this place set up and make it through the past few months."

"Amber gets a salary as Alpha Dominus now. We'll all be okay."

She plucked at the hem of her cardigan. "Not like I have any money anyhow. We're all in the same boat." She had been toying with options now that they weren't fighting for their lives but hadn't settled on anything. For the first time in her life, she felt like she almost had too many choices.

"I know, I just..." He scratched the back of his head. "Guess I just want to be able to give you things. And there is...well...I, uh..." He hesitated.

"Just spit it out." She braced herself for bad news. Some new problem to deal with.

"I talked to Amber about building another house on pack lands. Something just for us. If we ever wanted to have a family. One day. Not right now. I don't want to pressure you, I just−−"

She shut him up with a kiss. Thoroughly. When she finally broke away from the kiss, she grinned up at him. "I like that you have plans for the future for us."

"Do you even want kids? I realized while I was rambling that I've never asked."

"Yeah. Eventually." She stepped back and grabbed the broom leaning against that wall and tossed it to him. "Maybe once you get that house built."

He laughed. "And what do you plan on doing while I'm building a house for our brood of children? Want to learn how to work on engines?"

"Brood? How about one? *Maybe* two."

"Aw, man, and here I was hoping for at least a full dozen."

She tried to hit him with a cleaning spell, but he managed to dodge it. Those werewolf reflexes were the worst. "Definitely not."

He shook his head then pinned her with a look. "You're avoiding the real question, though."

She huffed out a sigh. "Maybe I don't have an answer yet. Tessa wants me to keep working with the coven. Make a real, permanent thing. Kate Ford approached me about starting some kind of training for witches without covens that are interested in joining a pack as a shaman. And…" She plopped down on the toolbox. "Icewind asked me to be a liaison with the Witch's Conclave."

Instead of being overwhelmed by the list, Derek just shrugged. "Maybe you can do a bit of all of it."

"What?"

"You like Tessa and the coven, right? I'm sure you can take on contracts together, which would make it easier to schedule, and they could help you train future shamans. And, because of our pack's status, there's not really any avoiding dealing with the Conclave, so you might be stuck with that job regardless." He paused in his sweeping. "Or you could turn it all down and do whatever the hell you want. Everyone is going to want to work with the witch that saved the world, right? You can do *anything*."

She bit back a smile even as a lump formed in her throat. "That easy, huh?"

"Yep. And you don't have to decide this week, either. I think we've earned at least a month to figure out our futures."

"You, Tommy, Deward, *and* Gen all already know what they want, though." She rested her chin in her hands. "And Amber is stuck with the whole Alpha Dominus thing. I'm the only one floundering."

"It's not a competition, Ceri."

"I know that, logically, but it's just…annoying."

"You'll find the right path for you, whether it's tomorrow, or in five years. I know you will." He propped the broom up and walked over then tugged her face up. "Until then, there's plenty of stuff to fill your time. Just because you take one of those jobs now doesn't mean it has to be what you do forever."

"Ugh, you're so full of logic and sound advice."

"Don't tell Amber. It'll ruin my reputation."

She snorted out a laugh and tugged him in for another kiss. The sweeping could wait.

CHAPTER 82

AMBER

After being trapped on bed rest for days and days, Amber was finally being allowed to do something *useful*. Even if she was still stuck in the house until tomorrow.

Alpha Kate Ford greeted her and Genevieve warmly before taking her place at the dining room table. "How are you feeling?"

"Restless," Amber replied with a groan. "I've never sat around this long without doing anything."

Kate laughed, the traitor. "I'm glad you have your pack here to keep you in line."

"It has been a full time, coordinated effort, but we've managed," Genevieve said with a solemn nod.

"Well, I appreciate you allowing me an audience during such a trying time." Kate's eyes sparkled with suppressed mischief. "I was a bit surprised when Amber so eagerly agreed to this meeting, but it all makes sense now."

Amber blushed. "I'll have to get used to meetings going forward. No avoiding them now."

"You'll do great." Kate patted her hand.

"So, why did you want to meet?" Since she'd been so painfully bored, she'd been antsy to find out the details of Kate's mysterious plan, but she hadn't been forthcoming about it over text.

Kate took a deep breath and folded her hands in front of her. "I've been doing some soul searching. My nephew accumulated quite a bit of wealth through his selfishness. The pack wants to do something good with all of that. We have bedrooms and houses sitting empty." She paused for a brief moment. "So, we took a vote yesterday, and all agreed that we want to take in as many omegas as we can and get them out of the System. They don't need to join our pack, but we can give them a place to stay. Perhaps form their own packs." She lifted her chin. "If Amber was able to form a pack on her own, then maybe there are other potential alphas out there who just need a little support." Kate handed her a folder. "That lists all the details of what we can offer."

Genevieve snatched the folder before Amber could grab it and flipped through the contents with wide eyes. "This is amazing. With Amber's influence, we can absolutely make this happen. My old boss would absolutely love to take on something like this. Advocating for werewolves in the System is right up her alley."

Kate nodded in approval. "It's about time we started making some changes. My wife has already started buying supplies, so I'm glad I can bring her back the good news."

"I didn't know you were married!" Amber exclaimed, wondering how much else she'd missed.

A blush colored Kate's cheeks. "Well, it's a recent development. I hadn't wanted to ask her while Carter was still alpha. She's human, and that just wasn't allowed."

Genevieve grinned. "I'm sure she was thrilled to finally tie the knot."

"She didn't speak to me for three days after I asked her, actually. After thirty years of waiting, I think she wanted to strangle me with the ring." She laughed. "The whole drive to the courthouse I wasn't sure if she actually was going to say, 'I do.'"

"I'm glad it all worked out in the end."

"Me too," Kate agreed with a smile.

"I think Ito will be thrilled with this plan as well," Genevieve said as she finally handed the folder over to Amber. "He's mentioned wanting to work on the issues between bitten and born wolves for a while. This is a start."

Amber nodded as she flipped through the folder. The plan was insanely comprehensive considering how recently Kate had put it all together. The woman had a knack for organizing. "This is amazing. I could never have come up with something like this."

"And I would never have dared try without you." Kate reached over to squeeze her hand. "You've shown me change is possible, if good people just *act*."

It was weird to hear how deeply she'd impacted someone else's way of thinking, but it also gave her hope. They would still have challenges. Not everyone would be excited for these sorts of ideas. But there were still good people, and together, they would find the strength to do the right thing.

CHAPTER 83

AMBER

Amber parked her truck and hopped out. This was the first time she'd left the house since she'd been released from the hospital-- and carried over the threshold like a child by Kadrithan. It felt good to be out on her own, but she couldn't quite relax. At every light, she was checking to see if she'd been followed, and she couldn't shake the feeling of being watched even though she *knew* she was safe. It was just hard to accept that after so long.

Taking a deep breath, she forced herself to ignore the urge to check for traps before she knocked on the warehouse door. Bram had invited her. This was *fine*. She was *safe*.

She rapped once on the door then stepped back and waited, but...it was silent inside. No footsteps or whispered conversations. With a frown, she tried the handle and found it unlocked. That was odd.

Her heartbeat ratcheted up as she opened the door and peeked inside. The ragged couches and flatscreen TVs were gone. Even the dust had been cleared out. No vampires were waiting to greet her or warn her away. With a frown, she stepped inside. The stairwell that led to the basement was open and the light was on, but that was the only sign of life. It looked like an invitation to her, so she made her way downstairs.

She paused on the final step. The basement was empty except for a single, blank canvas, and Bram himself, who awaited her by the small table with the supplies to draw the vials of blood he needed for this final portrait. "You're leaving."

Bram inclined his head. "Yes."

"Why?" She hadn't expected the sharp sense of loss that accompanied the news. Bram was too creepy for her to feel truly fond of him, but...she still didn't want him to leave.

He took in her expression and smiled. "You will miss me."

"I..." She huffed out a sigh. "Yeah, I guess I will."

"After our recent activities, it's best if I make myself scarce for a while. The balance of power amongst the vampires is delicate." He waved a hand toward the supplies. "Whenever you're ready."

She joined him by the table and went through the familiar motions to draw the blood. The prick of the needle didn't bother her, but she had to look away for a moment as her blood rushed down to the vial.

"It was interesting, that moment of humanity we experienced during the fight with Saraqael," Bram said quietly.

She glanced up at him. "Did you like it?"

"It was blissful, even while covered in burns, and yet..." His eyes softened as he watched the tube fill with blood. "I missed the call of blood even as I found peace in being free of it."

Her eyebrows drew together. "You missed the addiction?"

"It's exciting, both the wanting and when you finally give in to the temptation." He switched the tubes for her and held the first one up to the light. "You may find it surprising the things that you miss when you finally have peace. How something in you cries out for a fight, for the adrenaline to fill you once again."

She remained silent as she filled the last two tubes, his words running through her mind on a loop. Right now, she couldn't imagine wanting to go through any of it again, but...she could see missing the sense of victory. She could see how the bond between her and her pack was something other people may never understand, because they hadn't been there. Hadn't gone through what they had. Facing down your worst fears and coming out the other side was an experience that changed you, there was no avoiding it.

"I think I can live with missing it," she said finally.

He nodded then gestured at her hair and hands. "You look refreshed."

"I got my nails done with Ceri and Gen, then they forced me into a hair salon." It sounded so...weird to say out loud. She'd gotten them done for special occasions as a teen but hadn't bothered as an adult. But she'd also never really had friends she could do that sort of thing with. Now she did.

Bram lifted her hand and inspected her nails. "A dark red would have looked amazing on you."

She rolled her eyes. "Sorry to disappoint, but I'm *never* getting red. I'm sick to death of that color."

"A pity." He released her hand with a shake of his head.

She paced the room as he set up his morbid paint supplies. Watching him empty her blood onto his palette had always been disconcerting, but today she couldn't bear the idea of watching. "Did you toss all the paintings or just relocate them?"

"I relocated them with the utmost care," he said, sounding a bit offended at the thought of throwing them away. "You might as well ask if Picasso tossed his artwork before moving."

She bit back a smile. "Of course, how silly of me."

He grew silent as he placed the first stroke of "paint" on his canvas. She did her best to keep herself distracted, but signal wasn't the best down in the basement and her texts took forever to go through, leaving her with nothing to do but pace and try to avoid looking at whatever it was Bram was creating this time. Finally, she plopped down on the bottom step and laid her head on her knees.

"You'd think I was torturing you with how impatient you get during this process," Bram muttered from across the room.

"It's creepy."

"You don't find me emerging from my coffin scary, but this gets to you. Still." He shook his head. "You're afraid of all the wrong things."

"I think my fears are perfectly justified, thank you very much."

"You're afraid of trusting yourself. Of being seen." He replenished his brush and stepped back to inspect his progress before continuing. "Yet you throw yourself into battle with abandon."

"I think that's a bit of a stretch. Fighting Saraqael was terrifying for me."

He turned his gaze to her. "Yet you never looked away. You faced him without cringing."

"I'm not exactly running away from this, either," she muttered.

Bram sighed, clearly exasperated. "Only thanks to your sense of duty."

"You know what? I get to be afraid sometimes!" She threw her hands in the air. "I'm still just...me. I don't know what I'm doing, and I have all this responsibility now, and it's overwhelming. It's a lot. And I'm allowed to not want to deal with you doing your weird blood paintings and--" She trailed off as she caught sight of the portrait. It *wasn't* just a portrait. She stood there in the middle, but her pack was with her.

"You're right." Bram laid his brush down. "Don't ever forget it. Leading is hard, which is why the people you surround yourself with are so important. Cherish them, and you will never have to face your fears alone."

She couldn't speak as a particularly large lump lodged itself in her throat. There were possibly tears stinging her eyes, but she'd deny it to the day she died. She wiped her the back of her hand over her eyes, just in case, and forced herself to stand.

Bram said nothing as he cleaned up his remaining supplies. The portrait loomed behind him, both creepy and comforting, much like the old vampire himself.

"I, um..." She forced herself to approach. "Thank you."

"You will take this one home."

"Okay." For once, she didn't even have the urge to argue. Genevieve was going to throw a fit, but she needed to keep this one around. One final lesson from her strange mentor.

Bram helped her collect it and ushered her toward the exit.

She paused at the stairwell, feeling awkward. "Keep in touch. If you can."

He looked surprised, an emotion she didn't normally see on his face. "You really will miss me."

"I already said I would."

"Well, people don't normally mean it."

"I always mean what I say."

His held her gaze for a long, quiet moment. "Yes, you do." He shook his head as if amused. "I'll stay in touch. If I can."

She nodded in farewell, but Bram remained still as he watched her ascend the stairs.

CHAPTER 84

Amber stepped back and squinted at the painting. "I think it's crooked."

Genevieve shoved the left corner up even higher. "Oh? Is it? Is the creepy painting *crooked*?"

"It's a nice picture!" she objected, feeling strangely defensive about it now that she'd gotten it home.

"It's awful!"

Ceri shook her head with a smile. "Illya likes it, so it's not imbued with evil and curses, at least."

"See?" Amber waved a hand toward Ceri. "The magical, living house likes it."

"I hope Captain Jack tears it to shreds," Genevieve muttered as she angrily adjusted it to be level and climbed down off the step stool. "I can't believe you made us hang it above the fireplace."

She shrugged. "This is where we always gather. It felt right."

Derek strolled in and paused by Ceri, his nose wrinkling in disgust. "Why does it smell like blood in here? Is someone on their..." He trailed off as all three of them turned to him with identical looks of horror.

"Do not *ever* suggest you can smell that again, or I swear on the spirits I will *remove* your ability to smell," Ceri threatened, magic crackling at her fingertips. "And I know a spell that can do that."

"Just, um, forget I said anything." Derek laughed nervously and took a step back, his hands raised in surrender.

"However, that," Genevieve paused and cleared her throat, "*smell*...is THAT." She thrust an accusing finger at the painting. "And Amber made us hang it in here."

"The smell will fade!" She tapped a finger against her chin. "Or we'll find a way to seal it."

Derek stared at the painting then stared at her. "What the hell?"

"Look, it was a parting gift from Bram, okay?" She crossed her arms.

Her brother shook his head in shock. "I'm not even going to argue since that clearly hasn't had any effect." Taking a deep breath, he turned to Ceri. "Ready to go?"

Ceri nodded and smoothed down her hair. "Yes. Very ready."

Amber finally registered that Ceri was wearing a nicer dress than normal, and there was no cardigan in sight. And her brother's mop of hair had been combed. Sort of. "Where are you two going?"

"On a date," Ceri said, practically beaming with happiness. "Since no one is trying to kill us."

"Oh!" She grinned at them. "That's great! Is this actually y'all's first date?"

Derek rubbed the back of his head with a grimace. "I've already had an earful about that. Maybe we can skip a repeat." He placed a hand on Ceri's lower back and urged her toward the door. "And we have a reservation, so no time for chit-chat."

Ceri rolled her eyes but allowed herself to be ushered out to the cars with a wave goodbye.

Genevieve glanced at Amber. "Soooo, Steven and I actually have a date this afternoon as well."

"Oh?" Amber was surprised but pleased. It was about time everyone got out and did something fun now that they were done babysitting her.

"Yep. And Tommy and Deward are over at Deward's parents' house."

"I'll have the whole place to myself." She forced a grin even though that sounded terrible.

Genevieve let out a long-suffering sigh and grabbed her by the shoulders. "Maybe you should take advantage of the empty house and invite *someone* over."

She frowned. "Like Icewind?"

"No, you idiot!" Genevieve actually groaned in frustration this time and shook her. "Kadrithan! Your tall, dark, and handsome royal love interest!"

"He's probably busy, or––"

"I'm not listening to this nonsense. The two of you are *impossible*."

"We are not! There's just...it's complicated!" And she was confused. He'd been there every minute while she was in the hospital, but they never had a minute alone, and he hadn't said anything. After all the face touching and forehead kisses, she was at a loss.

Sometimes she wondered if she should be the one to make the next move, but for once, she wanted someone else to do that. Maybe that was dumb and he needed encouragement. But this was exactly why dating was complicated. She never knew what to do.

Genevieve shook her head with a look of complete disbelief. "And now you're brooding again."

"I am *not* brooding. I'm a grown woman. An alpha. I *contemplate* my *adult problems*."

That earned her an eye roll and a pat on her head. "Uh huh, sure. Just keep telling yourself that."

Amber did, in fact, keep telling herself that as she sat at the dining room table alone with a glass of cheap wine and leftovers from lunch. She was fine, happy for her pack, and was not brooding while abandoned at the house with only the cat for company. Even the pixies were gone since Deward's cousin had picked them up for a checkup.

She lifted her glass in a toast to Jack. "To not brooding."

He gave her a *very* judgmental stare before hopping off his chair and flouncing out of the room. Which was just plain rude. She took a long drink and drained the remaining wine from the glass then eyed her phone. If she just picked it up and texted Kadrithan, she could find out if he was busy or just sitting alone in his office taking care of his kingly duties.

She huffed out a sigh and grabbed it, flipping to her messages, but as she stared at the letters on the keyboard, her mind went blank. *Hey, want to touch my face again? You free to give me more confusing affection?* With a growl, she smacked the phone back on the table and slouched back in her seat, arms crossed.

"This is stupid."

From somewhere upstairs, Captain Jack meowed his agreement. She reached for her phone again, determined to follow through this time, when a knock at the door startled her into knocking over her thankfully empty wine glass. She righted it and forced a deep breath. Whoever was at the door was a *friend*. The security was too good for anyone weird to have gotten in. In fact, it was probably Velez or Ito wanting something important.

She jogged to the back door and pulled it open then froze. Sunflowers. Kadrithan stood just in front of her with a massive bouquet of them. And a bottle of wine in his other hand. And he was wearing a suit that fit him like a glove. And his hair was smoothed back in a style he'd obviously spent time on.

He cleared his throat and thrust the sunflowers toward her. "I heard you might be...lonely this evening."

She groaned in embarrassment. This was a set up. "Did Genevieve text you?"

"What? No, I..." He let the thought trail off, and his cheeks colored slightly, the bouquet drooping in his grip. "I've just had Leena watching the house."

"What?"

"To find time to catch you without an...audience."

She stared at him and the flowers and the wine and contemplated his admission to stalking. Swallowing down the nerves and embarrassment, she took the flowers with what she hoped was a smile. It was hard to tell. Her face felt wobbly. "Oh."

"Can I come in?"

"Of course. Sorry." She stepped back and let him inside. The subtle scent of his shampoo filled her nose. He never smelled of sulfur anymore, which was a huge relief. Now, it was something spicier mixed with vanilla. She wanted to bury her face in his neck and breathe it in.

Shaking off the impulse, she went to the kitchen and found a vase under the sink. He followed her and found a wine opener as she arranged the bouquet. It really was beautiful. She'd always been fond of sunflowers. They were so bright and happy.

"I hope you like the wine I picked. It's sweet. Reminded me of a cranberry vodka." He glanced back with a smirk.

She rolled her eyes but couldn't help a smile. "I'll drink fruity drinks until the day I die."

He handed her the glass. "I suppose I'll have to develop a taste for them, then."

Her heart skipped a beat at that. She accepted her glass with a slightly shaky hand. The wine smelled like pure sugar, which was a good sign as far as she was concerned. A sip confirmed it was sweet, fruity, and probably an affront to everyone who genuinely loved wine. "It's good."

Kadrithan grimaced as he swallowed his own sip. "I'm glad you like it, though it might give you cavities."

She laughed. "You don't have to drink it if you hate it, you know. We have a Malbec or something in the pantry. Ceri keeps bringing various bottles home when she gets groceries."

He shrugged and set his glass aside. "I didn't really come here for the wine."

"Oh?" She swallowed and stared very hard at her glass. "Why did you come over, then?"

He stepped into her space and took her glass as well. She stayed perfectly still as he set it on the counter then turned his full attention to her.

"I always imagined that when I set out to pursue a woman, I would shower her with gifts. After all, what's the point of being king if you can't use that to your advantage?" He tucked her hair behind her ear. "Instead, I fell in love in the midst of war, unable to offer anything but danger and demands to someone who deserved so much more." His fingers trailed down from her cheek, to her neck, then finally to the place her demon mark had rested. Her breath caught as he slipped his other hand behind her neck and pulled her in close. "I've lived a very long time, and I have never met someone that challenged me so much." His dark eyes filled with heat as he held her gaze. "I would sacrifice my realm all over again if it meant keeping you safe. I would give up my crown if it could make every wish you had come true. I would do anything to make you happy."

"You..." Her throat had gone very dry. "You already make me happy." The words came out quieter than she'd intended, but she couldn't manage anything more.

He traced the ridge of her collar bone. "I love you, Amber Hale."

"You love me?" she whispered.

His other hand dropped to her waist and slipped under the hem of her shirt. The heat of it seared her skin as desire flooded her. "I have been in love with you since the moment you told me I'd have to try harder to scare you."

"Oh?" she choked out, thoroughly distracted by the movement of his fingers on her bare skin.

"Yes." He pulled her into a searing kiss. His fingers curled into her skin and hair as if he was afraid she might slip away at any moment. They stumbled backward and slammed into a wall. Breaking away for a brief moment, he hoisted her up and held her there as his lips descended on hers once again.

All her doubts fled as they sank into one another, every barrier between them finally gone. There was no threat, no mark binding her to him, and nothing more important than his hands on her skin and lips whispering promises against her ear.

CHAPTER 85

KADRITHAN

Kadrithan woke up to sunlight and a tangle of red hair in his face. Someone was laughing in the kitchen, and the scent of breakfast had his stomach rumbling immediately.

Amber shifted in front of him and turned over to bury her face in his chest. "Early," she grumbled.

"I think it's nearly ten, actually." He curled around her and ran his fingers through her long hair, not in a hurry to leave her bed at all. "But we can sleep in today."

She huffed. "Hungry."

He grinned, amused. "You are so eloquent in the morning."

She jabbed his side, but he could feel her smiling against his chest. "Mornings suck."

"I don't know, I'm fairly fond of this one." He slid a hand down her bare back as desire curled in him again.

Her breath quickened, and she leaned into the touch but abruptly pulled away with a groan. "Ugh, they can hear us. Gen threatened to throw Captain Jack in here if we didn't stop." She pushed up onto her elbow and glared at the door. "Ceri has to put up her soundproofing in here or we're sleeping at your place from now on."

He laughed and sat up. Knowing the pack was listening in definitely killed the mood. Though, as Amber climbed out of bed, her smooth skin illuminated in the soft sunlight, he almost reconsidered. With considerable effort of will, he turned away and found his clothes where they'd been scattered around the room the night before.

They dressed, and he followed a blushing Amber out of the room. He bit back his grin, but her embarrassment over the simplest things would never cease to amuse him.

Genevieve popped open a bottle of champagne as they walked in. The rest of the pack had paper kazoos, which let out an obnoxiously loud sound. Someone had decorated a sign with an alarming amount of glitter that said ABOUT TIME in large letters.

Amber stared at the celebration in horror. "I need a new pack."

Shaking his head in amusement, Kadrithan grabbed her arm and tugged her into a passionate kiss. The kazoos blessedly stopped as the pack collapsed into groans of disgust. He pulled back with a grin. "We can always embarrass them more than they can us."

Amber grinned back at him with still-red cheeks. "I knew I loved you for a reason."

"Ugh, I should never have encouraged this," Genevieve complained with a wink at Amber. "But I'm a selfless beta, always looking out for my alpha."

"Ha. Ha." Amber grabbed two plates and thrust one at him. "Just for that, I'm taking the biggest pancake."

After a small tussle over the pancakes, which Amber, of course, won, everyone loaded their plates with food. It was a bit chaotic, but it worked for them, and Kadrithan couldn't picture their makeshift family operating any other way.

The pack gathered in the living room, finding whatever flat spot they could to set their plates. Laughter filled the air, and for once, he was part of it. He wasn't watching invisible from a corner, unable to touch and interact. He wasn't trapped in a dying realm.

He was here, and he was free. His gaze drifted to Amber, as it always did. The light was back in her eyes. Even though he had lost more than he thought he could survive, he knew in that moment that he would be okay because he wasn't alone, and he never would be.

CHAPTER 86

DEWARD

"Stop looking away! I'm going to screw it up," Deward complained.

Tommy refocused his gaze on the tiny glider Deward was putting the finishing touches on. Creating this using his ability to see through his pack member's eyes was probably a cop out, but he'd wanted to get it done as quickly as possible. He owed the pixies a lot and understood more than most how hard it must be on Woggy Jr. to not be able to keep up with his siblings.

With Steven's help, they'd come up with a lighter and smaller version of Woggy's glider. It wouldn't be able to travel as far, but it was a start for the tiny pixie.

Deward sat back and stretched out his tired fingers. "I think it's done."

"Time to test it out, then!" Tommy grabbed the glider as Deward released his connection to his sight.

The strain of seeing through Tommy's eyes vanished, and his tense shoulders relaxed. He waited for the usual fear to set in as he returned to darkness, but it didn't this time. He felt off-kilter for a moment, but disorientation was to be expected.

He followed Tommy outside, gathering the pack to come watch the test run as they went. The pixies were already waiting for them.

A light weight landed on his head, and Woggy tugged his hair in greeting.

"I hope it works for him," Deward said quietly.

Woggy gave his hair another tug of agreement.

"Here, you've gotta watch since you made the glider." Tommy put a hand on his arm, and once again, his pack mate's vision swam into focus.

Steven helped Woggy Jr. into the harness, leaving the tiny buckles to the pixie's nimbler fingers. Once the little guy was all strapped in, he stepped to the edge of the fence post and took a deep breath. It was a scary thing to fly for the first time, especially after spending your whole life grounded, but Woggy Jr. was brave. He didn't even hesitate before he leaped into the air.

The glider snapped out behind him and carried him up, away from the ground. The pack let out a whoop of celebration as Woggy Jr.'s sisters and brothers swarmed around him. They'd learned from mishaps with their father to *not* bump into him and kept their distance as he circled around the yard.

Deward grinned as he watched him fly. Going to college was his own leap of faith, but the pack would be his glider. They wouldn't let him fall.

For the first time, he let himself look forward to the future. All the dreams he had before the curse were still possible. He could do anything he wanted, and he would.

CHAPTER 87

The first full moon since the battle was an event. All the packs were here, even Ito's. Part of her had expected him to cut ties once the fight was over, but if anything, he was more determined to develop a friendship with her and her pack. They were stuck together until she died, so it made sense, but it was a huge relief nonetheless.

Genevieve stepped up onto a crate and whistled to get everyone's attention. "All right, everyone should have their buddies, but if someone doesn't, just come see me." They had bused in the werewolves from the nearest reserve that was part of the System. Tonight, hopefully some wolves would find a new pack or make their own. It was all part of Alpha Ford's plan for helping those werewolves, and tonight was the test run. "Remember, everyone shifts together, and everyone runs together. No fighting. No being a butthead. And don't knock over the humans!" Laughter rippled through the crowd as Genevieve climbed down from her makeshift stage.

Kadrithan slung an arm around her shoulder. "Leena challenged Deward to a race."

"That should be interesting. He's shockingly fast."

"I've already put my bet on him. I think she was offended."

Amber shook her head with a grin. "As long as you're betting on my pack, I'll allow it."

Her father approached, and Kadrithan gave her a quick kiss before slipping away to let them talk. The warmth of Kadrithan's kiss lingered on her lips, full of promise. It was so easy between them now. She knew his heart more surely now than when the mark had tied them together. If anything, the mark had always been a barrier. A debt that kept them from coming together as equals.

"You don't mind that I'm not gonna be running with y'all, right?" It was at least the fifth time he'd asked, but she appreciated the effort behind his questions. He was trying.

"Dad, you'd make it to the tree line and need medical attention." She patted his arm. "Grab a beer and relax. I'm not mad at you."

"A beer does sound good."

She nodded. "And this way you won't have to see me naked, either."

His face paled. "Maybe I should go grab that beer now."

"I'm tempted to join him," Jackson groused as he came up behind her and tried to put her in a headlock. She was strong enough now to just peel his arms off, but she pretended to struggle for a moment, for old time's sake.

"You can get naked with us, big brother. Feel the call of the moon." She waggled her eyebrows at him.

"Someone in this family has to stay human. And keep their pants on." He shook his head in mock disgust. "As the eldest brother, that responsibility falls on me."

She rolled her eyes. "At least it spares us all from the blinding glare that would reflect off your butt."

"Hey! I'm not that pale!"

"If you're anything like your brother, then yes, you are," Ceri said as she walked up with Derek.

Derek groaned. "Don't talk about my ass in public."

Ceri raised an eyebrow. "You're about to show it to everyone!"

"Yeah, but we pretend we don't see anything so we can all stay sane! The first rule of getting naked with your pack is *never talk about getting naked with your pack*. Especially if your alpha is your sister." He crossed his arms. "Besides, my butt isn't nearly as pale as Jackson's. He's the palest out of all of us."

Jacob jogged up. "What's this about butts?"

Amber shook her head and waved Genevieve down, leaving her brothers to their butt debate. "We ready to go?"

"Yep!" Genevieve bounced on her toes. "All the packs are in place, and everyone is ready. Where's Kadrithan?"

"He ran away when my family showed up," she said with a smirk. He was wary of her father and her brothers after they'd all had dinner together and he'd been thoroughly interrogated. They'd asked questions she hadn't even thought of. It had been hilarious.

"I did not run away," Kadrithan muttered as he rejoined them. "Your father clearly wanted to speak to you privately."

Genevieve snorted. "You're a terrible liar."

"I am an *excellent* liar," he objected.

"Don't even get started." Amber grabbed Genevieve by the shoulders and spun her around. "Come on, let's get this started. The sun has already set." The urge to shift was growing, so she knew the new werewolves had to be feeling it. There was no point in waiting around any longer.

They made their way to the front of the crowd along with the rest of her pack, her family, and Genevieve's family. Gen's mother was wearing a purple track suit with *Mother of a Bitten Wolf and Proud* in glitter on the back. They would definitely not lose her during the run.

Amber had refused all suggestions to give some kind of speech ahead of the event. No one hear needed to hear any more fancy words; they needed to shift and run. After all, when you got right down to it, they weren't really human anymore.

As the crowd's energy grew, she stripped out of the shorts and shirt she'd chosen for the night. Something she didn't mind never seeing again since, odds were, all this crap would be mixed up and lost in the chaos. Her pack followed suit. Even Kadrithan stripped down to his shorts, meeting her appreciative perusal with a smirk that promised, *Later*.

She lifted her gaze to the moon as the shift rolled up from her feet. The guilt of the past had been shed like an old skin, and she had been remade from the inside out.

The power of the moon sang in her veins. She and her wolf sank into each other, becoming more than they could ever be separately. There was no loss. No surrender of who she was. She shook out her fur and howled. Her pack answered, their voices joining into a triumphant chorus.

Then she ran. Free. Joyous. Complete.

MAKE A DIFFERENCE

Reviews are very important, and sometimes hard for an independently published author to get. A big publisher has a massive advertising budget and can send out hundreds of review copies.

Leaving an honest review helps me tremendously. It shows other readers why they should give me a try. It also shows Amazon that readers are enjoying the book.

If you've enjoyed reading this book, I would appreciate, very much, if you took the time to leave a review. Whether you write one sentence, or three paragraphs, it's equally helpful.

Thank you :)

P.S. Who's your favorite character? Let me know in the Facebook group.

https://www.facebook.com/groups/TheFoxehole/

Follow Me

Thank you so much for buying my book. I really hope you have enjoyed the story as much as I did writing it. Being an author is not an easy task, so your support means a lot to me. I do my best to make sure books come out error free. However, if you found any errors, please feel free to reach out to me so I can correct them!

If you loved this book, the best way to find out about new releases and updates is to join my Facebook group, The Foxehole. Amazon does a very poor job about notifying readers of new book releases. Joining the group can be an alternative to newsletters if you feel your inbox is getting a little crowded.

Facebook Group:
https://www.facebook.com/groups/TheFoxehole
Newsletter:
https://stephaniefoxe.com/#Follow-Me
Goodreads:
http://goodreads.com/Stephanie_Foxe
BookBub:
https://www.bookbub.com/authors/stephanie-foxe

MORE BY STEPHANIE FOXE

The Witch's Bite Series is a complete series that follows Olivia Carter –

I'm the only healer in a hundred miles, yet I'm probably the poorest in over a thousand.

Opening my very own apothecary is the only thing I really want in life, well that and a steady relationship. Lofty goals when you have a felony record for selling illegal potions. Healing neckers for the local vamps, while not all that glorious, has helped me build a good reputation. Then the cops show up at my door asking questions about a dead girl and trying to pin the murder on my employer. Next thing I know, I'm dodging fireballs in parking lots, and my favorite vampire is missing.

If you crave fast-paced, potion-slinging, snarky witch's, with a side of slow-burn romance, then you'll love Olivia Carter. This witch bites back, literally.

∼

Stephanie Foxe also writes with her husband Alex Steele. In The Chaos Mages Series you will meet Logan Blackwell and Lexi Swift as they solve crimes in a world full of magic and myths, much like in Misfit Pack.

What else could go wrong?

I'm a detective with the IMIB - International Magical Investigations Bureau. I eat good food, drive fast cars, and I work alone.

Because no one can keep up with me.

When my boss dumps an unwanted partner in my lap, I'm told to figure out how to play nice, or I can kiss my job goodbye. My job is my life. Losing it is not an option.

There's no time to complain before a vampire explodes, a werewolf beats the mayor's nephew to death with his own arm, and some very determined assassins start popping up everywhere where we go.

One misstep and it's not my job I'll have to worry about losing. It's my head.

I may not be a big fan of rules, but I sure as hell believe in doing the right thing. Whoever is hurting innocents will pay. One way or another.

What else could go wrong, you ask? Losing a bet and ending up with pink hair. Apparently.

www.StephanieFoxe.com
www.AlexSteele.net

facebook.com/StephanieFoxeAuthor
goodreads.com/Stephanie_Foxe
bookbub.com/authors/stephanie-foxe

Made in the USA
Columbia, SC
14 February 2023